I0710373

STROKE OF MIDNIGHT

MIDNIGHT'S CAPTIVE

HEATHER GREYE

Midnight's Captive

Copyright © 2024 Heather Greye

All rights reserved.

No part of this publication may be reproduced, distributed, or transmitted in any form or by any means, including photocopying, recording, or other electronic or mechanical methods, without the prior written permission of the publisher, except as permitted by U.S. copyright law.

If you would like to use material from the book (other than for review purposes), prior written permission must be obtained.

This book is a work of fiction. Names, characters, places, and incidents are products of the author's imagination or are used fictitiously. Any resemblance to the actual persons, living or dead, business establishments, events, or locales is entirely coincidental.

Published by Black Sheep Media LLC

Editor: Elizabeth MS Flynn, emsflynn.com

Cover Design: Deranged Doctor Design, www.derangeddoctordesign.com

BOOKS BY HEATHER GREYE

Stroke of Midnight

Midnight's Pawn

Midnight's Captive

For Patrice, Alexis, and Lillian
I always dreamed of dedicating a book to the strong
women in my family – my mom, sister, and
grandmother – and now I can

And for Thom, always

CHAPTER 1

ASH TOUCHED his nose to the cold, white linoleum, then straightened his arms. A bead of sweat rolled off his forehead, spattering on the floor beneath him. He barely noticed it, dropping into another push-up, his mind focused on the summons he'd received earlier.

Portia Tremaine required his presence in her office at eight A.M.

His breath caught, just as it had when he'd opened the message this morning. Was this it? Was this when his role in the death of her husband would be revealed?

The explosion at the New Amsterdam Hotel had changed the Seattle landscape more than physically. It had completely upended the Tremaine Corporation, exposing the family's dark secrets and leading to the disappearance of the CEO, Phillip Tremaine.

Portia had stepped into her father's position and had, by all accounts, spent the past six weeks settling into the role. Ash had spent the same time trying to solve the same problem he'd spent the last five years on: how to free himself and his sister from the Tremaine Corporation. He'd spent the days since the explosion frantically seeking a way out for him and Hope, while waiting for his role to be discovered.

Body on autopilot, he completed his workout—one hundred each of sit-ups, dips, and push-ups, no more, no less—and dropped to his knees. Hands on his waist, he waited for a rush from endorphins or the buzz of accomplishment, but neither came.

He didn't work out for any of those things. It didn't clear his head or help him think. It didn't do anything but keep his body strong so it could support his mind when it was otherwise occupied.

Too worried to eat, he skipped breakfast and quickly showered then donned the boring black pants and white shirt that served as his uniform. He tried not to let the summons throw him. Instead, he rubbed his hand over the back of his left shoulder, tracing the tattoo there. The raised design centered him. Reminded him of who he was and why he had to escape.

A female security guard waited for him at the executive elevators. Ever since the bombing and Phillip Tremaine's disappearance, there'd been heightened security on the main floors of Tremaine headquarters. Even the staff living quarters and common areas like the cafeteria, located at the base of the building, had a slight increase in security. Nothing like this, though. Everyone wanting to see Portia required special clearance and an escort.

Ash approached the guard carefully. Knowing about the extra security was one thing. Being called in to see the acting CEO put it in a new, worrying light. Until he knew more, he had to believe that the guard was there to escort him to Portia's office, not take him into custody.

Smile casual and his movements calm, he approached the elevator.

"I have an appointment with Ms. Tremaine," he said.

"Palm, please." The guard held out a scanner, her expression flat.

He pressed his palm to it and let the computer work its identification magic.

"Ash Cutter. Computer security specialist. Tremaine Corporation."

When the ID wasn't followed with directions to "Arrest immediately" or "Shoot on sight," the tension in his shoulders eased slightly.

"I'll escort you to the top floor." Her voice gave nothing away. They must teach that in security guard school.

"Okay." The less he said, the more unconcerned he could pretend he was.

The elevator doors slid open and the guard gestured for him to precede her. Ash stepped in and moved to one side. She followed, taking up a position on the opposite side of the car, her back to the wall. Her hand wasn't actually *on* her weapon, but it hovered too close for comfort.

They stared at each other for the entire ride. Willing himself not to fidget, he studied his escort. She wore her dark hair pulled back in a severe bun at the back of her neck and a bland expression on her face. He didn't know her, but he'd seen her around. Tremaine Security was hard to miss these days.

The elevator stopped with a happy *ding!* and the door slid open. Ash stayed where he was. Any sudden moves might make her jumpy.

"After you." She gestured at the open door.

He stepped into a mix of luxury and security. Half a dozen guards circled the room. The reception desk sat several feet in front of the elevator door. Sleek metal and opaque glass, it gleamed like new and stood out against the white marble floor. The woman behind the desk looked young and efficient.

She acknowledged him with a faraway gaze that instantly conveyed that she was plugged into the network. Jealousy flooded his system. He tamped it down with a struggle.

Ash hadn't been allowed to jack into a system in five years.

Five. Years.

There was nothing like streaming with the data. Becoming one with the pixels and packets. No barriers, no walls. It was better than any high he'd ever experienced and he missed it every damn day.

Tremaine Security had sealed up his port when they'd made him the offer he couldn't refuse. One that let him live and provided his sister with the medical care she needed. And there were *still* days that he'd throw it all away for a chance to surf a network again.

Watching the receptionist, he could almost imagine the rush she was experiencing. "Ms. Tremaine wanted to see me." He modulated his tone, keeping the jealousy out of it.

She eyed him curiously, the continuous movement of her eyelids the only sign that her attention wasn't fully focused on him. The fluttering paused for a few seconds. She must have found what she was looking for. "Ms. Tremaine is waiting for you. Go on in."

"Do you know what this is about?" he asked before he could stop himself. Some warning before facing the new head of a multinational corporation would be nice.

No answer. He'd already lost her attention.

Ash exhaled slowly. This was it. If Portia Tremaine had learned that he was involved in the bombing that had killed her husband, he'd need all his wits about him. And it still probably wouldn't be enough.

She'd never believe that he hadn't known the bombing was going to happen.

Frosted glass doors whooshed open as soon as he approached, providing his first glimpse of the inner sanctum. The Seattle skyline was visible from every window. The view was breathtaking.

Portia Tremaine sat in the center of the room, dressed in black as she had been since her husband's death. The stark color washed out her already pale skin and blond hair. When she looked up from her desk, the dark circles under her eyes reflected her deep grief.

Guilt hit like a freight train, a familiar feeling because he blamed himself for his sister's predicament.

She pinned him with an expression that said he was already wasting her time.

His gaze slid over the room as he stepped fully into her office. The doors shut automatically behind him, closing him in with Portia Tremaine—and no security.

What did that mean?

Her gaze—or was it the guilt?—pressed on him like a weight as he crossed the short distance to the chair in front of her desk.

When she waved him to it, he lounged carelessly in the chair, an intentional reminder that he dressed like a corporate drone, but he wasn't one.

Her fingers danced over the screen on her desk and he assumed she was flicking through his file. The silence was unnerving.

"Ash Cutter. Fēnix. One of the greatest hackers of all time. Until you got caught."

Derision coated her voice. It rankled, but he didn't let it show. His time at the company had taught him painful lessons about reacting to taunts.

"How long have you been working for Tremaine Corporation, Mr. Cutter?"

Ha. Working. That was one way to put it. "Five years." It was an effort to keep his tone polite.

"Five years of constant surveillance. And, according to your record, only one infraction." Every word in that damn superior tone.

One infraction. An ill-conceived escape attempt right after he and Hope had been captured by Tremaine Security.

Silence stretched between them and he realized that she was waiting for a response. *Okay. He'd play.* "That's correct."

Portia looked up from the file then, her gaze hard and steady as it met his. "Just one. That's quite remarkable for someone of your talents."

He tensed, but she didn't say anything else on that subject. That was good. Right?

"How much do you know about what happened last month?"

More than she probably wanted him to. Was she expecting a confession? "Some," he said slowly. "What the newsies reported. The little that the corporation's told us. Hallway chatter."

"Yes, we can't disregard the hallway chatter." She sighed and sat back. "As you may have heard, my father's assistant came into possession of some Tremaine Corporation secrets that should have stayed hidden. For all his business savvy, my father's assistant was an idiot when it came to computers and technology." After the cold recitation of facts, emotion colored her next words. "I know he had help."

His pulse jumped. He didn't like where this was going. At all. "Okay, why am I here?" He injected enough I-don't-care into his voice, like any good captive hacker would.

"Come now, Mr. Cutter. I know you're smarter than you look." She paused, looked at his file again. "I need your special skills."

Tamping down his confusion, Ash contemplated his next move. Was she *asking* for his help? That wasn't how this usually worked. But she wasn't accusing him of helping Leopold Brunswick either. Yet. "What's in it for me?"

Her laugh echoed around the room. He wasn't sure which of them was more surprised.

"Your file said you were arrogant. That's an understatement." Her smile didn't carry a trace of humor. "It also says we have your sister."

Her words struck like a blow, as she'd obviously intended. He clenched the arm rests, anchoring his body, instead of lunging at her. Fear for Hope's safety was the only thing that kept him from attacking her.

Portia didn't have the grace to look ashamed for using his sister against him. No surprise. She'd hit her own sister with a car. The world called her the Ice Queen for a reason.

"Yes." His words were clipped. "And I'm sure my record also shows that I've always done as asked and your father's people have upheld your side of the bargain." Only the bare minimum, though.

Ash was allowed to visit his sister twice a month. Seeing her in the coma, getting frailer and frailer, broke his heart every time, but he wouldn't abandon her. As painful as they were, the visits also allowed him to make sure they were providing her with the care she needed.

"The deal didn't change just because management did, Mr. Cutter."

Ash looked around the room while he reined in his temper. He breathed slowly, deliberately, and studied Portia's office. Her empty office.

No security guards. Not even one standing by the door. Unusual. Did Portia Tremaine have something to hide?

The Tremaine family maintained power by keeping control. They controlled everything. All the knowledge. All the secrets. Given what had happened with her father's assistant, he would have expected her to double down.

He met her cold blue eyes and held her gaze, while he took a wild stab at what she wanted. "You requested me specifically. And we're here alone." He gestured to the big bulky doors. "Tremaine Security is out there, not in here. Whatever you have going on is something that you don't want anyone to know about."

"Are you threatening me?" She tilted her head to the side, a tiny smile on her lips as she studied him like a flaw in otherwise perfect code.

He shook his head. "Stating facts. Whatever the job is, you need me. I want to renegotiate."

Would she call his bluff? He'd just taken a huge risk with Hope's safety, but he'd do anything for his sister. He had to free her before Portia discovered his recent crimes against the Tremaine family and made them both pay.

"You're right. This is important. And I do need you." Her fingers swiped over the screen again. "I searched within the company for someone else who could work on this project for me. Unfortunately, I don't know who I can trust."

She didn't break eye contact with him so much as look through him. "You have the best skills in the cybersecurity department and I have your sister. The way I see it, you have almost as much to lose as I do. That makes you perfect for my needs."

A pit formed in his stomach. He'd taken a big swing—and missed. There was no way that Portia would be willing to free Hope, not when she was using his sister as leverage the way her father had. "At least increase the visits to my sister."

Portia blinked in surprise. "What do you mean?"

Was she serious? She'd seen his file. "For the last five years, I've only been able to visit her twice a month. Please."

It killed him to ask a Tremaine for anything. But for Hope, he'd beg.

She didn't say anything for a long minute. "Fine, Mr. Cutter. I'll inform security and the hospital that you have permission to visit your sister." She paused. Considered. "Twice a week."

Ash's jaw dropped and his heart skipped a beat. Had he heard her correctly? "Twice a week?" he echoed.

"Yes." She nodded. "But understand me, Mr. Cutter. If you speak a word about this project, if you have any ideas about abusing my kindness and sharing anything you learn in this room, access to your sister won't be the only thing I cut off."

There she was. The Ice Queen didn't do anything without a reason.

"Fair enough." The threat was actually good news. If Portia knew about his role in the New Amsterdam Hotel incident, she wouldn't let him anywhere near Hope. "What's this big project?"

If he didn't know better, he'd swear she rolled her eyes. "Hacking, of course."

He started to smile, then caught himself. "Real hacking or the poor imitation you've had me doing the last five years?"

Computers were his first love and—besides Hope—his only love. Being cut off from them, only allowed to skim the surface through keyboards and voice commands, was like seeing the world without colors.

"Mr. Cutter, the 'imitation hacking' you've been doing with cybersecurity has been very important to the Tremaine Corporation. Why, I believe we can credit you with stopping several attempted hacks."

"Just doing my job." He managed to shrug. The last thing he wanted was credit for those captures. He, Fēnix, hacker extraordinaire, had burned other hackers to protect the Tremaine Corporation.

None of his opponents had been friends, but he'd known them. With every battle for control of the Tremaine system, Ash had hoped that they never learned who had been behind their capture. If anyone found out, he and his sister would be in danger from more than just Portia Tremaine.

"Will I be getting my access back?" He yearned to run his fingers over the back of his neck. Right after his capture, they'd sealed the port with a skin graft, leaving a bump of scar tissue where there used to be a jack. It didn't hurt anymore, although it haunted him like a phantom limb.

"No. You've been working perfectly fine without it."

"If you're going to hamstring me, find another hacker." Fuck, that was a stupid thing to say. She'd already threatened Hope; she held all the cards. He didn't have anything to negotiate with.

"Oh, Mr. Cutter. You amuse me. Making demands when you don't have anything to back it up." Her voice was pure condescension. "Be here tomorrow morning. I'll inform cybersecurity that you'll be reporting to me."

"Yes, ma'am." Ash choked on the venom he couldn't put into words. He'd already challenged her once today and lost. He needed to regroup, consider his options. There had to be something.

She glared at him. "You may go."

Ash didn't turn his back on her, backing up until the doors opened. He didn't take his eyes off her until he was through and the doors had closed again.

In the relative safety of the reception room—Portia Tremaine scared him more than the half-dozen security guards—he sucked in a shuddering breath.

Portia Tremaine had money. Leverage. Resources.

Ash may lack resources, but surely Fēnix still had some on the outside.

CHAPTER 2

TARYN CAST a cool glance over her bar, surveying the patrons and her employees. Maybe two dozen customers—at least two-thirds regulars—filled the poorly lit space, enough to fill the bar with the hum of activity. All in all, an average Tuesday night. No special events. No driving rain to either bring people in or keep them out.

Though she'd never turn down additional business, tonight's quiet was fine with her. She had late-night plans, but the bar would be in good hands with her second-in-command.

Still, there was a niggle of apprehension whenever she had to go out late. The bar was her future, one she'd never expected. A future with a steady income, employees, and friends. Some nights, nights like this when it was quiet enough to think, she couldn't believe how far she'd come.

And that was what drove her. What kept her risking it all. Other women deserved the chance at a real life too.

Unwilling to let worry and the past ruin the evening, Taryn walled off those thoughts before they veered into uncomfortable territory.

Her bartender was on break and Taryn was covering for her. She enjoyed being behind the bar. There was a rhythm to it, a flow that made it easy to stay in the moment. Regular shifts allowed her to keep an eye on the business, keep her finger on the pulse of the neighborhood, and maintain the Jack's reputation.

She carefully pulled a hot glass out of the sanitizer and ran a quick eye over it for chips or smudges before sliding it onto the shelf. Razor Jack's may be a dive bar, but it was *her* dive bar and she had standards.

A waitress rested her tray on the bar. "I need a draft and a house white," she said while she typed the order into the datapad inset in the bar top.

"They got a tab going?" Taryn pulled the beer and poured the wine. Patrons could pay for their drinks up front or provide a credit chip to run a tab—she didn't care which as long as they paid. Nobody got a free ride here.

"Yep, set it up earlier. They aren't loaded, but they can afford a few more rounds." The waitress smiled impishly.

"That's what I like to hear." Taryn set the drinks on the tray. The beer and the wine, chosen to be affordable by the clientele she strove to serve, were better than the swill served at other dive bars. It wasn't the way Razor Jack's had always been run, but when Taryn had assumed the mantle of the Jack, she'd made changes—some big, some small. Selling wine *she* enjoyed was one.

The other woman grabbed the tray of drinks with a smile and was off in a flash of color. Taryn shook her head at the rainbow her waitress wore. Blue pants, orange top, pink-streaked hair. Not that she was any less colorful or strangely dressed than the patrons.

Taryn turned her attention back to the sanitizer, emptying and refilling it. The movements were almost automatic and she enjoyed the breaks to fill orders and check in on the patrons seated at the bar.

She swept a couple of empties off the bar from in front of a regular. "You want another one, Jed?"

"No, ma'am," the older man said. "I've got to make my beer money last to the end of the month."

"You got work?"

He shrugged, the movement jerky as one shoulder moved more freely than the other. Jed had lost his left arm in an accident a few years ago. His replacement arm was nothing fancy —steel bones jutted out from his short-sleeve shirt and she could see the wiring that tied the mechanical arm into his nervous system. She didn't know if something had gone wrong with the replacement or if it hadn't healed right.

Jed wasn't the only one in the bar with replacement limbs. The people who frequented Razor Jack's usually couldn't afford more than the basic cybernetics that would keep them employed. Only the upper classes—and the corporate drones—could afford the fancy stuff.

"I got some leads," he said with another shrug. "Depends on whether I can get these two arms to work together."

"If you need it, you tell them the Jack will give you a reference."

Eyes wide, he bobbed his head respectfully. "Yes, ma'am. Thank you, ma'am." With that he slid off his stool. There was a spring in his step that she hadn't seen when he came in.

Taryn wasn't in the habit of helping her customers out. Jed, though, he was an old-timer—he'd had the same bar stool the whole time she'd been here.

She turned away to hide her smile. It wouldn't do for

anyone to get ideas and start thinking the Jack was getting soft. When she turned back, a newcomer sat in Jed's place, looking completely out of place.

"What can I get you?" She took in his shaggy and short dark hair, somehow completely at odds with his company-man clothes. He was cute—if you ignored the corporate vibes.

Corporate types only ever came to Razor Jack's on a dare. There were a lot of higher-end bars around the skyscrapers downtown. That was where the drones usually spent their money.

"Whiskey neat."

Well, well. Looked like he had a bit more personality than the usual worker bee.

Grabbing a middle-of-the-line bottle from the speed rack, she held it up for his approval. He nodded and she turned away to get a glass. While she did, she studied him in the mirror on the back wall, picking up little details that were out of place with his corporate air.

He'd turned to study the bar. His profile was strong and his posture was relaxed, but still alert. Like recognized like—this was a man who knew trouble could come out of nowhere.

Her instincts prickled. He wasn't your typical corporate employee. Why was he here?

She set his drink on the counter, but kept a hand on it. "Fifteen credits." A couple of credits more than it actually cost. She was testing him, but she wasn't sure why.

He didn't blink at the price, just slid a chip over the bar to her.

Taryn released the glass, disappointment flaring in her stomach. Maybe she was seeing things that weren't there.

Anyone familiar with this part of town would have known how much that drink should cost.

"Enjoy your drink," she said.

"Wait." He grabbed her hand.

Taryn froze. Years of practice were the only thing that controlled the impulse to yank her hand away. Violently. "Remove your hand before I do it for you." People didn't touch her without her permission. Most in here knew better. Just another sign that he'd stumbled into a place that he didn't know and didn't belong.

He dropped his hand. "Sorry. I have a question."

"What?" she snapped.

"Is the Jack in tonight?"

Taryn's jaw dropped. Well, damn, he really was new here.

CHAPTER 3

"WHAT'S your business with the Jack?"

Ash sipped his whiskey, his eyes never leaving the bartender's dark gaze. Her threat to remove his hand had been dead serious. When he'd spent time here before, the bartenders hadn't been so . . . flinty.

It was an interesting change on top of others he'd noticed. A subtle lightness in the air for all the bar's dim lighting. A less chaotic vibe. Small changes that spoke of larger ones. Ones he needed to understand and didn't.

Negotiating with the Jack was a delicate dance and he couldn't afford a misstep.

"That's between the Jack and me," he said, unwilling to share his business with anyone.

She'd obviously pegged him as an outsider since she'd tried to gouge him on the drink. He'd gotten the better of that deal, though. The payment details on his credit chip weren't linked to him. They pulled from the account of some rich asshole who wouldn't notice the extra charges. And if he did—well, it wouldn't trace back to Ash.

"You got an appointment?" She crossed her arms over

her chest, a move that pulled the black fabric tight against her torso, outlining breasts that would be plump handfuls. Damn, she was hot, with her long dark hair and dusky skin.

Rein it in, Ash. You can't afford to be distracted by a pretty face.

"What are you, his social secretary?" Was this one of the big changes? It hadn't been easy to see the Jack in the old days, but he didn't remember the man having a gate-keeper like this one. You tried your luck at the bar and if the Jack had time, you pled your case and made your deal.

His joke didn't go over well with the bartender. Her full lips pressed together.

"The Jack's busy tonight." Her tone was pissy and prissy.

And he was a sick, sick man for getting a little thrill from that. The woman had edges, ones he wouldn't mind exploring. Not tonight, though. He'd come here for a reason and damned if he was leaving without what he came for.

"How the hell would you know that?"

"I'm psychic," she said with a mocking smile.

"How about I ask the Jack myself?" He had to see the Jack tonight and if it took circumventing the pretty bartender, that's what he would do.

"Not going to happen." She broke eye contact, sweeping her gaze over his shoulder.

Ash set his drink down, then stood and braced his hands on the bar top. He leaned in, getting as close as he could, given the barrier between them. "Who's going to stop me?"

She didn't flinch. He had to give her props, the woman must have a spine of pure steel. He wasn't physically scary —wiry didn't seem to put the fear of anything into anyone— but he'd learned a few tricks about intimidation from corporate security over the last few years.

"They are," she said, her eyes focused behind him.

Ash shifted sideways and saw the two big burly guys approaching. He was probably the same height, but they each looked double his size. It didn't matter if their strength was real or augmented, they could easily put the hurt on him.

Deciding the bartender was the lesser threat, he turned to face them fully. He eased the tension out of his body and held his hands up. With guys this big, you had to move slowly and speak even slower.

"Problem?" The question wasn't directed at him.

"Do we have a problem, sir?" the pretty bartender asked.

The "sir" was snotty and Ash swiveled his head to glare at her. "I need to see the Jack tonight. Is that a problem?" He didn't dare take his eyes off the bouncers for too long. The big guy who hadn't spoken looked at him funny.

"And I told you that's not going to happen tonight," she said. "Better luck next time."

Ash ground his teeth together. She had an answer for everything and it was clear that the muscle looked to her for leadership. Maybe he should reevaluate his threat matrix.

Shit. After his meeting with Portia, he'd spent the whole day making and discarding plans. When he'd decided to approach the Jack for help, he'd worried about paying for assistance, not getting in. Getting stymied by a hot, stubborn bartender had never crossed his mind.

The bouncers stepped closer.

"How much?" he blurted.

The men stopped moving, so Ash focused on the bartender.

She stared at him, brow raised, a mocking smile on her lips. "How much what?"

Dammit, she knew what he was asking. "Everything for a price, right? How much to get in to see the Jack tonight?"

She didn't even pretend to consider his offer. "Not tonight."

"Why not?" Ash wasn't leaving until he saw the Jack or they dragged him out.

"Because the Jack is busy tonight." The chill in her voice rivaled Portia's. "Get him out of here," she told the bouncers.

"It's an emergency!" The words slipped out.

Security stopped where they were. One directed a questioning glance at the bartender. Ash's gaze bounced between them while "emergency" hung in the air.

Echoing his earlier pose, the bartender had dropped her arms and had her hands braced on the bar, leaning forward. "Seriously?"

"Dead serious."

"Yours?" Her tone warned him not to lie. The bouncers shifted behind him, ready to move if she demanded it.

Ash paused. How to answer that? This whole situation was his fault. But if something happened to him, Hope would pay the price. "My sister. She's sick and I need help getting her, well, help."

Something flared in her eyes and Ash knew he'd chosen correctly. He'd passed the first test. Maybe, just maybe, he'd get what he wanted from the Jack tonight.

"And you want the Jack to help? Rather than, I don't know, a clinic? Or your corporation?" She gestured at his jacket.

"The Jack may be our only hope." That was nothing but truth. "I don't think there's anything the clinics can do. And the corporation?" He shuddered and shook his head. "I already owe them enough."

All true. He owed the Tremaine Corporation plenty—and one of these days he'd figure out how to make them pay.

She stared at him for a minute. He met her gaze and didn't flinch. He didn't go so far as to let her see everything he was, but enough for her to judge his sincerity. Whatever she saw in his gaze seemed to convince her.

"Come back later, right before closing. The Jack will see you then."

How the hell could she know that? He considered the possibility that she really was psychic. Dismissed it almost immediately. Still . . . "How do you know?"

"You said it's an emergency." As if that explained everything. She jerked her head at the bouncers and after a few grumbles, they melted back into the main bar area.

When she turned away to help another customer down the bar, Ash grabbed his drink and tossed back the rest of it. The whiskey burned on the way down, but he didn't care. Couldn't care.

He'd set something in motion tonight. Something big. He hadn't done that in a very long time. It felt good.

CHAPTER 4

TWO HOURS LATER, Taryn slipped into an alley on the other side of town and cleared her mind. Or tried to. She kept thinking about the strange interaction with the man who knew about the Jack but didn't *know* the Jack.

She kept circling back to his story, the one that didn't quite gel for her. She shook her head. That was a worry for later. Right now, she had to focus on the job at hand. Weeks of planning had gone into the next few hours and she couldn't afford to screw it up.

Ignoring the creepiness of the dark alley, Taryn breathed through her mouth to avoid the stench and hurried through the space. She kept to the side of the narrow corridor, walking quickly.

Glass crunched underfoot. She looked down and grimaced. Slivers of glass caught the dim light of her phone and twinkled. She panned the light a few feet to either side. Tiny glass vials lay scattered amongst the other trash.

Vyne, the latest street drug, came in little vials like that. Rumor had it that the high was so intense, so addictive, that you might as well be dead after the first dose. True death came later, when your veins turned green, the side effect that gave the drug its name. Taryn had never seen it—she didn't allow that shit in her bar—but she'd heard too many stories floating around to ignore it.

None of that was what drew her out tonight. She sought a different commodity.

From the end of the alleyway, Taryn watched the cluster of women and girls on the street corner. In the distance, the bright lights and neon signs of downtown Seattle glowed, but here on the edges of the city, the lights were duller, the shadows deeper.

Her gaze landed on the youngest woman and her lips tightened. She looked to be barely into her teens, but had to be closer to sixteen based on the information Taryn had received. The others looked older, probably due to the harshness of life on the street rather than actual years. One of the women noticed Taryn and tipped her head slightly.

Taryn nodded back. Her stomach churned and she took a deep breath to settle herself. She couldn't afford nerves.

She pulled her jacket's zipper down far enough to show a hint of cleavage. The black synth-leather she wore was reinforced with lightweight Kevlar. It would stop small-caliber bullets and some stun weapons, while providing her with more freedom of movement than thicker materials would. If she was successful tonight, she'd need to move quickly. Everything she wore was well-made and expensive-looking and intended to give the impression of a wealthy woman out for a good time.

A hot pink wig covered her dark hair to draw attention away from her features. Her heels might look high, but that was an illusion. They were as sturdy as the boots that corporate security teams wore.

As ready as she could be, Taryn stepped out of the alley.

She put a wiggle in her walk as she approached the youngest girl. "Hi," she said in a breathy voice.

The other women stepped back a few feet, giving Taryn room to negotiate.

Fear flickered over the girl's face before a mask of boredom slammed down. "Hi," she parroted. "You looking for company?"

Her tone aimed for sexy, but all Taryn heard was fear. This was the part she hated. "You free?"

The girl pasted on what Taryn assumed was supposed to be a coy smile, but it looked frightened and distorted. "Not free, but negotiable."

Taryn could have recited those words in her sleep. Some nights, she was afraid she still did. She clamped down hard on the shudder of memory. Forcing a smile, she tossed her head, sending her pink curls swinging. "Great. Who do I talk to about getting you for the whole night?"

Something like panic crossed the girl's face. Taryn understood. Women could be crueler than the men.

"You want me for the whole evening?" she asked in a whisper.

Taryn dragged her fingers over the girl's jaw. "You're such a cutie, who wouldn't want to spend time with you?"

The girl swallowed hard then nodded. "Just a second." She toyed with a woven metal bracelet around her left wrist. It might look decorative, but Taryn was pretty sure that it communicated with the girl's pimp.

Her suspicions proved correct when three figures emerged out of the darkness. Taryn easily ID'd the white guy in the center as the pimp. Slender and without the muscle of the two men—bodyguards, probably—not to mention the air of self-importance surrounding him. Pimps were all the same, thinking they were hot shit and that they owned the people under them.

Tucking her hands into her pockets, Taryn did her best to look non-threatening. Out of sight, her right fist clenched and unclenched.

"You looking to spend the night with my Gazelle?" His voice oozed over her as he stepped toward her.

This close Taryn could see the glimmer of his pants, the threads either reflecting or emitting light as he moved. As tacky as she expected him to be.

She smiled. "For the right price," she said in the same breathy voice she'd used with the girl.

He slung an arm over Gazelle's shoulder. The girl flinched as his arm came around her neck, the tiniest of movements. Taryn bit back a growl.

The figure he named was lower than Taryn had expected. The girl with her youthful looks, long dark hair, and soft curves would fetch a higher price now than she would in a few years when she was used up. After that, she'd probably be traded away or thrown out on the streets, without the "protection" of a pimp. There was no retirement for the girls who worked the street and escape was nearly impossible.

Nearly.

"Done," Taryn said. When he held out a plain tablet, she slid her credit chip across it. The chip was unregistered; she assumed the tablet was too. Anonymity was the name of the game for both sides. As long as her credits were good— and Taryn knew they were very good indeed—Gazelle would be hers for the night.

The pimp kept his arm wrapped around Gazelle's neck and his eyes glued to the screen until the credit transfer was confirmed. His eyes lit up as soon as the transaction was done. "It was a pleasure doing business with you. Wanna join our frequent flier program?"

Taryn's stomach roiled. If she didn't get out of here in the next few minutes, she'd either punch him or puke on his shoes. Neither would serve her purposes.

"If I like her, maybe I'll consider it," Taryn lied. The girl's face lost all color.

"You treat my girl good." He smirked and pushed her toward Taryn. "She's gonna treat you real good."

Taryn wasn't expecting the sudden move and stumbled when the girl's body collided with hers. She managed to keep them both upright and on their feet.

"I'll do that." She faked a smile, hoping it covered the rage building inside her.

"You ready, honey?" Taryn looped her arm through the girl's elbow, deliberately keeping away from her neck. She didn't want to remind Gazelle of her pimp.

The girl nodded. Taryn was grateful that she didn't fight.

"Just a couple of girls ready to party," Taryn muttered under her breath and led Gazelle away.

"Hey, baby!" the pimp called from behind her.

Taryn stopped and flashed a flirtatious look over her shoulder. It took everything to tamp down the urge to wipe that smarmy look off his face. "Yeah?"

"You girls want some company?"

Taryn laughed. "I don't think you could handle it," she said with a flirty shake of her head.

He grunted, then he and his thugs slipped back into the shadows. Taryn walked slowly toward the alley, then stepped into the darkness.

Next to her Gazelle stiffened, but she didn't fight, allowing Taryn to lead her through the darkness.

Once out the other side, Taryn reached into her pocket and used the key fob to start the car. Another button opened the passenger door. Taryn helped the girl slide into the seat, thankful once again that she didn't struggle.

CHAPTER 5

"WHERE ARE WE GOING?"

Taryn shifted her gaze from the car's display to the girl in the seat next to her. "A hotel." Picking Up a Young Street Girl 101. It was in perfect keeping with the persona she'd adopted for the night.

The girl trembled.

"Are you cold?" Taryn commanded the car to turn up the heat.

The girl shook her head. Awkward silence filled the space between them.

"Your name's Gazelle?"

She shook her head again. Then, just when Taryn had given up on her answering, she whispered, "It's Giselle. He could never say it right."

Fuck. It wasn't bad enough that Giselle's whole life had been stripped away from her. She was taunted with her loss every time he used the almost-but-not-quite-right name. That sucked.

"Nice to meet you, Giselle," Taryn said softly.

Giselle gave her a funny look, then went back to staring out the window.

Several minutes later, Taryn pulled into the back lot of a no-tell motel on the fringes of the city. The flickering neon lights may have once enticed long-ago visitors to enjoy free Wi-Fi and in-room hot tubs. Now the only thing that kept the place in business was no ID requirements and a strict cash-only policy.

"Get out," Taryn said when they stopped in the darkened parking lot.

"Here?" Fingers on the passenger window, Giselle's voice wavered.

"You got a problem with this place?" She was curious how Giselle would respond.

The girl sucked in a breath. "No, it's perfect." Her voice was stronger than it had been.

Interesting. If Taryn didn't know better, she'd have said the girl's voice oozed sarcasm, but sarcasm was a dangerous game when you were a street girl.

Still, Taryn admired her gumption. It meant she'd made the right choice. "Good." It really was the perfect location for what she needed. "Follow me." Taryn grabbed a small overnight bag and a small metal carrying cage from the trunk and locked the car.

Tucking her arm into Giselle's, Taryn led her through the dark parking lot to the room she'd rented earlier on a burner phone.

She held the code up to the scanner and the old-school system flickered a weak green. Pushing open the door, Taryn studied the room. A big bed dominated the space. The faded bedspread covering it probably hadn't been changed in decades. Sadness and desperation hung in the air—they'd probably soaked into the walls.

It would do.

Waving Giselle to go ahead of her, Taryn set the cage outside, then closed and locked the door, setting the chain as well as a portable deadlock she'd brought with her. She intentionally didn't look at Giselle. The girl was terrified. Things wouldn't improve any time soon.

"Have a seat." Taryn gestured to the bed.

Giselle perched on the edge with a grimace. Her hands fluttered as she decided whether to fold them in her lap or brace them on the mattress and lean back seductively. She settled for placing them in her lap. In the room's bright lights, Giselle looked like a girl playing dress up.

Taryn wanted to cry. Instead, she channeled all those emotions into her resolve.

Digging into her overnight case, Taryn pulled out an untraceable tablet. She opened a popular music app, put it on the bedside table, and turned it up. It took a little fiddling to find the perfect volume: loud enough to cover her conversation, but not loud enough that the neighbors would complain. Like Taryn, the people who frequented these hotels didn't want to draw any attention.

Taryn stalked around the room one more time, studying the setup. Satisfied, she turned to Giselle. "Go into the bathroom and take off your clothes. Leave them there," she said in a cold steady voice.

Giselle stared at her, horror slowly wiping away the tentative smile that had been growing since Taryn hadn't immediately attacked her.

"What?" Arms wrapped around her middle, Giselle stared at her with wide dark eyes.

"Go into the bathroom. Take off your clothes," she repeated. "Wear a towel if you want." She knew Giselle was scared. That was what she wanted. Quiet and less likely to ask questions.

Giselle ran into the bathroom, slamming the door behind her.

Taryn smiled. Terrified or not, the girl still had a small defiant streak.

While she was alone, Taryn pulled a few more items from her bag and placed them on top of the rickety dresser.

She'd built an hour for coaxing Giselle out of the bathroom into her schedule. Fortunately, it wasn't nearly that long before the door opened and the girl stepped out. The worn towel mostly covered the girl's slim figure.

She approached Taryn and the bed timidly.

"Sit down," Taryn commanded.

Eyes wide, Giselle did what she was told.

Good. What Taryn was about to do was difficult. Unquestioning obedience would make it somewhat easier. She studied the supplies she'd laid out on the dresser. Picking up a scalpel and a topical anesthetic cream, she turned back to Giselle.

The girl's face paled. "Please don't hurt me."

Taryn crouched and placed her hand on Giselle's knee. The girl flinched, though she tried to hide it.

"I need you to listen to me very carefully. Do you understand?"

After a long moment, Giselle nodded.

Unfortunately, Taryn needed more. "Do you understand me?"

"Yes." Giselle whimpered. "Please don't hurt me."

"I'm not going to hurt you," Taryn said. Well, that wasn't true. She wasn't going to lie to her. "Scratch that, I am going to hurt you, but not for fun. I'm trying to help you."

"How?" The single word trembled.

"Do you like your life?"

The girl stared at her like it was a trick question. "Do you?" Taryn added more force to her voice.

"No." This time the girl's voice was stronger.

"Good. I can get you out of it, but you have to do exactly what I say."

Giselle looked around the room. Taryn was sure that she was looking for the trick. A hidden camera, unseen audio recorders. "The room is clean." She wrinkled her nose at the bedspread underneath Giselle. "Electronically, at least. Do you want out?"

Giselle swallowed hard. "Yes." Her voice was barely a whisper.

A wave of relief flowed through Taryn. If the girl had said no, she would have asked one more time, then returned her to her pimp after a few hours. She held Giselle's gaze. "Are you ready to do exactly what I say?"

With a deep breath, Giselle nodded. "Yes."

"Where's your tracking device?"

"In my thigh," Giselle said.

"Show me."

With another deep breath, the girl pulled the towel aside and extended her leg.

Taryn tucked the towel down to help preserve the girl's modesty. Giselle may have been on the streets long enough not to care, but Taryn believed it was never too early to help her rebuild her boundaries.

"Right here." Giselle ran her finger over a scar inches from her sex.

"Bastards." Not only did the pimps mark their prostitutes with fucking tracking chips like property, they made it as unpleasant as possible.

Taryn switched the scalpel to her left hand and grabbed the cream with her right. "I'm going to cut it out, but it's going to hurt. A lot. This ointment will dull the pain some. It also has antibiotic properties."

She handed the tube to Giselle. "Spread this over the scar and six inches around the area."

"You want me to do it?" she whispered.

Taryn nodded. "This is the first step toward your new life."

"Okay." Giselle shook her head. "Okay," she repeated, her voice stronger. She took the tube from Taryn and applied the ointment as directed. When she was done, she capped the tube and set it on the bed next to her.

"Do you feel the tingling?" Taryn watched her closely.

"Yes."

"That means it's working." Taryn pulled the sterile scalpel from the wrapper. "It'll help, but it won't block all the pain. If you scream, it could bring attention that neither of us want. Do you want something to bite down on?" Personally, Taryn wouldn't do it. She'd embraced the pain, accepted it as the price of freedom.

"No. I won't scream."

It was a vow. Taryn honored it as such.

"Okay, scoot back and lay down with your leg extended. I'll make this as quick as I safely can."

The girl did as she was told. Her fingers curled into the bedspread, but other than that she was still. Taryn hated to imagine the circumstances that had given her such control.

Taryn took a deep breath. She hated this part. Hated it every damn time. The only way she could get through it was to remind herself why she did it. She set up the rest of her tools, quietly narrating each step out loud. There was no need for Giselle to suffer and wonder what was happening.

Everything was in place. Taryn donned gloves and found her focus through steady breaths. She placed the tip of the scalpel slightly above the scar and pressed down. The skin beneath the blade resisted . . . until it didn't. Giselle's quick indrawn breath was the only sound she made.

Blood welled along the cut. Absorbent gauze clenched in her other hand, Taryn created an inch-long incision right next to the scar. With quick, practiced motions, she set the scalpel down on the sterile sheet she'd brought with the tools and picked up spreaders and a set of tweezers.

"This is the worst part," she quietly warned Giselle. Every time she dug a tracker out of another woman, Taryn remembered the pain of digging out her own tracking chip.

Blood welled from the cut and she wanted to gag. She'd rather face down the most thuggish of pimps on the street than do this. But it was the most important step. She didn't —couldn't—trust it to anyone else.

"I'm sorry." Her apology was the only indication that she was paying any attention to the girl on the bed. Taryn separated the incision with the spreaders, then blotted away the blood, revealing her first glimpse of the tracker. The tag was small, barely the size of her pinkie fingernail, and a mottled silver under the dark blood.

It didn't look like the chip had been in long enough to grow into the muscle. God, she hoped it hadn't. That was the worst. So many more chances to cause permanent damage to the girl she was trying not to hurt.

With a steady hold on the tweezers, Taryn forced everything but the task before her out of her mind.

The blood made the chip slippery and Taryn lost her grip on it twice. It had to hurt, but except for a hiss of pain, Giselle hadn't moved. Taryn was damn impressed. In the worst of circumstances, the young woman was bearing up well under the pressure.

That strength boded well for Giselle's ability to adapt. The steps from hotel room surgery to a brand-new life weren't easy.

"Yes." Taryn established a secure grip on the chip on her third try. She pulled it straight up, hoping to minimize Giselle's pain. When the thin metal bit cleared the incision, Taryn set it on the towel. As much as she wanted to destroy it, the tracker was crucial to her plans.

"The tag is out," she told Giselle. "I'm going to patch you up, then on to stage two."

As she'd hoped, the mention of the next stage caught Giselle's attention.

"What's stage two?" Giselle's voice was faint with pain, but carried a thread of that inner strength.

"After I seal up this cut, we'll dispose of the tracker and get you somewhere safe."

"How will you know it's safe?"

How much to tell her? Taryn understood her doubt, but she wouldn't risk the other women she'd rescued.

"Where we're going, you'll be able to stay out of sight as much as you want while you decide what you want to do next."

Taryn released the spreaders and carefully removed them from the cut. She cleaned the incision again and covered it with antibiotic cream and self-sealing skin adhesive. Unless Giselle developed an infection, the cut would heal with barely a scar. At least on the outside. Taryn would do what she could to make sure the girl had as few other scars as possible.

"There are other girls there—"

Giselle lurched upright, then fell back with a whimper.

"Easy now," Taryn cautioned. "The other girls are like you—off the streets and living new lives."

"Promise?" Giselle asked, sounding young and afraid.

Taryn's heart broke all over again. "Promise," she said, glad it was one she could keep. She shook off the melancholy and slipped back into Jack mode. "Let's get you up. Be careful. It's going to hurt—a lot—especially when the numbing agent wears off."

With Taryn's help, Giselle rolled to her side and sat up, clutching the towel against her chest. Then she spread her legs and tried to see the wound.

"Here." Taryn handed her a small mirror, then stood and turned her back while Giselle checked out the results of the impromptu surgery. Taryn had witnessed this ritual before. "I'll get you some clothes."

"Will it leave a scar?"

"Probably," Taryn admitted. "If you're careful and let it heal, it'll probably be a small one that gets less noticeable with time. Picking at it will only make it worse."

"Okay." Giselle's voice was stronger now.

Taryn pulled a pair of baggy black pants and an oversize blue sweatshirt out of her bag, as well as underwear and a tank top. All the clothing still had tags. "You decent?"

"Yes."

Taryn handed the pile of clothes to the girl. "Put these on." She added a simple pair of flats to the pile. They should fit the girl well enough to get out of here.

"What about my other clothes?" Giselle asked.

Taryn arched her brow. "Do you really want to put those back on?"

Giselle thought about it before she shook her head. "No, I guess not."

"These will keep you covered and warm until we get

you out of here. Can you stand?" A hard question for someone who'd just had surgery on her leg. Taryn's tone was brisk. She was itching to get out of here. The more distance—the more time—they could put between them and this room, the better she would feel.

She wanted to give Giselle more time, but the clock was ticking. If it ran out—if they were caught—then all Taryn's hard work and planning would be for nothing.

"I'll try," Giselle said. Once more Taryn was proud of this girl who kept fighting.

She watched intently as Giselle planted her feet on the floor and used her hands to push off the bed. When her legs took her full weight, Taryn caught the wince that flashed across her face, but other than a slight hiss of breath, Giselle made no sound.

The girl steadied herself with a hand on the bed, then flashed a beaming smile when she managed to stay upright. "I can walk."

"Good." The girl was slight, but Taryn didn't want to carry her. That would draw unwanted attention. It was better if no one noticed them and no one remembered them.

"Get dressed," Taryn reminded her.

Giselle dropped the towel and the dingy white cotton puddled around her feet. Bruises and scars marred her skin and she was too thin.

Pity and anger roiled within Taryn and she fought to keep calm.

One step at a time. They had to get away cleanly before she could help Giselle with her scars and anything else she needed.

The girl popped the tags off the clothes and dressed quickly. The oversize clothes swamped her.

Taryn dipped into her bag again and pulled out a prewrapped snack kit and a sealed bottle of nutrient-enriched water.

"Here." She thrust the packages at Giselle. "Eat and drink. You need to keep your strength up. It will help with the healing."

Giselle took them tentatively. She stared hard at them, then set them on the bed. Fists clenched, she asked, "How much do they cost?"

Taryn stopped what she was doing and studied her. Giselle must have taken her look as a challenge because she flinched and dropped her gaze. She looked up almost immediately and stared at Taryn defiantly. "What does this all cost?"

Ah. Taryn leaned against the dresser, arms crossed. About half the girls asked. The other half were usually too scared. The question broke her heart every time. "This rescue? It's free."

Giselle shook her head. "I don't believe you. Why are you doing this? Is it a trick?"

Taryn spread her hands wide. "It's not a trick. Not a trap. I'm doing this because I was once like you." She turned sideways and tugged down the neck of her shirt. "You see this scar?"

Her finger traced the thick, ragged scar on her left shoulder blade. "I got that when I cut out my own chip." Echoes of the pain she endured when she dug it out raced through her body. She closed her eyes and forced the agony back into the past where it belonged.

Giselle gasped.

"That was my first step to getting out of this life." Taryn didn't tell her that she'd been caught and chipped again. That would send the poor girl screaming.

She tugged her top back in place. "The rescue is free.

Mostly free," Taryn corrected. "Removing the chip, getting you a place to live, training you on new skills? All free. Once you're on your feet, we'll come to an arrangement. Each woman pays me a bit of their salaries."

Taryn held up a hand to forestall the accusation that she'd become their pimp. "Real jobs. Some work in offices, others get jobs in restaurants or hospitals. The funds are used to pay it forward and cover expenses for the next girl I rescue." She paused. "And each of them owe me a favor."

"What if they don't agree to that? What happens then?" Giselle asked, a tiny fire in her tone.

Taryn shrugged. "Nothing."

"Now I know you're lying. No one does something for nothing." Giselle surged for the door.

Taryn's right arm shot out to block her. "If a girl doesn't want to help after I've helped her, that's fine. I don't like it, but I don't take it out on her. When I say nothing happens, that's the truth. If her pimp comes after her, I do nothing. If she gets into trouble, I do nothing." She stared hard into Giselle's eyes. "Now do you understand?"

Giselle never dropped her gaze. Fear and hope and disbelief warred in her eyes. She nodded.

That wasn't enough. "Out loud."

"Yes, I understand."

"Do you believe me?"

Giselle hesitated this time, thought it over. Another positive sign. "I'm not sure."

"Fair enough. Now, do you want me to put the chip back in and you can forget all this happened?"

"No. No!" The young woman stared at the blood-covered chip laying on the bed in horror.

"Good answer," Taryn said. "Here's what happens next."

Wearing a clean pair of gloves, Taryn cleaned up the chip. Giselle's pimp might have coded it to her, but she wanted as much of the girl's genetic material off it before releasing it into the wild. She didn't want any trace of herself on it either.

"Please don't scream," Taryn said when she finished. "This is the kind of gross part."

"Grosser than cutting that out of my leg?" Giselle's laugh held the slightest bit of hysteria.

"Yeah, sorry." Taryn waved the girl toward the back of the room, then opened the front door. She scanned the area for people, then crouched and reached for the cage hidden in the shadows to the left of the door.

This was the last step before they left the hotel and it was the part Taryn hated most. She wrapped her fingers around the cage's handle and pulled it into the room.

She closed and locked the door, all while keeping the cage at arm's length.

"Oh my god, is that a rat?!" Giselle squealed and retreated into the bathroom.

"Shhh," Taryn warned. She set the cage on the dresser. It took discipline to not give in to the willies.

The cage held a big rat. One that was fucking huge and creeped her the fuck out. "Yes, it's a rat," she said with more calm than she felt, "and he's going to help us get you free."

"I don't have to touch it or anything, do I?" Giselle asked from the safety of the bathroom.

"No. I'm the one who has to touch it."

"Gross!"

Yeah, that summed up Taryn's feelings too. Unfortunately, it was the best way she'd found to take care of the chip.

"Take off your bracelet," she instructed Giselle. "You can do it without contacting him, right?"

Giselle nodded. Her gaze dropped slowly from the rat to her wrist. She slid it carefully over her hand. She held it out to Taryn.

Taryn hid a smile as she took in the distance the girl kept between her and the rat. Taryn opened her hand and the girl dropped the thin band into it.

"I'm going to put the bracelet and this," she held up the chip, "on it." Taryn pointed to the rat. "When we let him go, your pimp will be tracking it and not us."

"Isn't that dangerous?"

Now *she was worried about the danger?*

"No more than anything else. Plus, it gives us a chance to get away. Get you safe." She paused. "Any other questions, or are you ready to go?"

"Ready to go, I guess."

"Great." Taryn really hated this part. More than once she'd considered using some kind of drone or mechanical rodent, but nothing worked quite as well as the real thing.

She donned reinforced synth-leather gloves and grabbed the rat. It squealed and she was thankful that the music covered the noise.

Her hand wrapped around its torso and she shuddered as it wiggled. Although there was a full thick layer of material between them, it felt like they were skin to skin.

Ugh.

The rat wriggled and squirmed and all Taryn wanted to do was open her hand and let him go. Then wash her hands a million times.

Gripping the rat with her right hand, she slipped Giselle's bracelet over its head. Then she smeared adhesive on the rat's coat with her left. Then she grabbed the chip, careful not to damage the small circuitry and carefully, so carefully, she pressed the chip against the adhesive. That earned her a higher-pitched squeal. She startled and the rat bit her. She felt the faint contact even through the thick glove.

"Son of a bitch!"

"Ohmygod! Are you okay?" Giselle raced to her side.

"I'm fine." She pulled off her gloves to double-check. She stared at her right hand, nearly 100 percent sure that there was no way those little rat teeth could have penetrated the metal. Still, she had to make sure. It was a compulsion she'd never quite broken in the years she'd had the prosthetic arm.

"You . . . have a metal arm." Giselle sounded intrigued.

"Yeah." Though she frequently wore long sleeves that covered it, Taryn didn't hide it. The molded metal ran from her shoulder joint to the tips of her fingers. She had a good range of motion, fine motor skills, and could throw a helluva punch, but it wasn't a high-end prosthetic. It was the best she'd been able to afford when she'd needed it.

Taryn tested it a few seconds longer. No feeling, no harm.

"You ready to go?" Her voice was brusque, but the girl stared at her arm in fascination. "We need to get moving." She packed as efficiently as she had unpacked.

"Um, yeah, sure."

Taryn scanned the room and ran a mental inventory. Everything but the rat was back in the bag. "You want your other clothes?" she asked Giselle.

"No!"

Good. That was exactly the answer Taryn wanted. She'd leave them here in case there were extra trackers.

"One more thing." She reached into the bag and pulled out the final piece of her plan. The crystalline tube held a blue liquid under a high-pressure seal. When the seal the broke, it became a gas that dissolved organic matter, like the invisible bits of DNA that she and Giselle left in the room. Everyone said that it wouldn't dissolve people, but Taryn refused to remain in the room to test it. She'd purchased the tube on the black market and, well, you couldn't always be sure of the quality.

"Listen, I need you to do two things for me." Taryn didn't usually involve them in this part, but Giselle seemed to be holding it together better than other girls had.

She nodded, her eyes wide.

"Pick up the cage after I take the rat out. And take this." Taryn held out the cylinder.

Giselle didn't reach for it immediately. "What is it?"

Deciding "a highly concentrated chemical soup" would only freak the girl out, Taryn said, "A chemical eraser. It'll make sure there's no trace of us left in the room."

"That sounds dangerous." She tucked her hand behind her back.

Dammit. Taryn couldn't afford for her to get squeamish now. "Less dangerous than your pimp." The words were harsh, but true. "It'll make it harder for him to find you."

Apparently, those were the magic words. Giselle plucked the cylinder out of Taryn's grasp before the words were out of her mouth. "What do I do?"

"When we get to the door, I'll open it. You throw the tube at the back wall of the room. Hard. I'll close the door, let the rat go outside, and then we'll get the hell out of here."

Slinging the bag over her shoulder, Taryn grabbed the damn rat out of his cage. He wiggled and she resisted the urge to drop him. Not until they got outside. She opened the door the moment Giselle picked up the cage and the three of them stepped into the dark parking lot.

CHAPTER 6

THEIR EXIT from the motel had gone as planned and the ride back to the bar was uneventful. Once there, it took Taryn almost an hour to get Giselle settled into one of the back rooms. The excitement of the evening had masked Giselle's fear, but once they slowed down, she was understandably afraid that her pimp would find her.

Taryn didn't blame her. Escape was hard, often impossible. She'd tried over and over and had the scars to prove it. Only time and support would ease Giselle's fears.

She stood outside Giselle's door, waiting for the telltale snick of the lock. There it was.

"Good girl, Giselle," she murmured. The new girl was smart. That would increase her chances of being one of the ones who made it.

Exhaustion flooded through her. It wasn't last call yet and she debated about checking in with Dani. No, the bar was in good hands and Taryn was totally drained. Rescues were high stress. Any number of things could go wrong and she had to be prepared for all of them.

She turned down the hallway that led to her room and found Jenna, one of the waitresses, waiting for her.

"That guy's here."

"What guy?" Taryn stared at her blankly. It wasn't a date. She couldn't remember the last time she'd had a date. Or anything resembling one.

"The one who wanted to see the Jack. Dani said to let you know."

"Shit." Now she remembered him. The cute corporate drone who had been savvy enough to be aware of the Jack, but not who the Jack was. "He came back?"

Jenna shook her head. "He never left."

Fuck. She was so damn tired. Official meetings with the Jack required all her focus. Taryn forced a smile. "Give me fifteen minutes to clean up then bring him to the office."

"Will do."

Jenna turned to go and Taryn put a hand on her arm to stop her. "If you could get me a coffee, too, that would be amazing."

With her coffee in hand and the first gulps of caffeine hitting her system, she studied the man on the other side of her desk. Dark hair that gleamed in the brighter lights of her office. Boring clothes that didn't improve with better lighting. But it was his eyes that caught her attention. Gray eyes that held pools of shadow. She pegged him for about her age, but the dark circles under his eyes made him look older.

He'd blurted "You're the Jack?" when Jenna let him into her office and he'd continued to study her when she'd nodded. He hadn't said anything else after that.

Taryn wanted this over with so she could get to bed. She leaned back in her chair, enjoying the way it conformed to her body. "What is it you think the Jack can help you with?"

Supplicants to the Jack usually came in one of two types: those who wept and begged and those who demanded. The man before her did neither. He didn't even fidget.

The visitor's chair was intentionally uncomfortable, intended to remind those who sat there that she had the power, not them. It hadn't been Taryn's idea—the chair was a carryover from the previous Jack, and maybe even the ones before him. Taryn had only kept it because it worked.

When he finally spoke, it was something she could never have imagined. "Free my sister from the Tremaine Corporation."

"Oh, is that all?" The sarcasm slipped out because she was tired and her defenses were down. But since this man had no experience with her as the Jack, he likely wouldn't recognize how unusual, how out of character that was.

He was the second Tremaine employee to cross her path in the last several weeks. Most corporate types avoided this part of town. For him to be here . . . Her gut said something was up with that company, something more than just the new CEO. Could she use this to her advantage?

"That's a big ask."

He nodded.

"Big asks don't come cheap." She watched him closely. Was this a trap?

"I realize that. Can you do it?" His voice was strained, a crack in his cool façade. There it was—this was personal.

Or maybe that was her imagination. He was a cool customer.

Could she do it? Probably, but drawing the attention of a corporation wasn't something she did lightly.

She didn't know much about the inner workings of a multinational like the Tremaine Corporation. Whispers said that there was a way to buy out a contract. Dizzie, a Tremaine courier who had used the Jack's services, had definitely been working toward that. Personally, Taryn thought it was just for show. Letting people go wasn't in the best interest of the company.

"If you have enough money to purchase my services, surely you have enough to buy out her contract." Taryn watched him closely.

He flinched and lifted a hand to the back of his neck. He stopped halfway, clenched his hand into a fist and dropped it back into his lap. "That's the problem. She doesn't have a contract." He paused, stared at his hand. "She *is* the contract."

"Well, shit." The words whooshed out, tiredness once again getting in the way of her self-control.

"Yeah, that about sums it up." He laughed bitterly.

"How did that happen?"

He met her gaze, unflinching. "Does that matter?"

"If you want my help, then yes, I expect you to answer my questions." That was a hard line.

"She got caught in the middle."

That was a non-answer if she ever heard one. She'd let him finish, but Taryn couldn't see a reason to help him out. She wouldn't go up against a corporation on vague answers. "I assume because she's the contract, your sister can't leave Tremaine Corporation on her own."

He laughed, a bitter, angry sound. "Correct."

"Is she in prison?"

He shook his head.

Taryn set her coffee cup aside, then leaned forward, elbows on the desk. He watched her every move and she didn't speak until she had his full attention. "I don't have time to play twenty questions, Mr. Jackson. If you're going to waste my time, you can leave."

"Cutter."

"Cutter what?"

"My name is Ash Cutter. Not Eli Jackson."

Before escorting him to Taryn's office, Jenna had pulled the name from the credit chip he'd left at the bar. Another lie. Another strike against helping him.

She had to admit, though, "Ash" suited him better.

"Okay, Ash Cutter. I'm done with the games. Give me details or get out."

"Will you help me?" He looked slightly panicked.

"I can't see why I should. You've done nothing but play games and waste my time. I should charge you for the last ten minutes." She was tired, getting a headache. He might be good looking, but he was woefully unprepared.

"You want me to pay? Fine, here." He stood and dug into his pocket. Pulling out a handful of credit chips, he tossed them on the desk, where they clattered and bounced.

One, two, three, four . . . A dozen credit chips of various sizes lay before her. "You just wander around with a pocket full of credits?"

Not what she expected from a run-of-the-mill corporate drone. Damn him for getting interesting again.

"Yeah. Don't you?" he challenged.

Taryn smirked. Of course she did, but she ran a bar in Seattle's seedy underbelly. She wasn't beholden to a company like most people were. She didn't casually swipe her company-issued card to buy things.

She swept the credits up with one hand and dropped them in a drawer. "That should cover our conversation tonight."

It didn't matter how much they were worth. She didn't need his money. She'd take it—she wasn't crazy. The chips could be blank, but he had to know that was a bad idea. She'd never help him rescue his sister if they were worthless.

"So, you'll help?"

He was persistent. "Oh no. I haven't agreed yet. You've bought yourself another meeting." She smiled across the desk at him. The one that had made men in his position cry. He stood his ground. "Set something up at the bar on your way out. They'll let me know. Daryl will show you out."

"I need an answer now," he insisted.

Taryn stood and looked at him with a mix of pity and exasperation. "Think very carefully about what you just said. You won't like my answer if you insist on having it tonight."

Her office door opened and he didn't have time to respond before Daryl stepped in. Her guard looked at Ash and sneered.

Ash braced his hands on the desk and leaned over it. Taryn watched him, curious if he would threaten or beg. Despite her initial read, he was just like everyone else.

"I will convince you to help me. I'll do whatever it takes to get my sister out of Tremaine's hands."

"I'll give you another chance to convince me, Ash," she drawled his name, enjoying the way it rolled off her tongue, "but you'd best be much better prepared."

Very few people understood that this truly was a business. She may not run it exactly the way the previous Jack had, but she did run it just as carefully. Sob stories didn't move her. Cold hard cash did. Stories didn't protect her or the women she rescued. Money did.

She watched him, saw him struggle not to respond. Ash

didn't move for a long second, long enough that Daryl looked at her, a question in his eyes. She waved him off.

"Fine. I'll see you later." Ash turned and left the room.

Taryn admired the view until Daryl closed the door behind both of them.

Ash Cutter was interesting enough to earn another meeting. It didn't hurt that he was hot. Too bad neither were reason enough to help him. She had her hands full as it was.

CHAPTER 7

THAT COULD HAVE GONE BETTER. Ash wanted to punch something, anything, but mostly himself. He'd ruined his shot because he'd been too fucking gobsmacked that the hot bartender was the Jack. When had that happened?

He followed his escort back to the bar area. The pretty redhead with the pale skin was still behind the bar, wiping down the bar top and watching the patrons. She'd been there most of the night while he waited—others had helped out, but she seemed to be in charge. The Jack had told him to set the next meeting up at the bar. Ash needed that second appointment. Needed the chance to convince her to help him. He slid onto the same barstool he'd had earlier.

"Whiskey, no water?" the redhead asked.

"Yeah. Same tab too." All his credits were in the Jack's desk drawer. The one he'd left to cover his tab should have plenty left.

"Get what you needed?" She slid his drink in front of him.

"Not even close," he said and laughed cynically. He

sipped the whiskey, enjoying the way the alcohol burned on the way down. "The Jack said you could get me in to see her again."

She studied him, then waved his escort over. Ash couldn't hear what she asked, but Daryl nodded.

"You're telling the truth." She sounded surprised and he was slightly offended.

"So that next appointment?" He didn't want to be a dick, but he'd spent all night waiting for the first meeting. He didn't have time to wait that long again.

"Keep your shirt on." She paused, looked him up and down. "Or, you know, don't. I could use something pretty to look at."

She smiled and he couldn't resist smiling back. She was cute, but she didn't rev his engine the way the Jack did.

How fucked up was that? Today he'd met two of the most powerful women in the city and was totally hot for one of them.

One could help him and one could hurt him. Actually, both could easily ruin his life—ruin Hope's life. He had to figure out how to prevent that from happening.

"Soonest I got is two nights from now." She flipped through an old-school paper notebook. If it had been a regular appointment calendar, he'd have hacked it to get an earlier appointment.

"That's fine." It wasn't, but his options were rather limited.

He downed the last bit of alcohol. The warm burn hit again, this time followed by a head rush. Damn, was he drunk? He couldn't remember the last time he'd gotten drunk. It was too damn risky, especially in his room at Tremaine Headquarters.

He enjoyed the rush for a second longer, then refocused. He had to get back. "Can you close out my tab?"

"Sure." After she'd processed the payment, she handed him the chip.

"Is there anything left on that?" he asked.

"Sure is."

He grabbed her hand and turned it palm up, then dropped the credit chip back into it. "Keep the rest as a tip."

Suspicion flared in her eyes and the flush of anger colored her cheeks. She backed away quickly, dropping the chip on the bar top. "I don't do that."

"Do what?" He'd missed something.

"Whatever it is you're offering a lot of money for. I don't do that anymore."

What the hell? "I wasn't asking you to do anything. I was just leaving you a tip."

"Then you want information on the Jack." Her eyes wide, she remained pressed against the bar.

"No. Not that either." Though he wished he'd thought of it. Too late now. Though it obviously would have been the wrong move.

"Then why did you want to leave me a hundred-credit tip?"

"Shit! I didn't realize it had that much on it." Ash grabbed the credit chip off the bar and shoved it into his pocket. If she didn't want the credits, he wasn't going to throw them away.

"I'll see you in two nights then." He started toward the exit.

"Hey, what about my tip?"

Ash turned halfway and shrugged. "That's all I had on me. You said you didn't want it."

At the door, he slipped his hand into his pocket. Fingering the credit chip, he decided to spring for a ride instead of walking back to headquarters.

CHAPTER 8

TARYN STARED at the spreadsheet in front of her. She'd opened it an hour ago, intending to get some bookkeeping done. That hadn't happened.

What the hell was going on? She didn't get distracted, especially not when it came to the bar. Her focus on Razor Jack's was legendary.

Her knee jiggled. Why was she so damn antsy? She only felt this way when she was planning a rescue. Giselle was here, safe, so that wasn't it.

She'd been restless all morning. Could be lack of sleep. After Dani had told her about her interaction with Ash after their meeting, it had taken Taryn too damn long to convince the other woman that, most likely, he'd only intended a tip when he offered her the credit chip.

Her best friend and first rescue had calmed down and regretted not taking the money. Taryn shook her head. Dani should know better—when someone handed you money, you put it in your pocket and said thank you. Still, she understood Dani's reaction. The years on the street had left scars on both of them.

Between the proffered tip and the pile of credit chips he'd left with Taryn, Ash Cutter had been throwing money around all night. This morning she'd scanned the chips—they were all either unregistered or tied to names that weren't his.

When Taryn had finally crawled into bed last night, she couldn't get the man off her mind. Who the hell was Ash Cutter? And what the hell had he and his sister done to bring the Tremaine Corporation down on them?

"Screw it." She closed the document and shoved away from her desk. Bookkeeping wasn't happening today, at least not right now. A few minutes later, she strolled into the kitchen tucked into the bar's living quarters. "Hey, ladies."

Six young women turned toward her. Five called casual greetings.

Giselle, the sixth, sat frozen, a piece of toast loaded with butter and jelly raised halfway to her mouth.

The fear in her eyes pissed Taryn off. Her hands clenched and she wished Giselle's pimp were here in front of her so she could take her anger out on him. But he wasn't and Giselle needed a gentle hand. Needed to know that Taryn's promises of safety weren't a lie.

Taryn smiled gently, not wanting to scare the new girl further. It didn't seem to help.

Giselle set the toast on her plate and stiffly sat back in her chair.

Dammit. Last night, Giselle had acted like the girls Taryn had seen who thrived in their new lives.

Turning away from the table, she poured a cup of coffee. There was no way she could deal with a scared and abused teenager without caffeine.

She raised the cup and closed her eyes, inhaling the rich aroma. God, that was good. Out in the bar, she charged an arm and a leg for this stuff. Back here, rich delicious coffee was unlimited.

These living quarters were her home and she tried to share that sense of belonging with the women she took in from the streets. This space was the first stop on a long journey. From the very start, she wanted their lives here to be better than what they'd come from. To Taryn, good coffee helped with that.

So did abundant healthy food, new clothes, and a private room with a small bathroom and a door that locked from the inside.

She sipped in silence. The dark, earthy flavor awakened her taste buds, while the caffeine filled the empty places in her soul.

Sip and savor.

Then again.

Finally, she felt ready for the conversation she knew was coming.

Taryn turned back to the table and grabbed an empty chair. She flipped it around and sat with her arms wrapped around the chair back, cradling her coffee. She made introductions between Giselle and the other women who were staying in the back rooms.

Giselle stared at Taryn. "You're the Jack?"

Taryn sighed and nodded. "You can call me Taryn."

"Is that your name?"

"Yes, that's my name." The only piece of her past she'd hung on to.

Her pimp had loved her name. It sounded exotic and he'd charged more because of it. The Jack—the previous Jack—had called her a lot of things, but not usually her name. She'd used that distance to help her reclaim her name, her sense of self.

Only years of barricading those thoughts away allowed Taryn to hide her shudder. She didn't want Giselle to think she was bothered by anything she chose to tell her.

"Why did you take me last night?" She sounded so young.

The other girls around the table quieted. Every time a new girl asked the question, the rest listened intently, waiting to see if Taryn had a different reason than the one she'd given each of them. Each girl had a different story. Some Taryn had seen on the streets or huddling in a corner of the bar. Others like Giselle had been brought to the Jack's attention by other prostitutes.

But the reason she helped them was always the same.

"Because you needed help. And because I thought you could survive that help." Rescue wasn't for the fainthearted.

"What if I hadn't?"

Taryn never answered that question. Never would. These girls didn't need to know how ruthless she could be. Would be. Taryn protected what was hers. If someone didn't want to be here or caused trouble . . . well, she handled that, too.

"Not something we need to worry about, right?" Taryn watched Giselle's reaction, waiting for the girl's slow nod.

"Later today a doctor will be stopping by. A lady doctor," Taryn added before Giselle could panic. "She'll take a look at your wound and make sure everything looks good."

"Do I have to?" Giselle asked.

"Yeah," Taryn said. "I'm not a doctor and it's better to have a professional take a look. She visits every couple weeks—or sooner if we need her."

It looked like Giselle was about to argue again. "You can

have me or one of the other girls stay with you during the appointment if you want."

She held the teenager's gaze until she sighed and nodded reluctantly.

Changing the subject, Taryn gestured around the kitchen. "Help yourself to anything in the kitchen at any time, unless it has someone's name on it. Most everything is communal, but every once in a while, someone gets territorial."

She turned to one of the other girls. "Would you show Giselle around and give her the rest of the rundown?"

When the other girl agreed, Taryn excused herself. "Business calls."

CHAPTER 9

THE ELEVATOR DINGED at the same time the door slid open, revealing the executive floor. Ash had been allowed up on his own today, although there was a guard stationed both at the bottom and at the top. Maybe it was the lack of guards, but the ride had seemed shorter, definitely less tense.

Ignoring the guard, he stepped out and strode toward the doors to Portia's office. *Ms. Tremaine's* office, he corrected. He wasn't sure what the penalty for using her first name was, but he couldn't imagine that it was good.

Halfway there, he paused and spoke to the assistant. "Ms. Tremaine is expecting me." More like *summoned*, given the message waiting for him when he got home in the early hours of the morning.

She barely looked at him before she said, "Go on in."

Ash frowned. That wasn't very assistant like of her. Whatever other thoughts he'd had dissipated when the office doors opened.

Back to the door, Portia stood at the opposite side of the office, in front of the wall of windows. The city of Seattle sprawled out in front of her. On anyone else, the slumped shoulders would make him think she was lonely . . . Ash snorted softly. This was Portia Tremaine. He wasn't sure she *had* feelings.

No, that wasn't fair. Before the bombing, that might have been true. But he at least had witnessed her overwhelming grief at losing her husband. And the terrible anger that had followed. He dreaded the day she turned that anger on him. That was why he and Hope had to be out of the city as soon as possible. Why he needed the Jack's help so desperately.

Ash cleared his throat, uncomfortable witnessing this vulnerable moment. He couldn't afford to see the Tremaines as anything but his enemy.

She turned, back straightening, shoulders pulling back while he watched. Whatever hint of humanity he'd imagined had disappeared, leaving only the Ice Queen behind. He thought he saw a little moue of annoyance before that disappeared as well.

"Your workstation has been set up," she said, skipping hello or any courtesies. That was fine. He preferred to get down to business.

A very small desk that looked like it had been requisitioned from the orphanage sat between her desk and the windows. It looked like something you might see on bring-your-child-to-work day. Was that where she'd gotten the idea? Unlikely. Neither Phillip nor Portia Tremaine seemed capable of whimsy.

He stepped toward it. Stopped. "May I?"

"Of course." That cool tone—the Ice Queen granting him a boon.

Ash circled the desk. It looked nothing like the one he used in the cybersecurity center.

The chair was almost as tall as the desk. It was plain, with a metal back and worn cushions. Sure, to the untrained eye, it might look like a hacking chair. If you squinted.

He sat carefully. The chair creaked, but held. It was so uncomfortable, though. His knees hit the desk when he rolled up to it. With the added distance, his arms barely reached the keyboard and his neck bent awkwardly when he stared at the screen.

"I can't do this." He levered out of the chair with difficulty.

Portia stalked across the room. "The project?"

He almost nodded, then thought better of it and chose his words carefully. "I can't work with this equipment."

"It's a top-of-the-line computer. It won't officially be released until the end of the year." Her expression practically dared him to argue further.

Was it? He hadn't even looked at the computer. He did now and whistled. It was gorgeous. "Very nice. How'd you manage to score this?" He couldn't wait to test it out.

He didn't expect an answer, but she said, "I do have friends."

His jaw dropped.

Her icy gaze narrowed. "Don't try to tell me the computer is the problem."

"Oh, no. It isn't." He was sincere. "I wasn't talking about the computer. I can't wait to get my hands on it." Another truth. "That's the problem—I can't."

"Spell it out for me."

Arms crossed over her chest and dressed in her usual style despite the somber black, she was the picture of icy impatience. Even when the Jack had been impatient in their meetings, the fire in her gaze, her movements, drew him closer. Portia made him want to back away.

"I can't reach it." He sat back down, demonstrated. "You're hobbling me if you expect me to work on this system."

She circled the small desk. Her gaze was cool, assessing. He shivered.

"This was the best my assistant could do at short notice."

Ash doubted that. "Probably the easiest," he muttered under his breath.

She circled him again and he felt like a shark's next meal.

"It does look like a problem," she conceded when she'd finished her second loop.

The silence stretched between them until Ash broke it. "I can give you a list of what I need."

That glare again.

"A list of possible solutions," he amended.

"Show me." She gestured at his workstation.

Ash stifled a sigh. He'd hoped that she would let him use her computer. He wasn't completely sure he could create a back door to her system, but he'd planned to try. Portia Tremaine *had* to have secrets. There was no way someone that high in the company—a Tremaine!—didn't.

But in all his time at the company, all the time working with Leopold Brunswick to uncover Tremaine secrets, he'd found nothing on her. Which didn't seem possible. How could anyone raised by Phillip Tremaine have clean hands?

He scootched as close to the desk as he could get, angling his knees under to reach the keyboard. Ash made sure the chair creaked with each movement.

The computer walked him through setting up the biometric scanner and multiple passwords. "This machine is amazing." He didn't get a reply. Hadn't expected one, either. He glanced back to see how closely she was watching him.

Boredom and impatience looked back at him.

Taking a chance, he created an unregistered profile. It wasn't foolproof but it should prevent the majority of the Tremaine tracking software from watching his every move. Under the guise of setting up the profile, he pulled up the command line interface and reviewed the software that had been installed on this machine. He wouldn't put it past Portia to install in-house software to monitor his work.

After five years, he knew most of the programs Tremaine IT relied on—the ones he used and the ones he wasn't supposed to know about. Ash found two of them on the list as he scrolled through. Knowing they were there, he kept his initial keystrokes relatively normal. Nothing IT hadn't seen from him in the past.

He'd try the more complicated moves when she wasn't standing over his shoulder and he had the chance to circumvent the tracking software. Feeling her watchful presence, Ash realized that he knew absolutely nothing about Portia's computer skills.

She didn't know what he was doing—did she? What if she did? What if she'd understood every move he'd made?

Shit. That could be a problem.

"I'm surprised you don't have a computer like this." He tried to make the comment sound like casual conversation, not a fishing expedition.

"Who says I don't?"

Well, that told him precisely nothing.

Deciding that was a problem for later, Ash pushed those worries away and pulled up a furniture site. Still standing over his shoulder, she didn't say anything as he scrolled through desks and then chairs.

What he really wanted was his old port chair, the one that he'd been forced to leave at the warehouse. It was perfectly worn in, exceptionally comfortable. He could work in it for hours. If he still had a port.

Port chairs were out, though. Portia had made that clear in their first meeting. Asking her again would likely just make her mad. Working quickly, unnerved by her presence, he compiled a list of possible chairs and a couple of desks that would work. "I emailed you the equipment list and pieces that the company probably already has, either in one of the computer rooms or in surplus." Would she balk at being forced to choose his furniture or was that the level of micromanaging she wanted?

The soft chime from her computer let him know it had arrived. Ash looked up to meet her gaze.

She gave nothing away. "Very well. I'll review and ensure you get a more suitable desk. We need to get to work." Her smile was sharp and cold.

Ash shivered, thankful when she returned to her desk.

CHAPTER 10

ASH SHOWED up to visit Hope after hours. He'd made it through his cybersecurity shift—it looked like he would be doing double duty while working for Portia—and all he wanted was to see his baby sister. A visit would ground him. Remind him why he was taking all these risks.

Apparently, Portia had kept her word. They frowned a little and reminded him about visiting hours, but no one stopped him when he walked down the hallway that led to Hope's room.

He stopped outside her door and took a deep breath. He loved his sister, but every visit was so damn painful. The girl in his memories was vibrant and alive. The girl in the hospital bed . . . was not. Five years in a coma hadn't been kind.

Mentally preparing himself to see her took longer each visit. Gluing the pieces of his heart back together after each visit was harder and harder.

Ash had decided a long time ago to keep things cheerful for her—not that he always succeeded. The doctors had told him that she could hear everything he said. If she could hear him, he didn't want to be sad or angry.

He pasted on a smile and pushed open the door. The door closed quietly behind him and he dragged a chair to the side of her bed. The beeps of the machinery surrounding her provided the soundtrack to these visits. A melody as comforting as it was painful.

His heart ached seeing his little sister so still. She'd been a lively eighteen the night that everything had gone to hell. Lack of movement and the hospital's carefully controlled nutrition had removed her curves, turning her thin and bony, her muscles slack with disuse.

Ash pressed the knuckles against his eyes, preventing the tears from escaping. He wanted his sister back. Back from the Tremaines. Back from the living nightmare of this coma.

He gently took Hope's too-thin hand.

"Hi, Hope. I miss you." He leaned close. Every visit began the same way: letting her know he was here, telling her that he loved her. After that, it was pretty much whatever was on his mind.

"A lot's happened since I last saw you." He'd kept her up to date with what had happened at Tremaine Corporation, careful to omit his role.

"I met Portia Tremaine," he said. "She's as terrifying as she looks on screen. She wants my help to catch whoever helped her father's assistant try to bring the company down. But she won't give me access to my port, which sucks."

It was a struggle to keep his conversations light and high-level, but Ash suspected that the company recorded his visits. He would, in their place. Telling Hope about his role in the bombing would be idiotic.

"I met a girl."

Holy. Shit.

He hadn't intended to tell Hope about meeting the new Jack, but it felt right.

"A woman, really. She's pretty amazing, and I don't even know her name."

It had always been easy to talk to Hope. Now was no different. "She owns her own business and is well-respected in her field." And feared, but he didn't want to make it easy for the Tremaine Corporation to identify her.

"She's hot, too." He blushed admitting that to his sister. "And a badass."

Ash looked down to where he held her hand. His thumb rubbed gently over the delicate bones of her fingers.

"It's complicated, though. And probably not the right time to start something—I don't even know if she's interested." He laughed. "Things just feel . . ." he paused, searching for the right word. "Unsettled."

Yeah, that worked. He'd been unsettled ever since Portia had summoned him to her office. Change was coming and he had no idea whether he would survive it or not.

"I don't know if anything will happen between us." He leaned close and whispered in her ear. "I'd like to explore whatever it is that draws me to her."

A nurse cracked open the door and poked her head in. He sat up and nodded. He hated this part.

"They gave me the signal, Hope. I have to go."

He pressed a soft kiss to the top of her hand. Her skin was so translucent that he could see her veins. If she hadn't been hooked up to all the machinery, he'd have thought she was dead, she was that pale and still.

His heart broke again. "I'll see you soon," he whispered.

If not sooner.

Ash gently laid her hand back on the bed and tucked

the blanket around it. He watched the slow rise and fall of her chest for a few seconds longer. He ran his hand over her limp hair—nothing like the bouncy curls she used to have—then used the same hand to wipe away his tears.

"I love you, baby sister." He didn't care who knew that part. She was his only family. He'd already failed her once. He couldn't do it again.

Ash pushed out of his chair and exited the room quickly. It was slightly less painful than a lingering goodbye.

The nurse waited for him in the hallway.

"Any change?" He asked every visit.

"No better, no worse, baby." She gave him a sympathetic smile.

Ash smiled back, though his heart wasn't in it.

His brain was too full, too heavy, so when Ash left the hospital, he decided to walk. Maybe the night air would help him clear it.

Visiting Hope always made him restless and restlessness always made him reckless. That was how he'd been drawn into the bombing plot.

Not that he'd known their true intentions. He'd happened upon an ad seeking dirt on the Tremaine Corporation.

Over the years, he'd helped the company stop hackers and hide information, so he knew it existed.

His initial offerings—petty crimes by executives that were covered up and corporate espionage—had been deemed too mundane. He'd taken that as a challenge.

Now, due to his involvement, his sister was in danger —again.

Ash couldn't fail her a second time. He had to convince the Jack to help him. To help Hope.

CHAPTER 11

THE ANTSY FEELING was back and Taryn was grateful for the manual labor of working behind the bar. She'd sent Dani on a break and taken over. Slinging drinks had a way of emptying your brain. There was no substitute for focusing on doing it right, making the drinks as the orders came in. Keeping up with demand. Making conversation. Tracking payments.

She'd been brought to Razor Jack's unwillingly. The previous Jack had purchased her from her pimp and kept her for his personal use in one of the back rooms. When he wasn't using her in the bedroom, he put her to work behind the bar. Surprisingly, she'd taken to it. She was good at mixing the drinks and interacting with the customers. And she'd enjoyed it.

Despite the fact that the bastard who'd been the previous Jack had made her life a living hell, she'd never blamed the bar. Razor Jack's had provided a roof over her head and almost regular meals.

Thinking of her deceased tormentor, she slammed a glass down on the counter harder than intended.

"Rough night?" a voice rumbled.

A voice she immediately recognized.

She'd spent more time than she'd admit thinking about its owner last night. Taryn looked up and there he was.

"Naw, it's a pretty good one so far. How about you?"

"I've had better." Ash gave her a tired smile.

That urge to learn what was bothering him—because something clearly was—was stronger than it should be.

"Two beers and a couple of house shots!" A waitress called out her order.

She'd never admit it, but Taryn was grateful for the interruption. "Sorry, gotta take care of this."

She moved down the counter to pour the drinks and settle her thoughts. Why was she so interested in his day? He wasn't even supposed to be here tonight. They weren't supposed to meet again until tomorrow.

Setting the drinks on the tray, she filled a few more orders before there was a break in the crowd. Taryn pulled on her moderately interested bartender persona and approached him. "Whiskey?"

Ash shook his head. "Surprise me."

He was dressed more casually today, jeans and a long-sleeved tee. Tattoos peeked out from beneath the collar.

Her fingers tingled with the desire to reach over the bar and trace the thin lines. *Bad idea, Taryn. Bad, bad idea.*

Instead, she gathered the ingredients for a Flashin' Jack, a house special she could make on autopilot. Her focus was frayed and she needed every bit of it to talk to Ash.

She slid the bright yellow drink across the polished wood counter to him.

He looked at it, then at her. "Cheers." He raised his glass to her, then brought it to his lips.

Ash didn't take a tentative sip like she expected. No, he took a big swallow.

"Wow. That wasn't what I was expecting." He took another drink, savoring it slowly this time.

Taryn felt a rush of pride. Due to its garish color, no one expected the Flashin' Jack to be a quality drink. Idiots. Her bar didn't cheap out on the house special. Only quality booze went into that drink. "I know. Chip or tab?"

"Don't suppose I have any credit left from last night?"

She laughed. "Not unless you still have that credit chip you tried to leave as a tip."

Another drink order came in and she stepped away. When she returned a few minutes later, a credit chip sat on the bar in front of him. She wondered whose name the account would be under this time.

"You heard about that, huh?"

She swiped the chip. "J. Banderlee" popped up on the screen. Yeah, definitely not his chip. Not her place to worry about J. Banderlee and their credits, though.

"You want a tab?"

He shook his head, so she swiped the chip and returned it to him. Then, to make sure he knew she was dead serious, she braced her hands on the bartop and looked deep into his eyes. "I hear about everything in my bar."

And it was true. Part constant presence, part intensely loyal staff, Taryn knew everything that happened here. This was her home, her business, her future.

"I didn't mean whatever last night's bartender seemed to think I meant." Concern and confusion were reflected in his gaze.

She smiled. "Yeah, I explained that to her. I don't think she'll be quite so quick to turn down a tip that size next time."

"Good to know." He laughed, a deep earthy sound that sent shivers up her spine. Good shivers.

Dammit. Why was he affecting her this way?

"You never did tell me about that poor glass," he said, the humor still in his voice. "Why were you abusing it?"

Damn, he was charming. She shook off the unwelcome attraction. "You're right, the poor glass was innocent. I was thinking too hard."

"Credit for your thoughts?" He danced the credit chip over his fingertips.

She smiled at his antics and shook her head. "Already forgotten."

He leaned closer, studying her.

Her gaze flicked over the bar, and she made a pretense of checking on the other customers. Instinct told her that he would be more perceptive than she'd like.

"Can I tell you about my sister?" Serious words. A serious face.

Damn, he was persistent. "We're meeting tomorrow, Mr. Cutter. We can do story time then." She used his last name as a shield, a way to maintain distance between them.

"Ash," he said.

"What?" she asked.

"Just call me Ash. Mr. Cutter makes me . . . uncomfortable."

That was weird, but fine, she would call him what he wanted. "Fine, Ash, we're meeting tomorrow."

"I went to see her tonight," he blurted when she was about to turn away.

"Her?" Taryn asked, even though she knew what his answer would be.

"My sister. Hope."

Sorrow coated his words and tugged at her heart.

Enough so that she signaled to a customer down the bar that she would be with him in a moment. "At Tremaine headquarters?" Dammit, she really should wait to have this conversation.

But it was her job as a bartender to listen when customers spoke. *Dammit.*

"No," he said softly. "The Tremaine hospital."

Her jaw dropped open and she snapped it closed before Ash noticed. That was terrible. And would make it nearly impossible to get the girl out. She'd already been leaning toward rejecting his request. This would make that decision easier.

At least, that was what she told herself when she placed a comforting hand on his forearm. "I'm sorry to hear that," she said. "I'll be right back. I need to take care of another customer."

She poured two beers with an easy smile for the customer at the end of the bar and refilled Jed's drink as she passed by. Despite outward appearances, her brain was still struggling to process what Ash had told her.

She drifted back toward him, drawn by an unwilling need to hear more.

"This is my sister," he said as soon as she reached him. He slid his phone across the bar toward her.

Reluctant to take it, she nevertheless picked up the comm. A young woman with a hint of baby fat still in her cheeks looked out at her. If Taryn had to guess, she'd say the girl was around eighteen. Hope had an impish smile and gray eyes that sparkled. The dark hair that looked unruly on Ash fell into a tangle of curls threaded with blue, pink, and purple on his sister.

"Cute," Taryn said. It took effort to keep a sense of distance. And with the next words out of her mouth, she completely failed. "She's sick?" She set the phone back on the counter, turned away so Hope wasn't staring hopefully back at her.

"Brain burn." His voice caught with emotion. He flipped to another picture on his phone. If he hadn't told Taryn that the two figures were the same person, she never would have guessed. Lank hair, slack features. So much medical equipment. "She's in a coma."

"Oh, I'm so sorry." Ever since he'd mentioned the hospital, Taryn had assumed some type of injury. She knew next to nothing about brain burn, only that it happened to hackers and was never good.

Using Hope's injury and need for care to keep Ash in line was as effective as it was vile. The ruthless part of Taryn even admired it. She'd learned how threats could motivate people from the best.

"What happened?"

"It was a perfectly normal hack," Ash said, his voice sad. "We'd made it past the early defenses. They weren't too hard, weren't too easy. No different than any other hack. Except it was. We just didn't know it yet."

"Hope's a hacker too?" Dammit. Why had she asked that? Taryn didn't want to give Ash false hope. Especially now that she'd seen all the equipment required to care for her.

"Yeah." His sad smile broke her heart. "She wanted to be just like me. So we—I—trained her. She was good, proficient, but she was young and smart. Destined for better things than hacking."

Taryn nodded and was grateful—again—when more orders appeared in the system for her to fill. If you didn't come from money, it was so easy for this city to chew you up and spit you out. Hope, like so many other young girls, deserved more than what she'd gotten.

"You were hacking the Tremaine Corporation?"

He nodded. "Then, all sorts of firewalls popped up. We could stop some, but they were too fast. It was obvious that someone knew we were coming."

He paused, swallowed hard. "I told Hope to pull out. She was right beside me on the net. When I came out of it, my chair was surrounded by Tremaine Security. Hope was next to me in her chair, but she . . . wasn't there."

"And that's brain burn?" Taryn asked carefully.

"Nobody knows exactly," Ash said, "but that's my best guess. You get pulled out of a hack before fully disengaging your consciousness. You come out without actually coming out."

"I'm sorry." It sounded awful. Taryn placed her hand on his, a simple instinctive move that surprised her.

She pulled her hand away before he could react. *Where the hell had that come from?*

She wasn't a toucher and the Jack certainly didn't go around offering comfort. That could ruin the reputation she worked so hard to maintain.

Off balance, Taryn settled into her most comfortable role: the Jack. "We can discuss this further tomorrow."

Tomorrow she'd be ready for him. She'd have her talking points and would let him down as gently as the Jack could. Going up against a corporation was the definition of insanity and would threaten everything she was working to build.

CHAPTER 12

CRAP. He'd been too eager.

Ash nursed his drink and watched the Jack move.

The Jack. He still didn't know her name. But the title suited her. Purpose and efficiency radiated off her. She smiled at customers, bantered with her staff, but never lost that indefinable something that said she was in charge. There was nothing sexier than a woman who knew she was at the top of her game.

Looking back, Ash recognized that he had never understood exactly how Razor Jack's worked. That the name was a title. He'd just assumed it was pretension on the part of the owner, calling himself "the."

He'd been an idiot back then. Five years ago, he'd been on top of the world, no fear, all ego. And then he'd brought it all tumbling down on them.

Ash stared into his drink. He should have waited until their meeting tomorrow. But spending time with Hope always left him with a lingering sadness and need to burn it off. He'd been walking to Razor Jack's before he'd consciously realized it.

The window to free Hope—and maybe himself—was closing. Working directly under Portia Tremaine to discover who had hacked the system for Leopold Brunswick—to uncover his own crimes—younger Ash would have laughed at the challenge.

Older and wiser Ash practically pissed himself when he thought about it too hard.

The Jack was the only contact from the old days who might be able to help him. Except the Jack he expected wasn't the Jack he'd gotten. And now he had to convince her to help him.

But how?

Ash pondered the little he knew about the new Jack while he nursed the surprisingly tasty concoction she'd made for him. It looked—and tasted—like sunshine. She served much better liquor than the old Jack.

However, like the old Jack, she would solve problems for a price. And she didn't appear to dabble in the less-savory businesses that the old Jack had. Last night while he'd waited for his meeting, not once had he seen any hint of the prostitution and drug deals that had usually occurred here.

That was the one slim hope that he clung to. If she'd gotten rid of the prostitution, maybe she'd have a softer heart for his sister.

Someone stepped up to the bar, jostling Ash in their attempt to get the Jack's attention.

Ash flinched as the scent of sweat and days-old food assaulted him, throwing him into the past.

He knew that smell. Had worn it himself after a particularly long session ported into the computer.

Hand tightening around the glass, Ash fought the memories of Tremaine Security crashing into the hackers' den. They'd destroyed thousands of credits worth of equipment as they rushed him and he hadn't cared. Hadn't even tried to escape. Cross-legged on the floor, cradling his baby sister and begging her to wake up, he'd expected them to kill him on the spot. And he hadn't given a damn.

He could still see Hope's face, frozen in a little smile. She'd been right behind him when he'd pulled out of the network. But not fast enough.

Fuck! Get a hold of yourself!

He leaned away from the newcomer at the bar. He was no good to Hope if he couldn't pull his shit together and convince the Jack to help him.

Ash focused on slowing his racing pulse. His hand shook as he brought the glass to his lips and downed the last of his drink in one gulp. The glass hit the counter harder than he intended.

Raising his hand to get the Jack's attention, he drew his neighbor's notice.

"Busy night, huh? I've been trying to get her attention forever."

"Yep." Ash was in no mood for small talk.

"The bartender's smokin'," the guy said.

He couldn't argue with that. "Yep." Done with the conversation, he renewed his efforts to get the Jack to come back to his end of the bar.

The guy jostled Ash again and he turned to glare at him. The other man started to apologize then stared at Ash. "Hey, wait. I know you."

Shit. Ash recognized him too. Didn't remember his name. The guy'd been a decent hacker, but not as good as Ash. Definitely not part of the crew. "I think you've got the wrong guy."

So much for another drink. Ash had to get the fuck out

of here. He peeled the guy's fingers off his shoulder and stood.

The guy refused to give up and grabbed Ash's arm again. "No, wait. I do. You're a hacker. Dangit, what's your handle again?"

Ash shook him loose and looked away. No reason to give the guy a good, close look. "Sorry, you've got me confused with someone else."

"Some kind of bird or shit . . ." The other man snapped his fingers. "Got it! Fēnix! What happened, man? You were like the best of the best and then you disappeared. You and that sister of yours. Damn, she was hot!"

Ash's vision flickered and his ears buzzed. One minute he was standing by the bar, the next, his fist was connecting with the guy's jaw, slamming the asshole against the counter.

Goddamnfuck, that hurt.

He shook his hand out and ignored the throbbing.

Ash grabbed his opponent's shirt. All around them, other patrons jostled to get out of the way. Their claps and cheers were barely audible over the white noise of anger in his mind.

The other hacker threw a weak-ass punch toward Ash's middle. He sucked in his breath, bracing for the hit, and arched to the side. The guy got nothing but air.

Ash grabbed the guy's shirt with one hand and held him in place while he punched him repeatedly. "Nobody talks about my sister that way!"

"Shit, man, I'm sorry!" He couldn't defend against all the punches as Ash hit him in the face, side, and stomach with no apparent pattern. "I'm sorry! Okay? I'm sorry!"

The other guy started crying.

Hands wrapped around Ash's upper arms and pulled

him away from his opponent. He struggled against the restraint. "Hey, let me go!"

Ash kicked the person behind him.

"Oof!"

He kicked again, but his captor didn't release him.

Fingers dug into his biceps. "Stand down," a voice growled in his ear. Ash was dragged away from the other hacker.

Blood dripped down the man's face as Ash leaned into one of the bouncers.

That would teach him.

The buzz had faded some, but Ash's breath came out in harsh gasps.

And then the Jack stood in front of him, hands on her hips, a bar rag clenched in her fist. Her dark eyes shot fire.

"Damn, you're like a beautiful avenging angel." The words tumbled out.

She scowled. "What the hell are you doing?"

Ash stopped struggling. He had to make her understand. "He insulted my sister."

Her scowl turned into a glare. His chance for help was slipping away. Then he saw a crack in her façade.

A tiny one.

Maybe it would be enough.

She continued to glare at him, giving nothing away. Then she turned to the other hacker.

Blood oozed from the guy's nose and tears streamed down his face. He wasn't restrained the way Ash was.

"That true? You insulted his sister?"

The guy gaped like a fish. "What? No. C'mon, I just said she was hot." Or at least that was what it sounded like.

"Save me from fucking idiots," the Jack muttered. "Get him cleaned up and out of my bar." She pointed at

Ash's opponent. "I don't want to see you in here for two weeks."

"He started it!"

It sounded more like "He tharted it." Someone had a broken nose. Good.

"I'm finishing it," the Jack said.

Ash's opponent opened his mouth to argue, then snapped it shut when the Jack turned her full attention on him. "Two weeks," he mumbled in agreement.

"And you." Ash's smile faded under her withering gaze. "I don't fucking care if he grabbed your dick. You don't fight in my bar. *Nobody* fights in my bar!" She spoke loud enough for everyone in the bar to hear.

"Get him cleaned up, then take him to my office," she directed the man holding Ash. "I'll deal with him later."

Was that good or bad? Had he just blown his chance to get the Jack's help?

"I wouldn't do that," the other hacker said through his broken nose. "He'th a hacker. Uthed to be one of the beth."

The Jack froze. Barely long enough for anyone to notice. But Ash noticed. A side effect of being unable to take his eyes off her. That's when he knew.

She had secrets.

That familiar tickle of wanting to know them raced through him.

"Fuck." She cursed under her breath. "Take him to my office and stay with him. Don't let him go anywhere. Or touch anything." Her dark eyes gaze met his with that command.

Yeah, she had secrets, all right.

Ash followed the bouncer, the one who'd escorted him out of her office last night, into the Jack's office. But first they'd stopped at a first-aid room where Ash had cleaned up his hands and realized that he wouldn't be able to hide the signs of a fight when he returned to Tremaine headquarters.

The pain pills hadn't kicked in yet and his head throbbed like a sonofabitch.

The Jack stalked into her office, her wrath palpable, and he knew his headache was the least of his worries. She looked like what she was—a dangerous, deadly woman.

"Leave us," she ordered the bouncer. With a grave nod, the man acknowledged the command and closed the door behind him.

When they were alone in her office, there were no secrets in her brown eyes. Only anger.

Lots and lots of anger.

It probably made him an asshole, but she was hot as hell.

He wasn't stupid enough to say so out loud. The woman held his future in his hands. He watched her carefully.

"What the fuck were you thinking, starting a fight in my bar?" Even her raspy voice fit the image of a vengeful goddess, the kind you saw in comic books and vids and great tattoos.

He swallowed hard but met her gaze steadily. "He insulted my sister."

Holding her gaze was harder than he expected, she was that pissed. Last night, he'd wondered how she gained and held the title of the Jack.

Now he understood.

"I don't fucking care if he was talking shit about your mother. You come to me asking for a favor, and you fucking brawl in my business? Give me one good reason why I shouldn't kick your ass out now and ban you from the bar."

"I gave you several hundred reasons yesterday." He stepped closer.

Outrage flared in her eyes when he invaded her space. Outrage, anger, and a hint of something that might be attraction, but that couldn't be right. Could it? Because he was pretty sure the same emotion was mirrored in his eyes.

She snorted. "Oh no. I earned those credits listening to your sob story. I don't owe you anything else."

She didn't back down, not physically. Despite the blazing tension between them, Ash could tell the instant she disengaged.

Fuck! He'd blown his chance.

She confirmed it seconds later. "Get out, Mr. Cutter. And don't bother coming back tomorrow night."

CHAPTER 13

ASH ENTERED Tremaine headquarters on autopilot. He acknowledged other employees he knew, but his mind was elsewhere.

He'd fucked up. Big time. Now he had to figure out how to fix it.

The first thing he needed was information, and there was only one place in the building where he could find what he needed.

Instead of taking the route that would lead to his room, he took a familiar, circuitous detour. After traversing several floors and dark corridors, Ash stood in front of an active but forgotten computer tucked away in the heart of the building.

He'd discovered it early on, after his escape attempt had ended with him confined to the building. Exploring every inch of Tremaine headquarters, he'd met countless people and, one day, he'd encountered a computer terminal no one used. Forgotten but not decommissioned, he'd never have looked twice at it if he'd still had his port. Over the years, he'd dug deeper and deeper into the Tremaine system.

Into Tremaine secrets.

Unease skittered down his back. The last time he'd retrieved information from this terminal . . . Well, nothing good had come of it. Though he had been able to help Dizzie when he used it to hack into a satellite.

Was this a good idea? He shifted on his feet and stared at the terminal.

Probably not. But he couldn't think of anything else to do. Or of anyone else who could help him.

Shrugging off the indecision, he laced his fingers together and stretched his arms overhead. Releasing the stretch, he wiggled his fingers. He needed to be loose for this.

Loose and fast.

He never dared stay too long in the system. Too much time would be dangerous for him and his sister.

As ready as he could be, Ash laid his hands on the keyboard . . . and had no idea where to start. Normally he spent his time rummaging through hidden secrets of the Tremaine system. Or skimming money off the top of rich guys' accounts and funneling it to untraceable credit chips. But he wasn't interested in either of those things today.

The Jack. That's who he really wanted—needed—to know more about. But where to start the search when he only had a title and not a proper name?

Ash cracked his fingers again, for luck, and then started his search with the property address. He could picture the search in his head, the way he'd maneuver through the packets of data as if he was ported in. It took so much longer for the commands to travel from his brain to his fingers. He hated that his hands couldn't keep up with what he'd be able to do in a blink. Porting in was so much easier.

Ignoring the phantom ache at the back of his neck, he poured all his energy and focus into his hands.

The first commands were rote—accessing the system, cloaking his presence, and setting up a warning system in case someone noticed his activity.

His next commands bypassed the general internet and plunged him into the deep web beneath, where secrets were bought and sold and anything could be found for a price.

He laughed, because that part sounded familiar. Surely there would be a record of the Jack there. "All right, baby, let's see what you've got."

Fingers flying over the keyboard, he entered his parameters. The first results were crap. Gambling sites and decks of cards.

Not at all what he wanted. He wanted the story behind the intriguing brunette who owned the bar. The one whose touch had sent shivers straight to his heart. Whose husky voice made him long for hours of conversation. The woman who tied him in knots and hid secrets in her dark brown eyes.

Deeper down he found a years-old website, which was useless. Razor Jack's didn't need to advertise. If you knew about it, great. If you didn't, well, you probably didn't want to be there anyway.

"Okay, what next?" He tapped his fingers lightly on the keyboard and pondered his next move.

"Reviews, blogs, newsie sites." He added those as search parameters, but doubted they'd provide anything useful.

Nope. Nope. And nope.

"You are very well hidden, my dear Jack."

Had the previous Jack been this well-hidden? Ash had no idea. He'd never bothered to look—hadn't needed to.

Most people were an open book, posting every damn

aspect of their lives online. His respect for her and her business grew.

The Jack had intrigued him before. Now he was enthralled. He loved a challenge.

Where else to look?

Razor Jack's was a bar. Bars got rowdy.

He'd love an old-fashioned police report. Unfortunately, most public safety and security was run by corporations. He'd hack those if he needed to, but everything he'd seen pointed to the Jack not turning to corporations for help. She'd solve problems herself. He just needed to figure out how.

Other public records were still an option. Births, deaths, marriages, and disappearances. There had to be some kind of record out there.

Tweaking his search over and over, Ash scrolled through pages and pages of results, poking into the occasional record. Nothing.

"Fuck." If he hadn't seen her himself, he'd believe she didn't exist.

About to give up, something in the data scroll caught his eye.

A death certificate.

Not that unusual. Hundreds were probably issued each day in the region, and those were just the official deaths.

It wasn't the name that was familiar. It was the address. Razor Jack's address.

It could be coincidence—a bar fight gone wrong—but he had the feeling the Jack wouldn't be that careless. Any bodies falling in the bar sure as hell wouldn't be discovered there.

Ash delicately retrieved the file, careful not to leave any

tracks that would lead back to him or to the Tremaine Corporation.

Once he'd segregated the file into the section of the system he used for storage, he took a deep breath and opened it.

The medic involved had been meticulous in his notetaking, but despite all the time Ash spent in the hospital with Hope, the medical jargon didn't mean much. He understood enough to tell that it was a heart attack. The victim had been declared dead at that scene.

Ash closed the autopsy report and flipped to the profile of the deceased. He gasped and took and involuntary step back from the terminal.

The face of the old Jack—the Jack he'd known—stared at him from the screen.

Holy shit.

He skimmed the rest of the file.

He was survived by his wife. Huh. Ash couldn't imagine anyone marrying the old Jack.

Why hadn't the widow taken over the bar?

Curious, he flipped to the next page. It was filled with legalese that told him that the widow had inherited the bar. How had his Jack taken over?

He turned to the last page in the file.

"What the fuck?"

He blinked and read the brief profile of the widow again. Then stared at the attached picture.

Her name was Taryn. It suited her.

She was the old Jack's widow. She had inherited the bar.

Taryn was the new Jack.

His Jack.

The old Jack had been a bastard, willing to do anything

for a price. Ash wanted to puke when he thought about her —*Taryn*—married to the man. He'd seen the shadows in her eyes. What had she endured?

It took a few moments for the shock to wear off.

He returned to the beginning of the file, paying closer attention this time.

It was hard. Imagining her with the old Jack turned his stomach. He wanted to hit something.

She was a beautiful, vibrant woman. One who'd offered comfort when he'd shared the worst moment of his life. What had drawn her to the old man? Power?

It didn't seem possible. He'd met power-hungry people before. Despite the Jack's reputation, he didn't get that sense from her.

Okay, Ash, keep it together. What does the file tell you?

The old Jack had died nearly five years ago.

He had a wife.

That was it.

Ash jumped back to the search page and called up the public records again.

His fingers flew over the keyboard, inputting every combination of the names from the death report. No results.

There was no marriage record. No will either.

"So how did you inherit the bar?"

CHAPTER 14

TUCKED INTO A CORNER BOOTH, Taryn nursed another cup of coffee. She'd lost count of how many she'd had since she woke up. Enough that Dani had noticed and every other time Taryn asked for a cup of coffee, her friend brought Taryn a glass of water. Annoying, but she knew it was done out of love.

After kicking Ash out last night, Taryn had thrown herself into making the rounds in the bar. See and be seen.

The Jack had been extra snarly last night, especially when a group of corporate drones—probably there on a dare—had tried to get handsy with one of the waitresses. Rhonda had managed to extricate herself from their grasping hands and hightailed it to the bar. Taryn had swooped in like an avenging angel and escorted them out of the building. With force.

She'd enjoyed it, but it hadn't worked to get her mind off Ash. Or Hope.

It would be beyond foolish to go up against one of the corporations, especially Tremaine, Seattle's homegrown multinational. But she couldn't stop thinking about Hope.

About how—hypothetically—Taryn would get her out of a corporate hospital. It was madness.

And, well, she was feeling a bit mad. The coffee mug rattled as she set it on the table with more force than intended.

Madness was the only excuse for wanting to see Ash stroll through those doors. Because if he did—no matter how much she wanted to see him—she'd have to kick him out again. The Jack's reputation was only as good as the willingness to back it up. Last night, in the midst of her righteous anger, she'd informed her staff about his banishment.

She could lift it without reason, but if she did it now, she would look weak.

When her gaze skipped over the room and landed on the door again, Taryn knew she'd made a mistake. She could have—should have—found something else to do tonight. Get out and take the pulse of the city. Start scoping out her next project.

But no, she'd decided to watch over the business instead.

Idiot.

No matter how often she told herself it was because she was a hands-on boss, she knew it was a lie.

"I need to get a life."

That's what Dani told her—repeatedly. And every time she did, Taryn countered that she didn't have time, that the bar needed her.

Truth was, Dani was right. Taryn wanted a life, wanted a relationship. Companionship and sex with someone who knew her.

Her. Taryn. Not just the Jack.

But she'd never been on a date in her life. Her dating

options sucked. Either men were too intimidated by her title and power or they wanted to say they'd fucked the Jack.

"Assholes," she muttered.

Taryn sipped water because additional caffeine would rile her up more.

She'd clawed her way out of circumstances that had left her scarred but not broken and had taken control of her life. Even worked her way back to having and enjoying sex. But those nights out of town where nobody knew her hadn't been dates, they'd been therapy.

What would it be like to be with someone who cared?

And just like that, her thoughts circled back to Ash.

Dammit.

Two nights in a row she'd thought about him. Fantasized about him. Felt tingles in places she'd thought were dormant; it had been so long since she'd had sex.

Ash was a problem. Or a missed opportunity.

Who was she kidding? She'd banned him from the bar and most people were too scared of the Jack to challenge her.

The door opened and she looked at it again. Instead of the tall lanky man who occupied her thoughts, it was the last person she expected.

Ice slithered down her spine. Taryn scrambled out of her booth, but stayed in the shadows.

What the fuck was he doing here?

Giselle's pimp strolled into the bar, with a swagger of someone who thought he owned the place.

"Oh hell no." Scum like that had no place here.

She started forward, ready to throw his ass out, then stopped and studied the situation.

He was flanked by two men. Whether they were the same muscle from the night she rescued Giselle, Taryn didn't know. Didn't really care either. She'd make sure they all knew they weren't welcome in Razor Jack's.

The three men seemed pretty fucking clueless. They either didn't notice or didn't care that her security flanked them, ready to intervene at the first sign of trouble.

A fraction of her tension eased.

Her team was the best and she trusted them to handle this.

She watched from the shadows, ready to intervene if needed. The pimp radiated anger, his chest thrust out, his hands clenching and unclenching. She was sure he planned to use those fists if he found Giselle.

Thankfully she was still in the back—in her room or the living area—with strict instructions not to visit the front of the bar.

The pimp approached the bar and waved Dani over with the impatient movements of a man used to getting his way.

Dani approached with her usual smile. Taryn watched their interaction tensely. If he did anything to Dani . . .

Dani shook her head in response to whatever he asked.

His body language got more aggressive, but Dani never flinched.

Taryn knew what kind of will, what kind of strength, it took her friend not to flee.

This had to be bringing back unpleasant memories. *Dammit.* She should have stepped in to protect Dani.

Dani had been Taryn's first rescue after she'd taken over the bar. Dani had come in looking for a place to get out of the weather and her pimp hadn't liked that.

That had led to a fight. One Taryn had won.

That night Taryn had learned to keep a buffer between the bar and her other work. So how had Giselle's pimp found her bar? Taryn chose her rescues carefully, usually from the outlying neighborhoods. His territory was on the other side of the city.

Dani's brow wrinkled, but that was the only outward sign that she was getting bothered by the pimp.

Taryn hated sitting back while her people were in trouble. It went against everything she'd built since she took over the bar. Still, she'd realized early on that she wouldn't always be there, so she'd ensured they were well-trained.

Daryl moved within reach of Dani. He was close enough to stop the pimp if—when—he became a problem.

The pimp slammed his hand down on the bar. Dani shook her head.

Twice more, the pimp tried to intimidate Dani. Each time, security stepped a few inches closer.

Finally, Dani shook her head, shrugged, and returned to her duties, serving the next person at the bar.

The pimp watched her but she ignored him. With another slap on the bar, he pushed away from the bar and whirled around. "Bitch!" Taryn read his lips and it took every fiber of her being to not launch herself at him.

He stormed toward the front door, radiating such a cloud of menace that patrons slid their chairs back to get out of his way. She almost laughed at the train of people as his muscle and her security followed him.

The pimp and his cronies were barely out the door when Taryn approached the bar.

She stopped directly in front of Dani. "Are you okay?"

"I'm fine." She pulled a beer for a customer, outwardly calm, but Taryn noticed the fine shake in her hands.

"Are you sure?" After she'd delivered the drink, Taryn reached across the bar and grabbed Dani's hand.

"I'm fine, I promise." Her gaze drifted toward the front

of the bar. "That was Giselle's . . ." she paused, let the word hang unspoken between them. "Wasn't it?"

Taryn nodded. No need to announce exactly what he was to Giselle to anyone who might be listening.

Dani's eyes widened. "I thought so. How did he find you? Us?"

"I don't know, and that worries me. I removed her chip and the sensor didn't pick up anything else." Taryn bit her lip. "What did he say to you?"

"He described Giselle. Said his girlfriend had gone missing and he was worried about her." She excused herself to fill the order that a waitress brought to the bar. "There was something about him that seemed . . . off. Plus, I'll never answer a question about a missing girl."

"I never doubted you. I'm sorry I wasn't able to help you."

"Thank you for trusting me to handle it." She laughed. "I expected you to come running at any moment."

Taryn winced. "I wanted to. But I was afraid he'd recognize me and jeopardize all of this. I didn't intend to put everyone in danger."

"You didn't. You had no way of knowing he'd show up here. This place, the hope it provides, is more important. More important than me and," Dani smiled tentatively, "more important than you. Not that I want anything to happen to you."

Dani squeezed Taryn's hand. Her touch was comforting, but her words helped the most.

"Backatcha." She sucked in a breath, steadying herself. Dani was safe. The bar was safe. "Now I want you to take a break."

"I don't need a break," Dani protested. "I'm fine. I promise."

"It's not for you. It's for me. I want you to go write down everything you remember from your interaction with him. I need to figure out how he ended up here."

"Could be a coincidence." Dani's expression said she didn't believe it.

"Could be." Taryn didn't believe it either. "He shouldn't have been anywhere near this neighborhood."

CHAPTER 15

TARYN TAPPED LIGHTLY on the door. "Giselle?"

Not wanting to appear threatening or make any moves that frightened the new girl, she stepped back to the other side of the hallway.

"Yes?" A soft voice, barely audible, replied through the door.

"It's Taryn. Can we talk for a few minutes?"

"Um, okay." Locks turned, then the door opened a crack. Giselle peeked around the edge of the door. "Is everything okay?"

"Fine," Taryn reassured her. "But I need to ask you a few questions. Can I come in? Or we can go to my office."

The girl paled.

Dammit. She hadn't meant to sound like both good cop and bad cop.

"Or we can go to the kitchen," Taryn added.

"The kitchen." Her voice was still soft, but Giselle's response was decisive. She slipped through the crack between the bedroom door and the door frame. The flowing pants and baggy sweater made Giselle look even smaller than she had the first night. Having originally seen the girl in her skintight dress, Taryn wasn't surprised by the loose clothes.

Taryn kept a closet full of new clothes that she offered to the women who stayed here. They could pick anything they wanted and if they couldn't find anything that fit, Taryn purchased it. She truly believed it was the first step to reclaiming their lives and was glad Giselle had found clothes she was comfortable in.

Side by side, they walked to the kitchen. The lights flickered on automatically when they entered the room. "Want anything?" Taryn asked.

"I'll take a beer." Giselle looked everywhere but at Taryn.

"Yeah, um, no." Taryn bit back a laugh.

Giselle dropped into a seat and glared at her. "Why the hell not?"

"Because you're what, twelve?"

"I'm eighteen." Her tone dared Taryn to challenge her.

"Bullshit. At the most, you're fifteen." Taryn studied Giselle while she poured two cups of coffee. Her dark hair was caught up in two simple braids on either side of her face, adding to her childlike look. Taryn placed a mug in front of Giselle. She wrapped her hand around the other and took the seat across from Giselle.

"Almost seventeen," Giselle mumbled. She took a sip of the coffee and spit it back into her cup. "Oh my god, can't I get some sugar or something?"

Taryn slid the container of sugar cubes across the table to Giselle.

One, two, three, four went into her cup before she tasted it again. Then she dropped in another two. Taryn's teeth ached just watching her.

"How are you doing?" She watched the girl closely.

"Um, okay?" Giselle took a gulp of her coffee-flavored sugar.

"Good." Taryn wasn't sure how to have this conversation. Never in all the years she'd been doing this had someone come to Razor Jack's looking for a missing girl. That was how careful she was.

The fact that Giselle's pimp had started here . . .

Her stomach cramped and Taryn set the coffee cup down. The bitter brew probably wasn't the best idea right now.

"What do you want?" Giselle set the cup down on the table with a thunk.

"I can't just check in?" Taryn deliberately pushed her buttons.

"Sure, you can," she said sarcastically, "but you aren't. You want something."

Taryn hated that she was already so jaded, but that's what the streets did. Chewed girls up and spit them out. "You're right. I was trying to make you feel better first."

A snort from across the table. Taryn smiled. "You want it straight?"

Giselle nodded.

"Okay." Taryn sucked in a deep breath. She was about to seriously ruin this girl's day. "Your pimp came into the bar tonight looking for you. I don't know how he found you."

Giselle paled. The blood drained from her face so quickly that Taryn worried she'd pass out.

"Did you tell him? Are you handing me back to him?" She lurched back from the table and scrambled to her feet. Coffee sloshed out of her mug.

Before she could race out of the room, Taryn grabbed

her arm. Giselle struggled, but she couldn't break Taryn's grip. Her fear was almost tangible, and Taryn shivered. She remembered that feeling.

"It's okay. You're safe." Taryn spoke quietly, as if soothing a skittish animal. "Sit down. Please."

Giselle resisted, her body trembling. She strained toward the door.

Taryn gently steered her back to her chair. When Giselle finally sat, Taryn hooked her foot around the bottom rung and dragged the chair closer to the table, minimizing her ability to escape.

"I swear I didn't tell him where you were. I never would." Taryn leaned close. Made sure that the other woman looked at her. "That's why I wanted to talk to you. Do you have any idea why he would come in here asking for you? Have you been here before?"

"I don't even know where we are," Giselle said sullenly.

Taryn pursed her lips. That was probably true. She'd had the girl hide when they'd left the sleazy hotel and entered through the back of the bar. She knew Taryn was the Jack, but she obviously hadn't realized what that meant.

"You're at Razor Jack's," Taryn said.

"The bar?"

Taryn nodded. "The rooms are in the back."

"That's why you didn't want me wandering around."

That sounded like an accusation. Or maybe Taryn was just tired. "Yes and no. I wanted you to use this time to rest. Let your body heal. Let your mind accept that you're safe."

Giselle snorted. Her skin was still pale, but she'd stopped shaking. "Except he found me."

"No. He didn't find you. He asked about you, but he didn't get his hands on you and he won't. But did he ever bring you here? Did anybody?"

"No. He kept me and the other girls on the other side of town, over by the old high school."

There wasn't just one "old" high school in Seattle, but there were a lot fewer than expected for a city that was two hundred years old. Online school had rendered many of them obsolete and many had been demolished to make room for more skyscrapers. The area Taryn had assumed was the pimp's territory included an old school. She had no idea what it was used for these days.

Taryn reached out and patted the girl's hand. "That's what I thought his territory was, too."

She'd terrorized Giselle and still wasn't any closer to discovering why he'd shown up tonight. Frustration clawed at her insides.

"Did he have any rivals? Enemies who might have territory around here?"

Over the past few years, Taryn had leveraged the Jack's reputation to eradicate the pimps who claimed territory around the bar. Most people believed they'd left of their own volition—which they had, if you counted threats of bodily harm and disappearance as their own decision. When new pimps had tried to move into the territory, well, they didn't last long.

Giselle shook her head again. "I don't know. I'm sorry." She sounded frustrated, which was better than scared in Taryn's mind.

"It's okay. I wanted to make sure that I wasn't missing any information." Taryn took a deep breath and prepared to ask her last, worst question. "Could he have put a second tracking device on you?"

"No!" Giselle trembled and wrapped her hands around her middle. Taryn expected her to cry, but she was a fighter and held her tears back. She hated to think about how Giselle had learned that skill.

"No," Giselle repeated. "Do you think there's another one?"

Fuck. How was Taryn supposed to answer that? She didn't think so, but to risk everything she'd built on a hunch?

She chose her words carefully and tried to be reassuring. "No, I don't think so. But I want to be sure. Just in case your pimp was tricky and used a second one."

She braced for Giselle's reaction. Once again, she proved stronger than expected.

After several fortifying sips of heavily sugared coffee, Giselle clutched her mug in both hands and stared into it. "What do I have to do?"

"We'll need to do a second scan, with stronger equipment."

"Can I think about it?" Giselle asked.

Shit, Giselle wasn't going to like her answer. Taryn needed to be respectful of her feelings, but the answer was no. "I want to say yes, Giselle, but I can't. I need to know for sure so I can protect you and the other girls." Taryn looked her straight in the eyes. "Do you understand?"

She sniffled, but nodded. "I understand. If there's a second tracker, will you send me away?"

"Absolutely not." Taryn reached over and squeezed her hands. "We'll do the scan now and if there's a second one, we'll take care of it the same way we did the first one. Okay?"

With one last sniff, Giselle straightened and nodded. "Okay. Let's do it."

CHAPTER 16

AFTER TARYN COMPLETED THE SCAN—NO sign of a second chip—Giselle returned to her room and Taryn returned to the business of running the bar. She found Dani pacing outside her office.

"Everything okay?" Honestly, Taryn wasn't sure she could handle another issue tonight, but as the owner of Razor Jack's, that was her job.

Dani shrugged. "How was the scan?"

"Clear." Taryn sighed and let them both into the office. "I didn't expect another chip, but I really want to know how that fucker made his way here." She waved Dani toward a chair and pulled two bottles of fizzy water out of the small cooling unit she kept there. No caffeine, no alcohol. She needed to be clear-headed to deal with this new problem.

"Are you sure she didn't contact him?" Dani's voice was purely professional, but the pinch of her lips revealed how much she hated asking that question.

"Yeah, she was really freaked out. I'm sure it wasn't her. Everything okay out there after I left?"

The silence grew and Taryn dropped her head into her

hands. She'd really, really intended it as a rhetorical question.

"Crap." She lifted her head. "What happened? Was it the pimp?"

Dani set her water on the corner of the desk. "No, he didn't come back. It was . . ." She trailed off. "Never mind. It's probably nothing and you've got enough going on."

"No. If something is going on, I need to know."

"That's just it," Dani said. "It's nothing concrete. Just . . . a feeling, maybe?"

Taryn trusted her implicitly. "No. It's something. You don't get worried otherwise. I trust your instincts. Tell me."

Dani sighed and leaned back in her chair. "You're supposed to tell me that I'm wrong."

"Tell me what you've got and maybe I will. But I know better than to ignore your instincts."

Fiddling with her ring, Dani collected her thoughts. Taryn was impatient to know what had brought her friend and second-in-command here, but also appreciated the few moments of silence before the next problem hit.

"It's Rhonda. Something's going on," Dani said finally. She held up her hand to stop Taryn from asking any questions. "No, I don't know exactly what. I tried asking, but she completely shut me down."

"But?" Dani knew the bar staff as well as Taryn did, if not better. If she'd noticed something amiss, she was probably right.

"But . . . she's been late for shifts. Not flighty late or stuck-in-traffic late. Just . . . late. Less talkative. Not just when I ask her questions. With the other staff and the customers."

Taryn's lips pinched and she pondered Dani's information. Rhonda had been here six months and she'd always been quiet, self-contained. She was making good progress, but although Taryn didn't have a set timeline for anyone to get back on their feet, Rhonda wasn't as far along as Taryn would like.

That was okay, she reminded herself. Everyone dealt with trauma differently. Rhonda had refused therapy. There was no way Taryn would or could force her to go. She had to want to be there. Maybe she should have pushed the other woman a little harder.

"It's not your fault." Dani's voice was sharp.

"I didn't say anything," Taryn said harshly.

"You didn't have to. You're blaming yourself. I can tell."

True. But Dani didn't have to call her on it. Taryn huffed out a sigh. "I should have made sure she got therapy. Or, I don't know, socialized more."

"That's not the way it works," Dani countered. "You know that. You give them a safe place to land and an amazing support system. The rest is up to them. To us." She pressed a hand against her chest, including herself in the group of women Taryn had rescued.

Or rather, had helped to rescue themselves. Dani was correct. Taryn couldn't force them—they had to do the work themselves.

"You're right, you're right." Taryn held her hands up in surrender.

Dani laughed. Then both women sobered.

"What do you think we should do?" Taryn asked.

"I don't know. That's why I was hoping maybe you'd noticed. Maybe you'd have ideas." Dani sighed. "Rhonda's been here a few months and hasn't given us a reason to worry about her. It's just recently . . ." her voice trailed off. "That's why I'm worried."

Dammit. Now Taryn was too. "Do you want me to talk to her?"

Dani pulled her knees up and wrapped her arms around them. "I don't know. For now, could you keep an eye on her too? Maybe I'm just imagining it?"

Taryn was pretty sure Dani wasn't. "Sure," she said. "I trust you, but I'll watch her the next few days."

"Thanks," Dani said.

"Any other potential problems I need to worry about?"

"I don't think so. We did inventory tonight and the order should be here tomorrow afternoon."

Taryn nodded. That was good—weekends were always busy.

"The schedule's set and Rhonda will be here both nights."

"I'll definitely be on the floor, so I'll check on her," Taryn said.

"I think that's all I've got," Dani said. "Anything I need to know?"

"I'm going to rescue Ash's sister." Taryn's jaw dropped. She had *not* intended to say that. She hadn't even decided.

Dani looked horrified. "You just got Giselle out. You usually wait a few months until the next one."

"I know." Dani wasn't telling her anything Taryn hadn't already considered. "I know," she said more firmly. "And I'd decided against it. But . . . I just can't stop thinking about her." She clenched her fists. "I can't not help."

"Why did he come to you?" Dani leaned forward, her elbows braced on the desk.

Taryn laughed bitterly. "Remember how he didn't know I was the Jack? He used to come here when the old Jack was in charge."

Dani's eyes widened. "Wha—"

Taryn continued. "That's not even the best part. He works for a corporation. Tremaine Corporation." Taryn held her breath, waiting for Dani's reaction. Her friend didn't disappoint.

"No." Dani practically shouted. "No. No. No."

"Tell me how you really feel." Taryn could joke about it now, but Dani's reaction wasn't that different from her own.

"I don't like it," Dani said. "It's too coincidental. We had that dustup with Tremaine Security last month. Now one of their hackers shows up asking for help?" She shook her head. "It's a trap."

"I thought the same thing, but I don't think it is." Taryn sighed and leaned back in her chair. "His sister needs some serious help. How could I say no?"

"How did he know about the rescue operation?" Dani's voice still carried a thread of doubt.

"I don't think he did. I think he came here knowing that the Jack does—did—almost anything for a price." That question had kept her up. That and her unlikely and unwanted attraction to the man.

"Why doesn't he just use his corporate ties?" Dani asked. "He has to have some, right?"

"Um." Taryn hedged and squeezed her eyes shut. Dani wasn't going to like this part either. She looked at her friend reluctantly. "We'd be rescuing her *from* Tremaine Corporation."

Dani erupted from her chair. "That's insane. You know that, right?"

When Taryn didn't respond, Dani dropped her palms on the desk and leaned over it to stare at her. "We don't even know how Giselle's pimp found her here. And now you want to go up against a corporation?" She shook her head in confusion. "Why? Why would you risk that? What has he promised you?"

Maybe she should reconsider. Taryn hadn't decided —*thought* she hadn't decided—until she opened her mouth and the words came out. "We didn't discuss payment," she said sheepishly, ducking her head so she wouldn't see the disappointment in Dani's eyes.

"Is it because you think he's hot?" Dani circled the desk to Taryn's side and sat on the edge. "Because if you need to get laid that badly, we can get that taken care of, no suicide mission required."

"No! It's not because of that." *Shit.* That didn't come out right. Taryn threaded her fingers through her hair and clasped the sides of her head. "I mean, I don't think that's why. I think he really needs help."

Dani glared at Taryn another few seconds, then leaned back on the desk. "We're really doing this?"

"Yeah." Her voice squeaked. "Yes," Taryn said, putting more gravity into her tone. "Yes, we're going to help him. Her. Them."

"You're crazy, you know that, right?" Dani said.

"Yeah, probably."

"All right. I'm in."

Taryn raised a brow. "I don't have a plan yet."

"Oh, I know. That's why I'm in. You need help and someone you can trust. That's me."

She looked at her best friend. Dani had been invaluable in planning some of the rescues. Her strategic mind was damned impressive.

"Okay. Thank you. But only for the planning. I don't want you involved in the execution. I don't want you drawing the company's attention."

"Fair enough," Dani said after thinking it over.

"Plus I need you to run the bar."

"Of course you do." Dani laughed.

"And first . . ." Taryn paused, embarrassment tinting her cheeks. "I need to let Ash know he's not banned anymore."

"You're insane," Dani said through exasperated laughter.

Yeah, she probably was.

CHAPTER 17

"YOU SLEEPING on the job over there, Ash?" Mocking laughter followed the question.

Ash started, then glared at the man who'd said his name. "Real funny, Mendez."

Removing his hands from the keyboard, Ash laced his fingers together and cracked his knuckles. He'd been staring at his computer screen for what felt like hours, waiting for the cyberattacks that brought meaning to his day.

Over the satisfying pops, he taunted Mendez. "Asleep or not, I can kick your ass any day of the week."

"Yeah, I don't think so. You were over there with a goofy look on your face. New lady?"

Damn. He needed a better poker face. Mendez wasn't wrong. He wasn't completely right either. Ash had been focused on—okay, obsessing about—his confrontation with the Jack.

He'd fucked up.

"Maybe," Ash said. If he had a friend on the team—which he didn't—it would be Mendez. The other man had been here longer than Ash had. They got along but Ash didn't trust him. He didn't—couldn't—trust any of the other hackers who had been pressed into service by the Tremaine Corporation.

Mendez was clearly waiting for an answer and when Ash took too long to reply, he crowed, "You do! Spill, man!"

Ash sighed and shook his head. The whole team was looking at him now. He had to say something. "There's nothing to tell. Yet." There, that sounded mysterious, right?

Razor Jack's wasn't a team hangout—it was on the other side of town—but why take unnecessary risks, like giving any of these jokers real information.

"Let's bet on it." Excitement tinged Mendez's voice.

The crazy bastard's mind worked in mysterious ways. "How is this bet-worthy?"

"Give me a break, Ash. I'm dying of boredom here. So are you. Let's do something to make this shift less shitty."

That was why he liked Mendez: the other man wasn't completely under Tremaine's thumb.

"Fine. What's the wager?" The only way to get out of this was to go through it. Any more protesting and they would decide he really did have something to hide. That was the last thing he needed.

Some of the other hackers shouted suggestions ranging from dumb to downright pornographic. Ash swiveled in his chair to study the rest of the group. His team was small, a dozen or so hackers on duty at any given time, with a bona fide Tremaine Security grunt riding herd.

The security center was smaller than most people expected. It was set up like a theater, with three rows of workstations stair-stepped up one side of the room. Ash's desk was in the top row, Mendez's right next to him. Some hackers worked with a cluster of screens mounted around their station, hands practically strapped to their keyboards.

Others preferred headsets that put them right into the cyber battle. The only way to get closer to the action was to link up through a bodyport. No one on this team was allowed to have an active port.

Ash raised a hand to the back of his neck, brushing his fingertips over the skin at his hairline. His port was a hard metal nub, right below a layer of skin. So close to the surface, but sealed off as long as he was under Tremaine's thumb.

He thought about taking a razor to the skin and freeing the port almost every damn day. Each time he resisted the urge, knowing it wouldn't do him any good and might make things worse for Hope.

The curved wall at the front of the room was essentially a giant monitor. Computer code scrolled along the edges of the screen, with a digital map occupying the center of the display. Little red dots indicated where the nonstop barrage of attempted hacks originated.

The Tremaine Corporation was under nearly constant cyberattack every minute of every day. The majority of the attempted breaches were stopped by the company's firewall and automated defenses. Ash and the rest of this crew weren't called in until those measures failed. Then it was a race to prevent the attacks from making it all the way through to the juicy data at the center of the company.

Right now, a few of his team were busy blocking attacks. That was the thing about this job: there was always another attack incoming.

"Here's the rules," Mendez announced. "As soon as we're in our chairs, Ash and I will go head-to-head on the next ping. If I beat Ash, I get to hear about the girl."

Boos nearly drowned Mendez out.

"Fine. If I win, we *all* get to hear about Ash's new girlfriend."

Cheers echoed around the room.

Ash waved his hands to get them to quiet down. "What happens when I win?"

Mendez grinned and the rest of their team laughed. "Then you don't have to tell us."

Ash chuckled. "That hardly seems like a prize worthy of my skills."

Mendez rolled his eyes. "Fine, *if* you win—and that's a big if—I'll buy the beers tonight."

"Deal. But I'm going to make it cost you."

Ash would rather spend another evening with the Jack, but until he could figure out how to get unbanned, that wasn't an option. Spending time with his team was an almost worthy replacement. They usually grabbed drinks at least once a week and he couldn't afford to change his schedule too much. His work with Portia was already gaining unwanted attention.

Settling into his chair, Ash shifted so he could see Mendez out of the corner of his eye. He didn't know the other man's story. That was an unspoken rule among the hackers the Tremaine Corporation had captured and put to work: Don't talk about your past. Ash had worked with him for nearly the entire time he'd been at Tremaine Corporation and knew that Mendez had mad hacking skills and a wicked sense of humor. But the other man had been careful not to drop any other details about where he came from.

It didn't matter, though. Ash was better than anyone here.

"You ready?" Another hacker stood next to his chair. Someone else was next to Mendez.

"Always." More than ready. The competition with

Mendez was a good distraction from Portia's assignment and his utter failure to convince the Jack to help him out.

Ava, one of the two female hackers on the team, stepped into the space between Ash and Mendez so they both could see her. "Okay, boys. You know the terms. Whoever stops the next ping wins."

The room was quiet, something that rarely happened on shift.

Ash played his fingers lightly over the keyboard, keeping them loose, keeping them flexible. The big map on the wall should be his focus, but he spared a moment to glance at Mendez. Bundled into a padded chair like Ash's, the other man had strapped on his preferred goggles. Mendez turned his head and raised his fingers to his forehead in salute. Ash nodded back.

His gaze flicked over the map, watching the dots of light as they flared and died when they hit the firewalls.

Shouldn't be long now until one slipped through.

The thought had barely crossed his mind when the wall flared red and the screech of an alarm echoed through the room.

Showtime!

Information flashed on his monitor. Attack origination, suspected target, and bits and pieces of code that the hacker was throwing at the system. Ash's focus narrowed to the screen in front of him and the outside world faded away.

"All right, Takata Corp. Let's see what you've got," Ash murmured. He recognized the technique on the other end, knew they were part of the Takata Corp. They'd met before, multiple times, usually battling to a draw. The other hacker hadn't gotten in, but they'd made Ash work for the block.

Ash's fingers danced over the keyboard, faster than he'd even been during his pre-Tremaine days.

His moves were unconscious, motor memory and years of experience guiding him. The other hacker thrust, Ash parried. Ash attacked, they countered. Ash smiled, enjoying the routine. "You act like you're giving me something, but you take it away."

Cut the move off there.

"Ooh, a fancy misdirect. Still not fancy enough."

Then, suddenly, code on the other end got more interesting. More complicated. "That's new."

That didn't stop Ash from finding a pattern and blocking it.

The hacker on the other end tried to hide his attack via a series of reroutes and layers of more complicated code.

Ash snorted. It looked complex, but it wasn't. "Sorry, friend. That's not going to work either."

What was Mendez doing right now? Probably something very similar. Ash could spend time trying to watch Mendez, but he wanted to catch this hacker instead.

"Oh, I see what you're trying to do." Underneath the misdirects and the crazy code writing, Ash saw signs that he was getting close to the other hacker's firewall.

Good.

Ash was so close he could taste it. Mendez would be hot on his trail, so he needed to shut the intruder down.

Now.

Ash's fingers flew over the keyboard, a combination of keystrokes that would render the computer on the other end useless. It was an old trick, one he'd used before.

He waited a fraction of a second for a response from the other end of the line.

Nothing.

Ash launched a final attack, in case his last trick hadn't stopped the hacker. He slammed down on the final key and held his breath. Around him, he sensed the rest of the team holding their breath too.

Seconds later, the room burst into cheers. Ash thought they were for him, but it was possible—barely—that Mendez had owned the final block.

"Damn, Ash. You're fucking amazing."

"Yeah, I am." It wasn't bragging when it was the truth.

A different voice said, "Man, Mendez, you were so close."

"I know," Mendez said, his voice gruff with disappointment.

Ash swiveled to face him.

Mendez pushed his goggles to his forehead, shook his head in rueful acceptance. "Next time, Ash. Next time."

"Any time." Ash smiled his cockiest smile.

Mendez flipped him off.

Ash laughed, then looked at the big screen. He wanted to make sure that the attack vector really was stopped. Though he hated his job, he took threat neutralization seriously. Part of it was just the way he was wired: he hated doing a half-assed job. The rest was purely to protect his sister.

The board showed the threat gone, so Ash finally relaxed. "Sorry, Mendez, looks like you're gonna have to pay up."

He pushed out of the chair and stretched. His shoulders ached like he'd had a punishing workout, instead of just a computer battle.

Mendez grumbled, then said, "Fine, first round's on me tonight."

He'd won, so he didn't have to say anything, but in the

spirit of team building, he threw them a bone. "If it's any consolation, she's way out of my league and doesn't want to see me again."

They groaned. Mendez slapped his hand over his heart. "You're cruel, Ash. Cruel!"

He smiled. "I know. Imagine how boring I'd be otherwise."

The rest of the shift passed quickly. The mood remained light, the work steady and easy. After Ash's battle with Mendez, the team split their time razzing Mendez about the loss and Ash about his new "girlfriend."

The Jack as his girlfriend. That'd be amazing if it weren't so terrifying. In the brief time he'd spent with her, she'd been smart and funny, savvy and thoughtful, intense and scary. Add in those eyes that looked like they'd seen infinity and a body that wouldn't stop . . .

The Jack was the kind of woman you lost your soul to.

Ash shook his head and banished that daydream. That was the problem. He'd already sold his soul to the Tremaine Corporation. If even the tiniest bit of it was salvageable . . . well, that part belonged to Hope.

"Ready for those drinks?" Mendez ambled over when Ash logged off.

Ash shook his head. "Can't. Something came up," he said. He'd received an email an hour ago demanding his presence in the executive suite. Not wanting to draw unwanted attention to his arrangement with Portia, he'd ignored it in order to finish his shift.

Of course, Mendez took that as an invitation to give him more shit. "Ooh, is it your hot lady friend?"

More like the Ice Queen. "I wish. A work thing."

"Shit. What's wrong? Something happen on shift?"

Now he looked alarmed, the opposite of what Ash had wanted.

"No. It's probably nothing." Trying to lighten the mood, he added, "I probably screwed something up."

Mendez put his hand on Ash's shoulder and applied pressure until he looked at him. "Don't even joke about that. I've seen what they've done to hackers who screw up." He shuddered. "It's not pretty."

Ash already knew that. He'd screwed up once and those memories haunted him. The punishment hadn't been physical. Security had explained in excruciating detail what would happen to Hope if he stepped out of line again.

"Maybe it's gotten better under Tremaine's daughter?" Ash aimed for a super casual tone.

"I haven't heard anything," Mendez said. "You gotta wonder, is nothing happening or is it so bad no one can talk about it?"

Ash grimaced. He'd had those same thoughts even before he'd been called into Portia's office. "Well, that courier sure hasn't disappeared. Maybe that's a good sign."

Mendez sputtered a laugh. "Shit. She's banging that investor. I'd bang him too if I thought it would save me from the wrath of Portia Tremaine."

Ash stared at him for a second then burst out laughing. He was gasping for air by the time he got it under control. "Damn. I didn't peg you for a romantic, Mendez."

"I call them like I see 'em," he said, even as he flipped Ash off again.

The newsies were selling Dizzie and Killian as the love story of the century. Every damn broadcast was full of comparisons to the great love stories—Romeo and Juliet, Bogey and Bacall, Buffy and Spike.

Ash didn't know what part of the reporting was true

and what wasn't, but it sounded like one hell of a fairy tale. The kind that made you wish you believed in happy-ever-afters. Stupid fools.

Mendez had a funny look on his face. Ash had missed something. "What?"

"You all right? You spaced out for a minute there."

"Yeah, fine. Just, you know, late nights."

"You dog!" Mendez bumped his shoulder.

Ash didn't have a chance to respond. The doors to the room flew open and a pair of Tremaine Security guards stepped through.

"Ash Cutter. You need to come with us."

Next to him, Mendez stiffened.

"What's the problem?" Ash asked, trying to keep his cool.

The guard shrugged. "Ms. Tremaine wants to see you."

The entire room gasped. Ash hoped it was about the super-secret project she'd assigned him, the one he couldn't tell anybody about. No wonder everyone thought he was in trouble.

Ash consciously steeled his spine. "Ready when you are." He injected as much I'm-not-worried into his voice as he could.

He had to believe it was only because he'd ignored her summons. Anything else . . . he swallowed hard. Anything else would be catastrophic.

CHAPTER 18

PORTIA'S ASSISTANT waved Ash through the moment he stepped off the elevator. He studied her expression as he passed, but she was already focused back on her task. His stomach was a mass of knots as he pushed open the doors to the inner sanctum.

The head of Tremaine Corporation sat at her desk, her attention focused on the computer screen on her desk. He might have laughed that she was ignoring him so studiously, but sending security guards to pull him out of his shift had knocked him off-kilter.

"You didn't show up for your shift." Though she still didn't look at him, the chill in her voice indicated that he had the full attention of the Ice Queen.

His brows furrowed in confusion. "Yes, I did. That's where I was when Security found me."

"*This* shift," Portia said. "The project you're supposed to be working on for me."

That's what this was about?

"We never discussed an actual schedule," Ash countered carefully.

"I told you to make this a priority." She looked up, her blue gaze piercing him.

He still feared what she could do to him, but he wasn't going to take the blame for something that wasn't his fault. "You never told me not to show up for my usual shift on cybersecurity either."

Instead of taking his seat at the desk she'd procured for him since their last meeting, he sat in the chair in front of her desk. A small rebellion, but he wasn't falling into the role of Portia Tremaine's personal hacker until they set some expectations. He couldn't afford to piss her off, but he also couldn't allow Security to pull him away from other activities, like freeing his sister.

"Am I going to be working here all the time?"

Portia cocked her head, thinking over his question.

Before she could say anything, he continued. "I can't tell anyone what I'm doing, but you're not worried about how it will look?"

She blinked. "What do you mean, 'how it will look'?"

He had to carefully tread the line between convincing her and not pissing her off. "Well, if I'm supposed to keep this super-secret project super-secret, people are going to wonder what I'm doing in here all day long with you."

"They'll just think you're working for me." Her tone said she thought he was an idiot.

"Sure, some of them might believe I'm working for you. Others might think I'm 'working.'" He put air quotes around the word.

"What?" She paused. He saw the moment his meaning registered. "Ew!" She reared back.

"Wow, I'm offended," he said before he recalled that he wasn't talking to his team but to the woman who held his sister's life in her hands.

"You're joking, right? No one could possibly think that you and I would possibly . . ." She waved her hand between them.

Yeah, he was offended. She probably didn't mean it that way—and he wasn't interested either—but it still stung. "Why not? I'm a decent-looking guy and you're a lonely widow."

Horror, shock, and sadness flickered over her face in quick succession.

It was the sadness that cut him to the core. "I'm sorry, that was uncalled for." For all he wanted to poke at her, his apology was sincere. Especially since her loss was partially his fault. "I shouldn't have said that. But there are people who will."

She turned away to look out the window, but not before he caught the shimmer of tears in her eyes. Her pain pricked his conscience. He couldn't afford to feel badly for her—but he did.

The silence between them grew and Ash made no move to break it. Let her have all the time she needed to patch the cracks in her armor. "What do you suggest?" she asked finally.

"Since I'm supposed to be looking for the person who helped your father's assistant," his stomach turned at the words, "I should probably spend part of my time out there. If anyone asks, I can just tell them that I'm working on a special project for you. If they want to know more, I'll direct them to you. That should be the end of that." He chuckled darkly.

She seemed to be considering his words.

The silence finally got to him and he blurted out the question he'd been dying to ask since she called him to her office and demanded his assistance. "Why haven't you just asked Leopold Brunswick who helped him?" Her father's weaselly assistant had struck him as the kind of man willing to sacrifice anyone for his own gains. Just look at the New Amsterdam Hotel bombing.

Portia blinked at him as she processed the change of subject. "Do you really think I didn't? He was asked several times," and the way she said "asked" sent shivers up Ash's spine, "but he never broke. Said it would be a cold day in hell before he helped a Tremaine."

Ash grimaced, but was still grateful that the other man was stronger. No, not stronger. More *vindictive* than Ash could have imagined. "You don't think he'll eventually, um, change his mind?"

"No, I'm quite certain that he won't. Leopold Brunswick is dead." An emotion he couldn't identify threaded through her voice.

Shock—and was that actual fear?—coursed through him as he recognized how much more dangerous the game he was playing had just become. "You killed him?" Did his voice just squeak?

Her cool gaze and even cooler voice chilled the air between them. "Do you really think I would stoop to murder, Mr. Cutter?"

She paused longer this time, obviously waiting for a response. "Um, no?" Yeah, that was definitely a squeak.

Her smile was all Ice Queen and he shivered. "No, I did not kill Leopold Brunswick. Someone else did. And when I find that person . . . they'll wish they hadn't done that."

Ohfuckohfuckohfuck. Goosebumps covered his arms. He didn't want to imagine what she would do to him when she found out he had helped Brunswick. That was why he had needed the Jack's help. He had to get himself and Hope out of Portia's reach before she found out. But then he'd gone and fucked that up.

"That's, uh . . ." What the fuck did he say to that?

"Not truly a loss in the greater scheme of things."

Cold. Ice cold. Then again, the man had tried to kill her, had likely killed her father, and had definitely killed her husband.

"Did you ever meet him?"

Ash swallowed hard. "Brunswick?" How was he supposed to answer that?

"Mm hmm."

Her gaze was like a weight. Or maybe that was all the secrets he was keeping.

He cleared his throat. "I think so. Maybe. He came down to watch us in the cybersecurity room sometimes. Like he was inspecting us or something. I don't think we actually ever *met* him. Like officially."

Portia nodded. "That sounds like something he would do. He was always trying to be more important than he was. He wasn't a Tremaine, but he wanted to be one."

"That's . . . interesting."

Ash had never wanted to be a Tremaine. There was too much structure, too many downsides of running a big company, but he wouldn't mind the money upside. Ever since he and Hope had been left to manage on their own, thoughts of money and survival had been his constant companions. Until he'd been captured and freedom became more important.

Portia's laugh was bitter. "No, it's not. My father was never going to relinquish the company. Not to me and not to his assistant. He thought he would live forever. Now he's gone and I'm . . . here."

Alone. That was what Ash heard. Portia was the last

Tremaine left. Unless you counted Dizzie, which neither woman seemed inclined to do.

"I'll expect you here every afternoon after your morning shift." The change of subject made his head spin. "Do not keep me waiting—either for your shift or for the information I want."

"Yes, ma'am." Ash dipped his head in acknowledgment. Then, because he couldn't afford for her to be suspicious of him, he got up and moved to his desk.

Several hours later, Ash logged off, then stood and stretched. The setup wasn't nearly as comfortable as the one he used in the cybersecurity room, but it was better than the first desk she'd had installed.

Portia remained at her desk. Behind her, the cityscape had shifted from gray autumn sky to neon lights that shimmered through the raindrops on the windows.

"Where do you think you're going?"

"Back to my room. It's end of shift."

She raised her head. In the pale glow from her screen, her skin looked even paler. "Really?"

His head dropped back and he couldn't contain his sigh. "Look. I understand this project is important. But I am not my computer." His hand twitched and he shut down the urge to rub his port. "I need food and I need sleep or I'm going to be useless to you and to the company."

His days of living on caffeine and cheesy orange snacks were long gone. Not that he'd had either while working today. He hadn't eaten, period. His stomach rumbled, the sound loud in the quiet room.

"Very well," Portia said and returned to her work.

"Do you," he waved toward the door, "want me to bring you food or something?"

What the hell was he doing? He needed to come up

with other ways to free Hope. He didn't have time to bring Portia food. She had thousands of people on her payroll. Any of them could help her out. But she looked so worn that he felt bad for her.

He felt bad for Portia Tremaine? Had the world gone crazy?

Her mouth dropped open and she looked startled for a moment. "No, thank you." The note of finality in her voice said any other offers would not be appreciated.

"Have a good night." He turned and exited her office. The lobby area was quiet and slightly eerie, her assistant's desk empty. That was a surprise. He'd have expected her assistant to work as long as she did.

Not his problem. He pressed the button for the elevator. It had been a long, weird day.

He cracked his neck and rubbed his eyes. He was tired, but he had a lot more work of his own to do tonight. A beer sounded really good right now. As did seeing the Jack. Taryn. What would she do when he called her by her name? Did he dare?

Probably nothing good. He'd been banned from the bar. While that might not stop him at most places, even given the change in management, the Jack was not someone to fuck with.

Pissed that he'd screwed up the best avenue for getting Hope away from the Tremaine Corporation, when the elevator stopped, he strode out at a quick pace. And immediately barreled into someone, knocking them down.

"Shit, I'm sorry." One of the Tremaine Security guards —the one who'd ridden the elevator up with him that first day—was sprawled on the floor. "Here, let me help."

She grasped his extended hand and he pulled her

upright in one quick movement. "Thanks." The moment she released his hand, she continued down the hall.

He'd taken a few steps before he realized that she'd pressed a piece of paper into his hand. "What the—"

Ignoring it until he was well away from the executive elevator and any cameras in its vicinity, Ash ducked around a corner and carefully opened the folded note.

Ban lifted. The bold, broad writing emphasized the order. And it was an order. *The Jack* was scrawled beneath the command.

What did it mean? Was the Jack going to help? Ash's heart skipped a beat, and he didn't look too closely to determine if it was for the prospect of rescuing his sister or for the chance to see Taryn again.

CHAPTER 19

"WHISKEY NEAT, PLEASE."

Taryn looked up into gray eyes that she hadn't expected to see again. Warmth flared in her belly, but she was still pissed that he hadn't shown up yesterday. "Look who finally showed up." Dammit. That came out snippy. There was no reason for him to know that she'd missed him. No, she hadn't missed him. She'd just expected he would answer the Jack's summons.

She poured his drink—a top-shelf bottle because she wasn't letting him off easy—and set it in front of him without further comment.

Her fingers brushed his when she took the credit chip he offered and her skin tingled where they touched. The Jack's reputation was the only thing that kept her from jerking her hand away.

"I'm sorry, Taryn."

He whispered her name softly and it was easy, so easy, to imagine him using it like that in a more intimate setting. Except . . .

She grabbed his wrist and leaned close over the bar. "How do you know my name?"

His gaze searched hers. "You're not the only one who can find information."

That was true. Her name wasn't a secret, but she mostly went by "the Jack" these days. People respected the name—the title—and it served as a reminder of who they were dealing with. Her real name only came out in softer moments with friends or lovers.

Could she see Ash in either of those roles?

As a lover, yes. She suppressed a shiver, imagining all those delicious tingles everywhere.

As a friend? A man who dug up secrets? That required a level of trust she wasn't sure she could manage.

"I need two beers and a tequila shot."

The order broke the spell Taryn had been under. While she'd never admit it, she was grateful for the interruption. "Coming up."

The routine allowed her to settle her thoughts and steady her nerves. *Pull it together, Taryn. It's a transaction, like all the others the Jack makes every day.*

Nerves settled, she still braced herself to hear him say her name again. Instead, he said, "I was surprised to get your note. How did you do it?"

A half smile curved her lips. That had taken a little, no, a lot of thought on her part, but she was pleased that she'd managed to infiltrate the Tremaine Corporation. "Trade secret."

He smiled and saluted her with his glass. He didn't bitch, he didn't moan. Between that and his smile, she had the warm fuzzies.

"Why did you drop the ban?"

"We need to talk."

"About Hope?" he asked quietly.

She nodded. The bar wasn't the place for this conversation. "We'll talk in my office when Dani gets back."

"That's the bartender?"

"Yep, that's me." Dani appeared at her side. She frowned slightly at Ash, then turned to Taryn. "Thanks for covering for me, boss."

"No problem. You good out here?" Part of her hoped Dani would say no, would give her an excuse to *not* be alone with Ash in her office.

Dani studied the patrons at the counter and then swept her gaze over the wider bar. "Yeah, I'm good. I'll call you if there's trouble."

Taryn nodded, though she really hoped that trouble, whatever form it took, didn't show up tonight.

Ash's gaze swung between them. "You're having trouble?"

"No." Both women spoke in unison.

"Grab your drink," Taryn said, "and follow me."

Taryn waved Ash into her office. The entire walk from the bar area to the back, she'd felt his gaze, his presence, and it took effort not to squirm. She took a moment at the door to breathe, then took her seat behind the desk.

"It must be serious," Ash said.

"What is?" She was curious how his mind worked.

"Whatever caused you to drop the ban and send the note." His brows furrowed and the corners of his mouth turned down. "Are you planning to turn me in?"

Taryn blinked in surprise. "Why would I do that?"

"A better offer?" His concern was reflected in his eyes.

She laughed. "Right now, every offer is better than yours." When he opened his mouth to object, she shook her head. "You asked for my help, but you never said what you were willing to pay."

He swallowed hard and she watched his Adam's apple bob. "Whatever you want, it's yours."

She sighed. "Maybe it's better that you're on a leash if that's how you negotiate."

"I . ." Ash trailed off and snapped his mouth shut.

"I'm going to ask you some questions," she said, "and I expect answers. Truthful ones. Or the ban will be back in place before you can blink." Ash didn't know what she'd decided yet, and she was going to use that to her advantage.

Ash nodded.

"Yes or no?"

"Yes," Ash said.

"What were you going to offer me to rescue your sister?"

He set his drink on her desk and leaned forward, elbows braced on his knees. "Money," he said quickly. "I have some saved. Or I did before I was captured. I assume it's still there. And I've got a building."

"A building?" She hadn't intended to interrupt, but that was not what she was expecting.

"Yeah, an old warehouse near the water. We lived there sometimes." He canted his head to the side. "And secrets," he said finally.

"Secrets?" Secrets were always handy. But they were dangerous too. The old Jack would have taken them in a heartbeat. Taryn was more cautious.

He raised a hand to the back of his neck, then dropped it back in his lap. "Because you're the Jack. I figured you could do something with them."

"And you can't?"

He shook his head. "Not to get my sister out."

"Fair enough. You were a hacker and you were obviously good at it if you've got money and a building, so why didn't you ask someone from pre-Tremaine days for help?"

He finished his drink in one long swallow. "I've been out of the game for five years. I don't know who's around. Who to trust."

Taryn leaned forward. "Why do you think you can trust me?"

"I don't," he said. "But you're the Jack. Unless things have changed, the Jack will do anything if the price is right."

Ash wasn't wrong. Though he wasn't quite right either. She'd eliminated some of the more problematic aspects of the previous Jacks' business. Refused business in some darker gray areas.

"So why now? Why the sudden urge to leave? You've been there five years. Did they suddenly threaten your sister?"

He unclenched his jaw before answering. "It's time."

"That's not an answer," Taryn pressed. Sure, she'd basically decided that she was going to take the job, but they needed to establish some ground rules first.

"It just is." Ash leaned back in the chair, arms crossed over his chest like a recalcitrant child.

Taryn echoed his position and kicked her feet up onto the desk. "Look, you're the one asking for help. It's nothing to me if Hope gets out of the Tremaine hospital or doesn't. But you're wasting my time, and my patience isn't going to last much longer."

Ash looked everywhere in the room except at her before he spoke. "I . . . may have been poking around in places that I shouldn't have been."

"And?" she prodded.

"And I might have uncovered some Tremaine family

secrets that I shouldn't have." He looked pale admitting that.

Taryn sucked in a breath. Oh shit. Did he mean . . .

"So the timing," she chose her words carefully, "is related to the recent . . . revelations?"

He stared at her for a few long seconds, then gave a sharp nod.

Shit. The explosive news about the long-lost Tremaine daughter—and Phillip Tremaine's horrifying organ harvesting program—had dominated the headlines since the bombing. Everyone in the city had speculated about how the news had come out. "Do the Tremaines know?"

He leaned forward. "I don't know for sure. They've got someone looking into it."

"That's a problem." One she wasn't entirely sure how to solve. "Is that person any good?"

He smiled and her heart nearly stopped. "Yeah, I'm the best there is."

Her boots hit the floor as she shifted closer to her desk. "Portia Tremaine hired *you* to investigate yourself?"

His smile was a mix of proud and sheepish.

"Why you?"

"She called me into her office and dropped a bombshell on me."

"Let me guess. On Tuesday." The day he'd strolled into her bar.

He nodded. "Yeah. When I tried to get out of it, she threatened Hope."

"That's cold." Portia Tremaine was called the Ice Queen and personally, Taryn had no problem with a woman doing whatever it took to get ahead in business. No one else was going to look out for you. But, damn, threatening a coma patient . . . that seemed wrong.

Ash frowned. "She didn't threaten-threaten her," he said. "Just reminded me that they had her as leverage. Like I've forgotten over the last five years." His tone was bitter.

"What exactly is she having you look into?"

He looked away again before he spoke. "She wants me to locate whoever assisted Leopold Brunswick with his plans."

For the second time that night, he'd surprised her. "Not just the news about Dizzie, then." It wasn't a question.

He gave the slightest head shake.

Why the hell did all these people keep showing up at her bar? "You were responsible for the bombing?"

"No! I didn't know anything about that." Ash shot to his feet, his fists clenched at his sides. His chair rocked with the violence of his movement, then settled back into place. "He just asked me to find information he could use against Phillip Tremaine. He said he could help me get free from the company and I—" He shook his head and looked at his feet. "After hearing that, I didn't ask any questions."

Brunswick sounded like as much of an asshole as the previous Jack had been. And that was a pretty fucking high bar. "He won't turn you in?"

Gray eyes met her gaze. "Portia says he's dead. If she's telling the truth, he's not a problem."

"Have you considered just blackmailing your way out?" Blackmail was an effective tool, though personally Taryn didn't like to use it. It wasn't a permanent solution to problems.

"What?"

"You admitted that you dug up Tremaine's big secret." Secrets, probably. "Tell Portia that you'll keep quiet if she lets the two of you go."

Ash dropped back into his seat and stared at her like

she'd grown two heads. "If I tell Portia I've got her secrets, she'll know I was the one who helped him and I'll never see daylight again. I don't know what she would do to Hope." He shook his head. "No, I won't risk it."

Taryn studied the man in front of him. The love and care he showed for his sister got to her. What would it be like to have a champion like that? Someone who put you first?

It was a surprising and endearing trait in a man who was obviously willing to cross the line between right and wrong.

What other Tremaine secrets had he uncovered? Could she request those as payment?

Even as the thought crossed her mind, she dismissed it. She needed his skills and he obviously had them if what he was telling her was true.

Dizzie's fairy tale romance with Killian St. John, one of the hottest men in the world, overshadowed whatever other secrets might have been revealed. No one knew exactly what had happened between them last month, but they appeared inseparable whenever the newsies showed them.

The romance portion, Taryn happened to believe. She'd seen the two of them together when they'd been in hiding. The way St. John had looked at the courier . . . well, Taryn would never admit it, but it made even her callous heart race.

"Any other information I should know before I make a decision? Withholding information puts me at risk and it will put Hope at risk, too."

"No, I swear. That's why we need to move. I don't know how long I'll be able to pretend to be searching for myself."

"So back to my original question? What is this rescue worth to you?"

CHAPTER 20

ASH STARED AT THE JACK, processing everything she'd said. He was afraid to get his hopes up, but it sounded like she might be willing to take on Hope's case.

"Anything you want," he blurted. "I'll give you anything you want if you help me free Hope."

Fuck! What was he thinking?

Offering carte blanche to the Jack . . .

The old Jack had been formidable due to his willingness to do whatever it took to fulfill a request, whether it was a girl for the evening, a contract hit on a rival, or the latest drugs to hit the streets. He would have latched onto Ash's mistake and taken advantage.

Was that what she would do with the ridiculous offer he'd just made? And did he want to take it back?

He watched the wheels turn in the new Jack's head. Taryn was a thinker and that made her even more dangerous. She was also one of the most intriguing women he'd ever met.

"I want your skills."

"What skills?" he asked, dumbfounded by the request.

She couldn't mean his hacking skills, could she? But what other skills did he have?

She sighed. "Computer skills, Ash."

"You need something hacked?" He practically salivated at the thought of getting into the Jack's computer system.

Taryn swiveled side to side in her seat, then stopped. It was the first sign of uncertainty that he'd seen from her. "Maybe."

She looked like she was contemplating her words, so he didn't say anything, just waited.

"Someone came into the bar, shortly after I made an . . . acquisition. Someone who shouldn't have had a reason to visit Razor Jack's."

Ash stared at her. "Okay?"

"I want to know why he showed up here." Her lips were pressed into a thin line and her body radiated tension.

This was obviously important to her. More important than he probably understood at the moment if she was willing to trade rescuing Hope for something that sounded like an easy project. "So am I locating this person or am I hacking their system?"

"Yes."

Ash rubbed his brow with his thumb and middle finger. That wasn't really helpful.

"I know his territory," Taryn said, "but I need you to locate him electronically. Then I need to know why he showed up here. Has he been here before? Was he tipped off? Is there an electronic footprint we can trace somehow?"

As the scope of the "easy project" got more complicated, Ash understood why she was willing to make the trade. Except . . . "I can't do this at Tremaine headquarters. And I assume you wouldn't want me to, anyway."

"No, definitely not," she said, shaking her head vigorously. The sleek waterfall of her dark hair shimmered behind her.

"What about your computer?"

Another vehement *no*.

Shit. "I know I said I'd do anything, but . . ." He paused, searching for the right words. For an option that wouldn't nuke his chance of freeing Hope. "I don't have any equipment." He didn't tell her that he wasn't allowed to have any personal equipment. *Allowed*, like he was a child.

Sure, there was the warehouse he'd sent Dizzie to when she was on the run, but it was on the edge of town. Getting there, hacking, and getting back to Tremaine headquarters? The more time he spent there, the more chances someone would notice his absences.

"I'm sorry. I can't do it," he said. "Please. Is there something else I can do?"

Taryn pushed away from her desk and stood.

Ash tensed. Was she going to kick him out? Should he plead his case one more time? "Please, I'll do anything. I just . . . I can't do that. I don't have the equipment."

"Walk with me," she said.

CHAPTER 21

ASH FOLLOWED Taryn out of her office. She locked the door then led him deeper into the building. They turned down another hall lined with closed doors. Some were numbered, while others had little brass plaques that they passed too quickly for him to read.

"Where are we going?"

"To solve your problem," she said.

Sure, that wasn't mysterious at all.

Finally, Taryn stopped in front of a steel door. He nearly ran into her because he was too busy studying his surroundings.

His explorations of Tremaine headquarters had proven that interesting secrets hid behind mysterious closed doors. "What is this place?"

Taryn didn't answer right away. She looked past him, checking for a tail.

"Part of the old Jack's business." With that cryptic statement, she pressed her hand to a panel next to the door.

The door opened with a creak. She glanced around again and ushered him into the dark doorway. "Quick!"

The door closed behind them with an ominous slam. Darkness surrounded them along with a slightly musty smell.

"Um, should I be concerned?" The Jack had a reputation for dirty dealings, but Ash had begun to believe that this Jack—that Taryn—was different. Had he read her wrong?

"All will be revealed," she intoned. Her laugh echoed in the darkness.

He sucked in a breath. That simple sound sparked a flood of complex emotions. Joy, hope, curiosity.

Her footsteps moved away from him. Then, suddenly, the room flooded with light.

He blinked rapidly, letting his eyes adjust. He was standing in a small hallway.

Taryn stood in another doorway, her hand on what he assumed was a control box. "C'mon." She waved him closer, then stepped aside.

"Holy shit." His mouth dropped open when he got his first glimpse of the room and its contents.

A chair sat in the center of the room, surrounded by walls lined with monitors. It looked like a combination of the setup at his warehouse and the cybersecurity battle room.

"Is this . . ." His words trailed off. He couldn't believe his eyes.

"A hacking setup? Yeah. It belonged to the Jack before the last Jack. I think the one before me tinkered a bit. Or made a few updates, at least, but I wasn't allowed down here often." She shuddered.

Ash looked away from the chair and studied her profile. "He was a bastard, wasn't he?"

"You have no idea," she said quietly after a long pause.

The words hung between them, hinting at secrets that Ash longed to explore. Instead, he asked, "Is it active?"

Taryn shrugged. "It's got power." She gestured to a panel of switches on the wall. "I've never used it, so I don't know how well it works."

"Is it registered?"

Her laugh filled the room, chasing away the hint of melancholy. "You think the Jack has a registered system?"

Yeah, that was a stupid question. The Jack had always skated the edge of legality. "True. Wired in?"

She shrugged again. "I don't think the signal can be traced, but that's not my area of expertise. Will it work to fulfill my request?"

"You want me to use this?" Ash blurted. The words sounded harsh and ungrateful, but from the moment they'd left her office, he'd never expected Taryn to help him help her.

"Is that a problem?" Her voice was hard, flat and he knew he'd offended her.

He hurried to reassure her. "No, not at all. I was just surprised. Can I check it out?"

She nodded and he stepped past her and fully entered the room. He approached the chair, his head already spinning with possibilities.

He stopped by the chair, which barely looked used. He'd recognized its silhouette from a distance: a Johnson super chair, specifically designed for amazing ergonomics for hackers. Well, the marketing materials said they were for cybersecurity specialists, but everyone knew what they really meant.

If the Jack had been willing to shell out that much for a chair, maybe the rest of the equipment was as high quality.

Circling the room, he studied the rest of the equipment,

whistling in appreciation. Despite the layers of dust, it all looked to be in good shape. Except . . . something was missing. "No keyboard?"

Taryn looked surprised. "Do you need one?"

"I . . . I don't know." Ash rubbed the back of his neck, lingering over the scar tissue. If he didn't have a port and there wasn't a keyboard . . .

He dropped his hands in defeat. "I appreciate you showing me this, but I don't think I can use it." His stomach sank. He'd been one of the best. Before his capture, he could've made this equipment sing. Now he couldn't even use the best setup he'd seen in years.

Taryn's voice was gentle. "You don't need a keyboard. It runs off a port."

How could he explain how impossible that was? "I know," he said. "But I don't have one."

"You did." She reached up to tap the spot on his neck.

Her touch was gentle but it still burned. He hated the reminder that he wasn't the man he used to be. "Not anymore," he growled.

If he'd expected to scare her off . . . He'd forgotten who he was dealing with.

Instead of backing off, she pressed harder. "It's still in there, right?"

He jerked his head away and stepped away from her, already missing the warmth of her touch. "Yes." What was she up to?

"If you trust me, I can help."

Help? "How?"

"I can open the port."

He gaped at her. She made it sound so simple.

It wasn't like he hadn't thought about it. When he'd first been captured, every minute of every day, Ash had planned and plotted how to access his port. His fingers had scraped over the scab and picked at the edges. The only thing that had stopped him was knowing Hope would be the one to pay if Tremaine Security discovered he'd opened it. And that was still true today.

Still . . . it wouldn't hurt to know what she was thinking. "How?"

She rolled her eyes. "With a scalpel."

He might have blanched. Or made a sound. "What?"

"I have significant experience . . ." He had the sense she was censoring her words. "Cutting open wounds."

If she was trying to reassure him, it wasn't working. "Do you have official training?"

She laughed. "If I had training, do you think I'd be tending bar instead of working in a clinic somewhere?"

"You couldn't pay me to work in a clinic," he muttered. Bodies and blood. Ugh. He shuddered.

"Oh my god. Stop being a baby. Do you want my help, yes or no?" Hands on her hips, she stared at him.

In five years, she was the only person who'd ever offered to help him access his port.

God, what would he have done if someone had made the offer back then? He couldn't have had both his sister and the port.

But damn, in those first years, he'd missed surfing the networks like a lost limb. Even knowing the corporation would have punished her if he'd dropped offline, Ash wasn't sure he wouldn't have sacrificed Hope for access if he'd had the opportunity.

"No." His whisper sounded loud in the quiet between them.

When Taryn stepped back, her expression closing down, he reached for her, then dropped his hand, knowing her boundaries on unwanted touching. Instead, he stepped in front of her, willing her to look at him.

"I can't," he said, when she finally met his gaze. "I want to, but I can't. There's no way to hide even the smallest incision from Tremaine. They've reminded me over and over again that Hope will be the one to pay for any mistakes on my part. I can't risk it. I can't risk her."

Wrung out emotionally, he dropped his head. He jerked it back up when Taryn placed her hand on his arm. "It's okay. I understand."

He blinked at her through eyes blurry with unshed tears. Fuck, he wanted this over and Hope safe.

"What else do you need besides a keyboard?" she asked softly.

"That's a start," Ash said gruffly. "Can I turn on the equipment and test it out?"

She nodded. "Yes, that's fine."

Before she could remove her hand, Ash took a risk and placed his over hers. "Thank you," he said, and squeezed it before letting go.

Brushing away the moisture in his eyes, he dropped his hand and got to work.

CHAPTER 22

TARYN STUDIED the framework of the plan she and Dani had been working on. It wasn't perfect, not yet, but it was getting there. Ash had asked about it when he arrived earlier to play with the hacking equipment, and Taryn had been relieved to be able to tell him it was coming together.

Then he'd asked about a timeline. She sighed. Like she could just snap her fingers and get a person out of a bad situation just like that. Did he think she could extricate Hope from the Tremaine-controlled hospital like magic?

She'd wanted to tell him that her usual rescue took weeks and weeks of planning, but that wasn't a secret she was willing to share. So she'd just told him she was working on it.

The hospital looked like a fortress from the outside. Services were strictly for members of the Tremaine family, some employees, and, apparently, hostages. Ash had provided as much information as he could from his visits, so Taryn had the basic layout, including a map of Hope's floor and her room. He'd also listed off all the equipment required to keep her healthy.

Acquiring the equipment was her second problem.

Taryn tapped her finger against the computer screen. Outside of a few scalpels and first-aid kits, hospital-style medical supplies weren't usually on her shopping list.

It was solvable. She just hadn't figured it out yet.

Her office door slammed against the wall and she jumped. "What the hell, Dani?"

"You've got to get out there. Now." Dani's hands were clenched into fists at her sides. Her white knuckles were visible from across the room.

Taryn was already up and moving. She circled her desk. "What's wrong?"

"Giselle's pimp. He's back." Dani's voice was tight.

Fuck. This was the last thing Taryn needed. "Who's manning the bar?" she asked, keeping as tight a rein on her temper as she could.

"Jenna. Daryl's at her side."

Okay. Good. Daryl was big and intimidating.

"The rest of security?" Taryn didn't employ many guys, but the ones who worked for her were damn good at their jobs.

"Scattered around the room, keeping an eye on things." Dani paused, took a deep breath. "They're waiting for you, but if things escalate, they'll take care of it."

Yeah, that was what Taryn paid them for, but breaking up a good old-fashioned bar fight was one thing. Dealing with a pissed-off pimp who kept showing up where he shouldn't? That was something altogether different. Something completely unacceptable that Taryn needed to deal with herself.

Giselle's pimp had met her as a flighty city lady looking to get laid.

Tonight, he'd meet the Jack.

While she changed, Taryn peppered Dani with questions—the number of patrons, their locations, her sense of the temperature of the room.

Thankful she had on her shitkickers, Taryn pulled off her sweater and pulled on a thin armored undershirt. It covered her left side from shoulder to wrist. On the right, a capped sleeve covered her shoulder, but left the rest of her arm bare.

Her right arm didn't need protection. It *was* protection. The alloy could withstand heat and most projectiles. Plus, she hit like a badass motherfucker with that arm.

Taryn gathered her hair into a loose knot at the back of her head, then shrugged into a short leather jacket. Like the shirt, it was designed to leave her arm free.

While her arm was a weapon, it wasn't her only one. She slipped a stunner into her pocket and slid a knife into the built-in sheath in her sleeve. Additional weapons were stowed behind the bar and all her people were trained to use them.

She stretched her neck left and right. "Ready."

Taryn hurried down the hallway, Dani at her side. The situation could have escalated while she armed herself, but she trusted her people. They'd trained for this, for the day that someone tried to take her turf.

If things had gone to shit, her customers would be safe and the bad guys would be dead. She'd keep what was hers by fair means or foul.

Pausing in front of the bar area doors, Taryn took a deep breath and centered herself. She had to do this right and make an entrance. Maintaining the Jack's reputation was two-thirds showmanship and one-third backing it up with as much force as necessary.

"Stay back here," she instructed Dani.

Her second-in-command protested. Taryn cut her off with a look. "Good or bad, everyone's attention will be on me. I don't want you in the line of fire. Either stay back here or use one of the other entrances to get back behind the bar."

She hated the thought of Dani in danger. Still, the other woman was a big girl, able to take care of herself.

"I'm going to the bar." Dani practically dared Taryn to contradict her. Taryn wasn't surprised; she would have made the same choice.

Waiting until Dani was clear, Taryn pushed open the doors. Violently.

Silence fell over the bar. Taryn bit back a smile. She loved it when that happened.

Aware that all eyes were on her, she zeroed in on the troublemaker. The pimp was leaning over the bar, harassing Jenna. *Fuck that.*

Tension rode the room. Keeping her anger under tight control, Taryn strode to the bar.

He straightened and turned toward her with a swagger that was probably supposed to look dangerous.

Yeah, no.

Her gaze swept the room, picking out his bodyguards a few feet away from him. Whether the pimp and his friends had realized it or not, they were surrounded by her people.

"Problem?" Taryn stepped forward, crowding him against the bar.

He looked her up and down.

Her skin crawled. Men like him sickened her.

"Hey, baby." He squinted, stared a bit closer. "I know you?"

Taryn raised a brow. "You're in my place. Why?"

"The Jack's a chick? You're shitting me." He looked

around the bar like he got the joke. No one else laughed. The other patrons held their drinks close, while they waited to see how the Jack responded.

Another step forward. "Heard you had a problem." She didn't raise her voice. Not yet.

He put his hands in the air, gave her a mocking smile. "No problem, baby." He drawled out the word, leering at her. "I lost something, heard you'd found it."

"This look like a lost and found to you?" Her tone clearly called him an idiot. Taryn gestured around the room.

A few people snickered. She knew it wasn't her team, so it had to be her patrons. Good. She needed them on her side. If she lost face, she'd lose both their support and their money.

His eyes narrowed and his expression got mean. He puffed out his chest, playing at intimidation. If he thought he could cow her the way he did his girls—well, he'd best think twice.

The pimp stepped closer. Looked her up and down. "I know you." He narrowed his eyes, looked her up and down again.

She felt slimy and he hadn't even touched her. Poor Giselle, putting up with this on the regular.

"Yeah, I know you, bitch. You're the one who took my Gazelle."

The asshole mangled Giselle's name again.

"I don't think so." Taryn was willing to play this out for a minute. Was he smart enough to realize coming here was the biggest mistake he could make?

"No. You are. You're the bitch who stole my girl!" He was shouting now. "Where is she? I know you've got her here."

Everyone in the bar was watching now. That was fine. This could only end one way.

Her way.

"She's not your girl."

"I knew it. They told me you had her. Give her back." He slammed his hand down on the counter.

Okay, she was done. Taryn stepped closer again, projecting don't-fuck-with-me vibes. Weight balanced on the balls of her feet, she was ready to move if this went south.

Now he pushed away from the bar, his face inches from hers. From the corner of her eye, she saw his guards inch closer.

Taryn shook her head, a tiny movement telling her guys to hold.

"Bitch, give me the girl or I'll shoot this place up." His hand hovered near his hip. She didn't see a weapon but didn't doubt he was armed.

Behind her, patrons shifted, like they were trying to get a good view, rather than run. Good. They trusted the Jack to handle this.

"Bitch, I don't have your girl." She gave him the same up and down look he'd given her. "I can see why she left you, though." Her gaze lingered on his crotch a hair longer than the rest of him before she met his eyes and smirked.

"Get out of my bar." Her voice was steady. Solid. Cold as ice.

He flinched and took a step back.

Someone in the crowd snickered and the pimp seemed to realize what he'd done. He took a step closer and raised his hand.

Bastard. She'd dealt with his kind. Had the scars to prove it.

Raising that hand was a big mistake. She wasn't one of his girls. She wasn't under his power.

She had her own.

He lunged at her with a yell. Completely untrained, he telegraphed every move.

Taryn didn't flinch. Didn't even step out of the way.

She watched his hand as if he was moving in slow motion. She held perfectly still, giving nothing away as she gauged the moment it would strike and threw her hand up to block it.

Not just block it. Grab it.

Taryn wrapped her mechanical fingers around his hand and exerted slow but steady pressure.

It took him a moment to register what had happened. His expression morphing from surprise to pain was much quicker.

"Bitch!" he yelled, then his voice dropped to a squeak when she applied more pressure. It was almost comical.

His bones rubbed together in her grasp. The harder she pressed, the more it would hurt.

He whimpered and she tightened her grip. It'd be so easy to destroy him. It had taken her months to learn to control the unbelievable strength in this arm, to identify the fine line between making it hurt and crushing bones. Now she knew exactly how hard to squeeze.

That was when his two bodyguards moved closer.

As soon as they stepped toward Taryn, her guys intercepted them. Her team had them out of the way with barely a whisper.

Taryn changed her arm position slightly and he dropped to his knees. Only her grip kept it a controlled movement. She kept his arm straight while the rest of his body flopped to the floor.

Fear and anger warred in his eyes. The fear was winning.

And she wasn't even breathing hard.

Time for him to learn who was boss here.

"Now that I have your attention, I'll say this again. But slowly this time. Get. The. Fuck. Out. Of. My. Bar." She emphasized each word with a little squeeze. Rage simmered below her surface, her control on it as finely tuned as that on her arm.

He moaned.

"Do you understand?"

He nodded. A weak, pathetic effort.

"Out loud," she demanded.

"Yes." He spat the word.

"You will not come back here."

She waited. When he didn't respond, she gave him another little nudge.

"Yes, fine." He nodded again.

"You will leave Giselle alone."

Now he showed outright confusion. "Who?"

Save her from goddamned idiots. "Gazelle."

"She's mine—"

Whatever he thought he was going to say cut off with a scream.

"No. She's not yours. She belongs to no one but herself."

"Fine." He spat out the word.

"Come to think of it. Why don't you dismantle your entire operation?"

It was a pipe dream. As soon as he did, another pimp would pop up to take his place, like a game of whack-an-asshole.

"You stupid bit—"

Another scream.

"That's really not very nice." Like she fucking cared. "It does make me pretty determined to make it happen."

Every eye in the place was on her now. No one spoke. Half of them probably weren't breathing.

The entire bar waited to see what she did next.

The power was a rush.

It had surprised her at first. She'd learned to walk a very fine line. Too far in one direction and she would become just as bad as the man she had replaced.

She crouched down to his level, never releasing his arm, just moving carefully so she didn't do permanent damage. He would never understand how much thought she put into *not* hurting him. Guys like him never did.

Still gripping his hand—hard—she leaned close, her face inches from his. "You dismantle your business or I'll do it for you." She gave him her nicest, most terrifying smile.

He wet himself.

So glad that it still worked. She'd learned an awful lot from the previous Jack. Most of it bad. "I'll be watching you. I'll know whether you did. Or not."

Ignoring the smell of piss rising from the floor, Taryn leaned closer. "You don't want to see what happens if it's 'or not.'"

"I got it." He gasped. Anger flared in his eyes.

She released him and stood in one fluid movement.

The pimp lunged for her knees.

She'd been expecting it. Counting on it, even. Her booted foot met his chest and knocked his ass back down. He landed in a puddle of urine.

"You done?"

He scrambled to his feet. "I'm gonna make you pay, bitch." He kept talking but didn't make another move.

That could be a problem. Little assholes like him fed on their self-righteous anger. Her actions could make things worse for the girls he still had. She really hoped that wouldn't happen, but she'd keep an eye on the situation.

She turned her back on him, letting everyone in the bar know that she didn't consider him a threat. She waved Daryl and another bouncer over. "Get this trash off the floor. And escort anyone with him out of my bar."

Daryl clamped his hand on the pimp's shoulder—the one Taryn had used for her arm bar—and the man whimpered.

Dani slid a shot over to Taryn while she watched the trash get taken out. "That was pretty damn impressive," she whispered.

"Thanks," Taryn whispered back. She tossed back the shot and studied the bar. As soon as the pimp and his boys were tossed out and the puddle on the floor cleaned up, sound returned to the bar. Murmurs of approval and a smattering of applause told Taryn that the Jack's reputation was still intact.

CHAPTER 23

"EVERYONE GOOD?" Taryn surveyed the bar, taking in the regulars and the other patrons. Mostly, though, she was concerned about her people.

Adrenaline and excitement still ran high. The thick tension that had filled the air when she'd entered the bar had dissipated with the pimp's removal, replaced with a celebratory buzz. Her patrons were buying drinks and talking about what they'd seen. Dani was bartending and she and Jenna managed the chaos like the pros they were.

The story would spread, mostly through word of mouth. It might bring a bump of patrons, so she made a mental note to adjust the schedule, add an additional waitress. Maybe another bouncer in case the fight brought lookie-loos or wannabe challengers through the door.

During the fight, Rhonda had slipped behind the bar. Thank god. It would have been too easy for someone to take advantage of the chaos. They'd have to be idiotic when the Jack was in ass-kicking mode, but people were gonna people. Now she watched the door with concern on her face.

Taryn followed her gaze but didn't see any problems.

"It's okay, Rhonda. I don't think he'll be coming back." Taryn didn't have a solid plan yet if he did. She might have to consider more permanent solutions. She didn't like those.

"What?" Rhonda whipped her head around. She looked like she hadn't heard a word Taryn had said.

That wasn't like her. Was Dani right?

"You'd let me know if something was wrong, right?"

Rhonda nodded.

Taryn let it slide for now. It had been a weird night and everyone was still on edge. "Thanks for watching the bar for me."

"What? Oh, yeah, sure." A customer waved for Rhonda's attention and she returned to the floor.

Something was definitely going on with her. Taryn was about to ask if she was okay, then she saw Giselle peeking out of the employee entrance.

As Taryn skirted the bar, she smiled and nodded to patrons as she passed. A few congratulated her. It felt weird, but she thanked them. If watching her kick ass made them happy and kept them spending money at her bar, she was okay with it.

It took a few minutes, but she finally slipped into the back hallway.

Giselle pressed against the wall and looked at her, all wide eyes and terror.

"Are you okay?" The closer Taryn got, the more obvious Giselle's shaking was. She wrapped her arms around the girl as soon as she was close enough.

"He found me. How did he find me?"

There was so much panic in her voice Taryn was afraid she'd bolt. "I don't know." She refused to lie to her. "But I don't think he's coming back."

"He will," Giselle whispered against her neck. "He'll make me go back."

Keeping her arm around Giselle, Taryn shifted so the girl could see her face. She needed her to believe her. "You don't have to go back. I promise."

Taryn meant it. She wouldn't let that bastard take this sweet girl back.

"But what if he does?" Giselle was trembling so hard, she wouldn't believe anything right now. Fear had its claws in her too deep.

"Then we'll stop him."

"Everything okay?" Dani approached slowly so she wouldn't startle Giselle.

"Giselle was understandably upset about our uninvited visitor." Taryn kept her voice low, soothing.

"Aw, sweetie." Dani rubbed her back. "We'll protect you. The Jack's got your back."

"I heard the Jack was big and mean and not someone you wanted to piss off."

Taryn laughed.

Dani shot her a glare. "That's all true. But she has a soft squishy side, too. One most people don't get to see."

Most people didn't deserve to see it. Taryn kept her mouth shut. Dani was soothing Giselle and that was all that mattered right now.

"Did she rescue you too?" Giselle asked.

"Yeah, she did. A few years ago." Dani answered.

"And now you have to work for her?" Fear threaded through Giselle's voice.

That Giselle hadn't believed her when Taryn told her that she didn't work that way stung. But maybe hearing it from someone else would make her see the truth.

Dani laughed. "She rescued me, but she doesn't make

me work here. I do that because I like it here. I'm good at it. And . . ." Dani leaned close to Giselle's ear, then whispered loud enough for Taryn to hear. "The money's really good!"

Giselle smiled and laughed. Dani was so good with her. She'd make a great mom someday, if she wanted to.

Dani lifted her head and smiled. "Why don't I take you back to your room. You can ask me any questions you want about how the Jack rescued me."

CHAPTER 24

TARYN STOOD in the shadows near the bar, still watching to make sure everything returned to normal. Or as close to normal as it could be when the patrons had gotten to see the Jack in action. Dani had returned and was helping Jenna manage the apparently never-ending drink orders.

"Well, that was pretty damn spectacular." The now-familiar voice was close enough that her heart stuttered and warmth flooded her. She wasn't glad to see him, she told herself sternly. Just a residual high from her victory.

Taryn turned toward Ash.

"How long have you been here?" How the hell had she missed his presence?

"Got here just in time to watch you drop that guy." At her questioning glance, he added, "I finished inspecting the equipment. You weren't in your office, so I thought maybe I'd find you in the bar. I definitely did."

Heat flared in his eyes, warming her blood.

"That the guy who's been showing up where he shouldn't be?"

"Yeah." Her voice came out husky. Had he noticed?

"Since you got rid of him, you still need me to track him?"

Taryn swallowed hard and tried to focus on the conversation. The adrenaline from the fight was still buzzing in her veins. Fight was off the table, but maybe fuc—

Pull it together, girl! He asked you a question. A business question.

"Yeah, I need to know how he knew to show up here."

He nodded. "You'll need to give me the parameters of the search. You want to do that tonight?"

Was she the only one feeling this draw? "Let's do that tomorrow." There was no way she'd be able to focus, not with his presence affecting her so completely. So unexpectedly.

"Sounds good." His gaze traveled along the smooth metal of her arm. "Your hardware is pretty damn impressive."

She swore she felt his gaze like a touch. Metal couldn't shiver, could it?

His gray eyes lifted. "So are you."

Warmth suffused her face and she hoped the dim light of the bar hid it. This man, this damned hacker, brought out the young girl in her, the one who still believed in love and happily ever after, even after all the crap she'd lived through.

Taryn shrugged, reluctant to let him see how much his words affected her. "All part of the job."

She started to turn away. He put a hand over her modified one. For once, she didn't threaten bodily harm because he'd touched her without permission. Deep inside, in a place that she didn't want to examine too closely, she knew he'd intended the move to be comforting, not threatening.

His touch was gentle.

She felt the barest whisper of it. The touch receptors in the metal skin weren't top of the line. They hadn't even been near the top when she'd gotten it and she'd always assumed all she felt was the illusion of touch. Now . . . she wasn't so sure.

She held his gaze and decided to see where this moment led. Maybe it was the adrenaline. Maybe she was being stupid. Either way, she'd deal with that later.

Instead of making the smart move, she turned her hand over and laced her fingers with his.

Still holding his hand, Taryn flagged down Dani. "You okay?" Her color was good, but Taryn wondered about her nerves.

"Yeah, I guess."

"If I leave, will you be okay for the rest of the night?"

Dani's eyes widened. The moment the other woman saw their entwined fingers, her eyes got even wider and she offered Taryn a radiant smile. "Yes, definitely!"

Taryn pinned Dani with her best I'm-your-boss stare, but it had the complete opposite effect of what she wanted.

"Yes! We'll be fine. We don't need you at all," Dani said.

Taryn doubled down on the stare.

Her friend laughed. "Go on, get out of here."

"If you need me, come get me. No excuses," Taryn warned her. "Tell Daryl I want security on duty the rest of the night. I don't think he's coming back, but just in case."

Dani nodded.

Taryn tried to ignore her as she turned back to Ash. "Come with me," she said. Okay, ordered. "Please," she added.

"Yes, ma'am." He stepped close. Heat radiated off him and she leaned closer.

Taryn didn't stop to think or to consider her actions. She tugged on Ash's hand and dragged him through the employees-only double doors and into the hallway.

People were watching. Her staff was watching.

She didn't fucking care.

CHAPTER 25

"WHERE ARE WE GOING?" Ash asked as the doors closed behind them, cutting off the sounds of the bar.

Taryn paused and swung around to face him. "Back here," she said.

"Oh, okay." A smile slowly crossed his face and his eyes warmed with desire.

That smile did her in. Crooked, a little sly. It drove her wild. Before she could even think through her actions, her body took control. Hands on his chest, she pressed him into the wall.

"All righty then," he murmured.

Days. That's how long she'd been thinking about this. Now here he was. Lean and a bit taller than her, with muscles she hadn't expected.

Beneath her hands, he was warm, solid. She grabbed his shirt and rose up onto her tiptoes. His arm circled her waist and pulled her closer.

"This okay?" she asked, her mouth inches from his.

"Yes." His response feathered across her lips, their breath mingling.

Taryn pressed her lips against his.

It was supposed to a quick kiss. A taste to tide her over until they were in a more private place. Her office. Her room. She didn't care which.

His lips were firm against hers. Firm but soft, too. She nibbled at his lower lip. His groan made her smile.

Her palm cupped his jaw. She rubbed her thumb along his cheek, skating back and forth over the edge of his shadow, enjoying the play of textures against her skin.

He slid one hand from her waist to the curve of her butt and tugged her closer.

It was a surprising and audacious move. One that Taryn had practically torn guys' arms off for in the past. Tonight, she didn't give a damn. She wanted his hands on her ass.

She wanted his hands everywhere.

But not quite yet.

Taryn brushed her lips over his.

Once.

Twice.

This time he nipped at her upper lip and she squeaked in surprise. The rumble of his laughter reverberated through her whole body.

Oh, game on, she thought in delight.

She pressed her mouth deeper against his. Her right arm remained on his chest while she curled her non-powered one around the back of his neck. It had been so long that she didn't want to lose control. At least, not like that.

He echoed her move, sliding the hand on her waist up the curve of her back, gently trailing his fingers up her spine, her neck. Cupping the back of her head, he speared his fingers into her hair.

Mouth to mouth. Breath to breath. She wanted to devour him. She angled her head and deepened the kiss.

The hand on her butt tightened and pulled her flush against him. Her pelvis pressed against his, and it was impossible to miss the hard length of his erection. She pressed closer, rubbing against him.

He broke the kiss with a groan. "Stop," he said. "We've got to stop."

The word registered and Taryn immediately pulled back. She couldn't stop her whimper of disappointment, though. "Are you okay? Did I hurt you?"

She stepped back—tried to anyway—but his hands held her close.

His breath whooshed in and out. So did hers.

"I'm fine. Great even," he said with a smile, "but you didn't intend for this to happen in the hallway, did you?"

With her head still spinning, Taryn wasn't even sure what "this" was. She'd intended to kiss him. Maybe more. But ramped up on adrenaline, victory, and desire, the kiss had escalated faster than she'd expected.

"You're right," she said as soon as she caught her breath. "I hadn't planned on attacking you in the hallway." This time when she stepped back, he let her. Her gaze dropped to the evidence of his arousal, then surged upward again. "You're too damn attractive for your own good," she growled. She hadn't been that swept away in, well, ever.

"Backatcha."

His words brought a blush to her cheeks and sent a glow of pleasure rushing through her body. She received compliments daily from patrons who wanted to win the Jack's favor. They rolled off her, because as sincere as they might be, they were still looking for something.

Sure, Ash wanted something too. But his ragged breathing and obvious arousal weren't just business.

She smiled at him, letting him see how much she appreciated his words.

"Damn, girl," he said. "Wait 'til we're out of the hallway."

She'd been about to swoop in for another kiss, but stilled. Right. Out of the hallway.

"Yeah, um, this way." Taryn released his shirt and smoothed out the wrinkled fabric. It was polite. Not because she wanted to run her hands over his chest again.

His hands wrapped around hers. "Hallway bad," he said with a chuckle.

"Hallway bad," she repeated. She freed one hand and left the other where it was while she decided where to take him.

"It's okay if you changed your mind," he said.

"No, I haven't changed my mind." She met his gaze, let him see the undiminished attraction.

Her office was closest. Her bedroom, on the other hand, well, it had a bed. The bed sounded so good, it was probably undermining her judgment.

Office it was.

With their hands linked together, Taryn led him down the hall.

Quick steps took them to her office, and through the door, which she took care to lock behind them. Then she pressed him against the door.

With a growl, his mouth was back on hers.

"I can't get enough." He dropped his head into the crook of her neck, pressing his lips to the sensitive skin just below her jaw.

Her head dropped back with a moan as he peppered little kisses on her skin. Her eyes fluttered closed. His breath was warm through the layers she wore.

Wanting—needing—more, Taryn tried to shrug out of her coat but it caught at her elbows. "Dammit," she complained, a husky whine in her voice.

"Problem?" Ash looked up from where he was nibbling her neck, that sly smile in his eyes.

"Help me." She wiggled her shoulders, trying to shake the fabric loose. All it did was rub her breasts against his chest.

His gaze dropped to the view. "I'm not seeing a problem at all." His laugh was pure evil. Sexy, sexy evil. His gray eyes met hers, laughter and desire burning in their depths. "More of an opportunity."

With her arms pinned, breasts thrust forward, she was at his mercy. She wasn't helpless—she could rip through the fabric with her cyberarm—but freeing herself wouldn't be instantaneous. Taryn waited for the panic to set in.

It never came.

She wasn't worried about getting free. She wanted to get closer.

Ash didn't react the way she'd expected. Didn't immediately take advantage of the situation. Instead, he two-stepped them away from the door. Then he circled her slowly, a predator studying his prey.

Taryn had never considered hackers a threat until now. Their crimes weren't generally violent. They weren't trafficking women or robbing people on the streets.

Today, though . . . Ash was proving himself a predator.

She shouldn't find that so fucking hot.

Taryn stood still, letting him look his fill.

The little hairs on the back of her neck quivered in awareness. He was behind her.

He stepped close, his body heat warming her—burning her—even though he hadn't touched her.

She reached behind her with searching fingers. Between her coat and his caution, all she grasped was air.

He laughed, a wicked, wicked sound.

Chills shivered up her spine.

"It's killing you not to turn around, isn't it?" His voice close to her ear, his body still not touching her.

"Yes." Holy shit. Was that her voice? All breathy and husky?

"Thank you for trusting me." He stepped closer before he said it. The whisper of his words against her neck nearly made her jump.

She closed her eyes and concentrated on the sensations coursing through her. Her belly clenched in anticipation. Her pulse beat rapidly. She wanted . . .

"I want to kiss you," he whispered.

"Thank god." Because she wanted to kiss him too. "More kissing, less talking."

He laughed.

She could get addicted to his laugh. It made her all shivery inside.

"I like watching you tremble with anticipation."

Oh my god, she was going to kill him. Or he was going to kill her.

"I like watching you think about me kissing you." His words were warm against the delicate skin of her ear. His tongue flicked out, licking the shell of her ear. "I like watching you tremble as you keep strict control over your body. It makes me think about making you lose control."

Heat flooded her body, settling between her thighs, and she whimpered. She wanted that. All of it.

"But damn, I can't stop thinking about kissing you." His arm circled her and he ran the pad of his thumb running over her bottom lip.

She nipped at him.

That laugh again.

She squeezed her thighs together, clenching internal muscles against the ache he had created.

His thumb passed over her lips again before his hand slid down to cup her chin.

"Gotta kiss you," he growled. He released her chin and spun her around.

She wobbled, but he was there to keep her upright. Steadying her. Pulling her close.

This kiss was deeper, darker than the first. His mouth devoured hers, teasing and tempting her with nips and licks, soft caresses and sharp little nibbles.

"Want to touch you," she groaned when he paused for a breath.

His hands caressed her arms, working the coat over her elbows, his touch steady and firm. Finally—*finally!*—her arms were free.

Her jacket hit the floor with a thud. Her hands flew up and tangled in his hair.

"You. Are. An. Evil. Bastard." She punctuated each word with another kiss. Then on "bastard," she swallowed his laugh and kissed him like her life depended on it.

He didn't respond. Which was fine. Because he was still kissing her.

His hands roamed her body, cupping and shaping her curves. He growled.

Palms gripping the backs of her thighs, he picked her up.

Gasping in surprise, she wrapped her legs around his waist, locking her ankles. The move hitched her up, pressing her breasts flush against his chest and her core against his erection. In their new position, they'd practically be having sex if their clothes weren't in the way.

Using her crossed legs, she levered her body up, then back down, rubbing the junction of her thighs against him.

So good. So damn good.

Ash kept one hand on the back of her thigh and clamped the other on her ass. He used his grip to hold her still. Hold her pressed against him.

She was dying to move. If she couldn't do it that way . . .

Taryn clenched her inner thigh muscles. In and out against the hot, hard ridge of him.

He tore his mouth away from hers. "Are you trying to kill me?"

She loosened her arms from around his neck and leaned back to look at him. His eyes were hazy, half-lidded. His chest rose and fell like a bellows.

She shrugged. "Would that be such a bad way to go?"

His gaze never left hers and he peered straight into her soul. "Fuck no," he said, right before he captured her mouth again.

Hands locked under her ass for support, Ash started walking. With every step, she rubbed against him. Heaven and hell combined, it didn't last nearly long enough.

When they stopped, he tilted her backward a little. His mouth captured her squeak of surprise and she tightened her arms around his neck.

Her tailbone landed on a solid surface and his hands slid down the backs of her thighs as he released her.

Missing his touch, missing his kiss, she fluttered her eyes open to see what was happening. He'd set her in the middle of her desk.

"This is perfect." His sigh feathered against the delicate skin of her neck. His tongue skimmed over her flesh, then he nipped her with his teeth.

The slight sting of his teeth sent her reeling back into her own private hell.

Her stomach churned and she frantically pressed her hands against his shoulders. "I can't."

He stepped back instantly.

She scrambled off the desk as soon as he was out of the way. Memories assailed her. Too many times a sharp bite on her neck had ended with her bent over the desk or under it, servicing the last Jack. The man who'd owned her.

"Are you okay?" The question was laced with concern.

Breathing hard and choking back bile, she couldn't answer, just shook her head.

"What just happened?"

She shook her head again.

How to even start? The feelings were too raw, too present, for her to deal with.

Here she was, the big bad Jack and a nip on the neck had sent her running like a new girl on the street. It wasn't even the same desk!

Taryn wrapped her arms around her middle. God, she'd thought she was over it. Thought she was past those terrible years when the man she'd thought was her savior had turned into her captor. Turned out, only his death had made him a savior.

"Did I do something wrong?" he asked, his voice soft, gentle. He stood on the opposite side of the desk, giving her plenty of room.

That was good. She needed time to get her head straight. He looked so worried.

"Bad memories," she rasped out.

"Do you want to talk about it?"

Um. That would be a no. Possibly a never. Or at least never again.

She'd gotten therapy when the old Jack had died. Life was overwhelming in those early days, with the stress of keeping the bar going and the worry that people would find out he'd lied when he said they were married.

"You should go," she said, instead of trying to explain her complicated past. Her complicated emotions.

"Are you sure?"

She nodded her head vigorously. "Please." Yes. Right now, she was sure. Later, she'd probably miss him. Or maybe she'd be cussing herself out for letting it get this far. Or for not being over it.

He studied her, and Taryn couldn't imagine what he saw. Wished he hadn't seen the woman beneath the Jack's armor.

"I'm sorry I brought up bad memories."

"Me too." The words slipped out. He winced and it felt like kicking a puppy.

God, she was a mess. She needed to be alone to get her head together. He seemed to understand.

"I'm going to go," he said.

She nodded.

She stood between him and the door. When he moved forward, she stepped to the side, circling around, keeping a comfortable distance between them.

The closer he got to the door, the closer she moved toward her desk. She swallowed hard and didn't look at the desk. It was the last place she wanted to be right now, but it was the only way to maintain a safe distance.

"Good night," he said. "Take care of yourself."

"Night." She spoke because he deserved an answer.

He slipped through the door, closing it behind him and leaving her trapped in her office with memories she thought she'd dealt with.

CHAPTER 26

ASH STARED AT THE DOOR. *What the fuck had just happened?*

He couldn't get the image of Taryn, pale and shaking, out of his head.

Something he'd done had frightened her like a baby hacker hitting their first firewall.

Things had been going great until he'd crossed the room to her desk.

Had he invaded her space? Was it because he'd set her on the desk? Something had triggered her. Ash realized how little he knew about the mysterious Jack beyond how she'd inherited the title and the bar.

When he'd been here during his hacking days, the Jack had been an asshole who ran the place with an iron fist. Big, tough, and mean, he'd maintained his reputation through violence and cruelty.

If she'd lived here, under those conditions . . . It was a damn good thing the bastard was dead. Rage burned a fire in Ash's belly and he pressed his hand against the doorjamb.

Ash had spent his life protecting his sister from

assholes who thought that women were easy game. No one deserved to be taken advantage of, abused, or worse. And yet, he had a bad feeling that was exactly what had happened to Taryn.

"You coming or going?"

He turned toward the bartender. Should he say something? Taryn obviously had wanted him gone, but that didn't mean she wouldn't want a friendly face. Still, he was loath to expose her weakness to anyone else. "Just leaving. We're, uh, finished with our meeting."

Her eyes widened. She looked him up and down. "Finished already? That's too bad." She smirked.

"It wasn't like that," Ash protested, even though it totally was like that until the moment she'd pushed him away.

The bartender didn't say anything, just gave him an appraising look.

"Something upset her." He'd gotten the sense that the bartender was someone the Jack trusted.

In an instant, she turned from smirking at the guy in the hall to ballbuster. He was at least six inches taller than her, but that didn't stop her from getting in his face.

"What did you do?"

"Nothing, I swear!" As far as he knew, that was the truth. "Look—it's Dani, right?"

She nodded.

"Whatever upset her, Dani, I think it had to do with the room. Her office. If I'd been the cause, I'm pretty sure I wouldn't have left that room alive."

"True," she said, after a long pause while she processed his words. "Unless you killed her first." She looked him up and down, searching for bloodstains or other proof of his guilt.

He raised his hands in surrender and stood still. He didn't need another woman mad at him.

"I know who you are. I will find you if anything happened to her."

"Fair enough." He stepped away from the door and Dani circled around him.

She knocked softly on it. Whatever response she got was too quiet for him to hear, but it must have been permission to enter. Before she slipped into the office, she gave him one last glare. The door closed behind her with a thud.

Ash shoved his hands into his pockets and took a deep breath. He needed to remember why he was doing this. Hope needed to be his priority. Not Taryn, no matter how hot the heat between them was.

CHAPTER 27

"WHAT ARE we going to do about Giselle's pimp?"

"I'm sorry. What?" Dani's question startled Taryn. She rubbed her eyes, trying to clear the grit. She hadn't slept much after she'd freaked out on Ash and the little she'd gotten hadn't been great. How much of their conversation—Dani's conversation—had she missed?

Dani frowned. "Are you okay? You've been staring at your desk all like it was going to bite you all morning."

Taryn winced. "What? No. I'm fine."

A total lie.

The desk *had* bitten her. At least, memories from the old one had.

"Are you sure? I know you were upset last night."

Taryn had appreciated Dani's presence last night after Ash left, but she hadn't told her friend much about what had happened. Mostly, she'd reassured Dani that Ash hadn't physically harmed her.

If Taryn hadn't done that, she was sure Dani would have sicced one of the guards on him. It wasn't often that Dani saw Taryn that shell-shocked.

"I was," Taryn admitted. "But I'm fine now. Really." If she repeated it often enough, maybe she'd even believe it. This time it was only half a lie. She had been upset. Still was when she tried to untangle her feelings.

It wasn't only bad memories that had kept her up. Her mind—and her body—remembered Ash's every touch. And she was pissed as hell that the past had ruined such a promising encounter.

Taryn thought she'd gotten over her past. Apparently not.

Dani rolled her eyes, a sign she wasn't buying Taryn's bullshit.

That was the problem when employees became friends. Not that she regretted a moment of their friendship. Dani had kept her sane in those early days.

"I'll be watching you."

Dani's ferocity made Taryn smile. "You do that."

With a pointed look to let Taryn know that they weren't done with that conversation, Dani thankfully changed the subject. "Are you sure you want to go through with this? You can still say no." She pierced Taryn with a look.

Taryn choked back a laugh. She'd had no plans to say no last night. She cursed the old Jack again. When Dani looked at her funny, she said, "Sorry, just a random thought. Not enough sleep."

Sobering, she ran her hands through her hair. Her fingers caught on the tangles. "I can't say no. He's already paid. Well, he's paid half the fee."

"How much?" Dani asked.

"He's not paying credits," Taryn said.

"A favor?"

"No. He's—"

"Sex?" Dani squawked. "He's paying you in sex? Was that what last night was about? Did he hurt you? He said he didn't hurt you." She lunged out of her chair.

"Dani!" Taryn's voice was sharp enough to break through the other woman's muttering and stop her before she reached the door. "Sit back down if you want to continue this conversation."

Dani sat but didn't that didn't stop her rant. "Do you want me to have Daryl, you know, take care of him?"

"Take care of him?" She stared at Dani. "Take care of Ash?"

She didn't even squirm under Taryn's gaze. The woman had balls of steel.

"Yeah. Make him disappear. Eliminate him." She mimed taking a shot.

Taryn's eyes widened. "I knew what you meant. I just . . ." She wasn't sure what to say. "We don't do that."

In the five years she'd owned the bar, Taryn had never "disappeared" anyone the way her predecessor had, no matter how much she might have wanted to.

She'd been smart about getting rid of the competition and reinforcing her reputation without leaving a trail of bodies.

Taryn rubbed her eyes again, this time to stave off the headache that was building. "No, we are not going to get rid of Ash. No, he did not hurt me last night." Dani opened her mouth and Taryn knew what she was going to ask. "No, he's not paying me in sex. What happened between us was between two consenting adults and has nothing to do with rescuing his sister."

"Then why were you so upset?" She narrowed her eyes and studied Taryn. "Was he a bad kisser?"

"No!" Her cheeks flamed. "That was . . . He was . . . The kissing was great. I just got hit with some bad memories."

"Oh," Dani said quietly. "I'm sorry. I shouldn't have pushed."

"Pfft. That's what friends are for. Before I was so rudely interrupted," she gave her friend a wide smile, "what I was going to say was that he's going to help us figure out why Giselle's pimp was here."

Dani had settled back in her chair, but now she leaned forward again. "How?"

"He's a hacker, so he's going to use his computer magic." Taryn waggled her fingers in the air to indicate the magic.

"Didn't you say he worked for Tremaine?" Dani asked.

Taryn nodded.

"Won't that be a problem?"

"It would," she said, "except he's going to be doing it here. That old hacker chair in the basement. That's why he was here last night. He was updating it so he could use it."

Dani considered her words. "It still seems like it would be easier to just get rid of him."

"Ash?" Taryn's eyes widened.

"No, the pimp."

Taryn swiveled in her chair. "Yeah, probably. But we don't do that. And we won't make an exception," she growled, preempting Dani's suggestion. She hadn't seen Dani's bloodthirsty side in a while.

"He's going to be a problem," Dani repeated.

"I know. But first, Ash will help us determine how he figured out Giselle was here. Then we'll decide on next steps."

The fact that he had uncovered Giselle's location was

unacceptable. But she needed help to figure out where she'd made a mistake.

"I checked on Giselle this morning," Dani said. "She's still a bit freaked out that he tracked her down. Not to mention, still processing the fact that she's free."

Dammit. Taryn should have done that, but she'd been too caught up in her own pain. "Thank you for taking care of her."

"Of course. That's what we do." Dani looked like she was deciding whether to ask a question. "Do you know what you're going to do with her?"

Taryn rubbed her forehead. Dani had voiced one of Taryn's own concerns. "No. Not yet. She's the youngest we've ever rescued. She's too young to work at the bar. Do we send her to school? Find some family to foster her? I have no idea what to do with a sixteen-year-old. At her age . . ." She trailed off.

At sixteen, Taryn had been on the streets, living some of the worst years of her life. She rubbed her shoulder, where the prosthetic joined the skin and bone. "Do you have any idea what to do with a teenager? I sure as hell don't."

Dani shook her head. "At her age, I was turning tricks and drugged out of my goddamn mind. All I wanted was my next fix."

"If you'd had a choice at her age, what would you have wanted to do?'

Dani blinked in wonder, then stared past Taryn's shoulder. "I . . . don't know," she said after a while. "My family sucked, so I wouldn't have gone back to them. And I wasn't the type who liked school."

"I don't know what I would've wanted either," Taryn said. That was a lie. She'd wanted to know why her parents had abandoned her. But she'd finally made peace with not knowing. "Shit, I guess we ask her what she wants."

"Glad I'm not the boss." Dani laughed. "So, we've got one baby former prostitute. One stalker pimp. And one hot hacker. What next?"

CHAPTER 28

ASH TOOK a deep breath and pushed open the door to Razor Jack's. He'd thought long and hard about whether he should come back tonight, given what had happened yesterday. Seeing Taryn wasn't going to get any easier, no matter how long he waited.

The bar was hopping when he walked in. Every table was full and people were lined up two deep at the bar. What the hell was going on?

His gaze swept over the room. Had the person she was concerned about returned?

A wall-mounted screen caught his eye. Ah. Game night.

Ash wasn't a sports fan, but he had a soft spot for the local teams. They'd helped him build his hacking skills early on when he would slip bets into the gaming system long after the cutoff time. The winnings had kept him and Hope fed.

He wiggled his way through the crowd until he was pressed against the bar. It took several more minutes to get Dani's attention.

"What can I get you?" Her smile faded when she realized it was him.

"The Jack in tonight?" he asked, careful to keep his voice low.

"Maybe." With that, she slid down the bar to take drink orders.

Crap. He took a deep breath and dug deep for patience. He had to get past her to see Taryn. When she returned to his end of the bar, she didn't stop.

"Gimme a draft." Ash slid a credit chip on to the bar. "Please."

Since he'd ordered, she had no choice but to stop. "Is the Jack in?" he repeated. He didn't want to play games tonight. He just wanted to see Taryn.

Dani must have seen something in his eyes, because instead of blowing him off again, she nodded.

"Can you ask if she'll see me?" He really hoped she would.

She set the beer down and studied him. Then she gestured him forward.

Ash leaned over the bar and still had to strain to hear her over the noise of the gathered crowd.

"Go on back," she said.

"Really?" That Dani gave him a free pass . . . that had to mean Taryn was okay, right?

"Yeah." She tilted her head toward the employees-only door that eventually led to the Jack's office.

"Thanks, Dani." He slid the credit chip toward her. "Keep the change."

This time she didn't argue. The chip quickly disappeared into her pocket.

Ash grabbed his drink. It was easier to get away from the bar than it had been to get to it. People cleared a path for him, then rushed in to fill the space that he'd vacated.

He held the glass above his head to protect it as he crossed the room. Every few steps, he paused to take a sip and to glance around. The place was packed, which made it easy to look like he was trying to find a seat.

His glass was half empty by the time he reached the door and his patience was rapidly fading. Taking another drink—this one for courage—he slipped through the door. It closed behind him with a soft thud.

Passing the spot where Taryn had pressed him against the wall, he smiled. The need to see Taryn was like an itch he couldn't scratch and he knew it wasn't just because of Hope. That kiss had been . . . damn.

Ash reached the Jack's door and raised his hand to knock. Before he could, the door opened violently and a teenage girl barreled out, tears streaming down her face.

"Are you okay?"

She didn't answer, just brushed by him. He remembered when Hope was that age, half hormones, half attitude, with just enough sweetness that he always forgave her.

He watched the young woman run down the hallway. She turned left at the intersection and disappeared around the corner. She was younger than all the other employees he'd seen. What did she do here?

Ash had caught the door with his foot. He rapped on the door and poked his head in. "Can I come in?"

Taryn looked up, frowning. Then her expression cleared and she smiled.

His heart fluttered, and he was irrationally happy that he'd made her smile.

"Yeah, sure. Close the door."

He did as he was told. And then they were alone. He

prayed that it wasn't his presence that had upset her last night.

Ash didn't bring that up. He wouldn't ignore it, but it wasn't a good conversational opener.

"She looked a little young." He wandered toward her desk.

"For what?" She gestured for him to sit, then circled around and sat on the edge of her desk.

Ash tensed. The last time she'd been on the edge of her desk, bad things had happened. He said the first thing that came to mind. "To be in a bar?"

"You're not wrong," she said cryptically. She reached for his drink and he was so surprised, he relinquished it automatically.

Raising it to her lips, she drained the rest of it. "Thanks." She set the empty glass on her desk. "She's my current problem."

Yep, nothing mysterious about that. "Anything I can help with?"

She blinked at him, surprise written on her face.

"I have some experience with teenage girls," he felt compelled to add. Then realizing how that sounded, he scrambled to not sound like a creeper. "My sister, Hope, she was a handful." God, he was an idiot.

Taryn laughed. "I have experience *being* a teenage girl, but not dealing with them."

"Well, let me know." What was he doing? He wasn't a helper. All his life, every decision he'd made had been to benefit him or Hope.

And yet, he was completely sincere. If Taryn needed help, he wanted to be there for her.

"Thanks. I don't know. Maybe."

"Well, let me know when you do."

She smiled again, and it warmed him all the way to his toes.

Pulling her feet up, she sat cross-legged on the edge of her desk.

He took a moment to study her. Her black pants hugged her legs and her tank top showed off her arms. One arm was sleekly muscled and the other was crafted from sleek metal. The prosthetic was a beautiful piece of technology, sculpted like an arm, not metal bones like a skeleton.

He'd seen her in action, so he knew that the limb offered her exquisite motor control and bruising strength.

"Yes, I have a mechanical arm." Her easy posture had disappeared and her stiff tone brought his gaze to hers.

"What?"

"You were staring at my arm." Her tone was cold—pure Jack—but he swore it carried a thread of vulnerability.

"It's gorgeous." Ash never dropped his gaze from hers. "I hadn't seen it up close." He'd felt it, of course, felt the care with which she'd used it last night. But hadn't taken the time to appreciate it.

"It's metal and wire." The tension in her voice had lessened but hadn't completely disappeared.

"It's metal and wire turned into art. It's stunning. May I?" He should have touched her arm last night. Let her know that he didn't see it as a flaw, but as an essential, beautiful part of her.

Suspicion still filled her eyes, but she nodded.

He stood in front of her—a safe distance away—before she could change her mind. Moving slowly to not spook her, he reached out and gently slid the strap of her tank top higher up on her shoulder, revealing the seam between cyberwork and biology.

It wasn't the neatest work he'd seen, but it hadn't been done by a hack either. "Full replacement?"

Taryn nodded. "The shoulder socket was intact. Metal bracers along my collarbone help stabilize the merge."

He nodded. Despite all the advancements in metals, replacement limbs were heavy. Tremaine had some experimental stuff happening in their med labs that were supposed to be even lighter than anything on the market. The records he'd turned up in his clandestine research indicated the product was market ready, but the company was sitting on it for some reason.

Maximizing profits, probably. What would Portia do with all the tech the company was hoarding?

Not the time, Ash.

Hyperaware of her reaction after their kiss, Ash kept his movements slow. His fingers trailed over her shoulder and down her arm. The metal, a subtle copper color, blended smoothly with her skin tone. Her biceps and triceps were perfectly sculpted, with small details like muscle delineation etched into the metal. "This isn't company work."

"No. I couldn't afford that." She shrugged. Ash watched the arm move with her. "I paid for the best circuitry and software I could. The skin . . . It wasn't an afterthought, but it wasn't the priority."

"It's fancier than most, um . . ." Damn, he had no idea how to describe her arm without offending.

"Streetware?" Her tone was crisp.

His face flamed. "Yeah. Sorry."

"It *is* street. I just happened to know a really great artist."

"An artist did this? Damn, I've never seen that." Ash leaned closer, studying the detailed work. Discovering the hidden design on the inside of her biceps, he tilted his head and glanced up at her. "Is that a tattoo?"

Pink tinted her cheeks. "Yes, basically."

Straightening, he held her gaze. "A hummingbird?"

"Yes." Her blush deepened.

"What does it mean?"

"Nothing. I just liked it." Her gaze darted away.

Damn, he'd made her uncomfortable. "I have one too," he shared. "A bird tattoo."

Interest brightened her dark eyes, erasing the discomfort. "What kind?"

Now he felt color burn his cheeks. "A phoenix," he admitted.

She studied him. "Does that have something to do with your hacking?"

He nodded. "It was my handle. It used to light up when I was jacked into the network."

"Ooh, I want to see that. Oh wait, used to?"

Ash dropped his head and rubbed the back of his neck. "It's powered by the network. It was just something stupid I got when I was raking in the credits."

"It sounds very cool," she offered with a smile.

"It was." Ash wished he could show her the network tattoo in all its glory. Or even half its glory. He smiled slightly and wondered if they would have gotten there last night. "Yours is too. I've never seen anything like it." And he'd seen some fucking crazy body mods on other hackers.

Taryn rolled her eyes. "That's me. One of a kind."

Ash couldn't let that stand. He trailed his hand down her arm until he could take her hand. "You are."

"Stop it." She tried to tug her hand away.

Ash held on. It was important that she believed him.

"No, really. You are unlike any woman—anyone—I've ever met. Strong, beautiful. You're amazing."

She tugged again, and he let her go. "I'm just a woman, with a bar."

"You're so much more." Could she hear the admiration and appreciation in his voice?

Instead of smiling like he hoped, she withdrew into herself. "Whatever," she muttered and studiously didn't look at him.

She didn't take compliments well, apparently. Fine, he could take a hint.

"What happened?" He traced his finger over the seam between flesh and metal. Born and made. The amazing work still awed him.

She stiffened.

His touch or the subject? He withdrew his hand as surely as she'd withdrawn into herself. "I'm sorry. I didn't mean to offend you."

She sighed. A whisper of sound. "You didn't," she said, though it sounded more like she was talking to herself than to him.

He couldn't do anything right when it came to this woman. Two nights in a row, he'd hit raw nerves. "I should go."

"Wait." She laid her hand gently on his forearm.

He stilled, not wanting to scare her off and cause a repeat of last night.

She was touching him, asking him to stay. He wasn't going anywhere.

"I grew up on the streets." She stared straight ahead, not looking at him. Probably caught up in her memories.

He knew that stare. He'd seen it in the mirror so many

times, usually when he tried to figure out how he could have made the night of his capture end differently.

"I came home from school one day and my parents were gone. All our stuff was gone. It was the end of life as I knew it, and I still don't even know why or what happened." Her voice was heartbreakingly matter-of-fact.

Gently, not wanting to scare her, he curled his fingers around hers.

"I stayed with friends for a few weeks, bouncing from house to house. But I wasn't their kid, their family. I was just another mouth to feed."

His heart broke for young Taryn. He knew that feeling, of losing your parents and having to fend for yourself. At least he'd had Hope.

Her fingers clenched around his, squeezing the bones together. Whatever was coming, he wasn't going to like it.

"I was thirteen. A friend's dad said I was pretty. Said he'd let me stay a month if I let him—" She swallowed hard. "If I let him fuck me." She spit the last words out.

His stomach roiled. She didn't give him a chance to react. Which was good—what do you say to that?

"It wasn't quite a month until his wife found out. She kicked me out of the house. Told all my friends' moms so I didn't have anywhere else to stay. I ended up on the streets."

Rage filled him. Who did that to a kid? He imagined Hope in that situation and his blood thundered in his ears. His free hand clenched and unclenched. It took everything he had to stay still, to let her squeeze his hand and not react.

"I tried not to turn tricks. But it was cold and wet. I got so, so hungry." Her voice was a tiny mewl.

He tensed, knowing what came next. His heart broke for thirteen-year-old Taryn. He'd seen those girls on the streets and he'd fought to keep that from happening to Hope.

"One night, I wandered into someone else's territory. She beat me up pretty good. Then her pimp showed up." Her free hand ran over her cheekbone.

His gut clenched. He knew that move, understood the lingering memories of old injuries.

"He took me in, paid to treat my wounds. When I was back on my feet, he told me how much I owed him. Since I didn't have any money, I'd have to earn it."

His stomach churned. Red-hot rage flowed through his veins. It was a common story, but that didn't make it right.

The silence that fell between them wasn't easy. Should he say something? "How did you end up here? As the Jack?"

Taryn's bitter laugh did nothing to dispel his anger. "God, I never thought I'd end up here. Or anywhere that was like a home again."

She tugged him closer and rested her head on his shoulder. He froze in surprise but didn't pull away. He carefully wrapped his arms around her.

"I was maybe, I don't know, sixteen when the Jack came for me. He was looking for a girl of his own. He liked how I looked and the test drives he took. He and the pimp reached an agreement and I came to live here."

Bile surged in Ash's throat. He'd come here to ask that man a favor. He was part of the system that had wounded this beautiful, strong woman. If the old Jack weren't already dead, Ash would do the job himself.

Taryn sagged against him. "It was awful. He was awful. The only bright spot was the bar. I loved it. Bartending, waiting tables. It gave me the world." She started to shake.

"I lived and worked here for five years. Hell and heaven under the same roof."

It took effort to unclench his fist. Ash wrapped his arm around her waist and smoothed his hand up and down her back. She dropped her legs off the desk to bracket his, then released his other hand and wrapped her arms around him.

"One night I dropped a tray of glasses. I cleaned up the best I could, but it was busy and it caused a major slow-down. At the end of the night, he broke my arm."

Her trembling worsened and Ash wrapped his arms tight around her. To go from a broken arm to a replacement —that was a lot of damage. The old Jack had been a bastard, but damn. Cruelty for cruelty's sake.

"It didn't heal right, did it?" He didn't know if he wanted her to continue her story. He was barely hanging on to his temper as it was.

She shook her head. "He broke it in more than one place. One of the breaks got infected." She paused again. Ash was surprised she wasn't crying. "By the time he believed me that something was wrong, they couldn't save my arm."

Fucking asshole. "I'm glad the bastard's dead."

She buried her head in his neck. The shaking got worse. *Oh god, what had he done?*

He ran his hand up and down her back. "I'm sorry. I didn't mean to make you cry."

The shaking continued. Ash continued to hold her and tried to soothe her. Every second that passed, he hated himself for making her relive her trauma. He was a selfish bastard.

Then she lifted her head. Her face wasn't tearstained as he'd expected. She was laughing. "Me, too," she said between laughs. "Oh god, me too."

Her laughter got louder and a little out of control. Was she hysterical? Should he do something? "Are you okay?" A tentative question to match his tentative pats on her back.

"I'm fine," she gasped out between laughs. "Better than I have been in a while."

Since she said she was fine, he stayed where he was, enjoying the chance to hold her. Not in a creepy way. More of an I-can't-remember-how-long-it's-been-since-I-cuddled-anyone way.

His touch on her back became less tentative, until he was rubbing gentle circles. Her cheek was pressed against his shoulder, her cyberarm a cool firm presence against his back. Soft and hard, tough and tender—the perfect combination.

Her laughter slowly subsided and her breathing settled. "Thank you." The words were a whisper against his skin.

"For what?" he whispered back.

"This. Being here. Not flipping out. Take your pick."

Neither of them moved.

"The old Jack was a really shitty guy."

She laughed again. "You could say that."

This quiet conversation was the closest he'd come to a real human connection since he and Hope had been captured. It terrified and amazed him all at the same time. And now he was about to ruin it.

"Did you kill him?" he dared to ask. After the story she'd just told, Ash wouldn't have blamed her if she had.

She took a breath, then shook her head. "No. But I didn't save him either."

"Is he—" Ash paused, seeking the words to address the elephant in the room. "Is he the reason you, um, pulled away last night?" That should be safe enough. Right?

A flutter of laughter against his neck. "You mean when I flipped out?" Taryn pulled away and looked him in the eye.

Cool air replaced where she'd been warm against him. He immediately missed the press of her against his chest.

Ash nodded, not sure that bringing up last night had been the right thing to do.

"Yeah. You can say that." She sighed. "I have some really terrible memories of this room. Of being on a desk."

"If you hate it, why did you keep the office? You could work somewhere else." He didn't understand. He was ready to help her move. Anything to stop her pain.

"I believed I was strong enough to keep the bad memories at bay. I've made this bar my own. I thought I could make the office my own too."

That made a tragic kind of sense but he hated that she tortured herself with those memories every day. "You should at least change things around," he growled.

"Maybe. Maybe not."

"Tell me you'll at least think about it?" He hated the idea of her surrounded by painful memories.

"I will." She looked at him, her brown eyes serious. "I owe you an apology."

He shook his head. "No, never. I owe you one. I pushed too hard."

"No. You don't. You didn't." She pushed him back a step and, in one fluid move, dropped her feet to the ground and stood.

Close, she was so close. Ash tried to step back, to give her room, to protect her from the desk and all the memories it held.

Her hands rested on his hips and she stopped him. "Is this okay?"

"Yes," he whispered.

She pressed her lips to his.

Ash held still, not wanting to spook her.

Her kiss wasn't soft or tentative. Her hands were sure, the pressure steady as she pulled him closer.

"Kiss me back, damn you," she growled against his lips.

"Yes, ma'am." That was the invitation he'd been waiting for. Tightening his arms around her waist, he parted his lips against hers. She nibbled at his mouth, little nips that tested and teased.

Two could play at this game. Sliding his hand into her silky hair, he cupped the back of her head. Pulling her flush against him, he took control of the kiss.

He started as she had, little nibbles. Not really bites, though. More like little scrapes along her lips. Not enough to damage—he'd never hurt her. Just enough to sensitize already sensitive skin.

When she gasped in surprise, he took advantage and deepened the kiss. Her tongue darted out to tangle with his, shifting control back to her.

Her cyberhand grasped his shoulder and he marveled at her control. What would it feel like when she had that kind of control on his cock?

Their mouths played an erotic game of hide and seek. As her tongue teased his, she shifted her hips against him. Small movements at first. The warmth between her legs barely brushing over him. Little teases that sent the blood flowing from his head to his lap.

Not that his head had anything to do at the moment. He was running on pure instinct.

She tugged his shirt free from his pants with her other hand, then slid her palm against him. The press of her naked flesh on his back made him gasp. She captured the sound with another drugging kiss.

If one small skin-to-skin touch had that much power, full-body contact would probably fry all his circuits—biological and mechanical. He was okay with that.

TARYN MOVED SLOWLY, savoring the moment, remembering where she was and who she was with. Every cell in her body screamed for her to rub against him again and again, until they combusted. She took that as a good sign, but after last night, she still wanted to take it slow.

Okay, maybe just a little slower.

Her nails scraped lightly over the back of his neck. Once, twice, they passed over a small lump, just below the base of his skull.

Ash stiffened.

Attuned to his reactions, Taryn stopped and removed her hand.

"Did I hurt you?" She wanted to be as careful with him as he'd been with her, both last night and just now. Not many men would have taken last night's freakout so well. The last Jack never had.

"Phantom pain." His words were so soft she wouldn't have heard them if they weren't pressed so close together.

She knew all about phantom pain. Some nights she

swore she felt the breaks in her old, biological arm. Nothing but phantom pain. Memories of the limb she'd been born with.

But what would cause that pain on his neck?

It took her a second. "Your port?"

He nodded. Swallowed hard. "They sealed it up the night they caught me."

"The Tremaines?"

"Tremaine Security, yeah. Standard protocol, they said." The words came out a sneer.

"I thought standard protocol was to kill any hackers they caught." All the years she'd been at the bar, she'd heard stories about missing hackers, dead hackers. Rumors of deals gone bad. Whispers of what happened when hackers went up against a big corporation.

She was fiercely glad that Ash hadn't ended up dead.

He shrugged. "Guess it depends on the company. Depends on the hacker, too. The good ones they keep alive. I was the best."

No arrogance accompanied his words. No bragging. Just a pure statement of fact.

It was on the tip of her tongue to ask why he'd been captured if he was the best, but she didn't have it in her to be that cruel right now. To completely and utterly ruin this bond that was growing between them.

"What happened?" She kept her voice soft.

He pressed his forehead against hers, breaking eye contact.

She didn't care. The skin-to-skin contact felt more intimate. Like they existed in their own little bubble.

Although he didn't answer right away, the silence between them wasn't awkward. Being this close to someone else, this comfortable with someone, was completely new to her. She liked it.

"I don't know," he admitted on an exhale. "The information was good. The hack was . . . unstoppable. But the pieces never quite clicked."

"And you got out but Hope didn't?" He'd told her the story before, when she hadn't wanted to listen.

"Yeah." He pushed away from her suddenly. "It was all my fucking fault. I shouldn't have trusted the info. I shouldn't have let her come with me."

Taryn recalled the picture he'd shown her. The sparkling eyes and mischievous smile. "You were just telling me you knew teenage girls. Do you really think you could have stopped her?"

Ash shoved his hands into his hair. "Yes. No. Fuck, probably not." He laughed. "She was stubborn."

"Like her brother." Taryn stepped closer slowly, not wanting to spook him. She cupped his chin in the palms of her hands.

He took a quick breath, as if she'd punched him or tweaked a raw nerve. "She wanted to be just like me."

"You're a good brother, Ash." She pressed a finger to his lips when he started to protest. "You looked out for her. You still are. I'm betting a lot of people would have abandoned her when she got hurt. You didn't. She's lucky to have you."

He met her gaze. "Thanks. No one's ever said that before."

Raw emotion gleamed in his eyes. Some of it might have been residual desire from their kiss, but if Taryn had to guess, she'd say it was driven by the painful reminders of his past.

"You should, ah, go." She spoke softly, ignoring the disappointment that caught in her throat.

"I'm sorry," he said gruffly. "I didn't mean to kill the mood."

"I guess it was your turn," she joked.

He turned his head and kissed her palm. "Thank you," he said again.

CHAPTER 30

ASH SLIPPED OUT of the Jack's office and into the bar, regretting every step that took him away from Taryn. Exhaustion rode him, but he knew he'd get no sleep tonight. He was still processing what he'd shared.

He almost never talked about that night or about Hope but telling Taryn had felt . . . right. Every moment he spent with her felt right.

That should freak him out.

He couldn't afford to get attached, since he would be taking Hope on the run when she was free. There was no way they could hide in the Tremaine-controlled city.

He was trying to figure out why the thought of leaving Seattle—of leaving Taryn—bothered him more than it should when someone ran into his shoulder.

"Sorry about that, man."

"No problem. I wasn't watching where I was going." Ash aimed for the door.

"Fēnix?"

Shit.

Ash focused on the speaker. Recognition flared.

It was a hacker Ash had run with. They'd shared some jobs, some beers, but they'd never been friends.

Definitely someone that he'd prefer to avoid.

"Patches." Ash nodded, then started inching around the other man.

Patches had other ideas. He slapped Ash on the shoulder. "What the hell are you doing here, man? Haven't seen you in years!"

Ash cringed. He absolutely did not want to get into why he'd disappeared. Especially not with the real story so fresh and raw in his mind tonight. "Working. Hanging out. The usual." Anxious to get to the door, he tried edging around the other man.

Patches stared at him. "Huh. Seems like you're never around anymore."

"I got better," Ash said. "Trickier."

It was all somewhat true. He just had to hope that Patches was drunk enough not to think about it too hard.

"Cool."

"Good to see you, man." Ash slapped him on the shoulder like a buddy and angled his body to pass him.

"Uh, yeah, you too." Patches looked bewildered.

Ash wanted to be out of his sight before the other hacker thought too hard about seeing him.

He ducked into the crowd and wove his way toward the door.

Running into Patches was bad. Maybe he was drunk enough that he wouldn't remember seeing Ash. If he mentioned their encounter to the wrong people . . . If certain people learned that Ash was out and about, his life could get more difficult.

The pressure was building to get out of the Tremaine Corporation before Portia learned the extent of his betrayal.

Add in the hacker community suddenly becoming curious about him?

He'd be fucked. He'd burned some bridges—both before and after his capture by the Tremaine Corporation.

He couldn't trust anyone in that community.

CHAPTER 31

"WHAT IS YOUR STATUS, MR. CUTTER?"

Portia didn't waste any time with pleasantries when Ash entered her office. He was so used to it that a deviation would be cause for concern.

He'd come to respect her too. She put in the work and asked intelligent questions. Sure, she still treated him like a peon and he never forgot that she held his and Hope's fates in her hands, but he respected her.

If it hadn't cost a lot of innocent lives, he'd say the bombing and its aftermath was one of the best things to ever happen to the Tremaine Corporation. He knew from his own role in it that her father had his fingers in some very unsavory pies. Portia, on the other hand, had a shrewd business mind and a definite plan for the direction of the company. She'd be good for the Tremaine Corporation—and if she was able to dig out all the rot, she'd be great.

If she hadn't tasked him with unmasking himself, he'd love to help her turn the company around.

Wait. Why couldn't he "discover" some of her father's more heinous crimes and feed them to her?

Portia cleared her throat. He couldn't keep her waiting any longer.

"Found a treasure trove of stuff," he said, before he could change his mind. "But no sign of Leopold's accomplice."

Portia's expression didn't give much away. He watched her, curious how she would react.

She sighed. "What kind of stuff?"

Perfect. Now was his chance.

Mentally flipping through the files he'd discovered, Ash came up with five projects that seemed reasonable. Some were located in more easily accessible servers. Others would show that he'd spent serious time digging for them.

If she tackled any of them, she'd have already done more good than her father ever had.

"Want me to show you? Or send the files to your desk?" He'd prefer to show her the files.

If he made accessing them appear complicated, maybe she'd believe that he was working hard on her request.

"Show me," she commanded.

Ash dropped into his chair. He fiddled with the keyboard, typing quickly, and digging into the system where he remembered the projects lived.

It took a few minutes to access a couple of them. With a flick of his wrist, the files were on screen. He split the screen, then split it again so she could see more than one file at a time. With a pinch and a flick, he filled the quadrants.

She leaned closer to watch what he was doing.

She may have earned his respect, but her presence at his back felt too much like a death threat hanging over him.

"I think your father's assistant knew about some of these." Ash reached toward the screen and circled two of the files. "These showed up in the same file structure as the other . . . information."

He wasn't brave enough to actually mention her newfound sister Dizzie. Not on Portia's home turf. The whispers in the company hallway indicated that they still weren't getting along. Ash wasn't surprised. Even though she'd been unaware of what her delivery actually was, Dizzie had delivered the bomb that had actually killed Portia's husband. Ash squeezed his eyes shut for a moment. He hated the role he'd played in that.

"What are the projects?" Portia asked.

This was his chance. "Best I can tell, one is a failed drug. The other has . . . something to do with organs. I think."

"Organs? Is this the spare parts program? It's being dismantled."

Ash couldn't tell if the distaste in her voice was due to the program or because Dizzie was the one undoing it. "No, it appears to be a different program. Um, used organs."

"Another one?"

The horror in her voice almost made him smile. That she could sound so horrified, even after learning about her father's twisted schemes . . .

He hadn't expected decency from a Tremaine, but it appeared Portia possessed some.

"I think so. I haven't spent any time with the file. I just found it." Three months ago, but who was counting. He'd opened it—he'd opened all the files in case there was something he could use for leverage.

This one had been particularly disturbing. From what he understood, the seedy underbelly of the Tremaine Corporation had created quite a racket in the used organs market. People whisked right off the streets and into the organ market. He'd sent this file and the others to Mr. Tremaine's assistant when he'd believed the other man was seeking leverage to bring the company down.

Ash sighed. That certainly hadn't turned out the way he'd expected.

"Open it." Her voice was resigned.

A few keystrokes unlocked and decrypted the file. Images spilled onto the screen. He averted his eyes. He'd seen them before. The gruesome pictures made him queasy.

Portia swallowed hard.

As heir to the company, Portia had been involved in the business since she was a child. Ash had always assumed that she was as corrupt as her father, but she genuinely appeared shocked by every new reveal.

"How could you be an executive and remain unaware of these programs?"

Oh, shit. He hadn't meant to ask that.

Forcing himself to own the question he'd asked, he twisted around to see her reaction.

Her face pale and her jaw set, she gestured at the images. "You think I sanctioned this? Harvesting organs from indigents? From people too fucking sick or stoned to make rational decisions? Not to mention, their parts have to be in terrible shape."

Her voice wobbled on parts. Interesting.

He filed that tidbit away. It might be useful someday.

"Well?"

Shit. She wasn't going to let it go. He'd asked a brutal question—he owed her honesty back.

"Your role is way above my pay grade. And obviously, you've worked here way longer than I have," he said. "I have no idea what happens up here. You say you didn't do it? Fine, I believe you. But your name is on the building. You can't blame me for thinking that you're in charge of everything."

"I didn't know about this. Any of this." Resignation coated her voice, as if she were becoming accustomed to the hits.

"I believe you." He did.

"Thank you. But you're right. With my father gone, these are my messes now."

An apology from a Tremaine. He tried not to let his shock show.

She sighed. "You believe the other file is about drugs?"

"Yeah." Ash closed the organ harvesting file and opened the other. "It looks like it started as a legit program for cyberlimb transplants but they discovered serious side effects."

She pinched the bridge of her nose. "Any other bad news?"

"Not yet. I haven't fully decrypted all the files." He had, but no need to show all his cards at once. Plus, she looked like she couldn't take another hit.

"This is a nightmare." She ran her hands through her hair, leaving the blond strands disheveled.

It was the first time he'd seen her stressed.

"What can I do to help?" *Fuck!* Had he really offered to help the woman holding his sister hostage?

"Keep digging and find out who buried these files." She turned on her heel. The click of her heels was more of a stomp as she returned to her desk. "And locate the person who abetted my father's assistant."

Ash cleared the screen. "Which is the priority?"

"Both."

Nope, that didn't work for him. Ash pushed out from his chair and stalked to her desk. "You have to pick one. It takes hours to locate these files. I can focus on that or your original task. Or you can re-open my port." He was playing with fire.

"You dare tell me what to do?" Her blue gaze raked over him, leaving an icy burn.

"I can't do it all," he blurted. It might have been lack of sleep, it might have been years of feeling restrained.

"Perhaps you should curtail your bar visits."

His blood froze. "What?"

"Don't play dumb. You've been out a number of nights lately."

Blood rushed from his head, leaving him feeling faint. This was bad. Really bad.

He'd hoped no one had noticed his sudden affinity for Razor Jack's. He tried to laugh it off. "Some days you just need a drink to unwind."

"You suddenly decided you needed a drink in that part of town? Bullshit. I know what you've been up to."

Despite the churning of his stomach, Ash forced his stiff muscles to relax and his feet to remain where they were. She couldn't know why he'd been at Razor Jack's.

Could she?

He'd surely be dead if she had the slightest indication of his plan.

"Just having a drink." It took effort to keep concern out of his voice.

"The only reason to head to a bar that far out is a woman. Or a man."

Relief hit like a punch. His heart started beating again. That was what she thought?

It was true, but still. Ash shrugged. "The place has good beer and pretty girls."

"It's a woman." She paused and her gaze held his.

"Which is interesting. There's no report of any long-term relationships in your file. You're either very discreet or you're very into this woman." She tapped her finger against her chin. "And that makes me wonder. What kind of woman would keep your attention that long? Pull you out into the open?"

Portia Tremaine was a very scary woman. What would stop this line of questioning?

Ash gave in. "Fine. There's a woman. She works at the bar."

CHAPTER 32

"THE PRESSURE'S INCREASING," Ash told Taryn as he sat at the bar later that night. "Portia wants me to dig faster. I was able to put her off today, but I don't know how long I can keep it up." This was the part he wasn't looking forward to telling her. "Somehow, she knows I've been coming here. I don't know if she's having me followed or what. Please tell me you're close to freeing Hope."

She stared at him a long minute, then pulled a beer for someone down the bar. She looked pensive when she came back to him. "Almost."

Ash growled. That wasn't what he wanted to hear.

She glared at him. "Don't be an asshole. The pieces are coming together. We need to find the perfect time to put it in motion."

"Sooner is better." His impatience bled into his words.

She looked around, then leaned over the bar. "It's a lot of work moving a comatose girl," she hissed. "I can get her out safely, or I can risk everything for all three of us."

His brain stuttered. It was surprisingly easy to imagine the three of them together, creating a family, a life outside of

Seattle. Maybe Hope would never come out of her coma, but Ash wouldn't give up on her.

Deep in the files of the Tremaine system, he'd discovered a hypothetical cure. That file would be coming with him when he left.

"Why are you staring at me?" Her friendly smile carried an edge of concern.

"Just thinking about what it might be like to get out from under the Tremaines' control." It was too early to tell her he could imagine a future with her. Right?

She leaned her elbows onto the bar. "Where do you think you'll go?"

"I don't know. They'll be looking for me as soon as Hope disappears." His plan wasn't any further along than hers. Ideally, he'd use her plan as the jumping-off point, but since she hadn't shared it yet, that was difficult.

Her hand slid over his. "I'll miss you."

He flipped his palm up, catching her fingers before she could pull them away. "I'll miss you too. I'll miss this." He cupped his other hand over hers, holding her like she was precious.

Which she was.

Blushing, Taryn ducked her head. "You're just saying that because I'm helping you get free of the corporation."

Did she really believe that?

"You know that's not true, right?" When she didn't say anything, he repeated, "Right?"

Her shoulders lifted in a half-hearted shrug. "I guess."

He freed one hand from their tangle of fingers. He tucked two fingertips under her chin, gently tilting it up to see her eyes. "I'm serious. I'll miss you. This." He gave her hand a squeeze.

His hand slid up to cup her cheek and she leaned into his touch.

Her lips brushed over the heel of his thumb.

"You could come with us." He blurted out the words before his brain caught up with his body.

Ash expected to feel panic. Instead, peace settled over him. It felt right. Like they belonged together.

Taryn offered him a shy smile, tinged with sadness. She shook her head and her hair shifted around her shoulders. "I wish I could." Her voice was wistful, the words soft. She straightened and he reluctantly pulled his hand away from her face.

"Why can't you?" Was that childish whine really his voice?

It had to be. She stiffened and suddenly the softness was gone from her gaze, replaced with annoyance. "Not here." Though the physical distance between them was only the width of the bar, the emotional distance felt much wider.

"Why not here?"

"I'm working." Her voice was clipped.

"Pfft. You weren't worried about working a minute ago when you were kissing my hand."

"You weren't being an asshole then."

She was probably right, but he was in too deep now. Momentum, not logic, carried him forward. "I'm not an asshole. I just want an answer." He reached across the bar and grabbed her arm.

Taryn gasped, then tugged her arm free. "I told you never to touch me again without permission."

She stepped back from the bar, out of reach, and nodded to someone over Ash's shoulder.

Hands gripped his upper arms. Ash tore his gaze from

her, his head swiveling right to left. Two bouncers bracketed him. They dragged him away from the bar.

Ash leaned forward, trying to resist their pull. "Wait! Let's talk about this."

She shook her head but didn't look at him. "No."

"Tomorrow?" He dug his feet in, trying to slow his removal.

"I don't know." She sounded tired.

CHAPTER 33

TARYN TOOK the coward's way out, slipping into the hall to watch the guys take care of Ash through a crack in the door. She'd thought watching them drag him away would make her feel better.

Yeah, not so much.

Ash hadn't given her a choice—he'd been warned what would happen if he touched her like that again. She'd made that threat in public, so she had to back it up in public. Otherwise, word might get around that the Jack was all talk, no action.

She just hadn't anticipated how much protecting the Jack would hurt Taryn.

Dani joined her in the hallway. "I thought you two were at the touching stage."

"We are. Were." Taryn didn't know any longer. Had they just broken up? "I told him that first night, if he ever laid a hand on me without my permission . . ."

"You were right. You couldn't let it slide." Dani leaned into her, wrapping her arm around Taryn's waist. "I'm sorry that it happened."

"Yeah, me too." She laid her head on Dani's shoulder.

"Do you want me to take over the rest of your shift at the bar?" Dani asked.

She did. She really, really did. But Dani had been covering for her an awful lot lately. Since Ash had walked into her bar and her life. "No. I can't ask you to do that."

Dani hugged her. "You can ask anything. You know that."

She'd told Taryn that more than once. "I'm the boss. I'm supposed to take care of everything."

Her friend made a rude sound. "Fine. I know how stubborn you can be. If you need anything, all you have to do is ask."

"I know. I know."

"Now say it like you mean it." Dani leaned against the wall and watched Taryn with a serious look in her eye.

Taryn sighed again and did what Dani asked. It was the only way to get her friend off her back. "All I have to do is ask. And you'll be there." She paused. "Man, that sounds like bad song lyrics."

Dani burst out laughing. "At least you've still got your sense of humor."

Taryn smiled weakly. She wouldn't go that far, but making Dani laugh felt good. She appreciated that Dani worried about her, but it still felt wrong to lean on her. Or anyone. Taryn changed the subject. "Don't you have a date tonight?"

A pretty pink washed over Dani's cheeks and her eyes sparkled. For a brief, terrible moment, Taryn was jealous. Horribly jealous.

Fortunately, the feeling dissipated almost as quickly as it appeared, vanquished by Taryn's happiness for her best friend.

"Yes. He's taking me out for dinner." Dani's voice was soft and girly.

"Oo-ooh. This is what, your third date?" Dani didn't date often and Taryn couldn't remember anyone who'd lasted until the third date.

She nodded. An auburn strand escaped her hairstyle, curling in front of her ear. She moved to tuck it back, but Taryn stopped her.

"Leave it. It adds a bit of romance to your look."

If anything, Dani blushed harder. "Really?"

Taryn hadn't lied. The soft curl went perfectly with the top Dani wore. Soft cream-covered lace enhanced her slim build and soft curves and flowed into a rich velvet skirt the color of the fine wine Dani enjoyed. The skirt ended just an inch or two from the brown leather boots that covered her knees.

She looked like she'd stepped out of the pages of an old storybook. A heroine who could hold her own but embraced pretty things. Of all the people Taryn knew, Dani deserved a happily ever after the most.

Taryn was so happy for her. "You look amazing. What time is he picking you up?"

"Not for an hour or so. I was so excited, I got ready way too early."

Taryn grinned and her heart felt lighter. The sadness and confusion from how things had gone down with Ash wasn't gone, but now was the time to be happy for her best friend. She could deal with the guy bullshit later. "How about I buy you a drink at the bar while you wait?"

"Ooh. The Jack buying drinks? You better not say that too loud or people will start thinking you're a softie."

"That'll be the day." Taryn laughed.

She linked her arm through Dani's and they re-entered

the bar area. They parted ways at the edge of the bar so Taryn could take up her position behind the bar and Dani could take one of the seats in front of it.

Dani angled her body so she could see the door, a bright smile on her face.

Taryn held back a sigh. Who knew it was possible to be so damn happy and sad at the same time?

Business was brisk and the steady work helped Taryn banish Ash from her thoughts. Dani sat at the bar and nursed her drink. Whenever there was a lull, she kept up a mostly one-sided conversation with Taryn and fielded compliments from regulars who'd never seen her so dressed up.

Dani looked so happy and alive that it was hard to believe that she'd been a beaten-down girl from the streets just a few years ago. If anyone deserved happiness, it was her.

Taryn hadn't met Dani's guy yet and she was really looking forward to it. She watched Dani watch the door.

The smile that broke over Dani's face when she saw him practically lit up the room. His answering smile won him points, but Taryn still wanted to take his measure, maybe set a few ground rules. Starting with "I've got my eye on you" and ending with "Break Dani's heart and they won't find you. Ever. Not even the tiniest little piece of you."

They both watched him cross the room.

"You look amazing," Mason said, when he reached the bar.

Taryn watched Dani carefully as she stepped into his arms. Her friend's smile never dimmed—she really was happy.

"This is Mason. My date." Dani stepped back and smiled at Taryn. "Mason, this is the Jack."

Taryn watched for a visible reaction, but there wasn't one. She'd have to ask Dani what she'd told him.

Dani and Mason exchanged a look Taryn couldn't read. Then he stood and held out his hand. His gaze was direct, which she liked. "Nice to meet you."

His handshake was firm.

"You too."

Pleasantries done, she glanced at Dani. "So this is the boyfriend?"

She blushed beet red. "Date," Dani said. At the same time, Mason said, "Yes."

Taryn smiled. She'd still keep an eye on Mason, but she liked that he kept Dani on her toes.

"So, you're Dani's date." It wasn't a question. He seemed to realize that.

"And you're Dani's boss."

Touché.

"What do you do, Mason?" She pinned him with her gaze.

"I'm an analyst." He named a software company headquartered in Seattle. Decent place, based on everything she'd heard. At least he was gainfully employed.

He turned to face Taryn head-on. "I'm also single. I have my own place. I'm ready to be in a relationship and I think Dani is great. Anything else you want to know?"

If she'd overhead this conversation while she was bartending, she'd have smiled. Maybe even applauded.

But this was Dani they were talking about. Taryn couldn't afford to be amused.

"Since you did me the courtesy of being honest, I'll do

the same. If you hurt Dani, in any way, shape, or form, I will disappear you."

"I'm right here, you guys," Dani said.

Taryn had to give him credit, he didn't even flinch. "I would expect nothing less. I've heard about you."

"All bad, I hope."

He laughed and she could see why Dani had agreed to a third date. He was cute, quick on his feet, and didn't back down.

"Can I have my date back now?" Dani asked.

Mason turned to look at her, a bright smile on his face.

That weird combination of happiness and jealousy settled in Taryn's stomach again. "You two kids have fun."

Dani looked at her funny. "Do you need me to stay?"

"No. You're off the clock. Have fun."

Dani tucked her hand in Mason's elbow and led him toward the exit.

Shit. How could she be jealous of her best friend?

CHAPTER 34

"YOU HUNGOVER, ASH?" Mendez asked the next day, riding his ass.

"What?" Ash stared at his screen. His concentration was shit because he couldn't stop replaying the scene with Taryn last night. Fortunately, the pings were slow and infrequent today, because he was off his game. Even his coworkers had noticed.

"You're off today. What the fuck is going on?"

"I just . . ." Ash had no idea what to say.

"Aw, did you strike out with that girl of yours?"

He felt everyone's eyes on him, but Ash stayed focused on the screen. "We had a fight," he admitted.

"What did you do?" This from another member of his team.

Ash swiveled in his chair to face the speaker. "Why do you assume it's my fault?"

"Because you're a guy," Ava said.

Laughter filled the room.

He sighed. "Something I shouldn't have." The total truth, despite the lack of details.

He understood why Taryn had tossed him out. He'd grabbed her. He'd overstepped, mistaken their easiness, their closeness, for something it wasn't and abused his privileges.

"Damn, boy. That's a rookie mistake." Mendez's tone was half sympathy and half you're-a-dumb-shit.

"Yeah, I know." Once again, his fuckup could end up hurting Hope.

"You apologize?" the other woman on their team asked.

Ash shook his head. "Not yet."

"Mistake after mistake." She shook her head and tsked. "You like this girl?"

"Woman, and yes," Ash said. Taryn was a strong, tough woman.

She rolled her eyes. "Are you seeing her again?"

"Yeah, probably." He wanted to. And he had to—once Hope was rescued. The real question was, would Taryn let him back into her bar? Her life?

The questions came fast and furious after that. Ash felt like he was on one of those relationship shows that aired every afternoon. He gave up on trying to do his job and answered the questions mostly honestly and as quickly as he could.

"You've been a pretty busy boy, lately, though, haven't you?"

Ash looked at Mendez. "What?" Something in Mendez's tone put his back up and Ash studied the other man more closely.

"Between your new lady friend and all the time you've been spending with Portia Tremaine," Mendez said with pure stir-shit-up speculation in his expression.

Ash hid his wince. This wasn't good. He wasn't supposed to talk about what was happening with Portia.

Even though he'd warned Portia this could happen, he'd hoped no one noticed all the time he spent in her office.

"She asked me to look at something on her computer." That was close enough to the truth, right?

"Ooh, is that what they're calling it these days?"

"Screw you, Mendez." Heat colored Ash's voice. He turned back to his screen. The more he argued his innocence, the less they would believe him. Better to bow out of the conversation entirely.

The badgering and jokes continued, but he steadfastly ignored them. Finally, they found another target to tease. Fine with him. He just wanted the shift over, so he could work on a plan to get back on the Jack's good side.

Focusing on his job, he easily took care of a half-dozen pings against the system. Rookie-level stuff he could do even when he was distracted.

Then, suddenly, unexpected characters flashed across the screen. *What the fuck?*

He leaned forward and squinted at the screen. He was imagining things.

Wasn't he?

There it was again.

Fēnix. Hidden in the code.

"What the hell?" Ash mumbled under his breath.

"Hey, man, you know we're just giving you shit, right? None of these knuckleheads have had a proper date in forever."

"What?" Ash barely heard Mendez. His entire body was tense as he stared at the screen.

"It doesn't mean anything, ya know?"

"Oh, right. Whatever."

His name flickered across the screen again. Ash hissed out a breath.

"What's going on?"

If only Ash knew. The possibility that someone knew he was here spooked him. If they knew where to find him—and knew what he'd done—things could be about to get super fucked up for him.

"I thought I saw an attack," Ash improvised. "It was a blip, there and then gone."

Totally true, if by blip you meant his hacker handle, which had been essentially retired since the night he was captured. He'd heard it more in the last week than in the entire time he'd been at the Tremaine Corporation.

That couldn't be good.

"Where?" someone asked.

"Over there, in Europe." Ash pointed in the complete opposite direction.

"I don't see anything." Most of them had turned back to the screen.

"Must've been caught by the firewalls." Maybe if he repeated it often enough, he'd convince himself that it was just a blip instead of his hacker name.

Deep down, he knew what he'd seen. Was it a message or a trap? And why now?

He was so close to escaping his past. So close to freeing Hope from the corporation and getting out of Seattle.

Now it could all fall apart.

CHAPTER 35

"WHO KNOWS I'm working for you?" Ash stalked into Portia's office after his shift.

"I beg your pardon." Ice coated every word.

Ash ignored it. Too pissed—too freaked out—to toe the line.

"Who knows that you have Fēnix working for you?" He paced in front of her desk.

"Phoenix? Oh, that's right. Your charming little sobriquet." She glanced up and pursed her lips. "No one. Need I remind you this is a secret project? I don't need any leaks."

"Well, we might have one."

Her head rose sharply and she gave him her full attention. "When? How?"

Ash dropped into his chair and swiveled around to face her. "I don't know. But I think someone knows. Today . . ." He stopped, ran his hands through his hair. "Fuck. I don't know. It's mostly just a feeling, but . . ."

"But what?" Curiosity and urgency colored her question.

"I could have sworn I saw my handle on one of the attempted hacks today."

"What?" Her voice rose. "Why didn't you lead with that?"

For just a second he enjoyed knowing that he'd shaken her reserve. But when he closed his eyes, those characters hovered in his vision.

"It was gone in a blink. I'm not sure I really saw it."

Her gaze pinned him. "Did anyone else see?"

Would it better or worse if someone had? He shook his head. "I don't think so. Most of us weren't looking at the screen right then."

"What is that supposed to mean?" And she was back to frosty.

"They were giving me hell," he admitted. "About a woman."

"If you've spoiled everything because of that woman you're seeing—"

"I was distracted, yes, but no, I didn't ruin everything. Or anything." He hoped. "That's the only reason they missed it. Which I think is a good thing."

"How do you explain your handle appearing on the screen?"

"A fluke?" he offered, although he didn't believe it for a second.

She didn't either, judging by the pinch of her lips.

"I don't know. I think someone knows I'm here. But why now? The only thing I can think of is if . . ." Ash hesitated. He hated what he was about to say. There were only two ways that someone knew his location and he wasn't about to say one of them out loud. There was no way *he'd* screwed up. "What if it's a leak?"

"What do you mean, a leak?" Her Ice Queen voice was in play now. Ash would need to tread carefully.

"That's just it. I don't know. What if someone found out that we're looking around at what happened?"

"How do I know it isn't you?" Her blue eyes drilled into him.

His heart racing a million miles a minute, he held her gaze. Was she accusing him? "Why would I do that? That would put Hope at risk."

She studied him for a long—*long*—moment. "I'm sure you would, for the right reason." Portia tapped her finger against her lip. "But I don't think you'd risk your sister."

Maybe he was imagining things, but Ash thought he heard a question in her voice. Was she thinking about her own sister? Scuttlebutt was Portia had tried to take her out more than once after the bombing. That was cold.

"If it wasn't you, who was it?" she asked.

"I don't know," he admitted.

"You're not helping your case."

Ash tamped down his frustration. Taking it out on Portia was a bad idea. "Have I told anyone about the project? No." No reason for her to know he'd told Taryn. "Could I have made a mistake? Sure, but it's unlikely. I've been digging through Leopold's files. I've covered my tracks as much as possible." There wasn't much else he could do, aside from turning himself in, which wasn't going to happen.

Portia spun her chair around to face the windows. Rain streaked the glass, obscuring the usually clear view of the city below.

Ash automatically looked in the direction of Razor Jack's. Not that he could see it from here, even on a clear day. It was obscured by a number of buildings. But he knew where it was—where Taryn was—almost instinctively. What the hell did that mean?

"I don't know how my father juggled all this."

Ash held his breath. He had no idea what to say. Portia had never struck him as the sharing type, yet here she was, talking like they were friends.

Silence was the best—the only—response.

"I wanted all this, you know. The business. The position. I know everyone believes I got this position because of my name, but I busted my ass to get here. To get noticed by my father, to be named a worthy successor. And for what? To be named CEO because he disappeared, leaving a giant fucking mess to deal with. What a joke."

Holy shit. That was . . . that was the most human reaction he'd ever seen from her.

"That sucks." The words slipped out. It was something he'd say to a friend, but making friends had never been his strong suit.

Portia swung back around and stared at him.

He held her gaze, waiting for the inevitable threats.

Instead, she burst out laughing.

Of all the things he'd expected, that wasn't on the list.

"You're the first person who's dared to be honest with me. Yes, it sucks. A lot. A year ago I dreamed about running my family's company with my husband by my side. But one terrible night and I'm stuck in this nightmare of questionable loyalty, bitter memories, and never-ending grief."

It was hard to swallow past the lump in Ash's throat. His regrets about his role in her nightmare was a living, breathing weight. He opened his mouth to apologize, but he couldn't. Not yet.

Portia had noticed, though, and was waiting for him to speak. So he did.

"Have you talked to anyone about your feelings?" God, that was fucking laughable coming from him.

"Like my former best friend? The one who decided to fall in love with the half-sister I never knew about? Or maybe her?"

He nodded carefully. That was a . . . complicated situation.

She dropped her head onto the back of her chair. "Irony of ironies, they're the only ones I really do trust. How messed up is that?"

"Pretty messed up."

"Killian would bend over backward to help me. I think. Unless it involved that damn courier. He's already shown he'll choose her over me." Was that jealousy or anger in her voice?

She sighed and picked up the picture of her husband that sat on her desk. "Dizzie? I don't know. Don't care to. I'll never be able to look at her without remembering what she cost me. How Killian fell in love with her, I'll never understand."

Ash stifled a sigh. It was shockingly easy to fall in love with someone completely unsuitable.

"You fell in love?" Her tone was half curiosity and half actual concern.

He couldn't believe he'd said that out loud. "Pretend I never said that."

Was it even love? Or just gratitude?

"Is this the woman trouble they were teasing you about?"

"Yes." Of course, Portia wouldn't leave it alone. If anyone had told him that he'd be spilling secrets to Portia

Tremaine without being tortured, he'd have laughed his ass off.

Time for a subject change. "Do you want me to focus on the leak or on Leopold's trail?"

Portia raised a brow, her expression clearly indicating that she knew he was changing the subject. "Both," she said again.

He shook his head. "I can't do both. Not with our current setup. Let me have full access to the system." Full access meant porting in. He'd do just about anything she wanted for the chance to surf the network again. It was so close he could almost taste it.

"I can't," she said.

Was that real regret in her voice?

"I don't trust you," she continued. "I want to. You've given me good information. At least, I think you have. But as soon as I let you off that leash, you could do unimaginable harm to me and this company and I wouldn't know until it was too late."

She was right not to trust him, but that didn't mean her words didn't hurt.

He wanted to earn her trust. The woman who was using his sister as a hostage. How fucked up was that?

This must be Stockholm syndrome.

"Fine," he ground out. "I still can't do it all. What do you want first?"

Since he didn't bother to hide his annoyance, he expected a reprimand. Instead, she looked at him with pity.

Fuck her. He didn't need her pity.

"Finish with my father's assistant. I need to know how much damage he did that we haven't discovered yet." She paused, her gaze heavy on him.

He ignored it, focusing instead on the streaks of rain on

the window behind her. That was how he felt especially with Taryn mad at him. Gray and washed out.

"Fine," he said. "I'll get right on that."

CHAPTER 36

IN THE ELEVATOR, Ash sagged against the wall after finishing his time up in Portia's office for the day. His head hurt and he struggled to regain his focus on his next moves. Juggling Hope and Taryn and Portia, as well as all the secrets, was getting overwhelming. He feared the situation would come to a head before Taryn had extricated Hope.

He wanted a nap and a drink.

No. Scratch that.

It wasn't a drink he wanted, it was Taryn.

But he'd screwed up and that wasn't an option.

So, he should focus on his future. His and Hope's. One without Taryn in it.

Fuck, that was depressing as hell.

Ash stepped off the elevator and ran right into Mendez.

Crap. This day was getting worse and worse.

His brow nearly to his hairline, Mendez swept his gaze from Ash to the executive elevator.

"Moving on up, huh?" He waggled his brows in a suggestive manner.

Ash didn't bother to dignify that with an answer.

"Sorry. Just joking." Mendez looked him up and down. "You've been pretty fucking tense lately, man. What's going on?"

Ash rubbed his hands over his face. Where to even begin? Especially when Ash couldn't tell him the truth. He liked Mendez, but he wouldn't make the mistake of trusting the other man. Not when the stakes were this high.

Taking Ash's silence as an answer, Mendez scowled and stepped back. "My bad," he said. "Thought you could use a friend." He turned.

"Sorry. I just . . ." What the hell could he say? "You know those woman troubles everyone was giving me shit about today? Well, I just realized that I fucked up. It was completely my fault."

Mendez's eyes widened in shock. "You're not talking about Portia Tremaine, are you?" He jerked his head toward the executive elevator.

"Oh god no." Ash's tone was just as horrified.

"Good, because there was no helping you if you were." Mendez laughed and slapped Ash on the shoulder. "You thought everyone was kidding when they told you it was your fault and you should apologize?"

"Maybe?"

"Didn't your daddy teach you how to treat a woman?" Mendez asked as they walked down the hallway.

Ash blew out a harsh breath. "He wasn't around much." At all. Ever really. "Except when he needed money."

"Shit, man, sorry. I didn't know." Mendez actually looked like he felt bad.

What would it be like to have a friend he trusted enough to talk about this shit with? Since he'd been hauled into the Tremaine Corporation, he'd rejected—and distrusted—any overture of friendship. Maybe that had been a mistake.

"No way you would have. Unless that's in my Tremaine file and you somehow got into it."

Ash had meant it as a joke, but Mendez squirmed.

"Fuck. You have?"

The other man shoved his hands in his pockets and looked around the hallway. "I got bored."

"How the hell did you get that deep into the system?" Sure, Ash knew how to do it. It had taken weeks of careful poking and prodding and circling to make sure he didn't trip any sensors or set off any traps.

"I have my ways."

Ash laughed at the non-answer. "Yeah, I wouldn't share my secrets, either."

"Like I'm going to tell the guy coming out of the executive elevator anything." Mendez pursed his lips.

Ash stiffened at the implication. "It's not what it looks like."

"Either you're fucking her or you're ratting us all out." Mendez watched Ash skeptically. "I don't think you're doing either, but something is going on."

Crap. Ash had told Portia this would happen. "Maybe it was computer repair."

"There's a whole department for that." Mendez's tone said Ash was stupid for even suggesting it.

"She had a question." He couldn't say more. He wished he could confide in the other man. Helping Portia while keeping his activities under the radar would be easier if he had another professional to bounce ideas off of.

"Yeah, whatever," Mendez said. "Whatever you're up to, just remember, they're not like you and me. You can't trust them."

"Well aware," Ash said, letting his frustration with the whole situation color his words.

Mendez stared at him. "Good luck, man," he said finally and walked away.

If only Ash could do the same.

CHAPTER 37

TARYN LEANED over the computer screen. She was finalizing the plan to get Hope out of the Tremaine medical center without raising alarms. The last sticking point had been how to get her from her room to the ambulance, and she'd finally figured that out. She'd called in a series of favors to enact this rescue. Rescuing Ash's sister was costing favors she didn't want to spend. But if he upheld his side of the bargain and she was able to stop Giselle's pimp from showing up here, it would be worth it.

"Another rescue?"

Taryn looked up. Rhonda stood in the doorway.

"Yeah." She smiled at the other woman, glad she looked less concerned than she had the night Taryn kicked the pimp out.

"Can I help?" She stepped into the room and peered at the desk.

"No, I think I'm good," Taryn said.

"Seems awfully soon to be planning another one. The new girl, Gazelle, has only been here a couple days."

"Giselle has been here almost two weeks," Taryn corrected gently. It was an unusual name, but it wasn't that hard to pronounce, was it?

Still, Rhonda wasn't wrong. Taryn usually preferred at least a couple of months between rescues. The time allowed her to identify the woman who needed help and to make a plan that covered any contingency. If only that had been an option with Hope's rescue.

"It is unusual," Taryn admitted. "We've been asked to find a family member. Someone's sister."

"The hacker guy, right? The one you've been kissing?"

Taryn's face flushed. She could kiss whoever she damn well pleased. "Yes." She bit back a comment about Rhonda's overstep. While Taryn was friendly with all the girls who stayed here, very few became actual friends. Rhonda wasn't one of them.

Rhonda sighed. "Why does his sister need to be rescued?"

Taryn's temper flared, but she held on to it. Rhonda was pushing more than usual. Taryn didn't like it.

She almost refused to answer. Instead, she offered a tidbit, hoping it would make Rhonda go away. "She's in a bad spot."

"But why are we rescuing her? We've never done that before."

Taryn's jaw clenched, but she held onto her patience. Barely. "Because the Jack provides services to people for money. That's how this place works."

Rhonda looked like she wanted to argue further, but Taryn was done. Questions were a good thing, in her opinion, but the questioning? Yeah, not so much. "I need to get back to this, Rhonda. Was there anything you needed?"

Lips pursed, Rhonda glared at Taryn. "I just came by to

say hi. You don't have to be so rude." She turned and stomped out of the room. She probably would have slammed the door shut, but Dani grabbed it on her way in.

They both watched Rhonda walk away. "You're right," Taryn said. "Something's going on with her."

"Can I come in?" Dani's smile was rueful.

Taryn smiled back. "Of course. As long as you promise not to question everything I do."

"Done."

There was a bounce in Dani's step that Taryn hadn't seen before. "I take it the date went well?"

She beamed, her smile practically blinding Taryn. Dropping into her usual chair, she arranged her skirt daintily around her legs. "I really like him."

"He seems like a good guy." She'd only met him briefly, though, and was reserving judgment. Maybe she'd ask Ash to dig into Mason's background.

Having easy access to a hacker would certainly help the Jack's business. If only he wasn't planning to leave town as soon as Hope was free. It would be hard to hide Hope in Seattle, but not impossible. Razor Jack's certainly had the room.

As soon as the thought crossed her mind, she grimaced. She might have ruined her chances with him.

"He'll be back, Taryn." Dani spoke softly, her tone reassuring.

"I wasn't thinking about him." Her denial was almost immediate.

Dani's look said that she totally knew Taryn was lying.

"Fine. Maybe I was thinking about him a little." Taryn waved her hand, as if it would clear her conflicted thoughts. "Enough about me. Tell me about your date."

It was the perfect distraction and for the first time in

hours, Taryn relaxed as she listened to Dani gush about her evening. Every aspect of her meal was described in the smallest detail. The plot of the movie, lovingly described. Even the kiss they'd shared at the end of the night.

Taryn smiled. What told her the most about Dani's evening was the fact that her friend had taken the time to notice all those details. She'd relaxed enough around this guy to enjoy herself. That was priceless.

Dani's background was as fucked up as Taryn's. Although Dani had blossomed and grown over the last few years, she still had trouble letting herself get close to anyone, especially men.

Taryn completely understood.

But where Taryn had thrown herself back into sex with abandon and a fuck-you attitude during her second year of freedom, Dani was more tentative.

While Taryn had worried that Dani would never even date, she couldn't fault Dani for her hesitation.

"You really like him." Taryn watched Dani's reaction.

"Shut up!" Dani's face flamed, but she couldn't stop her smile.

"You're allowed to be happy, you know." Taryn looked her dead in the eyes, her voice completely serious. "You can also leave here at any time."

Despite Taryn's somber tone, Dani cracked up.

Taryn frowned. "I'm serious."

"Oh, I know," Dani said. "The whole 'you can be happy' speech is pretty rich coming from the woman who just broke up with her boyfriend."

"He isn't my boyfriend." The denial was automatic. "And we didn't break up. We just . . ." She still didn't know what the fuck had happened.

Or what to call it.

Or even how to deal with it.

Instead, Taryn refocused their conversation. "We were talking about you. There's nothing keeping you here. You can be happy. You can be free. You can be loved."

Taryn wouldn't require a favor from Dani when she left. If anything, she owed Dani multiple favors for all the times she'd kept Taryn sane when nightmares left her shaking. They'd huddled together, trading stories in the dark.

Dani was Taryn's sister in every way except blood. "I only want you to be happy," Taryn repeated stubbornly.

"I know you do and I love you for it. I'm happy here."

Taryn started to protest, then stopped when she recognized the look on Dani's face. It was her don't-you-dare-interrupt-me face.

"I like working here. I make good money. I have respect. Responsibility." She paused, looking pensive. "Where else could I get that with my background and no experience?"

Taryn growled.

Dani laughed again. "In time, I may want to look for something else. Stretch my wings. But I'm comfortable here."

"I love that you're comfortable here, but—"

Dani interrupted her. "This is my home, Taryn. I'm safe here. That's what makes it the perfect place for me while I try dating. I know you'll always have my back. And to answer your question, yes, I like Mason. A lot. But we're taking it slow. I don't want to get overwhelmed and make a rash decision that will ruin it." She shot Taryn a pointed look.

"I didn't ruin anything," Taryn muttered. "He did."

Dani rolled her eyes. "Sure, you had nothing to do with it."

"He asked me to go with him, when he leaves with Hope."

Dani's eyes widened. "Holy shit! What did you say?"

"I didn't answer and he pushed for one." Taryn sighed. "I can't leave the bar, Dani. No, that's not quite right. I don't *want* to leave the bar. I've made Razor Jack's my own."

"And here you are trying to convince *me* to leave? Don't think so." She waved Taryn off before she could argue. "That's a tough situation. You really like him, don't you?"

Taryn didn't want to lie. Not to Dani. Not to herself. Not about this. "Yeah. I do. I mean, I did." Her heart twinged.

"Then you should go for it," Dani said, like it was the easiest thing in the world.

Taryn shook her head. "I can't. The bar, what I do here, is too important."

"More important than love?" Dani's voice was soft, but her words were a wake-up call.

"Is this love?" Bewilderment washed over Taryn. Was that what all these feelings were? The pain in her heart when she thought about her last interaction with Ash at the bar? "I've never been in love."

"That's the perfect reason to follow it through."

"There's too many girls that I could still help." How could Taryn put her happiness first, when there were women who'd never felt it?

"You don't have to save them all," Dani said gently. It was an old argument. One that they'd never see eye to eye on. "You can't."

"I have to try." Taryn had to give them the chance that she'd never been given.

"You could move with him, start over," Dani countered.

Taryn had thought about that, but the logistics . . . "I'd have to build an entirely new network. In a new city. It would take me years to gain knowledge of all the players, make the connections. Too many things could go wrong. Too many girls would be hurt in that time." Taryn looked her in the eye. "It's too much."

"You can't let this run your life forever." Another old argument.

"Maybe not. But it's going to for now."

Dani sighed. "Fine. You know how I feel."

"I know. And I love you for trying," Taryn said. "But this wasn't supposed to be all about me. Are you going to see Mason again?"

Dani blushed. "Yes. In a couple nights. He's taking me to the theater."

"So fancy," Taryn teased. "Seriously, though, I'm so happy for you."

Pink tinged Dani's cheeks and her eyes got dreamy for a moment. Then she returned to the present. "What are you working on? Hope's rescue?"

Taryn nodded.

"We're still doing that?"

"I haven't heard otherwise. Plus, I told Ash that we would help." She might have broken up with Ash—maybe—but she wouldn't abandon a woman who needed help because of a broken heart. "And he's already started working on the payment."

"You're right. If he's already paid us, we can't back out." Dani's lips quirked in a half smile. "Have you figured it out?"

"Finally," Taryn said. She briefed her friend on the plan and Dani whistled when she was done.

"That's a lot," Dani said.

"I know. I knew it would be complicated, but . . ." She shook her head. "Remind me to never take on a case like this again."

"Done." Dani looked at the plan again. "When do you want to do this?"

"Soon, but I need to talk to Ash again. We need to know where to deliver her. We could set up a room here." Taryn paused, reminded of her half-baked thought to keep Hope and Ash here, with her. "But if he has a place or a vehicle to get her out of the city, we'll need to coordinate."

"Oh no, you have to talk to Ash again." Dani dramatized her statement with a hand pressed to her forehead and then to her heart.

"I hate you," Taryn said without any heat.

Dani leaned back in her chair and pulled her legs up, tucking her knees to the side. "You could just call him, you know?"

"I don't have his number," Taryn admitted.

"What?"

"He kept stopping by the bar. I didn't even think about it." And that should have been her first warning. The Jack never forgot details like that.

"I'm sure you can get a message to him."

"Yes," she admitted, trying to ignore Dani's scrutiny.

"Then put on your big Jack panties and reach out. Tell yourself it's only business if you have to, but you can't move forward—with this or with him—if you don't at least talk to him."

Dani was right. Taryn knew it.

"I'll think about it," she grumbled.

Dani laughed. "And think and think and think."

Taryn scowled. Her best friend wasn't wrong.

Dani pushed out of her chair. "You sit here and think. I'm going to bed."

"Thanks, Dani. I couldn't do this without you."

"I know, boss." She tossed Taryn a smile.

"Night, Dani." Her friend slipped out of the office and left Taryn alone with her thoughts.

CHAPTER 38

THE GUARD SHOVED Ash into Portia's office. He stumbled but managed to stay upright. She prodded his shoulder—hard—until he took one step, then another. The guard pushed him again, but this time Ash stood his ground. Ash expected them to shove him to his knees, the proper posture for a supplicant.

Fuck that.

If Portia Tremaine was going to take him out, she could fucking look him in the eye while she did it.

He stood up straight and did his best to radiate calm, but inside he was freaking out. Being dragged into her office by guards didn't tend to be a positive turn of events.

Portia stared at him, her expression serious. "Where is she?"

Of all the questions he'd expected . . .

"Who?"

Nostrils flaring, Portia pushed her chair back and stood. She circled the desk and closed the space between them slowly. Her heels clicked loudly, ominously on the tile floor.

"Where is she?" Her voice was cold. Quiet.

Whatever was going on, Portia was well and truly pissed. This was the Ice Queen, a woman he didn't want to cross. But he was telling the truth—he had no idea what she was talking about. "Who?" he asked again.

Her lips curled in a sneer. "Your sister."

His heart stopped and Ash swayed. "What?"

That was all he managed. Focusing on whatever Portia said next was impossible. He couldn't hear anything over the pounding of his heart. "My sister is missing?" he forced out.

Hope was free? Really?

"How did you do it?"

As reality set in, he realized that part of him had never expected Taryn to pull it off. And after their last fight, he hadn't been sure that she would.

He'd asked her to go up against the Tremaine Corporation and she'd done it. *She'd fucking done it!*

"I don't know. I didn't do it."

He owed Taryn an apology. No, not just an apology. He owed her everything.

Was that why Taryn had reached out? He'd gotten the message yesterday but had still felt too off-balance from their fight to return to the bar.

Ash grabbed the back of a chair, then lowered into it. Portia's glare had no effect. Hope was *free*.

"I think you're lying, Mr. Cutter." Portia crossed her arms over her chest and stared down at him, her head angled as she studied him. "Yet I also believe your reaction is genuine. That's a problem."

"And you don't like problems." He had plenty of experience with her dislike of problems.

Her smile belonged on a piranha.

"I didn't do it," he repeated. "I don't know where she is."

Taryn hadn't shared any details of her plan. Ash had never anticipated that the secrecy would bother him—she'd never even told him where she would be hiding Hope until they left the city.

The left side of his chest throbbed and he rubbed his hand over it. How was it possible to feel such joy and such loss at the same time?

Ash should be bouncing up and down with glee. They were so close to freedom. His heart broke because Taryn wouldn't be joining him on the next leg of their journey, wherever that was.

He stared at Portia and she stared back. Her blue eyes gave nothing away. Finally, she dismissed the guards and circled back to her desk.

Déjà vu washed over him. The last time he'd sat in this position, his life had been turned upside down. Now it was happening again.

"What am I supposed to do with you now?" There was nothing vindictive in her voice. Only curiosity and maybe . . . disappointment?

He shrugged. "Whatever you want, I guess." Suddenly, it didn't matter what Portia had planned for him. Hope was free. Taryn could get her the help she needed, as long as he could get her the funds to support Hope.

Ash had always imagined that when his time at the Tremaine Corporation was up, he'd go out fighting. He hadn't expected this . . . acceptance.

That felt like giving up and Ash had sworn that he would never stop fighting. A tiny flame flickered to life inside him.

"I still haven't uncovered how Leopold got the information to make his move."

It was a long shot, trying to bargain with the task she'd

assigned him. It was all he had left, though. Everything—everyone—important to him was safe outside this building.

"Twenty-four hours."

Relief rushed through him, but it was immediately countered by a touch of panic driven by the extremely short time frame.

"A week." It was a weak counter.

"Aren't you supposed to be the best?" She sniffed but he thought he detected a touch of amusement. "Thirty-six hours."

Better. Still not great.

Could he pull together a believable set of files for Portia and plot his own escape in a day and a half?

"Seventy-two."

"Forty-eight hours. Not a minute more." Her fingers flew over her keyboard and a clock appeared on the wall to his right. Forty-seven hours, fifty-nine minutes, and a few seconds.

An amusing trick, if it wasn't the time he had to get his affairs in order.

He wasted precious time watching the clock. Whether he got free or he got dead, his time at the Tremaine Corporation was truly limited.

"You've got a deal."

Ash stood, hopeful his legs would support him. "I'll just get started."

"Where do you think you're going?" Her tone was biting.

"Back to my shift." Security had dragged him out and the rest of the team would no doubt have questions. Ones he couldn't answer. But that was easier than trying to focus around Portia.

"You have less than forty-eight hours. That seems like a waste of precious time."

He hated that she was right, but he needed the time to pull himself together. Needed the time to decide which false trail to provide. He'd initially intended to frame one of his colleagues. It was still the smart play, but he felt like an asshole.

"I know," he said. "But it's my forty-eight hours, right?"

Portia shrugged.

"I'll be back after my shift," he told her as he stood.

"As you said, it's your choice."

Ash hid a smile. He'd actually miss working with Portia. The woman was whip-smart with a sense of humor he didn't think many people saw.

"I understand why you wanted to free your sister," she said as he approached the door. "Wherever you have her, I hope she's receiving the same quality medical care we provided."

His stomach cramped. Portia had pinpointed one of his major worries—that moving Hope would negatively affect her health. At the Tremaine medical center, she'd always appeared well cared for, but her condition had never changed. She'd just gotten thinner and remained unresponsive.

Ash's jaw clenched. He'd uncovered records on a possible cure for brain burn, but Phillip Tremaine had never approved its implementation. Ash had copied those documents and secreted them away for the day when Hope was free and they could attempt it.

"I didn't do it," he repeated. Taryn had kept the details from him for just this reason. He couldn't tell what he didn't know.

"I don't care," Portia said. "You've made a powerful enemy, Mr. Cutter. It didn't have to be that way."

He nodded. Without another word, he turned and walked away.

There was nothing he could say that would sway her to his side. He ignored the twinge of pain that thought brought. He'd grown to like and respect one of the most feared women in the city.

He'd fallen in love with the other one.

Ash itched to call Taryn and ask about Hope. How she was doing. Whether she needed anything.

Where she was.

He believed Portia when she said she wanted the best care for Hope. And maybe she was right, that Hope would be better at the Tremaine medical center.

But it was too late for second thoughts.

For the first time in years, he'd be responsible for Hope's health and safety again. He'd failed her the first time. Would he do so again?

His stomach churned with anxiety. Could he do this?

He'd been so focused on rescuing Hope and making sure he'd be prepared for her medical needs, he hadn't fully appreciated what moving her would mean. He alone would be responsible for her care. It had been one thing when she'd been an active teenager. But now, with her medical issues . . .

Ash swallowed hard and pushed the nerves away. Time to step up and play big brother again.

CHAPTER 39

ASH WAS BONE-TIRED. He'd worked his morning shift and then, as promised, had appeared in Portia's office for his shift for her. It didn't matter which project he was working on—protecting the corporation or excavating secrets for Portia—his brain had kept spinning. *Hope was free. Hope was free.* It was a never-ending chant in his head.

His phone rang and he ignored it. He was tired and cranky and couldn't remember the last time he'd slept or eaten.

The ringing never stopped. Even long past when it should have transferred to voicemail, it still rang. He finally picked up.

"What?" He spit out the word as he answered. He didn't care that he was being rude.

When there was no answer from the other end of the line, he growled. "Stupid prank callers."

"Don't hang up, Fēnix." A robotic voice, although it carried a familiar cadence.

His body went cold. No one called him that any more. Fēnix was as good as dead and he should stay that way.

"Who's this?" *Fuck!* Why hadn't he checked before he answered? Not that it would have done any good.

"Oh, Fēnix." The voice on the other end of the line chuckled.

Shivers ran up and down his spine. Like the voice, the laugh was distorted, sounding closer to a computer than to a human. And eerily familiar.

Ash knew that laugh. He'd never wanted to hear it again in his life. "What do you want?"

"Is that all you've got, boy? I'd heard you were a corporate bitch now, but I couldn't believe it. The old Fēnix would have known who was calling before the line even rang. How the mighty have fallen." That twisted laugh again.

Fuuck.

Ash knew who it was. His guess had been confirmed the moment he'd heard his hacker handle. He just hadn't wanted to believe it. "What do you want, Caspar?"

Caspar was the ghost in the machine. No one knew how old he was— if you believed the stories, he'd been around forever.

You didn't see him unless he wanted you to. A hacker had to be exceptionally good to find Caspar.

Ash was one of the people who had. That's how he'd joined the hacker collective.

"Is that any way to talk to a long-lost friend?" The computerized amusement gave him goosebumps.

Ash gritted his teeth. He'd hoped that Caspar had believed he was dead.

Unless . . . had Caspar sold them out? Ash didn't know one way or another, but if he ever crossed paths with the person who was responsible for Hope being in that coma . . . he'd make them regret it.

"Hang up now and we can both pretend that I'm still lost."

That crazy mechanical laugh again. "Oh, Fēnix. If you wanted to stay lost, you should never have gone into that bar."

"A man can't get a drink?" Ash was nearly completely sure that Taryn hadn't sold him out. The Jack might be ruthless, but his time with her had shown him that she was fiercely loyal to her friends and they'd gone way past friendly.

"Well, Fēnix," Casper said, stressing Ash's handle every time he said it. "If you hadn't set foot into that bar, no one would have seen you. If they hadn't seen you, I wouldn't have heard whispers that Fēnix was alive and still in Seattle. If I hadn't heard those whispers, I would never have started looking for proof."

An ominous pause. "You know what my search turned up, Fēnix?"

"What?" The sick feeling in Ash's stomach anticipated what Caspar was going to say.

"Your fingerprints, all over code from the Tremaine Corporation. Including the code that busted other hackers working on special projects for me."

Yep, that was what Ash had been afraid of.

He'd tried to keep his code clean, even generic, when he'd first arrived at Tremaine Corporation. That had quickly changed. Clean code didn't catch the bad guys who were way more advanced. And busting hackers was the only way to ensure Hope's safety.

His code—the twists and turns that his mind saw while he was coding—was pretty distinctive and he'd hoped that no one would notice it in Tremaine cybersecurity measures.

He hadn't been that lucky.

"Bad news?" Something in Ash's manner must have caught Portia's attention.

Ash briefly considered keeping the call private but that would take too damn much effort and make it look like he had something to hide.

He did, but it wasn't this call.

"If you'd managed to stay off my radar, Fēnix, we wouldn't be having this conversation. You'd be just a fond memory. A kid who worked for me and disappeared one day. Since you didn't screw me, I was happy to leave you in the past. But you just had to show back up."

Caspar was heading into repetitive territory. It was all part of his personality. He spun you in circles and then struck when you were confused. Ash expected it and concentrated on not giving him anything new to target. Hard to do with Portia watching him so closely. Both sides of his past were closing in on him.

Ash dug up his bravado. "Look, Caspar, you want to chat about the old days, just ask me out already and we can get a drink. Otherwise, I've got things to do."

"Oh, Fēnix. You haven't changed, have you? Still the same brash, blustery fellow who barged into my home demanding to be part of my crew."

Ash didn't respond. It was all true.

"You're missing something, aren't you? I mean, someone." The glee in the mechanical voice was doubly unsettling.

His heart froze.

Caspar didn't fuck around.

Taryn.

"Don't you hurt a hair on her head!"

Portia looked at him.

"I think we can come to a mutually agreeable trade."

How the hell had Caspar gotten to Taryn? Her security guys had been all over Ash when he'd touched her in the bar. Had they picked her up outside the bar? When she was rescuing Hope?

He gripped the phone so tightly his knuckles turned white. "Leave Taryn alone."

"Taryn? Who's that? No, dear boy, I have your lovely sister. Hope, isn't it? Of course, she isn't nearly as feisty as I remember."

Blood drained from Ash's face. The phone slipped from his fingers and hit the desk with a clatter.

Portia grabbed his phone and put it on speaker. She had come around to his desk when he hadn't noticed.

"You have Hope?" Ash barely choked out the words over the panic that filled him. Caspar could be cruel, and Hope was the definition of defenseless.

"Yes, I have your dear, sweet sister. Picked her up from the hospital today. A little bird provided me with a plan. I just moved up the timeline a little bit."

Taryn had given him the plan?

Bile surged. Ash choked it back. He'd practically declared his love and she did this?

Rage and worry warred within him. He didn't know what to do. He'd failed—again—at the only task that mattered—protecting his sister.

"Leave Hope alone."

"Of course, I'll leave her alone. She's hardly any fun, is she?" The eerie voice was filled with laughter.

Ash swallowed hard. "What do you want?"

"Oh, Fēnix. I really thought you'd get smarter as you got older. Tsk tsk. It should be obvious what I want. You're right in the middle of a very large pond. I want in."

"You want access to Tremaine?" Next to him Portia shook her head violently.

She could end this easily, but her ending probably wouldn't be a good one.

Ash picked up the phone and toggled off the speaker. "My sister returned unharmed for access to Tremaine?"

Portia tried to snatch the phone from his hand. Ash pushed away from his desk and crossed to the windows. Outside, the city was lit up like the holidays, thousands of lights from hundreds of buildings. It was pretty but he barely noticed.

"Of course. I always keep my promises. You know that."

Ash laughed bitterly. Caspar was a tricky bastard who kept to the exact terms of a deal. Any agreement had to be explicit and airtight or he'd find a way to wiggle around the terms.

"Why do you need in? I'm already here. I can get whatever you want."

Portia stalked toward him, a thundercloud on her face. He was trapped, literally and figuratively. There had to be a way out.

"No can do," Caspar replied. "I won't know what I need until I'm in there. So many lovely prizes hidden in that network, I'm sure. I bet the organ farming was just the beginning. No, if I'm there myself I'll be able to feast on all the delicious goodies."

"When?" Resignation colored Ash's voice. He was gonna to do it. He didn't want to. It would end badly for him, either at Caspar's hand or Portia's. Most likely Portia's, given the glare she directed his way.

"Soon. I'll contact you." He abruptly ended the call.

Ash stared at the phone in his hand, feeling dead inside.

His life was finally almost back under his control and the universe kicked him in the balls.

"What the fuck was that?" Portia was practically yelling—and she never yelled.

"My old boss."

She raised a brow. "From your hacker days?"

Ash nodded. Portia was no fool.

"He has your sister?" Her blue eyes pierced him.

"That's what he says." His stomach churned with the thought. Ash sagged against the window. Was she safe?

"You believe him?"

"Yeah. Caspar doesn't fuck around like that." He'd witnessed it firsthand.

"You were telling the truth that you don't know where she is."

Now she believed him. Yay.

"Yes." The word came out low. Dejected.

Ash had been sure that Hope was safe with Taryn. His girls together. Now his world was imploding in ways he'd never imagined.

"What did he want?"

"You heard him. He'll release Hope if I give him access to the Tremaine system."

"Do you honestly believe that? He's lying."

Ash considered what he knew about Caspar. "He'll do what he says. Exactly what he says, but he'll find whatever loopholes he can."

"And when will this visit take place?" She was pissed. It radiated from every pore, coated every word.

Ash shrugged. "Probably soon. He'll call when he's ready to make the exchange." Caspar would strike while the iron was hot. He wouldn't want to deal with Hope for longer than he had to. Not in her current state.

Portia stood directly in front of him, arms crossed. "From this moment, you are suspended from your regular shift and will remain under house arrest. If you aren't working here, under my supervision, you will be in your room."

Ash stared at her in horror. "He has my sister. She's in danger."

"I know. And it's terrible."

He interrupted. "What would you do if it was your sister?"

Her lips curled into a snarl. "*My* sister?" she asked archly.

Oh right. She'd tried to kill her sister a few weeks ago. *Stupid question, Ash.* He probably could have chosen a better example.

"Is it because she's in a coma? Is that why you think I shouldn't do whatever possible to save her?" Just when he was starting to believe Portia Tremaine wasn't the monster her father was.

"I didn't say that." Something flickered in her gaze, but it was gone before he could identify it.

"You didn't deny it either." He was going to be sick.

"I know you want her to wake up, but if it hasn't happened by now, I really don't think it's going to." Her voice had that tone that was intended to be kind, but in reality said that you were too stupid to understand what was actually going on.

"She still could," Ash insisted.

Portia's gaze was filled with pity. "I don't think so, Ash. I won't trade her life for the safety of my company. I'm sorry."

She sounded sincere but Ash was too horrified at the thought of losing Hope to care. "If you care so damn much about your company, maybe you should learn more about it."

There was a cure for Hope. Or at least the hope of a cure. Ash had read all the clinical notes and the lab trials and it sounded like there was real promise. Or that there would be if it was just funded further.

Of course, Portia would never believe that.

"What's that supposed to mean?"

"Figure it out." He was done. He had to get out of here before she sicced the guards on him again.

CHAPTER 40

TARYN WAS STANDING behind the bar when the front door burst open and slammed against the wall with a bang. Conversations stopped and everyone looked toward the entrance. Her bouncers immediately surged forward to block the threat. She really hoped it wasn't Giselle's pimp again.

She continued pulling the beer in her hand, but her attention never strayed far from activity at the front of the bar.

"I don't fucking care. I have to see her. Now."

Ash.

She caught Dylan's eye and nodded.

The guard stepped out of the way and Ash raced toward her. Her heart lightened. When he hadn't come back to the bar when she'd sent the message, she'd been sure that whatever was between them was over.

As he stormed across the room, Taryn realized he wasn't smiling.

"What did you do?"

She didn't know what he was accusing her of.

"I don't know what you're talking about." She set the beer on the counter in case she was tempted to throw it at him.

"Bullshit!"

When he neared, the look on his face was thunderous and for the first time, Taryn shivered in fear.

"Why did you give her to him?"

"I don't know what you're talking about," she repeated.

"He has my sister!" The pure anguish in his voice broke her heart.

"Who has Hope?" she asked again, trying to catch up.

"Like you don't know!" His cheeks were ruddy and his eyes were wide. His expression alternated between fear and rage. The fear broke her heart. The rage, well, that scared her.

But she was a big girl and knew how to protect herself. "Ash, I really don't know what you're talking about. Calm down and tell me what's going on. Dani, I need you." Taryn didn't yell but pitched her voice high enough to be heard over the noise in the bar.

Dani appeared at Taryn's elbow a few seconds later. "What's up?"

"I need you to cover the bar for me." Taryn jerked her head to indicate Ash standing on the other side.

"Okay." Dani stared at Ash. She must have sensed his anger because she straightened and stepped between them. "Do you want me to call security?"

"Thanks, Dani, but we're okay." She mouthed *I promise* to Dani then turned to Ash. "Let's go to the office," Taryn said, knowing he would follow her.

His accusations had stopped—for now—but tension radiated off him in waves. Her fight or flight instincts screamed that there was a pissed-off male behind her and she should run.

Fuck that. This was her bar. She wouldn't back down from a fight. Even with him.

She ignored him until she was in her chair with the barrier of the desk between them. Her power and the persona of the Jack were strongest here. "What's going on?"

She took a moment to study him. Perched on the edge of the visitor's chair, every muscle in his body was tight and he trembled with emotion. He looked ready to spring over her desk at any moment.

She swallowed. Hard.

"How could you do that to Hope?"

His accusation slapped her in the face. She clenched her hands and fought to keep her expression from betraying her pain. "I haven't done *anything* to Hope. You haven't told me where to take her once we get her out of the hospital." Her confusion was real, but she kept her tone calm.

"He told me! He said the plan to spring her from the hospital came from you."

Taryn froze as she processed his words. "Back up." She needed the facts, and she needed them without his emotional overload. "*He* who?"

Ash ignored her question.

"Hope isn't in the hospital?"

"No, she's out. Portia told me, but—"

Taryn raised her hand to stop him. He glared but stopped talking. Instead, he shot to his feet and paced the small office.

"Answer my question. He who?"

Ash practically exploded. "Just admit you had something to do with her disappearance!"

Part of her wanted to wrap her arms around him and

hold him tight. The other part wanted to punch him in the throat for speaking to her this way.

She kept her voice low and calm, like she did when she spoke to one of the girls fresh from the street. The ones so wounded that they couldn't quite believe they were free. "No. I'm not involved. The pieces are in place for this week."

"Why didn't you get her out sooner?"

She sighed. Taryn felt for him, she did, but goddamn, pick an accusation and stick with it.

Crossing her arms, she leaned back in her chair. "Your sister is in a coma." She chose her words carefully. Otherwise, she was likely to jump his shit the way he was doing to her. "I can't just whisk her from her hospital room and hide her in a hotel. You know how much care she requires." The list her sources had provided had been both extensive and expensive.

Apparently, being in a coma wasn't cheap.

"You said 'he.' Do you know who has her?"

"Caspar has her."

Taryn whistled. She'd heard of Caspar. He was like the hell lord of the hacker underground. You didn't cross him without consequences. What the hell had Ash done? "How do you know Caspar has her?"

Ash whipped his gaze up to meet hers. His emotional turmoil turned his gray eyes into a storm. "He told me."

"He told you," she repeated, as she struggled to process that piece of information. She'd known working with him against the Tremaine Corporation would be a problem, but this . . . This was next level. She'd never realized the depths Ash ran in. "Why would Caspar take your sister?"

"It doesn't matter." His voice was sharp. "Why did you give her to him?"

"I didn't do that. I *wouldn't* do that. To you or to Hope." Taryn was getting damn tired of defending herself.

"Then why did he say he'd gotten his plan from you?"

The accusation took her breath away, but she refused to let him know. "How did Caspar get her out?" It wasn't idle curiosity. If Taryn knew how Caspar had done it, she could compare it to her own plan.

"I spoke with one of the nurses on my way here," he admitted. "The hospital had already informed Portia that Hope was missing. The nurse told me what she knew. I might be able to access the videos later."

As Ash repeated what the nurse had told him, Taryn felt sick to her stomach. It was almost exactly the same plan she and Dani had created.

Her ire drained away and her shoulders slumped. "That's . . ." she paused. "That's *my* plan."

Ash didn't explode as she'd expected. He stared at her, the hurt in his eyes ripping her to shreds. "Why? Why would you give her to him?"

"It wasn't me." How did she make him believe her? "It's my plan, but Caspar didn't get it from me." The words hung in the air between them. The implications . . .

The situation pointed in a direction that she didn't want to believe. One that made her sick just considering it.

"If you didn't do it . . ."

Taryn was glad his anger had cleared enough to get his brain working again.

Her stomach churned. "I have a mole."

"Fuck!" His fists clenched and his jaw tightened. His anger was as visceral as hers. "Did you know?"

"That I had a mole? Of course not!" How the fuck could he ask her that? She rubbed her temples. It might explain a few things. Dammit. "Did you ever get the system here set up to detect Giselle's pimp?"

"What the fuck does that have to do with getting my sister back?"

Taryn took a deep breath, intentionally not reacting to his tone. Anyone else and they'd be done. "Yes or no?"

"No," he growled. "I needed you to set some parameters and we got distracted." His wild gesture at the room informed her about the distraction.

"Well, shit." Apparently neither of them had upheld their side of the bargain and here they were. "What does Caspar want in exchange for Hope?"

"Access to the Tremaine system."

Taryn whistled. That was a hefty price. "Does Portia know?"

Ash shoved his hands into his hair but didn't stop pacing. "Yeah, I was in her office when he called."

This situation just got worse and worse. She sagged back into her chair. "So, you have Caspar coming for you on one side and I'm assuming Tremaine Security on the other?"

He nodded.

"Anything else I should know about?"

"You're awfully fucking calm for someone who has a mole."

Ha! If only he knew. She may have looked calm on the outside, but on the inside, she alternated between wanting to punch something and wanting to puke. How had it come to this? And how could she get out of it?

"One of us needs a cool head." What a joke. "Sit down."

He growled and paced again.

"Sit. Down. We need a plan and I can't think with you pacing like that."

"Your last plan didn't work out so well, did it?" he snapped but dropped back into the chair.

The air between them pulsed with dark emotions that threatened to cloud her thinking. And she needed a clear head if she was going to get them out of this. The stakes hadn't been so high since she'd found the last Jack on the floor after a massive heart attack. The decision she'd made then had gotten her the bar. The decision she made now would help her keep it.

"When is Caspar supposed to contact you again?"

Ash sighed. "All he told me was soon."

"Fuck." She was quiet a moment, her mind churning. "You think he'll call?"

Ash shrugged. His shoulders were so tense they barely moved. The urge to comfort him was strong, though he'd probably shrug her off. She shoved the discomfort and doubt away, compartmentalizing them for now. There'd be time to lick her wounds later. Right now, Hope—and Ash—needed her clearheaded.

"I have a plan," Taryn said. "But you need to be all in."

He stared at her, his expression closed. "Depends on the plan."

She shook her head. "In or out? Do you still trust me?" Her breath caught and held while she waited for his answer.

Finally, a stiff nod.

"Out loud." She wanted no misunderstanding later.

His lips pinched, but he agreed. "Yes, I'm in. As long as it doesn't put Hope in more danger."

Taryn didn't think that was possible but wasn't going to poke the angry big brother. "It won't."

She took a deep breath, well aware she was about to

commit to the craziest plan she'd ever conceived. "Can you scramble your phone so Caspar can't trace you?"

Ash stared at her. "What the hell are you thinking?"

He'd find out soon enough. "Can you?"

A sharp nod.

"Right now?"

He pulled his phone out of his pocket. "Yes, if I can use your system."

Taryn pushed back from her desk and stood. She gestured to her chair. "It's all yours."

She swore he mumbled something under his breath.

He took her chair and within seconds his fingers flew over her keyboard with the expertise of a pianist. Taryn knew he was a skilled hacker, but this was beyond her wildest imaginings.

She watched the master at work. He must have been amazing before they took away his port. He could wreak havoc. And did, she realized, based on the trouble that had rained down on Tremaine Corporation a few months ago.

With a man like that at her side . . . they could do amazing things for the street girls. But she'd blown her chance at that.

"Done."

"You're sure?" Enough trouble had come her way lately.

"Yes. The signal will bounce around a bit. It'll look like I'm still in town but not here." He paused as if he were considering saying something else. "I also erased any information that might tell people that I've been coming here." He sounded sad about that.

The thought made her sad too. Would she ever see him again after she freed Hope?

CHAPTER 41

"I ASSUME you aren't going back to Tremaine headquarters now?" Taryn asked.

Ash flinched. He'd well and truly burned that bridge. In fact, he wouldn't be surprised if Portia tracked him down. She'd been pissed at the thought of him letting Caspar into the Tremaine network.

He logged out of Taryn's system and turned off the computer. It hadn't been lost on him that she'd let him use her network. He could have planted any number of bugs or backdoors and she wouldn't have noticed. Did that mean she trusted him? Should she trust him?

"What if Tremaine Security shows up here?" Had he brought trouble to Taryn's door? He was still mad at her for losing Hope, but he didn't want her harmed. And he was very afraid that corporate security would have no qualms about trampling innocents to get to him if Portia ordered it.

Taryn's smile was fierce. "I don't think so. It didn't work well for her the last time." He must have looked puzzled, because she added, "She sent them after Dizzie and Killian when they were hiding here. I don't take well to people coming into my bar and starting something. So, I finished it."

Well, damn. Ash hadn't realized that the Jack had been involved in Dizzie's escape. He'd tried to steer her clear of the bar, but maybe he shouldn't have. Taryn was a fierce protector.

"I can't go back to headquarters. Portia wants me under house arrest. If that happens, I may never leave the building again." He shuddered. "Once we rescue Hope, we'll have to leave the city immediately. In the meantime, can I stay here?"

Would she turn him away? The distance between them was growing, the accusations slowly tearing them apart and leaving ragged scars on his heart. He regretted his harsh words, but he hadn't been completely wrong. It was the fault of her people that Hope wasn't somewhere safe.

"I can show you to a room," she said.

"There's a cot in the hacker room. I can stay there," he said. "If that's all right?"

Disappointment flickered over her gaze, so fast he almost missed it.

"That's fine," she said.

"I can tinker while I'm down there. I assume your plan involves that setup?" he asked.

"You wait there for Caspar to contact you." She leaned her hip against the desk right next to him.

It would be so easy to pull her into his lap. But he didn't want her to freak out again—or to banish him from the bar. He had nowhere else to go.

"When Caspar calls you, ask for proof of life. He has to be expecting it, so he should be near Hope. We can track his location from that call. I'll take my team to rescue Hope. Meanwhile, you can use the hacking chair for the fight against Caspar. If you think it will work. Do you need to be at headquarters?"

Ash shook his head. "I've spent years in their system. I think I can use that knowledge to lure him in and then trap him the way they trapped me."

"That sounds dangerous," she whispered.

Ignoring the instincts that told him to take her hand and offer comfort, he just said, "Dangerous for him, with any luck. I'll have my team as backup, although they won't know it."

She stared at him, then exhaled. "Okay then. Sounds like we have a plan."

A team? A plan? It sounded more like a series of hopes but he'd take what he could get, as long as it brought the real Hope back safely.

"Once you go downstairs, you should probably stay there. Either Dani or I will bring you meals. That way no one at the bar sees you."

He understood her unspoken point. The mole in her business wouldn't know he was here. Except . . . "Dani saw me. And your bouncers."

"I trust Dani with my life." She didn't hesitate to defend her friend. "And the bouncer who tried to stop you is completely trustworthy too." She paused, her shoulders slumping slightly. "I think I know who the problem is. I need to take care of that."

She straightened and he watched her transition from Taryn back into the Jack. Taryn's softness was replaced by the Jack's hardness. Watching Taryn disappear into the role was more terrifying than the Jack alone.

"C'mon," she said. "Let's get this over with."

He should be agreeing with her, but why did those words hurt so badly?

CHAPTER 42

TARYN CLOSED the heavy door to the hacking room then sagged against it.

She'd accompanied Ash downstairs. They'd stopped for linens and a blanket, since the sheets on the cot down there probably hadn't been changed since before she took over. She'd waited around a few minutes, until it became clear that they weren't going to discuss anything that had just happened.

Being that close to Ash and yet feeling the distance between them had messed with her head—and her heart.

She'd used work as an excuse and left him down there. Even when she'd hesitated at the doorway, he hadn't turned around. Hadn't called her name.

Being close to Ash wasn't the only challenge she faced tonight.

She had a mole.

Someone in her bar—*in her home!*—was selling secrets to outsiders.

Though she couldn't bear the thought, Taryn had to take care of that problem before she could rescue Hope.

Strengthening her resolve, Taryn pushed off the door. The fact that Giselle's pimp had shown up at the bar—twice—had pissed her off. But once Giselle's second scan had come back clean, Taryn hadn't really considered her people as the source.

As she stalked down the hallway to the bar, Taryn considered her options. The old Jack had left a stash of less-than-legal instruments in one of the back rooms, but the thought of using them turned her stomach. She preferred less intrusive—less painful—methods.

Taryn knew her staff, many of them for years. That was why the betrayal broke her heart. One of her people—practically her family—had betrayed her.

And she thought she knew who.

When Taryn strode into the bar, Dani flashed her a huge smile. "Everything worked out between you two?"

Taryn's laugh wasn't a happy sound. "Not even remotely."

Dani's smile faded. "That sucks. I'm sorry. Anything I can do?"

Taryn shrugged. "Not about that." Maybe she and Ash would be able to work it out eventually, but there was a lot to do between then and now. "Would you give me five minutes then send Rhonda back to my office?"

Dani's frown deepened. "Sure. Everything okay?"

Taryn shook her head. She wanted to confide in Dani. Though her friend had noticed the problem first, it was Taryn's mess to clean up.

"Shit. Anything I can help with?"

"Maybe," Taryn said. "I'll let you know."

Taryn had just settled into her chair when there was a rap on her door. She took a long breath, then exhaled. She wasn't looking forward to this conversation.

"Come in." Her voice was heavy.

The door opened and Rhonda poked her head in. "You wanted to see me?"

"Take a seat." Taryn nodded toward the chair, just as she had a hundred times before.

While the other woman slid into the chair across the desk, Taryn took the opportunity to study her.

Rhonda's hair was limp. She wore long sleeves, something she rarely did, and moved slowly. All things Taryn should have noticed sooner. Dammit. She should've paid more attention after Dani brought up her concerns.

"When did you start using?" Taryn asked, skipping the pleasantries.

Rhonda paled and her shoulders drooped. She opened her mouth, then snapped it closed again.

"Think very carefully about how you want to answer that."

Rhonda straightened and crossed her arms over her chest defiantly. "Three months ago."

"What are you taking?"

"Vyne." Rhonda's tone dared her to make something out of it.

Taryn blanched. That shit was terribly addictive. It explained the long sleeves—continued use caused the veins to harden and turn green. That was what gave the drug its street name.

"Why, Rhonda? That stuff is scary bad for you." Despite her overall unhealthy appearance, Taryn still saw traces of the girl she'd rescued nine months ago. "You were doing so well."

She stared at Taryn. "Nightmares." Rhonda snapped out the word then her lips pinched closed again.

"Why didn't you come to me?"

She laughed. The sad sound made Taryn want to cry.

"How could you understand?" Rhonda asked in a shrill voice. "You've got this perfect life! No one threatens you. No one forces you to do anything you don't want to do."

"Rhonda." Taryn spoke softly and waited until she had Rhonda's full attention. "I've been in your shoes."

She gave Taryn a sour look. "Bullshit."

"I have. I started on the street. I told you that when you came here. All this," Taryn waved a hand in the air to indicate the bar, "was just a fluke."

Didn't she remember? Taryn told all the girls about her past when she brought them to Razor Jack's, so they'd know she understood the struggle they faced. Maybe not every detail, but enough that they'd know. That they'd believe.

"Is that why you bring us here? To rub our faces in it?"

Taryn fought the urge to bury her face in her hands. Where was Rhonda getting this stuff? Had she always been this angry, this self-destructive?

"I bring you here to help you get a fresh start." That was all she wanted for all the girls.

Rhonda was beginning to look like a mistake. But everything about her—her age, the length of time she'd been on the streets—had made her a prime candidate for Taryn's help.

Why had Dani and others succeeded where she didn't?

"Well, your fresh start sucks!"

The words hit Taryn like blows, but she powered through. "Where'd you get the Vyne, Rhonda?"

"From a guy."

This was like pulling teeth. "What guy?"

Rhonda shrugged.

Now that Taryn was paying attention, she saw how thin Rhonda had gotten. Her clothes hung on her frame.

Had she missed this because she was busy with Ash? Had getting involved with him been a mistake?

"A guy I met outside."

Hopefully that was the truth. The Jack had a strict rule about dealing in the bar. Taryn would come back to that. She needed more information before deciding Rhonda's fate. "Where did you get the money?"

Rhonda pouted. It might have been cute if she were a small child. Instead, she was just a woman who'd been dealt a bad hand and had made bad decisions on top of that.

"The money?" Taryn repeated her question when Rhonda didn't answer.

"Tips." She spat the word.

Taryn pondered her answer for a minute. It was true, the women who worked at Razor Jack's made good tips. Plus, Taryn paid them well. She didn't want returning to the streets to be an option.

Rhonda wasn't a bad waitress. She probably did okay. Dani likely did the best.

"How much are you spending?"

Rhonda spit out a number, then looked away.

Taryn assumed she was lying and immediately doubled that number. After three months, she had to be spending more than that. So where was the money coming from?

"How much did Giselle's pimp pay you?"

She hadn't been completely sure until Rhonda paled.

"I didn't . . . I don't know what you're talking about." Realizing she was digging a deeper hole, she clamped her mouth shut.

Dammit. Taryn had hoped she was wrong. "Cut the shit, Rhonda. Someone here gave him the information. You're the one with the expensive habit."

"What about your new boyfriend?" Rhonda sneered.

Taryn gave her props for trying to deflect suspicion. Even after their latest confrontation, Taryn had never worried that he'd sell her out. He was more likely to wound her heart.

Of course, Rhonda was doing a pretty fucking good job of that herself.

"That's not going to work." Taryn studied Rhonda. The other woman held her gaze for a few seconds, then dropped her eyes.

Taryn had won, although it was an empty victory. No one had ever rejected the fresh start before. Later, she'd analyze—probably overanalyze—what had gone wrong. For now, she needed all the information she could get.

"How much did he pay you?" she asked again.

The number Rhonda gave her seemed unbelievably low. Her habit must be worse than Taryn realized, if Rhonda couldn't judge the value of the information she sold.

"And the rescue plans?" A shot in the dark.

Rhonda mumbled another number.

Another *ridiculously* low number.

With a sinking stomach, Taryn asked, "Dizzie's location?"

Rhonda ducked her head.

Taryn's heart sank. All this time she'd thought it was a fluke. That a newsie or a patron had seen the fugitive courier and reported it to the Tremaine Corporation.

"How much?" she demanded. What Rhonda was doing —had done—risked everything Taryn had built.

This time the number was higher. Had Rhonda negotiated a better deal because she wasn't as addicted a month ago? Taryn would never know.

"Why?" How had she failed to help Rhonda?

Rhonda shrugged.

Taryn knew she wouldn't get anything more from her. "Oh, Rhonda. What am I going to do with you? I can't let you stay here." Saying those words nearly broke Taryn.

That statement made an impact on the other woman. She sucked in a sharp breath and her eyes widened. Rhonda's voice was barely audible when she asked, "What are you going to do with me?"

"I don't know." The absolute truth. This had never happened before. No one had ever refused the rescue, and no one had betrayed her like this. When women decided that working at the bar wasn't for them, Taryn helped them find their calling and wished them well.

What was she supposed to do now? Kick Rhonda back onto the street? Her stomach churned at the wrongness of that thought.

Taryn couldn't let her go. Rhonda knew too much now and had shown a willingness to sell whatever secrets she could. But she couldn't stay here, either. Taryn could never trust her again. Damned if she did, damned if she didn't. The old Jack had an easy solve—he'd make the problem go away permanently.

"You can't stay here," Taryn said gently. More gently than the other woman deserved.

"Why?" Tears welled in her eyes.

Real or fake? Taryn felt for her, she did. But her betrayal was too big and cut too deep.

"If you'd come to me when you started using, I could have helped you. If you'd come to me when you needed money, I would've helped you then, too." Taryn looked at her. "But you didn't. You dug yourself into a pit that I can't get you out of. People got hurt, kept getting hurt, because of you."

"Just some courier," Rhonda said with a smirk. "That wasn't even my fault. It was the crazy Tremaine lady's."

Strictly speaking, Rhonda wasn't wrong. Portia had run Dizzie over, but only after Tremaine Security had chased her from the bar.

That was beside the point. "Dizzie went on the run because you provided her location to the Tremaine Corporation."

"If it wasn't me, it would have been someone in the bar who saw them. Why shouldn't I get the money?"

"That's why you can't stay. You've put everyone here at risk. That's not okay." Had Rhonda always been this self-involved? Or was it the drugs? Probably a combination, Taryn realized with a pang of sorrow.

She could save people from the streets, but she couldn't save them from themselves.

Rhonda's lost look was quickly replaced by a glare that would've killed Taryn had it been physical. "Fine, I don't need you, bitch. I can make all the money I need from the secrets you've got here."

Taryn pressed her lips together. Well, this had taken a turn for the worse. She hadn't expected Rhonda to be a nasty addict.

Of course, she hadn't expected her to be an addict at all.

Taryn picked up her phone. "Daryl, could you come in here, please?"

Fear flickered in Rhonda's eyes until bravado replaced it. "You're bluffing."

Did Rhonda really think Taryn was playing games? She hadn't maintained her position as the Jack by being nice. "No, I'm not."

The door opened and Daryl filled the doorway. "Yes, ma'am?"

On the other side of the desk, Rhonda stiffened. This time, the fear in her eyes was permanent.

"Take Rhonda to the basement, please." Taryn's voice was cool, betraying none of the anger and regret that coursed through her.

To his credit, Daryl didn't flinch.

Rhonda did. "The b-b-basement?"

Taryn didn't owe her an explanation, so she just nodded.

Had everyone forgotten that the Jacks before Taryn had been utterly ruthless bastards?

Taryn gestured for Rhonda to stand. She did reluctantly.

"Take her to the cells," she repeated.

"Let's go." Daryl gripped Rhonda's shoulder and steered her through the door.

The door closed behind them. Taryn dropped her head into her hands. She hadn't solved that problem, only delayed it.

How was she going to deal with this mess on top of her other problems?

Hope's rescue was delayed until they located her. Ash was doing whatever it was hackers did. And she couldn't deal with the pimp until she saw him again.

How had things gotten so off track? She wanted to weep but couldn't spare the time.

CHAPTER 43

TARYN TOOK a seat at the far end of the bar. It was almost closing time and things were slowing down. Good. She wanted to sleep for at least a week but would be lucky to get a few hours with all the shit going on. If she could fall asleep at all.

"How'd it go with Rhonda?" Dani asked when she approached.

That was the last fucking thing Taryn wanted to talk about right now. "Give me a beer. Please."

Dani stopped what she was doing and focused on Taryn. "Everything okay?"

"Not even close." She would tell Dani everything, just not at this exact moment.

"You wanna talk about it?"

"Not right now." Taryn smiled her thanks when her friend set the beer in front of her. "What kept you here, Dani? Working at Razor Jack's?"

The other woman took half a step back, confusion on her face. "Why? What's going on?"

"I'm trying to understand . . ." Taryn took a sip of the

beer. Normally she'd take the time to enjoy the layers of flavor, but today had been nowhere near normal. "When I brought you here, why did you stay? Why didn't you run off? It's not a prison."

"You're freaking me out. Why are you asking me this?" Dani was pale and she'd lost her smile.

"It's not a trick or a trap. I really want to know. I need to know. To understand."

"I was a mess when I got here. The bar was warm." Dani shivered and wrapped her arms around her middle. "It was winter. It was so cold outside. And then I was warm."

"So, you stayed for the heat?" Taryn didn't judge. Whatever it took to keep her girls off the streets, she was for it.

"What?" Dani looked up, startled. Her gaze was far away.

"You stayed because it was warm. And you had food."

She gave Taryn a half smile. "Yeah, at first. Then it felt safe. Like you really meant it when you said I would be safe here. Over time, when you left me alone and didn't demand anything . . . Well, that's when I knew that it was better than life on the streets."

"Did you ever think about using?"

This time she hesitated. "Yes." Dani spoke slowly, drawing out the word. "More when I was on the streets, but a bit when I first got here. And when you put me in charge of the bar."

Whoa. Taryn hadn't expected that. "You never touched the alcohol."

Dani smiled. "No, by then it was only a thought. Not to mention, you keep really close track of the inventory." She pinned Taryn with a piercing gaze. "Why are you asking about this now?"

Taryn took a long drink while she pondered what to tell her. In the end, she decided on all of it. No one was nearby, but she still leaned close. "Rhonda's on Vyne. And she's been selling information."

"Oohh shit," Dani said on an exhale.

"Yeah."

"I hadn't noticed. I'm so sorry. I should have noticed."

Taryn shook her head. "My bar, my responsibility. Plus, you recognized something was wrong before I did."

"Is it bad?" Dani watched her intently.

"Yeah, really bad. She's the one who sold out Giselle. And Dizzie." Taryn was still struggling to wrap her head around the betrayal. What other information had Rhonda sold that Taryn wasn't aware of?

"Are you serious? How could she?" The outrage in Dani's voice echoed what Taryn had felt since she'd learned.

"Not to mention she sold the rescue plans and now Ash's sister is missing."

Dani's mouth dropped open but no sound came out.

Taryn laughed, though there was no humor in it. "Yeah, that was my reaction, too. She fucked us over a million ways."

"What are you going to do?"

That was what Taryn loved about Dani. She always bounced back and she was always practical.

"I have no idea. She obviously can't stay here, but she knows too much for me to let her go. I had Daryl put her in one of the basement cells for now. Where she hopefully can't do any more damage."

Dani paled. "Can we get her help?"

Taryn wrapped her hands around the pint glass. Her

head dropped and her shoulders slumped. "I don't know. It depends on how deep she is with the Vyne."

"Are her veins green?" Horror coated Dani's voice.

"She was wearing long sleeves, so I couldn't tell. I'm afraid that they are."

"Oh no," Dani said. "By the time that happens, it's always fatal."

"Yeah, that's what I've heard too. Although I've never heard of anyone living for very long after they tried it."

The silence that fell between them was pensive. From all accounts, Vyne was a horrible way to die.

Dani blew out a breath. "How can I help?"

"I need you to keep this place running, no matter what. Ash and I are going to try to locate Hope and then figure out how to rescue her. For real this time." She caught Dani's eye. "If you can handle it, I'd like to give you the list of supplies we'll need to set up a room for her here."

"Of course. Do you think it's safe to have her here?"

"Right now, I think it's best that she's near Ash until they can leave town. And I'm pretty sure he's not going back to Tremaine headquarters."

"Consider it done," Dani said.

Taryn grabbed her hand and squeezed. "Thank you. I can't do this without you."

Dani laid her hand on top of Taryn's. "You could, but you don't have to."

"That means more than you could ever know." Tears welled in Taryn's eyes and she blinked them away.

"Get some sleep," Dani said gently. "It sounds like you've got another busy day tomorrow."

CHAPTER 44

ASH SAT on the floor in front of the hacker's chair. He wasn't sure how long he'd been down here. After the meeting in Taryn's office, she'd provided him with some blankets for the cot in the corner and then left him. He'd come downstairs, dropped the blankets on the bed, and then puttered around the consoles and monitors.

There wasn't actually all that much to do. Earlier in the week, he'd taken care of all the upgrades, cleaned the dust off all the electronics and other surfaces, and generally made sure everything was in working order.

Now all he could do was stare at the chair. In some ways it represented his greatest wish: to hack into the network directly. Taryn had offered him that chance and he'd refused it. He ran his hand over his port. All that separated him from that now was about three feet and a little bit of skin.

The door above opened and he tensed. He wasn't ready to face Taryn yet. The scene in her office had been terrible. Worry for Hope had overridden every other thought. The things he'd accused her of . . .

Yes, Hope was missing because of her plan, but he couldn't blame her for someone else's betrayal. He knew too well how quickly plans could go to shit when you'd been sold out. He owed her an apology.

Ash stood and dusted his hands over his pants. He tilted his head. The footsteps on the stairs didn't sound like Taryn's confident stride. They were tentative. He stepped back into a shadowed corner. If it wasn't Taryn, who was it?

"Hello? Ash?" Dani's voice called out softly.

What was she doing down here?

"Yeah." He shifted so he was just outside the shadow.

"Oh good, you're down here." She came down the stairs the rest of the way, but hovered at the bottom, one hand on the banister.

"Is everything okay?" Was this a trick? Was Taryn wrong and Dani shouldn't be trusted?

She didn't say anything for long seconds. Her gaze traveled over him, although he wasn't sure what she could see in the dim light.

"Do you care for her?" she asked abruptly.

Not what he'd been expecting at all. "Taryn?" he asked while trying to suss out why she was asking.

"Yes, obviously," she snapped.

Why was it any of her business? But he'd noticed that Taryn and the people who worked for her rarely did anything without a reason. So he cautiously answered, "Yes."

"Enough to put your ego or whatever other shit this is aside?" She waved her hand at the room generally.

Was she asking him to put Hope aside? Because that would never happen. Almost anything else, though . . . yeah, he'd put it aside for Taryn. "What's the matter? Is something wrong?" Something had to be wrong, because no way would Taryn have sent Dani in her stead.

"She told you about the mole." It wasn't a question, but he nodded anyway. "She found her. And the leak was more than just your sister."

"Shit." That had to be a powerful blow.

"Yeah." Dani paused and steeled herself for whatever she was about to say. "She needs you."

"For what?" He didn't understand.

"To be with her. To comfort her. She's devastated, and I can't do anything for her." She clenched her hands at her sides. "I think you can. But you have to go to her. She won't ask. She's got too much of the Jack in her to ask for help or comfort."

Ash was gobsmacked. Of all the requests, he hadn't expected that.

Could he do it? They'd been fighting just a couple of hours ago. He hadn't had anyone to comfort him after the betrayal that led to Hope's coma and it had been awful. The guilt and worry had been overpowering. He hated to think of Taryn suffering that way.

"Take me to her," he said.

CHAPTER 45

TARYN TOSSED AND TURNED. The beer hadn't knocked her out like she had hoped and she hadn't been able to turn off her brain. She couldn't stop thinking about Rhonda and playing back the last few months over and over. Surely there was some clue that she'd missed. Some way she could have stopped this. Should have stopped this.

A soft knock on the door stopped the latest spiral into the past. Dammit. Nothing good ever happened at this hour.

Flinging the covers off, she shoved her feet into her boots and stomped toward the door. "What's wrong?" she asked as she flung the door open.

Dani stood in the doorway. "Nothing new," she said. "But I knew you'd have trouble sleeping. I brought you something to help with that."

She stepped out of the way and Ash slid into view.

"What the hell, Dani?" Taryn growled. She didn't have time for this right now.

Who was she kidding? Her walls were down and Taryn

didn't have the protections in place around her heart for this right now.

"You'll thank me later." Dani shoved Ash toward the doorway. He wasn't expecting it and stumbled forward. Taryn had to let go of the door to get out of the way.

Dani grabbed the handle and pulled it closed. Leaving Taryn alone with Ash.

Her best friend's matchmaking was truly inappropriate and they were going to have words.

"Dani said you identified the mole. She thought you might need some company." His voice was gentle. Quite the difference from when he was raging at her earlier.

"And she brought you here for what? To yell at me some more?" She was cranky and tired and sad. She didn't want to spar with him. She just wanted to crawl back into bed, pull the covers over her head, and pretend that this hadn't happened.

"That's not why I'm here." Ash turned his head, studying her room. Her private space.

What did he see when he looked around? Razor Jack's was hers, but this room really represented who she was. She'd combined two rooms to create her living space. The entire space was decorated in soft neutrals with hints of metallics and blues and greens threaded throughout. It was her home and her refuge and her safe space.

And now Dani had let in the biggest danger to her heart.

"Then why are you here?"

"I've been where you are, Taryn. I remember the rage and the hurt and the sense of betrayal like it was yesterday. I get it. I'm here to listen." He shoved his hands in his cargo pants. "Or I can go." He took a step toward the door.

"Wait," she said. If she let him leave now, she knew that

they would never be close again. She didn't want that, even if he was going to leave the city. "You're talking about your last hack." He'd told her about the betrayal.

He nodded.

"Does the feeling ever go away?"

His lips quirked in a sad smile. "It hasn't yet."

"Dammit," she said with a sigh.

Taryn padded over to her couch and kicked off her boots. She gestured for him to join her. He took the cushion next to hers.

She curled her legs under her and leaned toward him. "Is this okay?"

"Yeah," he said, his voice soft.

She pulled his arm around her and leaned close. The heat of his body warmed her. She didn't dress skimpily for sleep—she'd dealt with too many late-night emergencies—but she briefly wished she wore something sexier than calf-length pajama bottoms and a T-shirt.

"It was one of the waitresses," she told him quietly. "She's on Vyne and has been selling our secrets to feed her habit."

"That's some nasty stuff," he said.

"I didn't even notice. This is my fault."

"She's the one who chose the drugs. You can't blame yourself."

"I know. But it's hard not to." She rested her head on his shoulder. "And I don't know what to do with her. I can't keep her on, but I can't put her back on the street either."

"Back on the street?"

"I rescued her from the street. Gave her a place to live, a job. I would have arranged for any training she wanted, but she just never seemed to . . . thrive. I failed her." She choked back a sob.

Ash's arms tightened around her and he tugged her onto his lap. For once she had no desire to call out his manhandling. Snuggling into him felt so good, she might give him a permanent pass.

"Do you, uh, do that often? Rescue girls from the street."

"Every couple months," she said tiredly.

"The teenager I saw coming out of your office a few days ago?"

"The newest," she murmured.

"Huh," he said, his chin against her temple. "I really picked the perfect person for Hope, didn't I?"

Her only answer was a soft snore.

CHAPTER 46

ASH'S PHONE VIBRATED. He groped for it, encountering a warm body curled into his side. What the hell?

His eyes popped open. This wasn't his room. He didn't have a couch. Especially not one this comfortable. He shifted and felt the soft warmth all along his front. He looked down and nearly jumped off the couch.

Which would be a really fucking stupid idea. He was curled around Taryn's sleeping form, his arm around her waist, her head resting on his biceps. It felt . . . right.

The memory of Taryn falling asleep on his lap came back to him. He hadn't wanted to disturb her, so he'd sat there until he'd apparently dozed off too.

His phone buzzed again. Unfortunately, he didn't have the luxury of not disturbing her this time. He ducked his head close to hers and whispered, "Taryn, time to wake up."

Ash knew the moment she woke. Her body stiffened against him. Just as quickly, she relaxed again. "I didn't expect this," she said quietly.

"Neither did I. And I really wish I didn't have to disturb

this perfect moment, but someone's calling. I have to get it—it might be Caspar."

She scrambled to sitting and he immediately missed the press of her body against his. He followed her upright and dug into his pocket for his phone. The caller ID was blank.

"This is it," he said. He answered in audio-only mode. "Yeah?"

"Your manners need some work." Caspar's voice wasn't distorted this time.

Asshole. "I didn't realize you were calling about etiquette lessons."

"Oh, Ash. Did they take away your sense of humor when they took your port?"

His hand started to reach for his neck before he stopped. "Where's my sister?"

After an annoyed silence, Caspar tsked. "Not even a please?"

Ash said nothing. He wasn't sure how long he could hold on to his temper.

"Fine. You want your sister? Do exactly as I say."

"Proof of life first." Ash forced the words out. He hated using his baby sister as leverage. Taryn squeezed his hand. "If anything has happened to her, you're mine."

"You can't catch me, boy. But I anticipated this. Turn your video on. I'll show you."

Ash shook his head even though Caspar couldn't see him. "You don't need to see me. Send the video, I'll see it just fine."

For long seconds, nothing happened. Then the phone screen filled with an image of Hope in a hospital bed. Ash held the phone in front of him, his fingers curled tightly around the comm. Taryn leaned close, peering at the screen.

Familiar beeps and whirs told him the equipment was

active. His heart hurt, the way it did every time he saw her small, still figure. Hope had overflowed with energy and passion.

It was nearly impossible to take his focus off his sister, but Ash needed clues to her location.

It definitely wasn't her hospital room. Instead of gleaming white walls, grim beige ones surrounded the bed. The equipment was older, but he recognized the machines as the same types Hope had had at the Tremaine hospital. That was good. He hoped she was getting the care she needed.

The screen cut to black. "There, you've seen her," Caspar said gleefully.

"Bring it back." Pain surged through Ash.

"You wanted proof of life. I gave it to you."

Ash clenched his jaw. When he got his hands on Caspar . . . "You proved you have her, but that video could have been taken at any time. Show me the monitor with the current date and time to prove she's still alive."

The screen flickered back on, zoomed to an extreme closeup of the monitor. Ash confirmed that it was now and watched the lines and listened to the rhythm of the beeps. After five years of visits, he knew most of them by heart. He closed his eyes and focused.

Beep, beep. Beep, beep. Nothing unusual.

"Thank you." He had to play the game, even if he didn't know all the rules.

When he opened his eyes, the screen was black once again. Although it nearly killed him, Ash knew that he wouldn't get anything more from Caspar until he did what the other hacker wanted.

"What do you want?"

"I told you. I want into the Tremaine system."

"How do you expect me to get you that?" He gripped Taryn's hand hard.

He hated the thought of betraying Portia, but he had to save his sister. If only there was a way to do both.

Caspar tsked again. "You're a hacker, Fēnix. Hack."

"No shit, Caspar. I can get in just fine. How do I let you in? Where will you be waiting? How do I contact you? Are we supposed to do this side by side like partners?" Sarcasm coated Ash's voice. He was trying to get a rise out of Caspar. Maybe the other man would make a mistake.

After a short silence, Caspar spoke again. "Valid points. I'm sending you a piece of code. Use this to let me know you're in. At that precise moment, no sooner. Don't try to snoop around and ping it. It's alarmed quite heavily."

Ash's phone pinged and he stared at the file. He wouldn't know for sure what it did until he opened it, but odds were good he could use the packet to track Caspar. His warning was almost enough to stop Ash from trying. Almost.

Ash had too much on the line to ignore such a valuable lead. There had to be a way around Caspar's security. He just had to find it. Find his location, find his chair. Hopefully Hope would be in the same place.

"You have twenty-four hours to get me into the Tremaine system. After that, well, let's just say it becomes a lot more expensive to care for a comatose person."

Ash's stomach dropped. "How long will you need inside?"

"However long it takes."

God, how had he ever found this asshole worthy of emulating? Today, Caspar reminded Ash of a petulant child. "Give me a way to contact you inside the network."

The corporate network wasn't a physical space, but it

did have dimensions and a structure. With the right directions, you could maneuver easily through the space. But finding another person, especially one trying to stay hidden, was more difficult.

Caspar sent Ash a tiny piece of code. To the average user, it didn't look like much and it certainly wouldn't tell a non-hacker anything. But Ash had worked with Caspar and was used to things like this.

Like the first code, he segregated it from his main comm system as soon as he received it. Ash wouldn't put it past Caspar to send a virus.

"I'll let you know when I'm in and ready to receive visitors. It will be a small window of opportunity, so be ready," Ash said.

"I was born ready." Caspar's reply sounded like a cut-rate superhero.

"Who's watching my sister while you're under?"

"Lots of people," he said. "Your twenty-four hours have already started." With that threat, Caspar hung up.

"Fuck!"

For a second, Ash considered warning the Tremaine Corporation that they would be under attack. He might have considered it a few days ago, based on his growing friendship with Portia Tremaine. Even that had been put at risk with Hope's abduction.

No, calling the company wasn't in the cards. Hacking them was.

He was right back where he'd started five years ago. Ash hoped he didn't screw up the same way.

"Well, he seems delightful," Taryn said, startling a laugh out of him.

"That's one word for it." The rest of them weren't nearly as nice.

"What do you think? Do you know where Hope is?" she asked.

Ash shook his head. "I think he's got a camera feed on her. When he said lots of people are watching her, I think that's true. I think he set up a stream so members of the hacker collective can keep an eye on her."

"That was the sense I got, too. Can you hack into the feed?" She shifted on the couch so she sat perpendicular to him, one bare foot on the ground. But she never let go of his hand.

"I don't know." He leaned against the couch back. "Probably. But would that harm Hope?"

She raised a brow. "What do you mean?"

"I think it's a trap. He'll be watching for any attempts to hack that feed. Waiting for it. He warned me about doing any kind of trace on the code he sent me. I have to assume he's covered any and all electronic access points."

"That's it? You're giving up?" Her disappointed tone hit him deep inside.

"No." His denial was vehement. "I have an idea how to work around the code problem, but Hope is a different story. She's in a room somewhere. I couldn't see any distinguishing features in the room."

"Did you record it?"

"I did." He called up the recording.

"Give me a minute." She released his hand and popped up from the sofa. Curious what she was doing, he nevertheless enjoyed the view.

She returned a moment later with a notepad. "Play it again." She leaned close and he wrapped an arm around her so they could both view the tiny screen.

Taryn listened to the call and watched the video. Then she watched the video again. She bit her lip and stared at the device. She watched a third time. "Can you put the video up on that?" She pointed to the wall-mounted screen tucked into a corner.

"Sure." A few quick swipes and Hope's room appeared onscreen.

Taryn got up and stood right in front of him. "Zoom in on the equipment."

"What are you looking for?" he asked. Watching her work was fascinating, even though he had no idea what she was doing.

"Brands, models. We can use that information to identify where they're holding her."

"I don't have time to track all this stuff down. Even if I did, it would take me forever. We don't have time for this."

"Did I ask *you* to track anything?" Taryn asked.

"No."

"Exactly." She pinned him with a look. "I have someone who can look into it for me."

They worked together in near silence. She scribbled notes and pointed at parts of the screen and he captured the best-quality images he could.

Taryn was amazing. She pointed out details that he hadn't noticed.

"Okay, I think that's all of them," she said several minutes later. "Send them to me and I'll get someone on it."

That done, they stared at each other.

"Are you going to give Caspar what he wants?" she asked quietly.

Ash came to stand beside her. He stared at the frozen image of Hope in the hospital bed. "I don't want to. I hate the idea of Caspar getting what he wants."

"Can you warn them?"

He bumped his shoulder against hers. "I could. But I

don't think I should." He blew out an exasperated breath. "I know Tremaine's weaknesses. I can probably get in with no one noticing. The question is, do I let Caspar in and try to trap him? Or ignore his request."

She slipped her arm around his waist. "I think you have to plan to let him in. At least until I can get to Hope."

"We have less than a day," he reminded her. Taryn had proven herself to be extremely capable, but could she work miracles?

"The sooner I know she's safe, the sooner I can get on with making Caspar pay for taking her."

"We'll figure it out, Ash."

"I hope so." He rested his forehead against her temple. "I should have focused on getting us out of there sooner. Instead, I took the easy route and let the company hold on to her instead."

She placed her hand on his arm. "No one blames you for that. Taking care of a comatose patient is difficult. I've never done it, but the list of supplies we'll need is astounding."

"There might be a cure." He still had a hard time saying the words out loud.

"For brain burn?"

Ash nodded. "It's in one of the files I hacked."

"Why doesn't anyone know about it?" Brown eyes wide, she stared up at him.

"Because the Tremaine Corporation hasn't released it."

Her jaw dropped. He knew the feeling.

"How did you find it?"

"I've learned as much about the company—and its secrets—as I could. I wanted to find something I could use as leverage to free us."

"Did you?"

He laughed. It wasn't a cheerful sound. "Never the right thing. I thought I had it last month, but that went . . . badly."

"Dizzie and the bombing." It wasn't a question.

He nodded.

"Why didn't you use the cure on your sister?"

"I'm not a doctor. I didn't want to cause her any more harm." He smiled ruefully. "Plus, I couldn't understand most of the information."

Her answering smile was gentle. "What are you going to do about the cure once we've got Hope?"

He liked the sound of *we*. "Find someone who can help?" He really didn't know. For so long, his plans never extended past getting free of the Tremaine Corporation.

"And then?"

Ash's shoulders sagged. He didn't know if he'd even survive the next couple days. "If I beat Caspar, there's still the Tremaine Corporation to worry about." Portia would never forgive him for what he was about to do. "I have no idea. Stay away from any whiff of the corporations, I guess."

"There are opportunities outside the corporations." She may have been trying for neutral, but there was something in her voice that sounded an awful lot like hope.

Did she mean what he thought she meant? "Not if you're on the run."

She didn't say anything for a long moment. "Fair enough."

CHAPTER 47

CROWDED in the back of the ambulance, Taryn's friends and associates gathered around her. She'd called in nearly every favor for this rescue, but she'd made her peace with that. She owed Ash. His sister had been taken on her watch and she'd do whatever necessary to atone for that.

"Thank you." She acknowledged every member of the small but mighty team she'd been able to assemble on short notice today. One of her contacts had identified this building as a probable location through recent medical equipment sales. Although this was a rush job, Taryn had sent another woman to scout the location. She'd confirmed the presence of a patient but had been unable to get close enough to verify that it was Hope.

Ash had been ecstatic at the news and had wanted to come but she'd vetoed that. He needed to prepare for his showdown with Caspar. Plus, she didn't want to worry about his emotions overruling his common sense on such a delicate mission.

Sasha, who was an EMT, drove the ambulance. Taryn was thrilled she'd been available today because she had no idea how otherwise they'd transport a coma patient without medical assistance.

Gen was the computer technician. Technically, she was a hacker, although she wasn't on the same level as Ash. She was the one who'd backtracked the video feed and would loop the video feed and manage any of the other technical needs they encountered. Allie was a creative thinker and an accomplished thief. Daryl—the only man on her team—would provide the muscle.

Though Taryn had tried to cover every contingency, worry gnawed at her. This was the shortest timeline she'd ever worked under. What if she'd forgotten something?

"Let's go over this one more time," Taryn said. "Gen will loop the video and get us through the door. She'll also get Hope's machines ready to travel. Sasha will be the transportation out of here. Daryl and I will take first crack at any guards who might be in the room."

She studied their faces. "Keep your eyes open and jump in where you see a need. Questions?"

No one had any.

Taryn hoped they were ready. There'd been no time to practice. "Okay, let's do this." She quelled the nerves unsettling her stomach.

Gen huddled over her tablet in the back of the ambulance. A small laser projected a keyboard onto a smooth shelf and her fingers clicked the virtual keys.

"I've looped the video. I didn't find any alarms, but if this guy's as good as you say, they're probably hidden."

"It's a chance we'll have to take." Taryn hated the idea, but they had a very tiny window to make this work. She hated that they had to stage this rescue during the day.

"One of the rooms on the main floor is drawing a lot of

power. It's the same one we had a patient sighting in, so I think this is the right place."

It was a relief to have that confirmed. That the room was on the main floor was a bonus. It would be a lot harder to get a hospital bed or a stretcher down multiple floors.

"Ready?"

Everyone nodded.

Damn, she was proud of her people. Their success, their willingness to help, almost made up for Rhonda's betrayal.

Sasha circled the block and they exited the ambulance in ones and twos, approaching the building from different directions. No need to draw attention arriving in a big group.

Daryl and Gen went first so Gen could pick the lock.

Gen made quick work of it. Daryl flashed a thumbs-up.

Taryn walked quickly up the front steps and took the lead through the open door, trying to act like she belonged there.

Her jacket was lined with protective gear. Arms loose and hands free, she studied her surroundings, ready for anything. A number of apartment doors lined the hallway. She didn't hear much. Hopefully everyone was at work, leaving fewer people to notice them.

Halfway down the hall, Taryn stopped and turned. Which door to choose?

"Gen, would you scan again?"

Gen nodded and pulled a tech contraption out of her pocket. It looked homemade and probably was.

Turning this way and that, she aimed the device in every possible direction, including up and down.

"Not detecting any people. No live feeds except the one we looped. That's coming from the end of the hall. If there's anything or anyone waiting here, they're very well cloaked."

"Okay," Taryn said, still uneasy. Would Caspar really leave Hope unguarded?

Still quiet but with more purpose in her stride, she walked the long hallway until she arrived at the closed door at the end.

Taryn pressed her ear to the wood. Was that . . . beeping?

The steady beeps were similar to the ones she'd heard in Ash's video. But what if it was something else, like a bomb?

Taryn turned and looked at her team. She hated to risk them. "Gen, can you tell what's behind this door?"

Gen scanned the door and the surrounding hallway with a different device.

She shook her head. "No."

"Everyone get back. Just in case."

There was some grumbling, but no one argued.

"Get back." Taryn put her hand on the knob and turned slowly. The door opened quietly.

Without the barrier of the door, the beeping was louder.

Everyone took a position along the walls while Taryn took a cautious step into the room. One step, then another.

The monitors emitted an eerie blue glow and Taryn couldn't see much in the dim light. The open door blocked the entire right side of the room from view. The left was clear, so she stepped farther into the room.

The door swung toward her and caught her in the shoulder. "Ow." The impact knocked her back a few steps.

The momentum carried her to the left and away from the door. The impact reverberated along her metal arm. If they'd hit her flesh and blood limb, the pain would have likely incapacitated her.

Someone was here.

"You missed someone," Taryn growled over her shoulder.

"Shit! Recalibrating!" That was Gen.

Taryn focused on staying out of reach and locating her attacker in the dim room. The eerie light from the monitors cast shadows everywhere.

Taryn looked right and left as she stepped deeper into the apartment.

"Got it! To your right!" Gen's warning came just in time.

Taryn turned her torso and hips to face the threat.

A fist swung toward her face.

She ducked.

The fist whistled by, clipping her on the jaw rather than knocking her out.

Motherfucker!

Pain radiated through her jaw. She drew on her lessons from living with the previous Jack and forced the pain back.

Her assailant had landed two hits already. She wouldn't let him get a third in.

Rolling onto the balls of her feet, she stayed loose, ready to dodge the next time he took a swing. Right shoulder angled toward where she thought he was, she drew her arms into a defensive position.

Her eyes finally adjusted to the light and she saw the dark figure approaching. Based on his punches, he wasn't augmented.

Not the way she was.

Never taking her eyes off his shoulders, she watched for signs that he was about to attack.

His shoulder twitched.

Taryn leaned back to avoid the punch. Air rushed past her cheek.

She stepped into his space, planted her foot, and threw a punch with her right hand. A solid punch with all her body weight behind it.

Right on the button.

He dropped like a stone.

Taryn kicked him in the stomach and danced back.

No grunt, just dead weight.

Her shoulder throbbed, but the pain disappeared quickly. Her arm was designed to dissipate the kinetic force before it reached muscle and bone.

Her shoulder felt a hell of a lot better than her face.

"Can you see anyone else, Gen?" she asked quietly.

A soft curse and the rattle of equipment. "No one else. Sorry about that."

"It happens, Gen. Don't worry about it." Taryn surveyed the room. "Okay, people. Gen says it's clear and I don't see anyone else either, so let's get in and get Hope out."

Taryn led the way. The figure in the bed was so small, so still. Her heart broke for Ash. She stepped out of the way while Gen entered the room. She was followed by Daryl and Sasha with the gurney.

Taryn stayed out of the way, giving them room to study the setup. "We good?"

Sasha surveyed the setup for another minute.

"Yeah, we're good. We need to do this my way, though. Okay?" She looked at Taryn when she said that.

"You're the boss," Taryn agreed easily. She was all about letting professionals use their talents.

As if Taryn had uttered the magic words, Sasha took charge of the room.

"You need to pack up the equipment in this order, Gen." She pointed at every piece. "First, second, third, fourth. The first two can go under the gurney. The others will need to be tucked near her on top."

The tech worked quickly, carefully shifting equipment, until it was time to move the most important piece in the room—Hope herself.

Sasha arranged everyone around Hope's bed. "On three. Super carefully. Allie, make sure you've got that machine. It's the most important job."

"One. Two. Three."

On the final count, they lifted Hope on the sheet.

She was so light.

Ash said she was eighteen when they were caught, so she was twenty-three now. The same age as some of the women helping Taryn right now.

Poor Hope. She'd lost almost a quarter of her life. And might miss it all.

"Fucking Tremaines," Taryn muttered.

Taryn vowed to help Ash with the brain burn cure. She'd do whatever she could to help the still girl on the gurney.

"What's that?" Gen asked.

"Sorry, nothing." Generally, Taryn tried to stay neutral. It was better for business if she didn't get too close to any corporation.

But the Tremaine Corporation's treatment of Hope was making that difficult. Phillip Tremaine had a lot to answer for.

"We ready to go?"

Sasha didn't answer right away. She checked leads and connections, tubes and power cords. Taryn didn't think they'd broken anything. Hope's machines sounded like they were beating at the same tempo that they had in the beginning.

"Ready." Sasha held on to one side of the floating gurney and Daryl grabbed the opposite side.

Taryn took the lead, fists up, ready to take on anyone who challenged them. Gen came next, followed by the rest of the rescue party.

Leaving the building was just as eerily silent as their arrival had been.

Taryn paused at the front door. The ambulance was still parked where they'd left it.

Good. Taryn didn't have a plan B.

"Gen, you getting anything new?" Taryn kept her eyes on the street.

"The video is still looping. No one seems to have noticed. I'm not detecting anyone outside."

"Great, let's get the fuck out of here."

Taryn stepped out and stood watch as the others carried Hope out. She hated being in the open like this, but at least this neighborhood wasn't swarming with people right now.

Getting Hope out of the Tremaine hospital would have been doable—her plan had obviously worked—but it would have been twice as stressful.

The party made their way to the ambulance as quickly as they could.

No one approached. Nothing went wrong.

Taryn didn't like it at all.

Sasha took charge again when they reached the ambulance, getting Hope strapped down and settled.

Taryn stood on the back step, watching the action, studying Hope's face. She felt like she knew her after all her time with Ash.

"Everything okay, boss?" Gen asked.

"Yeah. Just grateful we got her out."

Taryn hopped into the back of the ambulance and sat

next to Hope. She took the young woman's thin hand in hers and held it tight. "We're taking you to your brother, Hope," she said quietly. "He can't wait to see you."

Sasha and Allie settled into the seats in the front of the ambulance and everyone else crowded into the back, taking care not to jostle Hope or any of the equipment.

"Take us in the back way, Sasha," Taryn said. "Gen, keep an electronic eye out for anyone following us."

Both women murmured their assent.

"Thank you. I couldn't have done this without your help," Taryn told her team once they were underway. "If you owed me a favor, your debt is paid."

CHAPTER 48

ASH PACED the hacker room while Taryn was gone. She'd left several hours ago after receiving information about Hope's whereabouts and he hadn't heard from her since. He'd tried to go with her, but she refused. No, it wasn't Taryn who refused. It was the Jack. He was learning the two sides to her. There was the softer side that worried about the women she rescued and then there was the ruthless side that got the job done—for a price. And the price in this case was Ash staying here.

Impatience warred with fear and the fear was winning. Was Taryn safe? Was Hope?

Dani had stopped by briefly to ask if he needed something and he'd snarled at her. She'd given him a look that she must have learned from Taryn and told him to stay down here.

Where else would he go? Right now, this room was the safest place for him if he wanted to stay off the Tremaine radar. Was this the future he had to look forward to if he stayed with Taryn? Waking up with her in his arms had felt so right, but this . . . This would break him.

"Fuck!" He shoved his fingers into his hair.

"Ash?"

He whirled around at the sound of Taryn's voice. "Is she safe? Did you get her?"

"Yes, we got her. They're settling her into one of the rooms upstairs."

"Thank you!" He surged forward and threw his arms around her. She stiffened briefly, then returned the hug. "Thank you," he said again into her hair. "Is she okay?"

Taryn nodded against his chest. "My EMT says she's fine."

He pulled back just slightly. "You have an EMT?" When she nodded again, he asked, "Did you rescue her too?"

Pink touched her cheeks. "I helped her start a new life."

"You are fucking amazing, you know that, right?"

"Hardly," she said.

He squeezed her again. "Can I see her?"

"Of course." Taryn stepped out of his embrace but grabbed his hand. He smiled as she led him up the stairs.

The room she showed him fit somewhere between Hope's stark white hospital room at Tremaine and the seedy location where Caspar had held her. The walls were light blue and the overhead light gave the room a bright glow. It was comfortable, homey with a light citrus scent that said it had been cleaned recently. "We have a doctor who visits regularly. She'll be here tomorrow to check on Hope."

Taryn handed him an old-fashioned key. "Here, so you can visit whenever you want. Just . . . be careful, okay? I've explained to the women who stay here that you'll be visiting, but they're still healing and I don't want to spook them."

Wrapping his fingers around the key, he recognized the enormous trust she was placing in him. "Thank you."

"I'll leave you to your visit." She slipped out of the room, leaving him alone with his sister.

He took a deep breath and watched the monitors. The beeps and lines and numbers all looked right. He wasn't a doctor, not by a long stretch, but over time, he'd come to recognize what the monitors said about Hope's health. They never changed, which was both good and bad. He still hated that she was stuck in limbo like this.

They'd obviously cleared out whatever furniture had once been in this room in order to bring in Hope's bed and equipment, but a chair had been left by her bedside. He appreciated that touch.

He sank into it and reached for Hope's hand. Her medical bracelet was gone, probably removed by Caspar. She wasn't very good as a hostage if she could be tracked. At least Ash didn't have to worry about her being tracked here. He hoped.

"I think you'll be safe here, Hope," he said, while stroking her fingers. "I'm sorry Caspar was able to take you. I never wanted you anywhere near that man, even when we were working for him. I should have kept you out of this life." He laughed. Like Hope would have allowed that. She'd wanted to do whatever her brother was doing and had a will of steel. She'd have found a way with or without him.

"I don't know what will happen next. I never really believed that we'd ever be free of the Tremaine Corporation. And I don't know if we are. And Caspar will probably come after us again. Not to mention Portia." He dropped his head to the bed. "I'll keep you safe, though. I promise."

He just had no idea how to keep that promise.

CHAPTER 49

"I NEED you to uncover my port."

Taryn looked up at Ash. He stood in the doorway of her office. "Why?"

"I'll need it to do the hack for Caspar."

Her brow wrinkled in confusion. "We have Hope. He doesn't have leverage over you any longer."

His sigh carried a wealth of frustration. "I know. But he knows I'm around and I don't think he'll stop coming for me."

"What about when you leave town?" Getting the words out was painful.

His gray eyes met hers. "It doesn't matter where I am physically when it comes to the network. He'll always be looking for me, always watching. I don't want to be always looking over my shoulder on a hack." Caspar was one of many loose ends he needed to tie up.

She sighed. "I understand. Are you sure you need your port opened? Can't you do this without being jacked right into the network?"

"I need every advantage I can get." He kept his tone

steady, not wanting to share his concerns. What if he'd forgotten how?

"Okay. Let's get this over with." She didn't sound happy, but he was glad that she didn't argue. He was afraid it might not be that hard to talk him out of it.

She led him to the small room she used as a clinic. It had a cot, a small cabinet that stored her first-aid supplies, and a tiny table and chairs. "Are you sure? I've cut trackers out of the girls, but I've never had any formal training."

He swallowed hard, but didn't change his mind.

"Take off your shirt and lie down while I get my tools ready."

"I wish you weren't telling me that with a scalpel in your hand." She chuckled, but he was serious. This would be a lot more fun if he wasn't about to head into battle.

Ash pulled his shirt over his head and wadded it into a ball. Then he settled on the cot, using his shirt as a makeshift pillow. Resting his head on his arm, he turned so he could watch her.

Taryn grabbed her equipment with efficient movements, then turned to place them on the table. Her breath caught when she met Ash's gaze.

His lips curved into a smile. "If you wanted to see me shirtless sooner, all you had to do was ask."

"Ha ha." She stepped close and studied him.

Ash knew what she saw, but didn't know how she felt about it. He wasn't bulky and muscular like her bouncers. His body had always run to wiry. Black ink tattoos marked the skin along his torso and on his biceps.

Her eyes flickered to his back, to his favorite tattoo. The wings of a bird stretched from between his shoulder blades and curved lovingly over his shoulders. The bird's tail feathers trailed in delicate swirls to the small of his back. Shapes reminiscent of flames surrounded the figure.

"Your back is spectacular. A firebird?"

"A phoenix."

"That's right, for your hacker name. May I?" she whispered.

"Yes." His response was low, guttural. The thought of her hands on his skin . . . was nothing compared to the real thing.

Her fingers trailed over the shape—slowly, gently—burning him like the flames in the design. "Oh! It feels like metal. I've never felt anything like it."

"An alloy," he corrected. "Tiny filaments laid into my skin. When I'm connected to the network, they light up."

Taryn traced her fingers over the tattoo again, then lay her hand on his shoulder. He shivered under her touch. "That's right, you told me. I'd like to see that someday."

He eased out his breath. "If this works the way it should, I'll let you."

"Well, let's do this right. The port's in the back of your neck, right?"

"Yeah." He shifted, lacing his fingers together and resting his head on them, exposing his neck.

She ran her fingers over the small scar. "Right here?"

"That's it." His voice was muffled. He tried to keep his breathing as shallow as he could and to move as little as possible.

A cool cloth with an antiseptic smell passed over the skin of his neck and upper back several times. "That was to clean the area and this should numb it." Her touch was gentle as she smoothed a topical cream over the skin that covered the port and the surrounding area. "Do you feel the tingling?"

"Yes." The tingling sensation was muted by the electricity of her touch.

"It won't take all the pain away, but it should help." Taryn kept her hand on his neck while she gave the cream some time to do its job.

She picked up the scalpel. "Ready?"

"Do what you need to do." His voice was thick with emotion. Eyes closed, he took one final deep breath and then focused on separating his mind from his body, the way he did when he surfed the network.

"This will probably hurt like a son of a bitch."

Ash sucked in a sharp breath when the point of her scalpel broke the skin. She paused and it was bearable until she moved the blade deeper. "Motherfucker!"

Her movements didn't slow, but she placed her free hand briefly on his shoulder. "Relax. It's worse when you tense up."

Between the blade and her touch, he couldn't believe that she expected him to remain calm. He tried to get out of his own head. When that didn't work, he tried to imagine his life with the port open. He was getting everything he'd ever wanted over the last five years, but it was nothing like he'd expected.

After what seemed like forever, he finally felt the blade withdraw from his neck. The pain didn't recede, though.

Taryn's hand was back on his neck, this time with something soft. "Take a deep breath," she instructed him.

After a few breaths, his muscles started to relax.

"You have a choice to make," she said. "I can't bandage the wound up because that defeats the purpose of uncovering the port."

"Okay." He shifted his head so he could see her. His

neck was on fire, but he didn't want to have a serious conversation like this, not without seeing her.

Her arm stretched to keep the temporary bandage in place. "I can put some salve on it and leave it open. It's bleeding a little right now, but that should stop soon."

His stomach turned at the thought of porting in with an active wound. "Gross. What's my other choice?"

She paused. Her silence was long and ominous.

"Worse than the open-wound option?" What could be worse than that?

"Yes." He'd asked as a joke, but her voice was completely serious.

"What is it?" Maybe she was wrong. Maybe it wasn't that bad.

"Cauterization."

He was wrong. His skin crawled just thinking about it. "You're fucking joking."

"Sorry." She sounded sincere, but that didn't ease his concern on how awful it would be. "I have a laser. It's not like I'd be using fire."

"You want to use a laser on my wound to cauterize it?"

"Stop being such a baby."

Easy for her to say—she didn't have a gaping hole in the back of her neck and someone begging to laser it closed.

"Cauterization will lessen the chance of infection, too."

Intellectually, he understood the argument. Emotionally? He was not ready for this. "Laser it," he said before he could change his mind.

When the laser hit his skin, he flinched. It hurt so much, he couldn't scream. He'd never felt pain like that before.

The next minutes were a blur. His shirt had teeth marks. His neck felt like he'd been branded. But that was nothing compared to the nausea that racked him.

"Can you sit up?"

"I think I'd rather die." The truth slipped out.

"I can put numbing cream on the edges. Not sure if it will do more harm than good." She leaned over him to inspect the wound. While her presence soothed his nerves, it didn't help the waves of pain. "If you can sit up, I can give you a pain pill."

Possibly the only thing she could have said to get him to move. "Fine. Help me sit up."

Taryn stood beside him. She braced his head with her metal arm, carefully avoiding the area around his port. With her other hand she rolled him onto his side. "Bend your knees."

He did as she instructed.

"When I start to lift your head and shoulder, swing your legs over the side of the bed. On three. One. Two. Three."

They moved in unison. The pain was intense. Although he never wanted to move again, Taryn's arm kept him steady.

He could see a future like that, her providing a steadying influence. She was a badass and he loved that about her.

He loved her.

Shit.

The words didn't come with the sense of panic he expected. That surprised him, too. And made him sad. He wouldn't be able to explore what loving Taryn every day meant.

"Okay?" She still watched him. He was glad that she couldn't see what was going on in his head.

He nodded. A wave of pain raced around his neck. "Fuck, that hurts."

"Don't move. Let me get you that pill." She moved her hand from his neck.

He swayed and gripped the side of the bed. "Please hurry."

Pulling a bottle out of the cabinet, she read the ingredients to him. "One pill or two?"

"One." Even though the pulses of pain were crying out for two, he would need his wits about him to deal with Caspar. The pain throbbed with every beat of his heart. He could think through it. Mostly.

She dropped the pill in his outstretched hand, then opened a bottle of water and handed it to him.

Popping the pill in his mouth was easy. Drinking from a bottle without bending his neck? Nearly impossible. More water rolled down his chest than made it into his mouth, but that was fine. He got enough to swallow the pill.

"Let me get you a towel." Taryn's eyes were glued to his chest. Of all the times for this to happen, this was the worst.

"Thank you."

Her cheeks flushed before she turned away to grab a handful of paper towels. Eyes averted, she started to pat his chest dry.

He covered her hand with his, stopping her movements. "I think you got it all," he said.

"You must think I'm an idiot." She tugged her hand away and he let her go.

"Not at all. If I could move my neck, I'd kiss you." He sighed. "But right now, I think I'd rather die."

Taryn's laughter filled the room. "How about a raincheck?"

He smiled, although he was too afraid to tilt his head to look at her. "I'd like that. A lot."

"What do we do now?" she asked while retaking her seat.

"I'm going to sit here until the pain meds kick in, then I need to see a man about a computer."

CHAPTER 50

HER CYBERARM WRAPPED around his waist, Taryn helped Ash down the final step into the hacker's room. His head and neck ached and he could have sworn he'd already sweated through the borrowed sweatshirt Taryn had provided.

"Are you sure you're ready for this?" she asked.

Ash had explained his worry that Caspar would keep coming and his fear that he and Hope would bring trouble to Taryn and the bar. She'd tried to argue that they had time. That Caspar might not have even noticed that Hope was gone yet.

Ultimately, though, it was his decision.

"Let's get you over to the chair." Slow baby steps brought them to the hacker chair in the center of the room. The chair wasn't far, but each step felt like a mile. The throbbing in his neck was worse than any hangover or post-surf crash he'd ever had. Worse even than the pain of getting it installed in the first place.

When they reached the chair, Taryn guided him in a

little dance that ended with him eventually sitting. As soon as his ass hit the cushion, she released him. Leather—real leather—embraced him.

"What do you need me to do?" she asked.

"Um . . ." Was this a bad plan?

He fiddled with the arm rests, making minute adjustments until they felt right. "Would you help me adjust the head rest?"

"Sure." She moved slowly, sliding the head rest close to the back of his head, carefully avoiding the port area.

"What next?"

His head and neck weren't even touching the back of the chair, but he knew it was there. Knew that the port that would connect him to the system was there, too.

Inches away.

It was the closest he'd been to porting into the network in years.

All he needed to do was align the newly freed port with the plug on the chair. It was that easy.

Just a head butt away.

So why was he hesitating?

"Everything okay?"

Taryn had obviously picked up on his delay.

"Fine." An automatic response. Ash wasn't fine.

He was afraid of a fucking chair.

For five years he'd had an excuse for not surfing the network. That excuse was gone. A golden opportunity was staring him in the face and he was terrified.

What if something went wrong? What if he'd forgotten how to do this? What if he got brain burn like Hope?

He loved his sister, but the thought of losing himself in the system was more terrifying than the thought of losing her.

What if he got stuck in the network?

"Is that what you're worried about?"

Ash turned his head slowly because it still throbbed like a son of a bitch. Had he said that out loud?

Ash nodded, even though the movement made him queasy.

Taryn's hand brushed his forehead, shifting hair away from his skin. Then she trailed her fingers down his face until she cupped his chin, her fingers resting on his cheek. He closed his eyes and leaned into the comfort of her touch.

"You'll be fine," she said.

Ash wanted to believe her. He really did.

"Tell me how I can help. I've never done this before." She stepped back and gestured to the chair.

"It's pretty straightforward," Ash said, struggling to sound confident. "That pin slips into the port."

She grimaced.

"I know, but it's not as bad as it seems." If only he could make himself believe that.

"Do you need me to help push your head onto the spike?"

The gruesome image startled a laugh out of him. "No, I can do it. It's easy—just slip tab *A* into slot *B*."

Holy shit. He'd never considered how sexual the whole damn thing was until just now. When he couldn't do anything about it.

"I've never done it with a head wound." Ash changed the subject, before he needed to adjust his pants.

"Not even when you first got it?"

Instead of nodding, he twisted his body so he could see her. "I wasn't allowed to port in until it was fully healed. I didn't know what I was missing, so there was no rush."

Now he knew what he was missing, so the anticipation was almost worse than the actual experience.

"I don't think I can watch," Taryn said and turned away.

He reached up with his right hand and felt for the spike. As his fingers slid over the thin metal spear, another thought occurred. "Hey, you got anything to sterilize this?"

Taryn turned around, her face pale.

"You mean . . ." She paused and her hands fluttered, a move he never expected from the usually calm and collected Jack. "You mean, that thing?"

She'd cut him open without blinking, but this bothered her?

"The thing that goes in my brain? Yeah. I don't know where it's been."

"Uh, yeah." She paled further and sprinted across the room. Sounds of retching echoed back to him from the bathroom.

She returned not long after, holding a spray bottle out to him.

"This is the best I have here. Let me know if you want me to get something from the main bar."

"That's fine. I trust you."

She blinked several times, her eyes wide like an owl's.

"Oh. Okay."

When she didn't say anything else, he added, "Would you spray it down for me?"

"Um, sure."

Ash leaned forward, causing little ripples of pain to flow through him. This was such a bad idea.

Taryn moved closer. Her shoulder brushed his.

He gave into the urge to lean into her.

She turned her head and smiled. Just for a second. Then her expression turned serious and she focused on her task. Behind him, he heard the release of the spray and caught the flutter of a cloth as she wiped the spike down. "Done. What's it feel like when you're in there? Are you in there? What do you call it?"

He thought for a moment. How to explain the network to someone who'd never experienced it? "I think it's different for everyone," he finally said. "For me, it's like you're racing in the fastest car. Speed and strategy and competitiveness."

Ash dropped his voice. "Hope used to say it was like swimming through the stars."

Taryn gasped. "That's so beautiful."

"The data flows look like bits of light. The more data, the bigger they are." He hesitated. When he spoke again, his voice was thick with loss. "I always wonder if she's lost in there, swimming among the stars."

"Oh, Ash. I'm so sorry." She wiped away a tear, then leaned closer and peered at his neck. She swallowed hard but didn't back away this time. "Are you sure you can do this? It looks like it will hurt."

"I don't have a choice." He already knew it would hurt. The constant throbbing in his neck was evidence of that.

She blew out a breath. "How can I help?"

"You've done everything you can. Now it's my turn. I'll contact Caspar and hopefully I'll be able to lead him into a Tremaine trap."

"You want me to leave you here alone?" She sounded horrified.

"Is the room secure?"

"Yes."

"Then there's really nothing you can do here." Ash hoped he was good enough to beat Caspar. He wasn't sure if he could. He plugged his phone into the system to activate Caspar's code and prayed he had the skill and the stamina to best him.

CHAPTER 51

"PUT ME TO WORK, DANI." Taryn entered the bar area, needing a distraction. Otherwise, she'd worry about what was happening downstairs.

Leaving Ash alone in the hacker room had been hard. Harder even than cutting his neck open. It was good he hadn't been able to see her while she worked. Her hands had been shaking the entire time and she'd worried constantly about cutting too deep. What if she'd hit a nerve and done permanent damage?

Now he was preparing to shove a metal spike into a socket in his neck that hadn't been used in years. What if the technology had changed? What if she'd screwed up?

Dani stopped unloading glasses and studied her. "You okay?"

"Fine. I promise. I just really need a distraction right now."

"Well, I'm not going to turn down free help," she said, winking at Taryn, "so why don't you finish unloading this. Then, there's a bunch of liquor and wine that needs to be restocked. It was a busy weekend."

Taryn grinned and felt a little bit lighter. Watching Dani take charge, watching her bloom, always made her happy. Unofficially, the other woman managed the bar and was the Jack's second-in-command. Maybe it was time to make that official. What would she even call her—the Jill?

She laughed out loud.

"If putting glasses on the shelves makes you that happy, maybe you should do it every day."

"Maybe I will," Taryn sassed back.

She missed this. The banter, the time with her friend. "We need to do this more often."

"Prep the bar?" Dani asked.

"No, hang out. I've forgotten how much fun we have."

"Me, too." Dani smiled. "I know it's hard when we're busy—"

"But that shouldn't be an excuse. Don't get me wrong. I love the bar. Love being a business owner, but I don't want to spend my whole life working. There's got to be more to it than that."

"Count me in," Dani said.

She could do this, Taryn thought. No, she *would* do this. She could have a life. All work and no play made for a very sad Jack. Hadn't she taken over with the intent of changing how business was done here? Maybe she wouldn't have Ash in her life, but she could have a fulfilling life if she wanted to.

Taryn had just opened the first box of booze when her phone dinged, notifying her she had a message. She pulled it out of her pocket.

SOS

Shit. That was Ash's number—she'd made sure he could reach her before she'd left him. Something must have gone wrong.

"Dani, I'm so sorry. I've got to go check on Ash."

"Is he okay?"

"I don't know. He just sent an SOS."

"Go." Dani shooed her away. "I can finish this up."

"Thank you!"

Taryn felt bad abandoning her friend when she'd begged for a distraction, but what if she'd screwed up and Ash was hurt? She raced down the hall, for once not worrying about security for the hidden room. Even if one of the women saw, they still couldn't access it without the code.

She pounded down the steps. The hacking room was eerily quiet when Taryn stepped through the door.

"Ash?"

"Here." His reply was muffled.

Taryn entered the chair room, nervous about what she would find.

The lights were low. A big screen had dropped down over one wall.

Huh. She hadn't even known that was there.

Ash sat in the chair where she'd left him, still hooked into the chair.

The thought made her queasy. It would be hypocritical to rage against human–machine interfaces when she had one as well. But if she had to screw her arm on every day, that would make her sick too.

And that was just her arm. This was his brain!

The images—squiggle? symbols?—that were projected onto the screen meant nothing to Taryn. They weren't even really images, just impressions. Is that what Ash saw? It didn't look like speed or stars to her.

He cursed.

"Everything okay?"

"Fuck, just a little bit more." His voice was tense, like he was in pain.

That made absolutely no sense. Was this his battle with Caspar? She'd expected something more . . . battle-y.

Could she talk to him when he was like this? "Can you hear me?"

"Yes," he ground out. "But I can't focus on this and you at the same time."

"Why send me a panicked text if you don't need me?" Taryn snapped. She hated not knowing what was happening. As she spoke, she watched him work.

His head was practically immobile. She assumed the pin that inserted into his neck caused that. His fingers twitched on the arms of the chair.

If she didn't know that he'd voluntarily put himself in the chair, she'd think he was being tortured.

"Are you having a seizure?" Had she screwed up when she'd opened the port? He'd said he was in the middle of the fight. If he passed out in the middle of it, the fight was over.

"No," he ground out. "I'm used to keyboards. It's been five fucking years since I've had this much brain interface. I'm out of practice. And I'm losing."

Oh shit.

He had to beat Caspar. It was the only way he and Hope could truly escape and live free. If anything happened to him . . .

Her heart twisted at the thought.

It would be hard enough living without him when he left town. Living without him because he was dead or brain burned? That wasn't a world she wanted to live in.

Taryn circled the chair and studied the cables and plugs.

She didn't know when it had been purchased, but she

knew it had been top of the line when it was new. Like the Jack before her, the hacker Jack had enjoyed the best things in life. He would have purchased the best chair he could, which would probably mean the most advanced at the time.

"What the hell are you doing back there? Why are you circling me like a shark?"

"I'm looking for something."

"Look for it where I can't see you. I can sense you moving and it's distracting as hell."

Distracting him was bad, but Taryn was irrationally glad that her presence disturbed him. He disturbed the hell out of her. "I'll do my best," she said.

Taryn crouched down and took a closer look at the base of the chair. "Gotcha."

The panel was dusty and the printing was tiny, but she found the symbol she was looking for—the one that indicated peripherals could be attached. Ash had told her that he was used to a keyboard these days. So, she'd get him a keyboard.

She bounced to her feet and faced Ash. "I think I can help. I'll be right back." She raced out of the room without waiting for his reply. She knew what she needed and where to get it.

How long would it take Ash to do whatever it was he was doing? Hacking sounded like magic to her. How else could you insert yourself into a computer?

Shaking off those thoughts, Taryn sprinted down the corridor to her office. She grabbed the keyboard off her desk, hoping that it would be able to pair with the chair. Taryn tucked it under her arm and yanked her office door open.

Dani waited the other side, about to knock. "We have a problem."

"Can you handle it?" Taryn begged.

"It's better if you do. Giselle's pimp is in the bar."

"Not again!" Why now? Taryn had no time for his shit. "Who's minding the bar?"

"Neecy arrived right after you left. She was hanging out when he walked in, so I asked her to watch the bar while I got you. She's got the guys with her." Dani glared at her. "I've been looking all over for you."

"I was taking care of Ash."

Dani looked at the keyboard in Taryn's hand then back at her, a million questions in her gaze. "Well, I hope you've solved that problem, because we've got a bigger one out there."

Fuckfuckfuck.

Taryn focused on the bigger problem. "I need to drop this off, then I'll be back. Ten minutes, tops."

"What is wrong with you? The bar is getting full and a man you told not to come back has come back. The fucking office supplies can wait!"

"You don't understand, Dani. This is more important than it looks. I've got to get back to Ash."

"You say you care about these girls, but you're putting a keyboard ahead of rescuing one? Screw you, Taryn. Go play secretary or whatever the fuck you're doing. I'll figure it out."

Whoa. Dani rarely lost her temper.

She grabbed Dani's arm. "I'm sorry. All the shit is hitting the fan at once."

"There's a big old pile of it out front. If you want to keep Giselle and the bar, you better get out there." Dani turned and walked away.

"Hold on, Ash," Taryn whispered under her breath. "I'll take care of Hope if it goes wrong for you."

Keyboard in her left hand, she followed Dani down the hallway.

A week without some kind of crisis. Was that too much to ask?

CHAPTER 52

TARYN WALKED through the door to the bar and into the middle of a brawl.

Someone took a swing before she was halfway through.

She grabbed the door with her free hand and shoved it into his face. With the power of her cyberarm behind it, she knocked him out cold.

Taryn looked down as she stepped over him. One of the pimp's buddies.

Sonofabitch. The whole place was chaos.

Jed and a few other old timers sat at a high table at the edge of the action. He saw her and raised his glass in a salute.

Taryn would've smiled if she hadn't needed to duck.

Another fist flew at her.

This time she raised her left forearm deflect the blow.

Tiny keys scattered all over the floor as the keyboard caught the punch.

Fuck!

Taryn dropped the keyboard frame. She'd find another for Ash later.

Right now, she had to end this motherfucking brawl in her goddamn bar.

Broken keyboard guy came at Taryn again. This time she was ready for him.

A right cross shattered his jaw. A knee to the balls dropped him to the floor.

He curled into a fetal position, easy to step over as she advanced toward the bar.

Another black-clad figure charged her.

She sidestepped and he rammed into a table.

Idiot.

Taryn dodged, punched, and kicked her way to the center of the brawl.

Like the eye of a hurricane, nothing was happening there. The pimp stood in the middle, Giselle's beautiful dark hair wrapped around his hand.

He watched the chaos around him, a smirk on his face.

"Let her go."

He turned a quarter way around to look at Taryn. The movement put Giselle's head at a sharp angle and she cried out in pain.

The sound amped up Taryn's rage, but she couldn't let concern for Giselle distract her. All her attention had to be on the monster hurting the girl. "Let her go," she repeated, her voice soft and cold.

"No. She's mine," he said with a sneer.

His words took Taryn back to a time and place she thought she'd escaped. The previous Jack had done the same to her. Claimed her like a piece of property.

She'd broken free. Now she helped others. It was that sense of rightness, of purpose that shook her free of the memories.

"Wrong answer. She's mine." Taryn imbued the word

with all her feelings—rage, protectiveness, love. The pimp would never understand the difference in their world views. Giselle was Taryn's to protect, not to own and abuse.

Taryn reached for the hand he'd speared through Giselle's hair.

The fine motor controls of her arm had been the best she could afford at the time. Since then, she got them upgraded regularly for occasions just like this. She grabbed his hand and exerted pressure.

Controlled pressure, carefully calibrated to squeeze until his fingers opened. He hissed in pain.

"Can you get free?" she asked Giselle.

The tiniest of nods.

Taryn could tell she was afraid of getting hurt, but the fighting spirit Giselle had shown from the beginning was still there.

Giselle tilted her head and tried to free her hair without moving her body.

Nothing happened.

"I need you to hurry up, honey." Taryn could hold him for a while, but she hated having her back exposed like this.

"You're going to pa—"

She exerted more pressure on his knuckles and the pimp's threat cut off.

His grip loosened some more and Giselle freed herself. She scrambled backward like a crab to get out of his reach.

Taryn continued to hold his hand while she pondered what to do with him. He kept turning up. She couldn't allow that any longer.

He struggled in her grip. "I'm coming for both you bitches! You're gonna regret this!"

"Shut up, asshole." Taryn twisted his arm until he whimpered and hunched over.

Giselle took advantage of his position and slammed her fist against his jaw.

Bone crunched and Taryn winced. That didn't sound good. Not that he didn't deserve it.

Giselle's exclamation of pain was drowned out by the pimp's wail.

"Shit, that hurt!" Giselle didn't let the discomfort stop her. She cradled her right hand for a moment and then kicked him in the balls.

"Nice!" Taryn said with a nod. She approved of kicking assholes when they were down.

He squealed in pain and sagged to the ground. One hand cupped his balls and he tried to tug his other hand free.

Taryn let go because she didn't want her hand anywhere near his balls.

He moaned and rolled on the floor.

Giselle slammed her foot down on his hip, holding him in place.

Damn, Taryn was proud of her.

"Behind you!"

Giselle's warning gave Taryn the time she needed to duck. She spun on her heel and slammed an elbow into her attacker's throat.

He dropped too.

Fists at the ready, confident Giselle would keep the pimp down and warn her if anyone else approached, Taryn turned a slow circle.

The pimp's crew were all sprawled on the floor in pain.

"Anyone else got a problem?"

The room fell silent.

Someone clapped.

What the hell?

Taryn surveyed the room again. It was Jed. His clap was uneven and obviously caused him pain, but he kept going.

Then more and more people joined in.

Dani, Giselle.

Other patrons.

Her bouncers.

What was going on?

"Stop it." The applause got louder. "No, really, stop it." Taryn pitched her voice above the applause and put her meanest tone into it.

This time it worked.

The clapping slowed. Got quieter.

Then sputtered until it was only a few of her employees.

"That was amazing," Dani said.

Giselle wrapped Taryn in a hug.

Taryn didn't know what to do with her hands, so she awkwardly patted the girl on the back. Hugging would definitely ruin her rep.

Taryn disentangled from Giselle.

Jed stood next to them. Taryn really hoped he didn't want a hug too.

"That was pretty badass, Jack," he said.

Taryn looked around the room. Most people were getting back to the business of drinking. A lot of them were on their phones.

Ugh. That couldn't be good.

"Are you sure? I think the Jack's reputation is going to take a hit."

Jed barked out a laugh. "Oh no. Your rep will skyrocket if it hasn't already. You kicked his ass, girl. Plowed right through the crowd, knocked out all comers, and kicked his ass. People are going to be talking about it for days, how you protected your own." He pierced her with a shrewd look. "You're going to get more business out of this, not less."

"Probably lookie-loos who just want to walk on the wild side."

"Lookie-loo credits spend just as well as everyone else's." He looked skeptical. "I think you'll be surprised, though. They'll come and they'll want to be a part of this. They'll want to be part of the Jack's, too."

Credits were a bright side. The rest . . .

"I don't know, Jed. That sounds like I'm weak. None of the other Jacks worried about protecting anything but the bar and themselves."

"Look where it got them," he said quietly. "Dead and alone. You're definitely not dead, and even before this you weren't alone."

He was right. Even before the bar was hers, people had helped her. Sometimes just a little, but it had kept her going. That was what she tried to bring to the girls and to the regulars.

"Are you one of mine?"

"Damn straight! As long as you don't give away my seat at the bar to any of the newcomers."

"Never," she promised.

Taryn felt better after talking to Jed. Who'd have guessed?

She'd built a family. A reputation. And now it looked like those two worlds were colliding.

She didn't know how to feel about that.

She couldn't dwell on it because Dani chose that moment to give her another hug.

"That was amazing. I'm so glad you're not dead."

Taryn held the hug another second, then stepped back. "Sounds like you didn't have much faith in me."

"I did! Compete faith. But I figured the pimp and his guys would cheat."

"Yeah, me too."

Dani looked at her in surprise.

Taryn had surprised herself. "Can you handle the cleanup?"

Dani looked around the bar and nodded. "What do you want to do with the trash?"

"Tie them up—tight. And put them in the basement cells. We'll have to come up with a more permanent solution later."

"Where are you going?"

"I need to finish this thing with Ash." She hoped he was still fighting.

Dani's face fell.

Taryn added, "In a good way."

If Taryn could have her reputation and her family, maybe she could find a place for Ash and Hope in that mix. A way to use her reputation to make them hers.

Taryn patted Dani on the shoulder then retraced her steps. The keys were scattered all over the floor. Some had been crunched under feet. Others were probably lost. She didn't have time to pick them up. Fortunately, she had an idea that didn't require the keys.

CHAPTER 53

ASH STRUGGLED to find his footing against the Tremaine cybersecurity measures. He knew what they were, where they were. He'd even spent hours thinking about how to beat them over the last five years.

And right now, none of that was working.

He needed to get deep enough into the system to trigger the big traps. The ones that could catch and keep Caspar.

Right now, his only advantage was knowing his old teammates' styles.

He dodged Ava when he encountered her first. Ash felt bad when he slipped by her easily. These were the people he'd spent his time with. His people.

Betraying them turned his stomach. But right now, they stood between Ash and his sister's long-term freedom. Never a good place to be.

"Looks like you've slowed down some, boy."

Caspar. Ash would recognize that fucking drawl anywhere.

What the hell? Ash was supposed to let him into the system.

"Decided to make sure you didn't set up a special welcoming party for me."

"You've been here the whole time?"

His laugh told Ash everything he needed to know. Caspar had been trailing him inside the system and he had completely missed it.

"I'm sorry, Hope," Ash whispered into the darkness. He couldn't handle the corporation and Caspar at the same time.

It felt like he'd been here for hours, but the tiny clock ticking away in the corner of his display said it had only been one.

Ash's heart rate suddenly sped up. He wasn't alone. "Taryn?"

He had to concentrate to only speak to her in the real world. Projecting his thoughts about her into the network stream would only bring more trouble to her door. He'd complicated her life enough.

"I brought you something."

"Water?"

She paused. "I can get you some."

"Yes, please." His voice was scratchy.

Taryn returned quickly and pressed a bottle of water into his hand. He gulped it down gratefully, not caring that some of it dribbled down his chest.

He handed the glass back and prepared to face Caspar again.

"Are you ready?"

Had she read his mind? "Not even close," he admitted.

There was a long pause, then she said, "I promise it will help."

"What?" He wasn't following their conversation.

"Lift your hands."

He did as she asked, completely confused. It was hard to concentrate on both worlds when he was riding the network.

She slid some sort of tray over his lap. Part of the chair or something else?

"Give me your hands."

He lowered them slowly. She met him halfway, taking a hand in each of hers.

His shoulders relaxed and he let her guide his hands where she needed them.

She set his hands on something plastic, with ragged edges and textured holes across the top.

It felt like a keyboard, but . . . "Where are the keys?"

"The keys . . . had a little run in with the pimp and his muscle. But I don't think you need them."

"Why? What are we doing?" Taryn wasn't making sense. What did a broken keyboard and a pimp have to do with hacking into the Tremaine Corporation?

She must have read his confused silence. "You haven't ported into the system in several years, right?" She didn't wait for an answer. "You're used to a keyboard. Well, I brought you a keyboard."

She didn't get it. She completely misunderstood how porting worked. "I, ah, appreciate what you did, but I can't use a keyboard for this hack."

"I'm not an idiot, Ash." There was a bite to her words. "I know you can't use it for the hack. It's here for your mind to use it."

"What the fuck are you taking about?" He needed to end this conversation and refocus on Caspar.

"You've trained your brain to think about hacks in terms of the keyboard, right? That's how you do what you do now. Since you're rusty, put your hands on the keyboard like you're used to, then channel those actions into the network."

It sounded crazy. But sometimes the craziest plans worked.

Did he trust her enough to try?

Yes. Definitely.

Ash placed his hands on the keyboard. It felt weird because of the missing keys, but he found a familiar position.

He blew out a long breath. "Okay, here goes."

Before Caspar had shown up, he'd been trying to get through the second-level firewall. Mendez's defenses had been giving him fits. He hadn't been fast enough to beat them.

Putting Taryn's theory into practice, he imagined what he'd do if he were countering the attack from the control room. The commands came easily to his fingertips.

Fingers flying across the broken keyboard, he imagined the commands in his head and manifested them on the network. Was it faster?

Maybe. He wasn't getting as hung up thinking about what he needed to do instead of doing it.

This time he was able to slip past Mendez and could sense Caspar on his tail. Two more barriers and he could spring one of the more dangerous traps on Caspar.

Bridging the gap between his port and the keyboard got easier with each command. With every keystroke, Ash envisioned the command and it manifested in the network.

He used all the knowledge he'd learned from defending the corporation to attack it, ignoring the pangs of guilt. He'd deal with the fallout later.

At the next barrier, he threw up a shade to blend in with the surroundings, a trick he'd learned from one of the hackers who'd tried to compromise the Tremaine system. He'd studied their moves and taught himself to do them.

One millisecond he was fighting Tremaine cybersecurity, the next he'd gone invisible, bypassed their counterattacks, and entered the final level. "Can't see me, can you," he murmured, making sure to keep that thought out of the network. While security searched for him, he stepped into a data stream.

The data stream would take him close to where he wanted to go. And close enough to what Caspar wanted that maybe Ash could convince him that was where they were.

"Neat trick, boy." Ash heard Caspar but couldn't see him.

Did that mean he couldn't see Ash?

He still didn't have a plan. That didn't matter, now that both Taryn and Hope were safe. Taryn would take care of his sister if something happened to him. He could be as ruthless as necessary.

Ash hadn't expected his strange friendship with Portia. He would do his best to protect the company.

He raced toward another stream of data. He knew where he was now. And he knew how to beat Caspar. He just needed time and maybe a little luck.

Whatever tricks Caspar had up his sleeve, Ash could counter them. Taryn had given him a new perspective and he would use every analog trick he'd learned.

With that confidence wrapped around him, Ash triggered Caspar's piece of code and let himself truly slip into the zone.

CHAPTER 54

ASH'S HEAD flopped back against the chair, his eyes closed and his breathing shallow. On the chair's health monitor screen, his pulse was fluttery.

Oh shit.

"Ash!" Worry coursed through her and Taryn ran to his side. "Are you okay?"

"Thirsty," he mumbled. His eyes opened and he looked around blearily.

She grabbed the water bottle that he'd been drinking from and tilted his head up. She'd fetched a straw from the bar so it would be easier for him to drink this time.

He swallowed greedily, his throat working as he emptied the bottle. He closed his eyes again and slumped against her.

She had to get him out of this damn chair.

To do that, she had to get him out of the network.

During the battle, she'd watched him slip deeper into that world. Every once in a while, he'd shout. She rarely understood what he said. Unable to do anything, she'd paced the room, not knowing—or understanding—what was going on. She never wanted to feel that helpless again.

Taryn gently tipped Ash's head back. Now she wished she'd watched him insert the port. She pressed a kiss to the top of his head. "I hope I do this right," she whispered.

She kept his forehead pressed against her shoulder. His hair was damp. Slowly, so slowly, she slid her fingers over his neck, seeking the junction where his port met the chair.

Ah, there it was.

The skin around the port was slick with sweat. Taryn pinched the jack between the thumb and forefinger of her cyberarm and wrapped her other hand around his neck. "Here goes nothing."

She applied steady pressure and pushed her hands apart. Millimeter by millimeter, she disengaged Ash from the chair. She was barely aware of the light under his shirt fading.

Oh, his tattoo. She'd wanted to see that in action, but this wasn't the time.

He slumped against her, his forehead still pressed into her shoulder. She pulled her hand back and saw that her fingertips were red. Blood mixed with the sweat. This was her fault. She'd cut the port open.

She studied the back of his neck. It wasn't bleeding steadily, just some mild weeping from the wound.

If only he'd let her cut the port open when she'd first asked. The wound would've had time to heal and she wouldn't be freaked out that he'd plunged a mess of dirty wires into the gaping hole in his neck.

"I'm sorry, Ash."

She couldn't lean him back against the chair, not with that wound and the bloody jack protruding from it. She could drag him out of it, but he was dead weight. What if she dropped him?

Taryn draped his arm over her shoulder and wrapped her right arm around his waist for the best support. For a wiry guy, he was solid. She could ask Dani or Daryl for help, but she didn't want to reveal Ash's weakness.

Bending her knees, she tugged him out of the chair, then she half walked, half dragged him to the cot.

She put one knee on the thin mattress and tried to swing his weight around so she could lower him. Miscalculating, Taryn tumbled onto the cot, with him on top of her. "Sorry!"

Even though he was dead weight, there was something comforting about having him pressed against her.

Trying to disturb him as little as possible, Taryn shifted their positions so they were side by side. She smushed down a pillow and rested his head against it, making sure that the back of his neck wasn't touching anything.

Then she curled up on the edge of the cot, her head on her arm, watching him.

Dark circles sat under his eyes and his cheekbones stood out sharply. He looked old and worn out from just a few hours in the chair.

How could he do this to himself?

She knew the answer. He'd do anything for his sister.

"Ash. Wake up." She reached across and laid her hand on his chest.

CHAPTER 55

ASH WOKE SUDDENLY. His throat was dry and he felt like he'd been hit by a bus. "Where am I?" he rasped.

"Whoa, go slow." Taryn's voice came from somewhere in front of him.

Relief whooshed through him. He was safe. Or at least alive.

Her hand rested on his chest, a reassuring weight.

"What happened?" His brain felt staticky.

"You can try to sit up but go slowly. I think you should lie down a bit longer."

"Where are we?" He tried to focus on his surroundings, but all he saw was Taryn and the concern on her face.

"Still in the Jack's hacking room. I dragged you out of the chair and over to the cot when you passed out."

He passed out? What the hell had happened?

Ash rolled to his back, intending to sit up. Instead, fire raced through his nerve endings. "Ow!"

The edges of the cut Taryn had made throbbed. Fuck, that hurt. At least the pain cut through the rest of the fuzziness in his head.

"Let's get you up and then I can get you more pain killers."

Even with her help, he struggled to sit up. He should be embarrassed to appear so weak in front of her, but he was too damn tired to care.

"Did we win?" he asked.

Silence.

He grabbed her hand and tugged her back down onto the cot next to him.

"Don't you know?" she sounded worried.

Shit. Did he? He thought back to his battle with Caspar. He'd led him to an inner core, then triggered the security system. That was why he was so wiped out. He'd had to evade the same trap and then make his way out of the network without being caught.

"Yes," he said slowly, memories coming back to him. "I trapped Caspar in the system. Tremaine Security should be tracking him down now." A rush of pride flowed through him. For a while there, he hadn't thought that he would win. The woman beside him was the reason he had.

"What will they do with him?" Taryn asked.

"I don't know for sure. I can't imagine that they'll use him like they did me, but it could happen." The best thing, in Ash's opinion, would be brain burn, but he didn't say that.

"Do you think any of his people will come after you?"

Despite the throbbing in his neck, he turned his head and looked at her. "I don't know," he admitted. "But I don't think so. I think going after me was Caspar's personal project. And I'm not going after anyone else."

Taryn slid her arm around his back. "What now?"

He wrapped his arm around her waist and sighed. "There's still the Tremaine Corporation to deal with."

"Tell Portia you stopped a major hacking syndicate from taking over the Tremaine network and to leave you alone."

Ash imagined walking into Portia's office with that message and laughed. Ouch. Even laughing hurt. "I don't think that would go over very well. Especially since I was the one who let him into the system."

"There has to be a way." She rested her head on his shoulder.

He would miss this when he left. They fit together so perfectly. "I've thought of nothing else for the last five years. If there's another way, I don't see it."

"That's because you didn't have me on your side."

Was this amazing woman thinking about battling a corporation for him?

"If you could, would you stay?"

Yes, his heart shouted. *Yes!*

"It depends," he said slowly. "Here in this basement, hiding? No, I can't. It would be too much like being trapped before." Just the thought panicked him. "Here in the city, without looking over my shoulder for Tremaine Security all the time? Yes, of course."

She lifted her head and looked him in the eye. "What about here in Seattle and here . . . with me?"

His breath caught. "Here, like one of your rescues or here?" He placed his hand over her heart.

She covered his hand with hers. "Here."

Ash leaned close and brushed his lips over hers. "Yes," he whispered. Then he sat back and let reality take over. "I don't see how that can happen."

"As long as it's what you want, we'll figure it out. Anything is possible—"

"—for a price," he finished. The thought of a future with

Taryn, with Hope, a future free of the Tremaine Corporation sounded like a miracle. An impossible miracle.

CHAPTER 56

TARYN GLANCED at the clock again. She'd never been much of a clock watcher—time really had no meaning in a dimly lit bar—but she was anxious to see Ash. After she'd bandaged him up last night, he'd slept on a cot in Hope's room. If she were being honest, she was a little disappointed, but it was understandable. He hadn't spent more than a couple hours at a time with his sister for years. She'd peeked in on them earlier, just to make sure everything was okay.

"What are your plans for today?" Dani asked. "Any more big battles I need to worry about?" She was joking, but Taryn caught the bite in her tone.

"I hope not," she said vehemently. "I'm really sorry about yesterday. There was so much going on. Forgive me?"

Dani paused and studied Taryn over the table in the small kitchen. The bar was in good hands right now. They both would check in later. "You're forgiven. But you can't tell me that you aren't spread too thin. You need to get your priorities straight."

"You're absolutely right. I am spread too thin and I can't

do it all. I have some thoughts about that I want to share with you later. When we're sure things have calmed down." When Dani started to ask about it, Taryn shook her head. "Later. I promise."

Taryn rubbed her eyes. "Both Ash and Giselle are priorities. Unfortunately, last night they clashed. I think, no, I hope, that they both become permanent fixtures here." She pressed a hand to her stomach. That was the first time she expressed her thoughts—her hopes—out loud. The relief she felt was just as unsettling as the nerves.

"Ohmygod." Dani clapped her hands. "You two worked things out?"

Taryn shook her head. "Not yet. The Tremaine Corporation is still hanging over our heads. Not to mention I still need to deal with our mole. And our pimp and his friends. But I'm hopeful," she said with a smile.

"Excellent news!" Dani said.

"I agree," Ash said from the doorway.

Color flooded Taryn's cheeks. It was one thing to tell Dani her plan. It was another to tell Ash. She'd wanted to ease him into it. "How much did you hear?"

His slow, sly grin made her heart race and her blood warm. "Enough."

"How are you feeling?" She hurried to change the subject.

"Like someone drilled a hole in my neck," he teased. "But better than I have in a long time. Thank you again for rescuing my sister." He gestured to one of the open chairs. "May I?"

"Of course," Taryn said.

"I'll let you two talk." Dani stacked her dishes.

"You don't have to go," Ash said.

"I think you two need to talk. Besides, I need to take lunch to, ah, someone."

Taryn mouthed her thanks to Dani. She was taking a meal to Rhonda. Taryn planned to visit her later. It was one of the problems she needed to solve.

"Taryn told me you readied a room for my sister with no notice. Thank you. Really."

"You're welcome," Dani said, as she stood and cleared the table. "I'll see you around. I hope."

Ash smiled and took her seat.

"Sorry I slept so long," he said. "My body just crashed as soon as I hit the pillow. Then I spent some time talking to Hope before getting up."

He paused and looked at her. "You're still serious about keeping us. Me and Hope?"

"If you want to stay, yes." She stretched her hand across the table. He grasped it.

"And you have a plan?"

Did she? Not really, not yet, but they'd figure it out. "Working on it," she said. "I usually focus on one rescue every few months. Not three in a couple of weeks." She laughed.

His return smile was half-hearted. That was okay. She'd make a believer out of him.

CHAPTER 57

ASH STEPPED off the executive elevator, regretting every decision that had brought him to this point. But his one-sided conversation with Hope this morning had brought clarity. If he wanted to start a new life with Taryn and with his sister, he had to make peace with his old one. He could only hope that Taryn would understand if this all went wrong.

He'd received a few funny looks when he'd entered the Tremaine building, but no one had stopped him, so maybe it wouldn't be as bad as he thought.

Yeah, right.

The executive elevator opened at Portia's floor and he wiped his sweaty palms on his pants before exiting. He'd stopped to change clothes before facing Portia because he'd need every advantage if he wanted to come out of this meeting little worse for wear. Of course, he'd also grabbed his copy of the potential cure for Hope.

Head up, shoulders back, he faked confidence he didn't have and strode right past her receptionist. She didn't even look at him, her attention obviously focused on the network.

Over the last two weeks, he'd spent so much time up here, he was a regular visitor.

Ash watched her work for a moment, resisting the urge to rub his own port. It was still healing. Plus, he didn't want anyone to know that it was active again. The back of his shirt carefully covered the newly opened port.

"Go on in." She didn't even check the calendar first.

He stepped around the receptionist's desk and crossed to the big, metal doors. They were still impressive, but they didn't intimidate him the way they once did. The woman behind them still did, though.

Portia looked up sharply at the interruption. "You have a lot of nerve showing your face here."

"We need to talk." Refusing to be intimidated, Ash dropped into the seat across from her with a casualness he didn't feel.

"Have a seat." Portia's laugh was bitter rather than amused.

Ash studied the woman across from him. He'd known this conversation would be difficult, but now that he was here, he didn't know how to start. How did you blow up your own life and hope to come out the other side unscathed?

"I'm surprised to see you here."

"Why?" He didn't want to give her more ammunition. Not just yet.

Her blue eyes bored holes in him. "You disobeyed my orders, disappeared for two days, and created a door in our network security big enough for the enemy to slide through. Am I missing anything?"

Ash swallowed hard and didn't respond. Yeah, she was missing a few big pieces of information.

"And now you have the nerve to stroll into my office without the courtesy of even knocking."

"I can explain about the attack," he started.

Portia cut him off. "Oh, don't bother. I know you'd do anything for your precious sister, up to and including betraying me."

Ash blanched. Deep down he'd known that Portia would see his behavior as a betrayal. It absolutely was. But he'd forgotten there was a living, breathing woman behind the Ice Queen. One he liked and respected. Once again, in trying to save his sister, he'd left a trail of carnage for Portia Tremaine to deal with. And that was why he was here. To repent.

"You're right. I had to get my sister away from Caspar." His forced "employment" at the Tremaine Corporation had sucked, but being forced to work for Caspar in return for Hope's safety would have been worse.

"How did he get her away from the hospital?"

"He had a very clever plan." Ash refused to say more. He wouldn't risk Portia learning about Taryn's involvement.

"Is she okay? Is she safe?"

The concern in her voice was so surprising, it had to be sincere. He hadn't expected that from the woman who'd held Hope's well-being hostage to get what she wanted.

"She's fine." He added, "Thank you for asking."

"You need to bring her back to the hospital. Who knows what being away from there could have done to her condition."

"That's not necessary." He shook his head. "She's getting medical attention and isn't any worse for the brief time she was in his care."

Portia stared hard at him. "How did you find care for her so quickly?"

When he didn't answer, she sighed. "You had contingency plans. Of course, you did."

Ash didn't move, barely even breathed. Portia was incredibly astute. Giving her any additional information could endanger the two most important people in his life.

"You and your sister were both free. Why come back?"

Ash had been asking himself that from the moment he'd walked through the building's front door.

"We have unfinished business," he said finally.

The Ice Queen was back and her smile didn't reach her eyes. "I'm glad you recognize that." She leaned back in her chair. "Explain to me why you helped a known criminal break into my network. Make it good and maybe I won't toss you in the cells for very long."

Ash shook his head. "You already know why. He kidnapped my sister. I would have done anything for her freedom." He paused and collected his thoughts. "I always have."

"What does that mean?" Portia leaned forward. She'd definitely picked up on his word choice.

This was it. Confessing could change his life forever. It wasn't too late to keep silent.

Except it was. He had to do this.

Ash blew out his breath slowly. "Since the night Hope and I were captured, I've been trying to find a way to free myself from your family's clutches."

"Yes, your file was quite clear about your escape attempt." Her tone was snappish.

His lips curled into a not-quite smile. "Yeah. I stopped trying when my sister's life was threatened."

Portia paled. "I had nothing to do with that."

"I know." That hadn't stopped him from blaming the entire Tremaine family. All two of them. "Your father was in charge then. I don't know if the orders came from him or if someone in the cybersecurity department thought it up. But you know what an effective leash my sister's presence provided." He pinned her with a stare.

Portia squirmed slightly before returning to her upright posture.

Ash felt a glimmer of satisfaction. It probably wasn't smart to antagonize her right before confessing to ruining her life, but he couldn't help it. She may not have threatened Hope's life at the beginning, but she'd willingly used his sister as leverage.

"Once escape was off the table, I thought maybe I'd be able to blackmail my way out."

Portia's mouth dropped open. He'd surprised her. Not what he'd expected.

She recovered quickly. "How?"

He gave her a questioning look. "Your system is filled with secrets. I'm a hacker." He shrugged. "Uncovering them is what I do."

Had he said too much? Ash had no idea how to break this next part to her.

"I started digging through the system. There's a lot of useful information buried once you get past the first few levels of security."

Ash took a deep breath. His stomach churned. He'd delayed this next part for as long as he could. "Information like the cure for brain burn. Secret projects. Secret sisters."

Portia sucked in a breath. Her mouth opened and closed. "It was you? All this time and it was *you*?"

She clamped a hand over her mouth and scrambled away from her desk. Her heels clacked unevenly as she raced across her office to the bathroom tucked into the corner. The door slammed behind her.

"Fuuck." That had sucked. He didn't feel any lighter for confessing, but he knew it had been the right thing to do. All his secrets were out in the open now. Except for Hope's location and Taryn.

If he were a complete and utter bastard, Ash would leave now, while she was otherwise occupied. Disappear before she sicced security on him.

A bitter laugh escaped. He might think he could disappear, but the arms of the Tremaine Corporation were long and Portia's pockets were deep.

One way or another, if he ran now but stayed in Seattle, Portia would find him.

And staying in Seattle was the only way he could be with Taryn.

He rubbed his hands over his eyes. It had always just been him and Hope. Now he had Taryn and Dani. And even Portia.

The restroom door opened, and Portia stepped out. Her face was pale and her eyes were red. "I didn't expect a coward like you to still be here."

He stood and faced her. "Portia—"

"Ms. Tremaine," she corrected him through clenched teeth.

"Ms. Tremaine. I'm sorry for what happened. I had no idea what the information I provided would be used for."

"You didn't intend to kill my husband and others? It was just a happy accident?" Her voice was scathing.

Ash flinched from the verbal blow. "Your father's assistant told me that he would use the information to blackmail your father into a more favorable position in the company. He promised me that when that happened, he would use his power to free both me and Hope."

"I asked you to help me find my husband's killer. And

you sat here—*in my office*—and said you would. You must have gotten a good laugh about that."

He shook his head. "I didn't. I felt terrible."

"But you did it anyway?" Her blue eyes were like lasers. He wanted to look away, but she deserved his full attention.

"I had to rescue Hope before anyone caught me. Her freedom was the most important thing to me. I hoped to be with her, but I knew it might not be a possibility."

"For her sake, I hope she's truly safe, because you're never leaving this building again."

Shit. He'd been expecting it, but that didn't make it better. Ash took a step back.

He hadn't decided what to do before the office doors burst open and half a dozen Tremaine Security personnel surrounded him.

Ash dipped his head in acknowledgment. No matter how devastated she was, underestimating Portia Tremaine —even when she was throwing up in the executive restroom —was a mistake.

"Put him in a cell," Portia commanded.

Two of the guards grabbed his arms. The others gathered around him.

His muscles tensed, but he didn't struggle. Taryn would come for him. He had to believe that.

CHAPTER 58

THE SMALL JAIL in the basement of Razor Jack's was one of Taryn's least favorite places. She'd never been held here—the old Jack had preferred to punish her elsewhere—but its mere existence hinted to the dark history of the bar. And until this last week, she'd never had cause to use it. Twice in a single day.

The pimp and his crew had only been held overnight. She'd arranged with one of her contacts for them to be transported far, far away from Seattle. Killing them probably would have been easier and less expensive, but she never wanted to be like the old Jack.

She took a deep calming breath and approached the cell where Daryl had put Rhonda. Dani had warned her that it was bad, but it broke Taryn's heart to see the woman she'd once trusted.

Rhonda huddled in the far corner of the cell. She'd dragged the mattress from the frame and pulled it into the shadowed corner of the small room. Her hair hung stringy and limp around her too-pale face. Twenty-four hours without the drug had left its mark.

"What's wrong with me?" She thrust her arms into the dim light.

Taryn gasped.

Rhonda's arms were streaked with green lines. The telltale sign of Vyne.

That wasn't good.

She'd asked Dani to attend to Rhonda's needs. Now Taryn felt terrible for burdening her friend with that task. In her defense, Taryn hadn't expected the drug to act so fast. Of course, she'd only seen Rhonda in long sleeves. The marks could have been there for a few days, but not much longer than that. Word on the street was that once your veins turned green, you had about a week.

Taryn had still been pissed at Rhonda when she'd entered the basement. But seeing her like this . . . The feelings hadn't necessarily melted away, but Taryn wouldn't wish this on her worst enemy.

"Oh, Rhonda. I'm so sorry." Unlocking the door to the cell, Taryn crouched near the other woman. She kept her cyberarm between them, ready to fend her off if necessary.

Rhonda wrapped her arms around her waist. "I don't feel good."

"Can I get you anything?" Taryn's fists clenched. She hated feeling helpless like this.

"I need it," she moaned. Rhonda abruptly tumbled to her side and started rocking back and forth. "I need it."

Taryn prided herself on handling any situation, but nothing had prepared her for this. Should she get her the drugs and make her more comfortable?

"It's bad, isn't it?"

Startled, Taryn stood and whirled around. "You about gave me a heart attack, Daryl. What are you doing down here?"

"Dani asked me to come get you. There's a message for you at the bar." He watched Rhonda over Taryn's shoulder.

Taryn dropped her head for a moment. It never ended. She really should talk to Dani about taking on more responsibility.

"I don't know what to do for her," she admitted. "Do you?"

The big man's appearance was scary if you were messing with anyone in the Razor Jack's family, but gentle as a lamb when it came to protecting those who needed it. "We can get her the drugs she's asking for and make her as comfortable as possible for as long as possible." Sadness filled his eyes. "I don't think it will be long."

Taryn studied the still-rocking Rhonda. "Do you know where to acquire Vyne?" She hated to ask him, but her interests focused more on trafficking people than drugs.

"Yes, I can take care of it. Take care of her."

She placed her hand on Daryl's forearm. "You don't have to do this," she said fiercely. "I need your help with the drugs, but you *do not* have to be here with her. That's on me."

"Thank you." He brushed the back of his hand over his eyes. "I can help, though. I will help."

"I won't argue with you, but if you change your mind, let me know." This wasn't part of his job description.

"It's what you do for family."

Family.

She'd never thought of it like that until today. But he was right, the people here at Razor Jack's . . . they were a family. Her family.

Taryn looked down at Rhonda huddled on the mattress and blinked away the tears that welled in her eyes. She'd given Rhonda a chance at a new life, but the other woman hadn't been strong enough to take it.

"Thank you." She looked at the woman rocking on the floor. "We'll make it better soon, Rhonda."

CHAPTER 59

"HE DID WHAT?" Taryn stared at the woman standing next to the bar. The Tremaine employee was the same woman who'd delivered Taryn's message to Ash. Now here she was in Razor Jack's bringing Taryn the worst news of her life.

"He returned to Tremaine headquarters and Portia Tremaine had him taken to the detention cells."

The brunette was obviously nervous, but Taryn appreciated her initiative. While she'd been in her office trying to decide what to do with Rhonda, Ash had decided to go see Portia Tremaine.

The idiot.

While she respected his desire to confess his role in the events leading up to the bombing, he was insane to go alone. If he'd shared his plans with her, she'd have insisted on accompanying him. Or made him take Daryl or one of the other bouncers with him.

"I don't suppose it's an easy place to stage a jail break?" she joked.

"Um, not really," the other woman said. "Dizzie got out, but she had help."

Taryn bit back a laugh. That was one way to describe Killian St. John's rescue of Dizzie.

"Thank you for bringing me this news." Not long after the bombing, the woman had come into the bar and offered her services. Taryn generally didn't trust corporate employees, but so far, her information—and her help—had been useful.

"You're welcome. I don't know if I can get a message to him again, but I can try."

Taryn was already shaking her head. "No, I don't want you to get in trouble. I'll take care of it." How? She had no clue.

She paid the woman for her information and then watched her leave. "I'm going to kill him," she told Dani.

"Why would he go back?" Dani asked while she poured a drink.

"Trying to do the right thing." She sighed. She'd fallen in love with all of Ash—even this stupid, noble streak he'd decided to show—but couldn't she have a few peaceful nights with him?

"How are you going to get him back?"

"I've got an idea," Taryn said, "but I'm going to have to call in a favor."

Dani wrinkled her brow. "Who?"

"The big favor."

"Oh!" Dani's eyes widened. "You must really like Ash."

That startled a laugh out of Taryn. "Yeah, you could say that. You good here or do you need me to stay and help?" It was after ten and the bar was in full swing. Business had been especially good since the fight with Giselle's pimp. Jed had been right—lookie-loo money was just as good as anyone else's.

"We've got this," Dani said. "Go call in your favor."

"Thank you."

"Wait." Taryn reached out and touched her best friend's wrist. "Are you okay with this?"

Dani quickly poured the drink she was making, then gave Taryn a funny look. "Okay working in the bar, yes."

"Okay with Ash and Hope maybe becoming permanent additions to our family?"

Dani gave her an incredulous look. "Am I okay with you moving the man you love into your home? Of course." She twisted her hand beneath Taryn's so she could lace their fingers together.

"It's a lot of change," Taryn blurted. Oh god, she was sharing her insecurities again. "For all of us."

"I love you," Dani said.

Taryn didn't know what to say. Her face must have revealed her stupefaction because Dani continued. "You're the sister I always wanted. All I've ever wanted was for you to be happy. And now you are. So yes, I'm completely okay with this."

Her heart lighter, Taryn made her way to her office. The basics of a plan were starting to come together in her mind. She had all the pieces except the first one: getting in to see Portia Tremaine.

As far as Taryn knew, the average person couldn't just make an appointment to see the head of a multinational corporation. And even though the Jack was far from average, she didn't think she could either.

Unless . . . you knew someone. Someone who could get you access.

"Dammit, Ash. This would be a lot easier if you were here to hack into Portia's calendar."

Taryn picked up her phone and punched in a number she hadn't expected to use so soon.

"Killian, it's the Jack. I'm calling in that favor."

CHAPTER 60

TARYN STEPPED into the glass and metal first floor of Tremaine Corporation headquarters. The jaw-dropping architecture was stunning and only years of schooling her expression kept her from gawking.

Shoving the awe aside, Taryn strode through the public entrance, fighting not to rush. Nearly twelve hours had passed since Ash had returned to this building and she had no idea what was happening to him.

Heads turned at her approach and she hid a smile. Damn straight. She looked fierce as fuck.

Her black leather pants were custom made and fit like a glove. Matching black, knee-high heeled boots slicked over her calves. Like the boots she wore the night she rescued Giselle, they were sky-high but were made for moving fast and kicking ass.

She wore a custom-tailored jacket—black leather, of course—over a black shirt made of real silk. The combination of leather and silk landed her at the crossroad of high-end corporate and street. Exactly where she wanted to be.

The don't-fuck-with-me vibe the outfit radiated was a bonus. From the glances she was getting, the clothes were doing their job. The woman behind the front desk swallowed visibly as Taryn approached. That made her smile.

The security guard near the desk stepped closer.

She made them nervous.

Good.

"Ca-can I help you?" the receptionist stuttered.

"I have an appointment with Ms. Tremaine." Her tone was polite. She'd start there and only pull out the attitude if it was warranted.

"Um . . ." The receptionist swallowed again. "Your name?"

"The Jack."

The receptionist had dropped her gaze to her screen. Now it jerked back up to Taryn's. Her eyes were wide and slightly terrified.

Good. She knew the Jack's reputation.

"Your last name?" she stuttered.

Taryn smiled again, this time with genuine amusement. The other woman was trying to stay on course despite the unexpected. Taryn appreciated that. It was a valuable skill.

"Just the Jack," Taryn said.

"I don't think . . ." The receptionist's voice trailed off as her fingers flew over the screen. "Oh, you do."

Thank you, Killian. He'd stepped in to help run the company when Phillip Tremaine had disappeared. He'd used that access to get her onto Portia's calendar this morning, and she'd cleared his debt.

The woman looked from the security guards to Taryn and back. "Please escort the Jack to see Ms. Tremaine." Her voice remained steady.

That had to be why they put her in such an outward

facing position. She'd been thrown by Taryn's appearance but managed to keep it together.

"Thank you," Taryn said with a smile.

Security stepped closer then directed Taryn through a metal detector.

Of course, she set the damn thing off.

They stepped back and pulled out their weapons.

Shit. She'd wondered if this was going to be an issue.

Taryn raised her hands. "I have a cybernetic arm." She kept her voice calm while she wiggled the fingers of her right hand. "See?"

"Take off your jacket."

She moved slowly, every cell in her body aware of the weapons trained on her. She pulled the jacket off her right arm first and made a show of demonstrating it was metal. She reached over and slowly tugged the jacket off her left arm.

Security snatched it out of her hands and subjected it to yet another scan.

When it came through clear, one guard—her visitor from last night, Taryn was surprised to see—holstered her weapon and stepped close. She waved a wand over Taryn's arm and the rest of her while her comrades kept their weapons out.

Taryn wasn't sure what they scanned for, but the results came up green.

"You're clear," the guard said.

Security slowly put their weapons away, although a few rested their hands on them. Not her fault that they didn't realize the real danger of her arm was in pure strength. Taryn didn't expect to use it. She probably wouldn't leave this building if she did.

"Let her through," the receptionist said. The security guards obeyed and ushered her into a black-doored elevator.

"Thank you." Taryn slipped her jacket back on.

One of the guards rode up with her. He kept slipping sideways glances at her, but she ignored him and focused on the task at hand.

The elevator doors opened to a grand view and a stylish but cold office. Her breath caught. Even as a little girl with a family, she'd known that there was no way she would make it into the hallowed halls of one of the corporations. Living on the streets, those odds had been even slimmer.

And yet here she was.

Taryn might not be running the place—something she didn't want, anyway—but she'd made it into the corporate offices. She was as close to an equal as anyone not corporate born probably ever got. It may be small, but she ran her own empire too.

The admin looked up with a curious expression. "Yes?"

"Ms. Tremaine's appointment is here," Taryn's escort said.

"Of course. Please take a seat. She'll be with you momentarily." This one didn't look nearly as concerned as the woman at the entrance. Maybe they'd called to warn her. Maybe she just didn't care.

Taryn sank into a soft chair along the wall.

She didn't have to wait long. The big glass doors swung open. At the same time, the admin said, "You may go in."

Taryn stood smoothly and nodded her thanks to the receptionist. She pivoted to enter the room.

This time she didn't have an escort.

Portia Tremaine's office was immense. Stunning views of the city dominated the room. It was an office created to intimidate. One that allowed its owner to survey her kingdom.

Taryn was impressed, but not intimidated. Not by the office. Not by the view. And not by the cool blonde who sat behind a giant desk.

Without waiting for an invitation, Taryn took the seat opposite Portia and her big desk. The visitor's chair was lower than the desk to unsettle the supplicant.

Taryn bit back a smile. She was pleasantly surprised that she could identify all the tricks that a corporate CEO used. The old Jack could burn in hell, but he'd schooled her well in intimidation tactics.

Ignoring the other desk in the room, the one she assumed Ash had used, she settled into her chair. Arms stretched along the back and one leg crossed over the other, she was the picture of comfort.

"You're a long way from your little bar." Portia spoke without looking up from her computer.

Taryn inclined her head, acknowledging Portia's recognition. She also noted the dig but refused to show it. Portia had obviously never crossed the threshold if she thought Razor Jack's was so easily dismissed. "You should visit some time."

"And you'll buy me a drink?" There was a hard-edged sweetness in Portia's voice.

Taryn laughed. "There's no profit in that."

Portia finally looked at her. A genuine smile cracked her lips, just barely, before her pinched look returned. "Profit, hm? Aside from your name . . ." Portia paused. "Your title? My calendar doesn't have any additional information. That's not the way my admin schedules my time."

One corner of Taryn's mouth tipped up. "She didn't make the appointment."

"Oh." After a moment, she said, "I hadn't realized that the Jack was a woman." Portia's tone was neutral.

Taryn shrugged. "Does it matter?"

Portia pondered the question for a moment. "No. Your reputation is . . . strong."

Taryn wondered what descriptors Portia had discarded in that slight pause.

"Thank you. As is yours."

"What brings you to my office?" Portia steepled her hands. "If you're looking for some kind of payment for helping my sis—for helping Dizzie, you'll have to talk to her."

Portia dropped her gaze to her computer, obviously dismissing Taryn. "If that's all, I need to get to work."

Damn, she'd definitely earned her reputation as the Ice Queen. Taryn had to respect that.

Except there'd been that little slip when she almost called Dizzie her sister. Between that and the fact that Ash liked her for some reason, Portia Tremaine might have a heart.

"Good to know, but that's not what this appointment is about."

That drew Portia's attention back to Taryn. She enjoyed the look of surprise on the CEO's face.

"If it's not about Dizzie, then why are you here?" There was a hint of curiosity under her bored tone.

"I'm here to negotiate for the release of Ash Cutter." Taryn crossed her legs in the opposite direction and watched Portia.

Portia's nostrils flared. "You're wasting your time. Release isn't an option."

"Of course it is," Taryn countered. "Everything has its price. We just have to find it."

"You don't understand. The man killed my husband. He'll never see daylight again."

Taryn had been afraid that Portia would be intransigent. She wouldn't denigrate the woman's grief—Taryn would feel the same way if she lost Ash. "I understand and I'm very sorry for your loss," she said sincerely. "But you and I both know that Ash wasn't responsible for that bomb and your husband's death." She paused. "He worked with Leopold Brunswick. He was *used* by Brunswick, the same way Dizzie was."

Rage flashed in Portia's eyes.

Dammit, bringing up Dizzie had been a misstep. She tried another tack. "Leopold Brunswick was the mastermind of the New Amsterdam bombing. He used at least two members of the Tremaine Corporation to do his dirty work. Can you honestly say there aren't more?"

Portia's lips tightened, the only sign that Taryn's question had hit the mark. "What does that have to do with anything?"

"Wouldn't it be nice to have at least one person you trusted? Someone who can help you root out Brunswick's supporters? Solve other problems?"

"And that's supposed to be you?"

"Oh no," Taryn said with a laugh. "That's Ash."

Portia leaned back in her chair and crossed her arms over her chest. "That's ridiculous. I could never trust that man."

Taryn knew she had to tread very lightly here. "But you can, Ms. Tremaine. What sort of man turns himself in, even when he knows it could be a death sentence?" She was still so pissed at him for that.

"That doesn't mean I can trust him. He made a laughingstock of me, pretending to work for me."

"Didn't he give you actionable intelligence about some of your father's projects?"

A thoughtful look crossed Portia's face. "You're very well informed."

Taryn smiled. "I am."

"For a bartender, you're showing up in the middle of Tremaine business with a concerning frequency."

Taryn rolled with the subject change. Negotiations were delicate.

She shrugged. "I run a good bar." Prior to the bombing, Taryn's policy had been to stay off the corporate radar. Now here she was, voluntarily in the heart of the Tremaine Corporation.

"Right. What would I find if I sent Tremaine Security to check it out?"

Oh, goodie. Threats. "A dozen beers on tap, more by the bottle. A decent selection of booze and wine." Taryn paused, like she'd had a sudden thought. "And a bunch of regulars who don't take kindly to threats against their favorite place."

She looked at Portia and continued. "Walk in the front door like any other customer, you'll get a drink. Stick your nose where it doesn't belong? You'll run into trouble."

"You really think the people in your bar will give a damn?" Portia sneered.

Last week, Taryn wouldn't have thought so. But after the confrontation with Giselle's former pimp and her conversation with Jed, she realized that yes, she could count on her patrons.

"Yeah, they would. They're my people. Loyal. But you wouldn't know anything about that, would you?"

Portia flinched like Taryn had struck her. "I reward

loyalty," she ground out. "I would have rewarded Ash if he'd done his damn job."

"Really?" Taryn asked. "He'd have gotten his freedom? Or would you have continued to hold Hope over his head?"

Dammit. She was probably ruining any chance of negotiating Ash's freedom, but Portia had pissed her off. "As far as I can tell, he did his job. He found the hacker you were looking for and turned himself in. He also stopped a hack this weekend. Remotely."

"He let them in," Portia said through clenched teeth.

Taryn nodded, acknowledging her point. "Yes, he did. But he could have let Caspar all the way in the system. Instead, he got him far enough in for your security measures to capture him."

Portia sucked in a breath.

"Go ahead, check with your people. I'll wait." Taryn trusted that Ash had provided sufficient details to sell this story. He'd willingly let Caspar in, but he'd fought hard to keep him just at surface level and out of the important stuff.

Portia's fingers flew over her keyboard. A few seconds later her phone rang. "Portia Tremaine." She nodded. "What caused it?"

Taryn couldn't hear the other side of the conversation, but Portia's side was pissed. Taryn would hate to get on her bad side.

Then again, she was probably already there.

"And who stopped the attack? Why wasn't I informed?"

Watching her, Taryn understood why Portia had taken over the business when her father disappeared.

She didn't slam the phone down or make any other kind of move that would indicate that she was angry, but her entire body radiated tension. "My people have confirmed the attempted hack. Both how far they got in and where they were stopped."

"Did they stop it?" Taryn knew the answer, but she wanted to know how Portia's team had responded.

"No."

Taryn didn't think she was going to say anything else. Then Portia said, "They said there seemed to be another presence—besides the intruder—but they could never get a visual."

"Are you willing to negotiate now?"

Portia sneered. "You want me to negotiate for Ash's freedom when he abandoned his post and let a hacker into the system? Don't be ridiculous."

Taryn settled into her chair. Now they were getting to the fun part. "He only left because your people—the ones at your supposedly secure hospital—allowed his sister to be kidnapped. Plus, he stopped that incursion."

Portia pinched her lips. "After he caused it."

Taryn would never be able to prove it, but she'd swear that Portia was having fun too. "All that matters is that it was stopped and Hope is safe," Taryn countered. "Now he wants to be free from Tremaine Corporation to spend time with her."

"Whether he stopped Caspar or not, he still plotted to kill my husband."

Taryn held onto her temper by a thread. "No, he didn't. He uncovered a bunch of corrupt programs run by your piece-of-shit father."

Portia's mouth fell open. "He really was a piece of shit."

Now it was Taryn's turn to be surprised.

"Say I do this," Portia said. "Say I let him go. What's in it for me?"

Now they were talking. "What do you want?" Taryn

countered. Her goal was Ash's freedom and a promise to leave him and Hope alone. She had to believe that Ash would trust her to make a fair deal.

"I want to know all my father's dirty secrets. I want to clean house of anyone else who worked with Leopold Brunswick." Her tone promised a reckoning.

Taryn almost felt bad for anyone who got in this woman's way when that day came. Almost. "Let's get started, then."

CHAPTER 61

OVER COFFEE AND POINTED DIGS, Taryn and Portia hammered out a deal.

Ash would get his freedom, along with papers—real and electronic—that outlined his release to protect him from any overzealous Tremaine security personnel.

Hope was free as well, although Portia didn't seem concerned about losing her, only her well-being.

In return, Ash was banned from the Tremaine network unless he was specifically working on a contracted project. He and Portia would arrange any consulting projects. He'd be paid an hourly rate for any consulting work and would solely be responsible for choosing projects and determining his hours. One of the projects he would work on—for free—was Portia's secret project. The one where he was supposed to identify himself.

After spending time with Portia, Taryn discovered she liked the other woman, icy prickles and all.

"Why are you doing this?" Portia asked as Taryn stood.

"Doing what?"

"Why are you so invested in Ash's freedom? Why put

all this effort in for one hacker? Do you want him to work for you?"

No way would Taryn share her true feelings with Portia Tremaine, especially not before she shared them with Ash. "I care about him."

Portia blinked. Blinked again. A soft look crossed her face but it was gone before Taryn could be sure she really saw it. "Oh. I should have fought harder then."

Taryn laughed. "I can see why he likes you."

"Ash does?"

"Yes." No matter what happened next, she deserved the truth about that. Taryn sensed that she didn't get close to many people. She'd lost her husband tragically and then her best friend had hooked up with her hated illegitimate sister. It was like a soap opera.

"Why?" Portia asked.

"Why does he like you?"

She nodded.

Portia's question was one Taryn had asked herself. "I don't know. He just does."

"But I kept his sister captive."

"Yeah, that would make it very difficult for me," Taryn admitted. "If you really want to know, you'll have to ask him."

"Did you take her?" Portia asked suddenly.

Did Taryn detect a note of concern in her voice? "Not the first time. I'm the one who got her back from the hacker collective."

"Is she safe?"

"Yes. She is."

"I'm glad."

They'd concluded their negotiations, but there was

something else. "Ash said there was a possible cure for brain burn in the network."

"Yes, he mentioned that in passing," Portia admitted quietly.

Taryn nodded. "Apparently your father decided that there wasn't enough value in the idea and shelved it. I'd like the cure as well."

"What's it worth to you?" Portia asked.

"Knowing I helped a woman trapped in a coma get her life back." Her voice carried a bite. Shouldn't that be enough?

Apparently, Portia got the message. "Fine. If he doesn't have it already, he can copy it from the system. I would also like it sent to me, so I have the data available."

"Fine." Taryn extended her hand. Portia stood and didn't hesitate to shake Taryn's cyberarm.

Portia rose another notch in Taryn's estimation. She knew Portia was un-modded, but she hadn't known how she reacted around enhanced people.

"It was a pleasure doing business with you," Taryn said. Sure, it was half sarcastic, but it was also half true. Portia Tremaine was a savvy businesswoman. Taryn had held her own and rescued the man she loved.

Portia's smile reminded her of a shark. "Until next time," she said.

"Can you please have Ash waiting for me in the lobby?"

With a regal nod, Portia agreed. She escorted Taryn all the way to the elevator.

CHAPTER 62

ASH PACED BACK and forth in the Tremaine headquarters lobby. When Tremaine Security had come to his cell, he'd been sure he was done for. Instead, they'd escorted him up here. They were still loosely gathered around him, but no one had drawn their weapons. "What am I doing here?" he asked for the millionth time.

Like all the other times, they ignored him.

The elevator opened and his breath caught. Taryn stepped out, looking 100 percent like the Jack.

"What did you do?" He hurried toward her, half expecting security to restrain him. They didn't.

He engulfed her in his arms. "Where were you?" His voice was gruff and slightly muffled since his face was pressed into her hair.

Her arms wrapped around his waist. "Meeting with Portia."

He let her go and stepped back. "What?" He couldn't possibly have heard that right. "Are you okay? What did she want?" He had so many questions.

"It wasn't about what she wanted. It was about what *I* wanted." She looked triumphant.

"What did you want?"

"You," she said. "And Hope. I know you're a package deal."

"But how?" None of this made sense. "What did you do?"

"I got your freedom. And I kind of got you a job, too."

Ash's jaw dropped. "What?"

Taryn's smile was soft. "Look. I'll fill you in on all the details later. Let's get your stuff and get out of here. Before she changes her mind."

Panic welled in his stomach. "It's just stuff. Let's leave it."

"Are you sure?" She leaned close and pressed her lips to his ears. "What about the cure?"

"I've got it," he said. They hadn't bothered to search him when they'd taken him to a cell. After all, he hadn't been going anywhere.

She tucked her hand into his elbow and led him to the exit. He kept looking over his shoulder, waiting for someone to stop them. Someone to raise the alarm. While security watched them leave, nothing else happened.

Once outside, Ash took a deep breath. "Is it real? Am I free?"

Taryn stopped them on the sidewalk and pressed a kiss to his lips. "Would I lie to you? You're free. Hope's free. Well, you'll still have to do some work for Portia. She wants to know who else helped Brunswick. And all the other stuff her father was hiding."

His eyes widened. "What?"

"Oh, and you'll get paid for most of it. I hope that's

okay. I needed to give her something in exchange for getting you out." Her smile lit her up from the inside.

"I'm . . . I'm in shock. Thank you. That's amazing." He blinked and tried to corral his thoughts. "Later, when my brain is functioning again, I want to hear all about it."

"It was interesting. She's a tough negotiator." She paused, then added, "I liked her."

There was wonder in her voice. Ash knew exactly how she felt. "She grows on you, doesn't she?" He grabbed her hand and she smiled at him.

"Yeah, maybe." Taryn pressed a kiss to his cheek, then started walking again. "There's something about her that reminds me of the girls from the streets."

It was his turn to laugh. When he saw she was serious, he asked, "What do you mean?"

She led him to a car parked on the next block. "There's this lost quality to her that I think she's trying to hide. Maybe you didn't see it, but I did. I recognized it."

Ash thought back over his interactions with Portia. Maybe there had been something . . . He wouldn't have ever pegged her as having anything in common with young prostitutes. "Still not seeing it," he admitted.

"Because you've always had your sister." Her voice was pensive.

"What do you mean?" He didn't like it when she sounded sad.

"You and Hope are close, right?"

He nodded.

"You had family. You faced everything together. I didn't," she said. "I don't think Portia did either. Now she's all alone."

"She was raised by her father. She had Tommy and

Killian. And now she has Dizzie." As far as Ash could tell, Portia was surrounded by people.

"Her father was an asshole, right? I'm guessing he really wasn't there for her as family." She stressed that word. "Tommy was her family, but she lost him in the bombing."

Ash flinched. He would live with that regret for the rest of his life.

When they were in the car, Taryn placed a comforting hand on his leg. "Killian was family, but I think she believes that he abandoned her for Dizzie. That's got to be hard for her to swallow. Not to mention she's probably got a lot of guilt about surviving when Tommy didn't."

Christ, another jab in the heart.

"Dizzie may be her biological sister, but they don't have a relationship. Maybe they never will. Right now, she feels all alone. And still, she wakes up every damn day and gets things done. That woman is strong."

Ash cupped Taryn's cheek. She pressed against his palm and looked up at him. "I love you," he said firmly. "You are amazing."

The words felt right coming out of his mouth.

Her cheeks flushed. She turned her head and pressed a kiss against his palm. "I love you too," she said softly. "But what was that for?"

"You're this amazing person who helps others. There aren't too many people who would look at Portia Tremaine —look close enough," he emphasized, "to see that she was hurting. That she might have been hurting for a long time."

She dropped her eyes.

He'd embarrassed her. That hadn't been his intent. "I'm so lucky to have you in my life." Then Ash stopped. She hadn't said how exactly the meeting with Portia had gone. "I do have you in my life, don't I?"

"I'd like that," she said. "Shall we go home?"

"I like the sound of that."

Ash asked questions the entire way back to the bar. And all the way back to her room.

"So, do I get my own room? Or can I stay here with you?" he asked. He was really hoping it was the latter, but he would respect Taryn's decision. He never wanted her to regret spending time with him. Regret freeing him.

"I'd like you to stay here," she said shyly. "If that's what you want."

"Oh, I want." With a wicked grin, Ash shifted his weight and tumbled Taryn backward onto the bed. He braced his head on his arm and stared down at her. "I'm free. We're free." He leaned in for a kiss.

His lips met hers, scattering soft kisses over her mouth. Each one was filled with the emotions he didn't have words for. Excitement. Terror. Uncertainty. Ecstasy.

She'd faced the Ice Queen to free him. The thought staggered him.

When he'd walked into her bar, freedom for Hope was all he could dream of. Taryn had managed so much more than that.

She'd given him his family back. His freedom. And her love.

He was the luckiest man in the whole world.

He slipped a hand under her head and threaded his fingers through her hair. "You are amazing," he repeated.

Ash kissed the little divot at the top of her lips and she gasped. He took advantage and nipped at her upper lip.

She arched toward him. Nipping him back, she fully engaged his lips with hers.

Their tongues tangled. The hand that had pressed

against his cheek now grabbed his shoulder and pulled him closer.

He went willingly, his lips glued to hers. His tongue caught in a delicate dance with hers.

His heart was filled to bursting. This was his life now. With her.

He pulled back and pressed his forehead against hers. "I can't believe I get to spend the rest of my life like this, here with you."

TARYN ARCHED HER NECK, giving Ash access to the sensitive spot behind her ear. She sat on his lap in her chair in her office. "This is way better than spreadsheets," she said breathlessly.

Ash's laughter rumbled through her. "That's a pretty low bar."

"True." She wiggled closer. "Work harder."

His lips captured hers and his hand slid under her shirt, caressing her stomach. She dug her fingers into his hair, deepening their kiss. Office sex had become one of her favorite things.

A cough sounded in the background. "Um, boss. We need you out there. There's a . . . There's a problem?"

Taryn broke the kiss with a groan. "Dani, this is why I promoted you. So *you* could handle problems for me."

It had been a long week since she'd rescued Ash from Portia Tremaine. For Taryn, the sadness of Rhonda's passing from Vyne-inflicted injuries had been tempered by Ash's presence. Having a man live with her—live with *all* of them—had been an adjustment. There were still kinks to work out, but all in all, it had been a positive change.

Ash swiveled the chair so they both faced the door. Dani definitely looked concerned.

"What's wrong?" she asked, slipping into the Jack role.

Dani's mouth opened and closed like a fish. Finally, she said, "You need to see it. Both of you."

Taryn exchanged a concerned look with Ash. "The Jack's work is never done," he said wryly.

"Fine. But you better not be messing with me, Dani." Taryn stood. "We'll be right behind you."

Dani closed the door with a nod. "Good. And hurry."

Ash stood and she watched hungrily as he adjusted himself. "She better have a good reason for interrupting us," she said. "I had plans for you."

A wicked grin crossed his face. "Hold that thought. We can pick this up later."

They were at the bar a minute later. "Okay, what's the problem?"

Dani looked at her then pointed toward a table tucked into the corner.

Taryn's gaze panned over the table. What was the— She looked at the table again, recognizing the woman.

"I think it's Portia Tremaine," Dani whispered.

Ohmygod. What was she doing here? And why was she dressed like that? Taryn shared a look with Ash before they moved as one toward the shadowed corner.

"What a surprise," Taryn said when she reached the table. She didn't say Portia's name. "I never expected to see you here."

"I was told the bar had good drinks. A dozen beers on tap, more by the bottle, and a decent selection of booze and wine?"

Hearing her words parroted back at her, Taryn smiled. "You heard right. What can I get you?"

Panic crossed Portia's face. "Surprise me," she said finally.

"Get her the house special," Ash said. It was the first time he'd spoken since Dani had pointed Portia out.

"Sure, one house special coming up. Will you be okay here?" Taryn asked him quietly.

"I'll be fine," he said.

Taryn walked back to the bar and quickly mixed up three of the drinks. When she returned, Ash was sitting at the table with Portia.

Taryn studied the two of them as she approached. Portia's signature fair hair was pulled into a severe braid that she'd tucked under her shirt. Her cargo pants had so many pockets they would have done a street rat proud. They were worn, too. Worn enough that even if her outfit had started life as designer clothes, there was no way to tell now.

Despite the camouflage, Taryn never forgot how dangerous the other woman was.

"Flashin' Jacks all around." Taryn set the drinks on the table and grabbed an open seat. "Welcome to Razor Jack's." She raised her glass. The others echoed the toast and clinked glasses.

Portia looked at the bright yellow drink and took a tiny sip. Then she looked around the bar. "Tommy and I used to come to a place like this. Not here. Never in Seattle." She stared into the distance while she spoke. "We were both too recognizable around the city. We'd dress down, take an inconspicuous car, and drive for hours just to get a beer."

Taryn reached over to squeeze Ash's hand. He looked as pensive as Portia and she knew it was the mention of the other woman's husband. "That sounds like fun," she said to fill the growing silence.

Portia looked up. When she caught Ash staring at her, she smiled. "What, you think I don't know how to have fun?"

Ash opened and closed his mouth a few times before words came out. "Well, yeah. No one thinks you know how to have fun," he blurted.

She frowned. "Because I'm the Ice Queen?"

Ash nodded. "That's one reason."

Taryn coughed to cover up her laugh.

"So, what can we do for you?" Taryn asked. "Are you here about a job for Ash? Should I expect a pack of newsies to follow you in?"

"No job. No newsies. I just came to get a drink." Portia took another sip of her drink. "Do you know how long it's been since I've been out in a bar just for a drink?"

"How long?" Taryn watched the other woman.

"More than a year. The last time Tommy suggested we slip out of town, I put him off. Said I was too busy." Portia raised her glass to her lips, hiding her expression. That didn't hide the tears that welled in her eyes.

Until Ash, Taryn hadn't fully understood the impact of something like the attack that had killed Portia's husband. Intellectually, sure. Emotionally? Not even close.

Ash had only been in her life a few weeks, but Taryn would be devastated if she lost him. She'd survive—it would suck, but she'd get through it with work and friends like Dani—but it would leave an empty space in her heart.

She couldn't imagine what it must be like for Portia.

"We'll leave you alone," she said quietly.

"Thank you." Portia's sharp tone was back. Good.

Drinking and grieving didn't mix well. Taryn would keep an eye on her, though, just in case.

Rising from the table, Taryn said, "Let Dani know if you need anything. She can always find me."

"I'm sure I'll be fine," Portia said.

"I'm sure you will," Taryn said quietly. "But we're here if you need us."

As they made their way back to the bar, Ash asked, "Why do you think she came here?"

"Here? It's a safe place. You and Hope have proven that. And no one would think to look for her here." Taryn glanced over her shoulder. "I feel bad for her."

When they reached the shadows near the bar, Ash pulled her to his side. "Why?"

She leaned forward and pressed her lips against his frowning mouth.

"Portia Tremaine is not a woman who loves easily. Neither am I." Taryn raised her other hand to the back of his neck. "Losing you would devastate me."

He growled a protest. His arms wrapped around her and pulled her closer.

Taryn leaned back to look him in the eye. "It would destroy me. I'd go on. I'd have to because people depend on me. Just like people depend on her. I'd carry on, because that's what I do, but I'd be broken inside. And I'd want someplace I could lick my wounds in private." She kissed him again. "I think that's what Portia's looking for. And why she'll be welcome here unless she tries to harm me and mine."

Ash cupped her face. Tears shone in his eyes. "I . . ." He shook his head. "I love you. I don't know what else to say. I love you and I never want to leave you."

———

What on earth had driven her to visit a bar? Any bar, let alone this one?

Portia was already regretting her decision.

Almost.

No one had recognized her. Except the bartender and she'd gone to fetch the Jack and Ash. Portia didn't blame her. She'd want someone to tell her when an enemy entered her territory.

But the Jack didn't feel like an enemy. If not for her choice of partners, Portia thought they could be friends.

What a ridiculous thought. The head of the Tremaine Corporation friends with the owner of a seedy bar?

It would never happen.

THE END

ENJOY THIS BOOK?

Reviews and ratings encourage other readers to try out a book and I'd love your help spreading the word!

If you could take a quick moment to rate or leave a review for this book on Goodreads or your favorite book site, I'd be forever grateful!

ABOUT THE AUTHOR

Once she stopped being stubborn and learned to read, Heather always had a book in her hand. Or in her bag. Or under the pillow.

Anne McCaffrey, Nora Roberts, Agatha Christie, and Tamora Pierce. Heather devoured anything and everything, from sci-fi and fantasy novels to historical romance and Harlequins. Her favorites, though, were the stories that combined swoony romance with fantastic adventures. Now she creates her own worlds and plays "what if...?"

Heather lives in Seattle with her husband and two cats. When she's not writing (or working at her day job), she can be found reading, traveling, or enjoying a quiet cup of tea—sometimes all at once!

Find her online at heathergreye.com or on social media

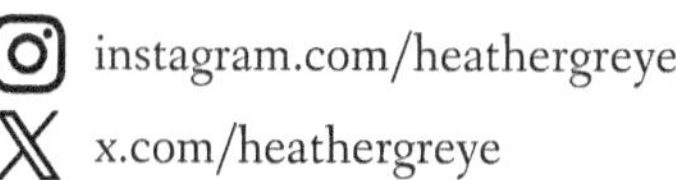

ACKNOWLEDGMENTS

Sitting down to write a book can be a lonely job. That's why I am so grateful for all the amazing people who have supported my publishing dreams.

Thom, who's always willing to talk through story problems with me. Love you!

My mom, for early reads and encouraging text messages.

Christina Sol, my amazing critique partner, who read this in a week because I was running behind schedule. Thank you!

Shelli Stevens, for friendship and support.

Michelle, for grabby hands and proofreading.

Stephanie, for being so amazingly supportive!

Eilis, who wrangled this book and Midnight's Pawn into their best selves.

Everyone who read and enjoyed Midnight's Pawn! Thank you so much!

www.ingramcontent.com/pod-product-compliance
Lightning Source LLC
Chambersburg PA
CBHW020331010826
48973CB00005B/1212